"TALK TO ME, SPYDER. TELL ME THE STORY. . . ."

"You already know the story, Robin."

But Robin squeezes her hand hard, sudden, unexpected pressure, and her eyes flutter open.

"Please, Spyder?" she asks, "please? I need to hear it again, I need to hear *you* tell it."

"It's very late," Spyder says, brushing Robin's bangs from her eyes. "You look so sleepy."

"I need to hear," Robin says and now she sounds desperate, close to tears. "I need to hear."

Spyder sighs, hugs Robin close.

Outside the house, Spyder's rambling junk-cluttered house where it is never anything but Halloween—the late October night is still and satisfied. No wolf-howling wind or bare branches scritching window glass, nothing but the sound of a car passing on the street. Spyder waits until it has gone and then she clears her throat.

"Before the World," she begins, "there was a war in Heaven. . . ."

"KIERNAN WRITES LIKE A GOTHIC CATHEDRAL ON FIRE. HER UNFOLDING OF STRANGE EVENTS EVOKES NOT HORROR, BUT A LARGER SENSE OF AWE."
—Poppy Z. Brite, author of
Lost Souls and *Exquisite Corpse*

Silk

Caitlín R. Kiernan

A ROC BOOK

ROC
Published by the Penguin Group
Penguin Putnam Inc., 375 Hudson Street
New York, New York 10014, U.S.A.
Penguin Books Ltd, 27 Wrights Lane,
London W8 5TZ, England
Penguin Books Australia Ltd, Ringwood,
Victoria, Australia
Penguin Books Canada Ltd, 10 Alcorn Avenue,
Toronto, Ontario, Canada M4V 3B2
Penguin Books (N.Z.) Ltd, 182–190 Wairau Road,
Auckland 10, New Zealand

Penguin Books Ltd, Registered Offices:
Harmondsworth, Middlesex, England

First published by Roc, an imprint of Dutton Signet,
a member of Penguin Putnam Inc.

First Printing, June, 1998
10 9 8 7 6 5 4 3 2 1

 REGISTERED TRADEMARK — MARCA REGISTRADA

Printed in the United States of America

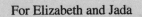
For Elizabeth and Jada

Author's Note

The section headings have been taken from the successive stages of the arachnid molting process. To quote Dr. Rainer F. Foelix (*Biology of Spiders*, 1982): "In a strict sense molting comprises two different processes: (1) *apolysis*, the separation of the old cuticle from the hypodermal cells, and (2) *ecdysis*, the shedding of the entire old skin (exuvium), which corresponds to what most people think of as molting. Apolysis precedes ecdysis by about one week."

I would also like to acknowledge the works of Drs. Joseph Campbell and Carl G. Jung (and in particular *Synchronicity*, 1960) as indispensable resources during the writing of this book.

"All the events in a man's life would accordingly stand in two fundamentally different kinds of connections; firstly, in the objective, causal connection of the natural process; secondly, in a subjective connection which exists only in relation to the individual who experiences it, and which is thus as subjective as his own dreams. . . .That both kinds of connection exist simultaneously, and the selfsame event, although a link in two totally different chains, nevertheless falls into place in both, so that the fate of one individual invariably fits the fate of the other, and each is the hero of his own drama while simultaneously figuring in a drama foreign to him. . . ."

—Arthur Schopenhauer

Prologue

Parlor Game,
And Flies With Faces

Two nights before Halloween, as if it matters to anyone in the house, as if every day in this house isn't Halloween. As if every moment they live isn't the strain and stretch, the hand reaching back, groping through bottomless candy bags down to where front porches glow with orange flicker grins and skeletons dance hopscotch sidewalks and ring doorbells. And they are all here, here around her where they belong.

When someone passes Spyder the little pipe and the plastic lighter, she pushes her bone-bleached dreadlocks from her face, matted as close to dreads as her stringy, white-girl hair allows, virgin black showing at the roots. She sucks, pulls the delicious, spicy smoke into her mouth, and the embers in the bowl glow warm and safe as jack-o'-lantern light.

She holds the smoke inside until it seems she might never have to breathe simple air again, and then releases it slow through her nostrils, passes the pipe to Robin. Robin sprawled on the floor at her feet, almost naked, black panties and black lace wrapped loose around her shoulders, hair dyed the color of absinthe.

"Ummm," Robin murmurs, accepts the pipe, but her wide, acid-bright eyes never waver from the television screen, from the silent gore and splatter of a pirated, second-generation Italian zombie flick, sound all the way down so that everything becomes an impromptu video for the Skinny Puppy or Marilyn Manson pounding from the stereo. But Robin knows where all the shrieks and moans belong and on cue she opens her mouth wide, perfect teeth and pink tongue, and Spyder shuts her eyes, feels the scream tear itself from Robin's throat and wash over her, filling up the room until the jealous music pulls it apart.

Someone claps loudly and Byron glares from the sofa where he's still making out with the pretty black boy from Chicago, the boy who brought the sheets of blotter. Spyder smiles at him, runs her fingers through Robin's improbable hair, dares him to say a word. Then Robin laughs and spills gray smoke from her lips, gives the pipe to someone else before she nestles snug into Spyder's lap. And Byron turns away, hides his face deep in the boy's neck.

Spyder squints through the gauze of marijuana and cigarette smoke hanging a few feet above the hardwood floor, through the strange half-light, salt and pepper TV glare blending into the gentler glimmer from the candles scattered around the room. She lingers, admires the tattoos that cover both her arms from shoulder to knuckle, dark sleeves, tapestry of webs rendered in silvery blues and iridescent highlights against a field of deepest black and indigo.

On the screen, another latex disembowelment and the sudden seethe of maggots like boiling rice.

"Oh," and Robin flinches like she hasn't seen this tape fifteen times before, like there's anything left to shock. Spyder closes her eyes again, tight, savoring the smoky aftertaste and the industrial throb and crash from the speakers, the soft snarl of Robin's hair.

This moment, she thinks and her head is clear, no acid or X and certainly none of Walter's ugly little mushrooms. Only enough of the rich Mississippi pot to deal with the distractions, the blurry edges of her attention. *This one moment,* and behind her eyes, she imagines bottling the seconds, one whole minute, in antique green glass or amber vials, drives the cork in deep before it goes to past like vinegar or slips away.

Everything, she thinks, *and everyone here around me.*

"Ohhhh," Robin says, almost whispers, "Oh fuck, oh fuck, that's so *beautiful.*"

* * *

Later, the last precious hour before dawn, and the sable-skinned boy from Chicago has gone, and the hangers-on have gone, the girl from Atlanta with her tarot deck and the nameless child treading on her shadow, both so skinny it hurt to see. The two drag queens who dropped by looking for Walter, looking to score a quarter bag after their last show of the evening.

Just Spyder and Robin all but asleep in her lap, still tripping deep and hard on her three hits, three tiny white tabs stamped with prancing blue unicorns and dissolved like sugar on her tongue. Byron sits alone on the sofa now, staring at the television, Murnau's original *Nosferatu* in scratchy blacks and whites like celluloid watercolors, and his eyes are somehow vacant and expectant at the same time.

And Walter, squatted like a ragged gargoyle before the stereo, digging noisily through her CDs and cassettes, singing or mumbling to himself. He settles on something, slips it into the deck and The Cure's "Plainsong" pours like honey and raindrops from the speakers.

The girl rises from her bed like a living ghost and sleepwalks along the edge of a balcony; her bare feet, jerky tiptoe stride, barely seem to touch the stone balustrade. Byron picks up the remote, presses pause, and she freezes in midstep. He holds her that way until the song's overture is done and Robert Smith releases them both.

"Spyder?" and Robin's voice slips from her like an echo of itself, something shouted far away and faded thin and hollow by the time it finally crosses her lips.

"I'm here," Spyder answers.

"Talk to me, Spyder. Tell me the story."

"You already know the story, Robin."

But Robin squeezes her hand hard, sudden, unexpected pressure, and her eyes flutter open.

"Please, Spyder?" she asks, "Please? I need to hear it again, I need to hear *you* tell it."

Byron has set the remote down, watches them, arms crossed and waiting. Walter pretends to organize the careless scatter of jewel cases on the floor, pretends he hasn't heard.

"It's very late," Spyder says, brushing Robin's bangs from her eyes. "You look so sleepy."

"*No*. No, I don't want to sleep yet. Please, Spyder."

When Spyder glances at Byron, he shifts his eyes quickly back to the television, back to the terrified solicitor and the vampire, and Walter shrugs and stacks the CDs.

"I need to hear," Robin says and now she sounds desperate, close to tears. "I need to hear."

Spyder sighs, hugs Robin close.

"Yeah," she says, nothing more, but already Byron has reached for the remote, flips the set off and now the room is very dark, only a few guttering pools of yellow candlelight. Walter turns down The Cure until the music is just a murmur of guitars and keyboards, and he sits with his back to Spyder and Robin and Byron.

Outside the house, Spyder's rambling, junkcluttered house where it is never anything but Halloween, the late October night is still and satisfied. No wolf-howling wind or bare branches scritching window glass, nothing but the sound of a car passing on the street outside. Spyder waits until it has gone and then she clears her throat.

"Before the World," she begins, "there was a war in Heaven . . ."

PART I

Apolycis

"There's this thin place behind my ear
Where time is getting heavy and as you say
'I always meant, I always meant to open up'
My skin starts to tear."

"Imperfect"
Stiff Kitten

CHAPTER ONE

Daria

1.

Daria sat by herself on the sidewalk, fat spiral bound notebook open across her lap, back pressed firmly against the raw brick, pretentiously raw brick sandblasted for effect, for higher rent and the illusion of renewal, the luxury of history. The cobblestone street was lined with old warehouse and factory buildings, most dating back to the first two decades of the century or before and sacrificed years ago for office suites; sterile, track lit spaces for architects and lawyers, design firms and advertising agencies.

The felt-tip business end of her pen hovered uselessly over the paper, over the verse she'd begun almost a week ago now. A solid hour staring stupidly at her own cursive scrawl, red ink too bright for blood, and she was no closer to finishing, and the cold, real Christmas weather, was beginning to numb her fingers, working its way in through her clothes. Daria closed the notebook, snapped the cap back on her pen, returned both to the army surplus knapsack lying on the concrete.

This time of day, in this light, latest afternoon and the sun sliding like butterscotch from the pale November sky, she could almost make an uneasy peace with the city. Almost find a little comfort, something enough like comfort to do, in the mismatched cluster of taller buildings that passed themselves off as a downtown skyline. She ignored the stares and sidelong glances from the secretaries in their ridiculous heels and the men in suits who looked at her suspiciously; dumpy, rumpled Daria

Parker growing from their sidewalk like a monster fungus. Thrift-store cardigan beyond baggy, shar-pei of cardigans, the unreal yellow of French's mustard, tattered white t-shirt beneath. Black jeans worn almost straight through the knees and ass.

Her bass leaned against the wall next to her, the hulking rectangular case betraying no hint of the Fender's sleek Coke-bottle curves. The case was almost completely covered with stickers pushing local bands, a few goth and grrrl groups, conflicting political slogans and Bob Dobbs and the Church of the Subgenius. The newest addition, plastered dead front and center, confectioner's pink and black filigree borders, was Daria's band, Stiff Kitten. The zombiefied rendition of Hello Kitty had been her idea, brought to life by the band's drummer, Mort.

Daria fished her last Marlboro from the crumpled pack in her sweater pocket. The cigarette was bent and she frowned as she carefully straightened it with her fingertips. The smoke masked the oily smell of peanuts roasting down the street, tumbling like agate in their steel barrel vats. Two young black men hefted burlap sacks from the open doorway of The Peanut Depot, shouldered them out onto the sidewalk and left them like greasy sandbags beside a parking meter. Above the peanuts, there were pricey apartments and she wondered how anyone could stand the smell. All the windows were empty, no curtains or blinds, and dark, so maybe no one could.

Tailpipe farts and the gentle rev of engines made in Japan and Germany, the office monkeys calling it a day, reclaiming their cars from the parking garages spaced out along the length of Morris Avenue. Daria closed her eyes, exhaling slow smoke through her nostrils, listening to the bumpity sound of wheels on the polished unevenness of the street. Behind her, behind the offices, the sudden air horn blat and dinosaur herd rumble of a freight train, hurrying along one or another of the six tracks that divided downtown Birmingham into north and south.

Daria opened her eyes, squinting through the matted tangle of her hair and the soft gray veil of smoke that hung like a shapeless ghost, undisturbed in the chilly twilight air. She kept her hair long, down past her shoulders and cut no particular way, bleached clean of any trace of its natural color and dyed cherry red with Kool-Aid or, when she could afford it, the Manic Panic cream rinse she bought around the corner at Spyder Baxter's shop.

The men brought more peanuts out to the curb. There would be a white panel truck soon to take them away.

She glanced at her wrist, at the clunky silver dreadnought of a man's wristwatch she'd found a year or so ago, groundscore, lying in the road and obviously run over but still counting off the seconds on a liquid-crystal display the color of dirty motor oil. She'd worn it continuously ever since, when she slept or showered, every time and everywhere the band played, and it had become a sort of running joke, a bizarre contest of wills, whether Daria would eventually devise a torture that even the watch could not survive or if perhaps it might go on forever.

Beneath its scratched and pitted face, the watch said 5:15 P.M. in squarish numbers and that meant fifteen more minutes before she was late for practice, less than seven hours until her graveyard shift at the coffeehouse began. She pulled a last drag from the cigarette and crushed it out on the sidewalk, thumped the butt halfway across the street, narrowly missing a Nissan's tinted windshield.

"Three points," she said out loud, smoke leaking from between her lips, and stood up, shouldering the knapsack, brushing sidewalk tracks off her jeans. The sun was almost down now, just the slimmest fireball rind silhouetting the city's brick and steel and glass carapace. Daria hugged herself, shivered as she buttoned the sweater's only two remaining buttons. When she was done, she slapped her hands together a couple of times to get the blood flowing again, picked up her bass and crossed the street.

* * *

Spyder Baxter's shop looked like something dis-
placed, something stolen from the streets of New Orleans maybe, and wedged in tight between Steel City
Pawn and First Avenue Rent-2-Own. Daria paused before the display window, fly-specked and ages of dust
gathered in the corners like little dunes, parabolic drifts
against smeared glass and rusted frame and a handful of
dead bugs thrown in for good measure. Weird Trappings' handpainted sign swayed and squeaked faintly
on its uneven chains, approximate Gothic in clumsy
black and purple slashes across whitewashed tin.

Something new, or at least something that hadn't been
there yesterday, caught her attention. Or maybe she simply hadn't noticed the album before, *Anthology of Tom
Waits,* almost hidden in the clutter, the confusion that
Spyder let pass for window dressing. Used leather jackets, tie-dyes and Guatemalan trinkets, a stack of battered
art books, heaped around last year's life-sized nativity
scene, paint-chipped plastic, electrical cords snaking
from the butts of wise men and camels. And dangling
above the shabby manger, a holy host of rubber bats and
the severed head of a concrete cherub, pilfered from
some cemetery and sporting wrap-around shades and
fuzzy green earmuffs.

The LP was propped against the kneeling Virgin
Mary and Daria could just make out $4.50 in Spyder's
measured, careful script, ballpoint on the dime-sized
price sticker. Not bad at all, if there weren't a lot of
scratches. And she'd been good, hadn't spent a penny
on herself in weeks, everything she made at The Fidgety
Bean going for bills and rent, whatever was left over
going into the band. And Jesus, she needed something
to wake her up, to jog her out of this dry spell, something that she didn't already know by heart. The album's front cover was a shadowy portrait, indistinct
profile in black and grays, the perfect image of Waits'
voice, growl and rasp, soothing jangle.

Overhead, the street lights buzzed to life, mammoth
fireflies flickering dirty sodium white from their tall

poles. Inside Weird Trappings it was very dark, and the
sudden light made a mirror of the plate glass, hid the album and everything else behind her reflection. Daria
glanced at the door and the sign said closed, but she
could come back for the record tomorrow evening, as
soon as she got up. Would even have a few hours free to
listen to it before work since Stiff Kitten didn't practice
Friday nights.

When she looked back to the window, she saw the
patrol car, cruising slowly, watchfully, along, and she
turned away from Weird Trappings, her boots loud and
deliberate on the deserted street.

Stiff Kitten practiced, and when rent couldn't be paid,
lived, in the empty space above Storkworld. A sort of
baby's K Mart, Storkworld sold everything from disposable diapers to cribs that rocked themselves, safety
pins by the gross and rolls of pink and blue wallpaper.
The cloying smell of talcum powder sifted up from below through the old floorboards, and their lease strictly
forbade rehearsal before five-thirty p.m. every day except Sundays, but it was roomy and just barely within
their budget.

This late, the store was locked tight, salespeople closing out their registers, an old woman pushing her dust
mop from aisle to aisle. Outside, the sidewalk was
washed in the glow of the huge neon stork perched over
the doors, neon bundle of joy hanging from its beak.

Daria walked quickly across the employees' parking
lot, past the two or three cars still waiting patiently for
their drivers, tried hard not to notice the "Equal Rights
for Unborn Women" and "Pro-Family, Pro-Life" bumper
stickers on the rear windshield of a banged-up Chevy
Nova. She squeezed herself into the narrow space between masonry and the sagging chain link fence that
separated the building from a Texaco station, barely
room enough to breathe, much less walk. Back here, the
streetlights and shine from passing cars couldn't reach,
and already the night was pooled like runny tar. But the
door was braced open, half a brick wedged there, and

she was glad that at least she wouldn't have to stand around in the cold and the shadows digging in the knapsack for her keys.

Daria pulled the heavy steel door open, careful to leave the brick in place on the slim chance she wasn't the last, the latest, and stepped inside. For a moment, it seemed even darker, despite the thin and yellowy incandescence from a bare bulb strung way up at the top of the stairs, 40-watt light at the end of the tunnel. She followed it up, her bass bumping once or twice against the edge of a step, her breath, her footsteps, close in the gloom. Finally, the door that Mort had painted in charcoal grays and chalky whites, hints of crimson, a ring of tiny, winged skeletons, bone rattles clutched in bone fists, leering fetal grins, and "Baby Heaven" inscribed in the perfect mimic of tombstone chisel. Mort loved Edward Gorey and Gahan Wilson, Tim Burton and Mexican folk art, and it showed every time he put down the sticks and picked up a brush or pencil.

Daria pushed open the gates to Baby Heaven, and there was warmer air and real light on the other side, the steamy hiss of radiators and rows of fluorescents suspended from the high ceiling, a couple of shadeless old floor lamps like tiny suns on gooseneck stalks.

And Mort, sitting behind his drums in the middle of the mostly empty room, framed in amps and completely absorbed in the business of rolling a more than respectable joint from the Ziploc baggie of pot balanced on his knee. He looked up, saw Daria and smiled his wide, perfect smile, flashed broad teeth stained dingy with tobacco and neglect.

"Daria," he said, the way a chintzy magician might say "Presto-chango!" or "Abracadabra!," and made a grand show of tipping his ratty baseball cap in her direction.

Theo, Mort's girlfriend, latest true love of his life, was camped out in the permanently reclined La-Z Boy chair halfway across the room, smoking and prowling through a stack of *Duplex Planet* and old *Rolling Stone* magazines. Theo had come down from Nashville late in the spring. She dressed like Buddy Holly with a stumbling hangover and claimed that she was an artist, although Daria had yet to actually see anything she'd painted or drawn or photographed. She wore her hair piled high in an oily pompadour, dyed so painfully black it sometimes seemed almost blue.

Daria closed the door behind her, shutting out the shadows and the clammy stairwell chill.

"He's not here yet, is he," she said, no room for question marks in her voice; Mort shrugged his bony shoulders in reply and went back to rolling his smoke. She watched as he sealed the paper with a single, expert lick, twisted the ends tight between thumb and forefinger, and tucked the bomber in snug behind his left ear.

"I am so surprised," and she set her bass on the dusty hardwood floor, sat herself down next to it and flipped up the slightly rustscabbed latches on the big case. The inside was lined with nappy, wine-colored velvet, a burgundy cradle for the black Fender Precision she'd rescued years ago from a local hockshop. From her knapsack, she pulled the shoulder strap she'd cut from an old belt, midnight leather and studs like robot teeth, and fastened it to the instrument, slipped her head through. She removed a snaky coil of cable, plugged the quarter-inch jack into the bass.

"Mort, you *are* going to tell her, aren't you?" Theo asked, looking up from the jumble of pages in her lap. Daria froze, faint prickle of dread stroking the back of her neck, the deepest part of her gut.

"Yeah, I'm gonna tell her. Christ," but instead, he leaned forward, began to fiddle nervously with a wing nut on the snare's tripod stand.

"Tell me *what,* Mort?"

"I was gonna tell you that Keith's pulled another fucking boner on us."

The prickling inside her swelled, ballooned into raw and gnawing alarm. Keith Barry was Stiff Kitten's guitarist, had in fact been the one who'd approached Daria the year before, shortly after the band's original vocalist got wasted on vodka and speed and tried to play limbo with her Camaro and a moving freight train. The wreck was local legend, the sort of thing that was destined to be savored for generations, and although it had felt a little strange at first, being the replacement part for a dead girl, she'd jumped at the chance.

Of course she'd known that Keith Barry was a junkie, that he'd been shooting smack since high school, but no idea that she would wind up falling for him ass over tits. Just that he could do things with his guitar that left her speechless, could pull sounds from the strings that left her crying like a goddamned old woman, like the child she spent so much time trying to forget she'd ever been.

"Will you please just tell me what you're talking about, Mort?"

"Keith told me this morning that he's sublet this place to some guys in another band." Mort had stopped fussing with the wing nut, sat very still now and stared up at the ceiling, past the ceiling to some invisible point beyond.

And the old anger swept over her, then, hot and immediate and utterly devoid of focus, as perfectly indifferent to who it hurt as Keith's addiction. The small voice, silly, timid whimper that always made her think of some milksop's cartoon excuse for a conscience, ivory white and angel wings flitting around her head and shoulders, the voice that raised its hand politely, that begged her to think first. But Mort was convenient, Mort was here and now, and the hurting words were already slipping across her lips.

"Jesus Howlin' Christ, Mort. *Fuck!* Do you just sit around with your thumb up your skinny ass while he's out pulling this shit?"

"*Hey,* Daria," Theo said, rising up slowly from her nest in the La-Z Boy, "Don't think you're gonna take this one out on Mort. It's not his fault your boyfriend's a piss-for-brains junkie."

"It's all right, Theo. She's just mad—"

"*No,* Mort. It's not all right, goddamn it. If she wants

to scream at someone, she can wait until Keith decides to drag his butt up here."

The door swung wide, impeccable slapstick timing, slammed hard against the wall, and Keith, as tall as Mort was thin, tall and hard for his habits, stepped across the threshold. He carried his guitar case in both hands like a tough in an old gangster film, violin hiding a tommy gun. Had carried it around that way for months, since he'd used the case to take a swing at a skinhead and the handle had broken off. Keith kicked the door shut behind him, and something tacked to the wall, one of a hundred fliers or handbills, came loose and fluttered to the floor like a big paper moth.

Daria managed to draw a deep breath, wasted attempt at scrounging some sort of calm, and leaned her bass gently against the nearest speaker. Very slowly, she turned to face the guitarist. And saw at once the stupid glaze, pupils like saucers and his face slack as hot butter behind its goatee and stubble shadow. It would be worse than useless arguing with him now, she knew that, but the angry thing had wound itself so tight inside her, and she imagined its electric hiss and crackle, power lines down on wet tarmac, blacksnakes coiled on scorched earth.

For a moment, no one said anything, and there was only the anger and her heart, and the faint sounds of the last work traffic stragglers down on the street, a car horn filtered through the foam rubber and egg cartons stapled to the walls.

"So, what's your plan, Keith," and her voice sounded detached, ugly distance, and she thought again of something deadly and black underfoot. "We gonna start rehearsing in the fucking street now?"

"What?" and his blank eyes, lids at half-mast and cold gray stones barely visible beneath the overhang of his thick eyebrows, couldn't have looked more innocent, more surprised. "Oh, hey, Mort . . . Jesus, man, didn't you explain this thing to her?"

"I just told her what you did, man." Mort wasn't

looking through the ceiling now, stared down at his tennis shoes.

"Jeez, man, you were supposed to tell her how it *is*." Keith's words came out slurred, fuzzy with the junk slogging through his veins. "Look, Dar, it's only for Mondays and Sundays, okay? It's not a big deal—"

"*Fuck you,*" Daria spit back, cutting him off. "Just shut the fuck up, okay?" and she was on her feet now, the free end of the cable dangling threateningly from her hand like a weird bullwhip.

"Me and Mort are out busting our asses trying to hold down jobs to pay for this place *and* get a few decent shows together and what are you doing, Keith? *Huh? Why* don't you just tell me what exactly the fuck it is you think you're *doing?*"

Keith rubbed at his chin, shook his head slowly.

"Mortie, man, will you please talk to her."

"No, Keith, this time I want to hear a goddamn answer from *you!*" and she took a sudden, vicious step in his direction, snapping the tangled cable tight. Her bass fell over, clatter and *clong* to the floor, and she winced at the noise, but kept her green eyes steady on Keith.

"Hey, Dar. I was just tryin' to help some guys out, okay? They need a place and I was just tryin' to help some guys out."

"*Bullshit!* That's a load and you know it's a load, Keith," and she turned away, picked up her bass from where it had fallen and began checking it over for damage.

"You don't even give a shit about us, Keith, about your *own* music." Her cheeks felt hot past flushed, angry-burn, blistered inside-out by her rage, and she spoke with her back to him as she carefully tested volume and tone control knobs, each brass tuning peg.

"You expect us to believe that you're out there posing as some kind of rock and roll angel of mercy, that you *care* whether or not—" but then she found a fresh scratch an inch or so above the output jack, hairline violation of the smooth, ebony resin, and ran a callused index finger softly over it.

"Tell me how we're supposed to get ready for a show when you've rented this place out from under us. We've got Dr. Jekyll's this Saturday night, and then the big show at Dante's. Or did Dante's just kinda slip your mind?"

"Just forget it, okay, Daria," Keith mumbled, still holding onto his guitar case, holding it like James Cagney. "Just forget the whole fucking thing. I'll call Jack and Soda and tell them the deal's off."

Daria hooked the bass over one shoulder, closed her eyes, and spoke slow, choosing her words more carefully now. The rage had almost passed and she felt shaky and a little ill, the dimmest threat of nausea squiggling around in her belly like tadpoles.

"You do that, Keith," she said. "And listen, I swear to god, if you ever pull anything like this again, I don't care how bad you need money for a fix, you're out on your ass. Do you understand?"

"Hey, whatever you say, Dar. You're the boss lady."

And then Daria marched away to the skanky little toilet at one end of the room, trailing the black cable out behind her. She shut the bathroom door hard, but the cable, half in, half out, got caught in the way, and the door swung slowly open again.

Keith set his guitar down, ran one hand through his spiky, mudbrown buzzcut.

"So, Mortimer. I guess you think I'm one mondo asshole too."

"I think you went way too far this time, man, that's all. I've always known you were an asshole."

"Yeah. Thanks, man."

"Hey, that's what I'm here for," and Mort lightly smacked the edge of a cymbal with two fingers.

Theo pushed the magazines aside and climbed over the arm of the La-Z Boy, wide corduroy gash and bulging tufts of white stuffing, chair hernia. Neither Mort nor Keith said anything to her as she got up and followed Daria and her black rubber excuse for bread crumbs to the john.

* * *

Theo stepped inside the bathroom, little more than a shit closet really, and pushed the door quietly shut behind her. Daria's bass cable was wound loosely around her left hand like a ropy bandage; she slipped it off and laid it on the edge of the sink, feeling awkward, knowing she was absolutely no good at this, wise-ass Theodora Babyock, never any good at consolation or the sympathetic shoulder to cry on bit. Just like now, worrying more about her inability to be the good mother goddess, dispensing tenderness and understanding like Easter jelly beans, than Daria's need for comfort.

"Hey, are you gonna be okay?" she asked, and god, that was lame enough all right, Daria sitting there on the edge of the crapper, arms tight around her bass, face buried in her hands and everything hidden beneath her blood-red hair. She wasn't crying; Theo had never seen Daria cry and she had a feeling no one else had either. She was just sitting there, breathing too hard and too fast, a dry and graceless sound stranded somewhere useless, the stillborn expression of something she knew Daria would never even admit to feeling.

"I am so goddamned sick of this," she said, the words squeezed out like toothpaste between her clenched teeth, and her voice only made Theo feel that much more ineffectual.

"He's just gonna keep jerking us around like this, and pretty soon I'm gonna be too tired to even care anymore. Christ, I hardly give a rat's ass *now*," the last word hissed and she kicked the wall, drove the toe of her Doc Marten into the bare sheetrock.

"Then maybe it's time to cut him loose, babe," and there it was, out quick before she could back down, before she lost her nerve.

Daria looked up through the red straggle, slash-mouthed lips pulled tight and those eyes, red-rimmed but tearless, their twin fires banked for now, but the last green coals still dancing around her pupils, and Theo looked away.

"We're nobody without Keith. Do you honestly think people are gonna pay to hear Mort, or to listen to another froggy-voiced chick with a bass? Even when he's so high he can't find his dick to take a piss, he plays like . . ." but she trailed off and her face disappeared back inside the shaggy veil of her hair.

"You can't save him," Theo said flatly, and she heard the tone of her voice slipping, no longer straining to sound supportive, pretty sure she was at least as fed up with Keith Barry as anyone could be.

"And if you guys think you can, he'll wind up dragging you and Mort down in flames with him."

And then neither of them said anything else for a moment. Through the closed door, they could hear Keith tuning, rambling discord, stray chords segueing cruelly into a snatch of something that might have been funked-up B. B. King or Muddy Waters. And then the riff collapsed in a sudden, tooth-jarring twang and feedback whine, and Keith, cursing the broken string.

"What an asshole," Daria muttered, released a stingy, strangled sound that might have been meant for a laugh, and Theo flinched, afraid for a moment that Daria might cry after all. Instead, she leaned back against the toilet tank and sighed loudly, inverted V of dark water and ruststreaky porcelain showing between her denim thighs.

"It wasn't supposed to be like this, Theo," she said, soft as a whisper. "I mean, I never thought it was gonna be the fucking Partridge Family, you know, but I also never figured it was gonna be like this."

There was a hesitant, soft rap at the door, just once, as if whoever it was had thought better of it at the last minute, and Mort, sounding cautious and impatient at the same time.

"Daria? We're ready whenever you are."

"C'mon, girl," Theo said. "Nothing else is gonna make you feel any better." And she knew at least that much wasn't bullshit, had been through this scene enough times, scenes enough like it, to know that the only way back up for Daria was work, her music or just the coffeehouse thing she'd taken to keep the bills paid. Work that absorbed her and left absolutely no room for distraction, no room for anything but itself, and always ended in merciful exhaustion.

Daria fingered the new scratch on her bass, freshest scar, so many dings and scrapes there already that one more couldn't possibly matter, and Theo thought about all the stickers on the instrument's case, glossy Band-Aids hiding a hundred scuffs.

"Yeah, Mortie," Daria said, "I'm coming," and Theo felt unexpected relief, the knot in her stomach beginning to loosen a little. Daria stood, flushed the toilet for no reason Theo could see, turned on the tap and splashed her face with cold water.

"I'm right behind you," she said, drying off with the front of her t-shirt, and Theo opened the bathroom door.

2.

As McJobs came and went, Daria had certainly done a whole lot worse than The Fidgety Bean. Whenever the crowd of yuppie poseurs, the wanna-bes and could've beens, began to eat away at her fragile resolve not to get canned, all she had to do was remind herself of the months she'd put in at the Zippy Mart, two armed robberies in as many weeks, and that last time, the slick and shiny barrel of the .38 or .45 or whatever so close to her face. Or the fast-food nightmares, scalding showers after every shift, scrubbing with sickeningly perfumed soaps and shampoos until her skin was raw and her hair worse than usual, and still stinking like deep-fried dog turds.

There were no drug tests or polygraphs at the Bean, no security cameras. And at least Claire and Russell, the two aging deadheads who owned the Morris Avenue coffeehouse, allowed her to dress like a human, the less threadbare of her own clothes instead of some middle-management fuck's idea of dress-up, somebody's poster child for corporate identity.

Tonight, Friday morning already, the Bean was quiet; there'd be a little rush toward dawn, when the clubs along 21st Street emptied out and the rave crowd, sweatsticky and half of them sizzling on ecstasy, wandered in. But so far, things had been calm, lots of Nina Simone and Alison Moyet sighing through the stereo, and a handful of night owls sipping at their pale lattés, hardback books or laptop computers open on the tables in front of them. One conversation toward the back, a black woman and two men with gray beards and pipes, smoke like burning cherries and occasional laughter. And Russell, stomping someone's ass at chess across the bar.

Daria finished setting out the careful rows of freshly washed mugs and glasses on top of the big, silver Lavazza espresso machine, squat mugs the color of old cream and the crystal demitasse like cups from a child's tea party. The Lavazza was sleek and utterly modern, efficient Italian engineering, none of those antique Willy Wonka contraptions at the Bean. She'd heard enough gripes and horror stories from baristas who'd worked with those funky, old brass octopuses to be thankful that Claire had insisted on function over flash. She'd never had any trouble with the Lavazza, except once or twice when someone else had forgotten to turn the thing back on after cleaning it and she'd had to stand around waiting for the boiler to build up steam, watching the pressure gauge's slow creep into the red as orders backed up and people began to grumble and complain.

"Hey, Daria," Bunky shouted at her from the register. "Make this guy a double with lemon." Bunky Tolbert was the worst sort of slacker, scabkneed board weasel, late more often than not and Daria couldn't believe Russell hadn't fired his ass, that he'd actually hired him in the first place.

The "guy" was tall and lanky, expensive suit that hung off his shoulders like scarecrow rags, and she thought immediately of Keith, of the shitty, spiritless excuse for a rehearsal and the way that he'd finally just packed up his guitar, not a word, and left her and Mort and Theo in Baby Heaven.

Daria nodded, removed the filter and banged it

upside-down over the dump bin until the old grounds fell out as a nearly solid disc, miniature hockey puck of spent espresso. She rinsed the filter clean beneath the scalding jet on the far right side of the machine and scooped a cup's worth of the fine black powder from the can on the countertop. The espresso flowed from the scooper like liquid midnight, dry fluid so perfectly dark, so smooth, it seemed to steal the dim coffeehouse light, to breathe it alive and exhale velvet caffeine fumes.

Daria added a second scoop and packed it down with the plastic tamper, slid the filter back into the machine and punched the "double" button above the brewer. She glanced at the register and the scarecrow was counting out the dollar-fifty for his drink in quarters and dimes and nickels, a handful of change spilled on the bar and his long fingers pushing coin after coin across the wood to Bunky.

He didn't really look anything like Keith, too healthy despite his thinness, much too alive. Sometimes she thought the only part of Keith that had survived the junk was his eyes, his strange granite eyes trapped in there alone, and that everything else was just clumsy puppet tricks with string and shadow.

The espresso drained from the brewer's jets, twin golden streams, smooth as blood from an open vein; Daria caught the steaming coffee in a demitasse, waited until the machine had finished. In the glass the liquid was as black as the powder had been, black as pitch, and the layer of nut-brown créma thick and firm enough to support sugar crystals. She took a strip of lemon peel from a plastic container and rubbed it around the rim, passed the glass to Bunky and the scarecrow carried it away.

Daria looked up at the huge Royal Crown Cola clock, vintage plastic glowing like a full moon above the fridge and the shelves crowded with their heavy glass jars of freshly roasted beans. Half her shift gone already, and she hadn't so much as stopped for a cigarette, driving herself, finding things to do when there were no orders to keep her busy. No doubt Bunky would think she was just brown-nosing Russell, trying to make him look bad in front of the boss. But the night was catching up with her, Mr. Jack Baggysuit having somehow managed to unravel all her defenses, the rough mantra of movement and distraction that kept the crap in her head and the ache in her muscles from taking hold and dragging her down.

"I'm taking a cig break," she said, stepping past Bunky, handing him the soppy rag she'd been using to wipe down the bar.

"Oh. Yeah, sure," Bunky said, sounding sullen and supremely put upon.

"Try not to hurt yourself for five minutes."

As she walked away, Bunky mumbled, muttered something she didn't quite catch, but enough meaning conveyed in the sound of his voice that the words didn't much matter anyway. Russell looked up from the chessboard, one white plastic bishop in his hand, flashed her a grandfatherly scowl, his *everybody play nice or else* face, bushy, white Gandalf eyebrows knotting like epileptic caterpillars.

Daria shrugged, dredged up half an apologetic smile that she hoped would pass for sincere. Tonight, it was the best she had and was going to have to do.

She fed two dollars and fifty cents into the cigarette machine, too much to pay, but it was her own fault for not having picked up a pack on the way over after practice. A booth she liked near the back was still empty, back where the two men who looked like professors and the black woman sat talking in their shroud of pipe smoke. Daria slid into the cool naugahyde, fake leather the unlikely color of eggplant, and tapped the fresh red Marlboro box hard against the palm of her hand before peeling away the cellophane wrapping.

"Mmhmmm . . . ," the woman said. "In the Sumerian and Babylonian fragments. The Semitic tribes were still worshipping their rocks and trees."

Daria had purposefully sat down with her back to the

discussion, had always hated listening in on other people's conversations, even by accident.

"Watch her, Henry," one of the men warned the other, his voice low and full of mock admonition. "Let her go and change the subject now and she'll have you arguing patriarchal conspiracy theories 'til dawn."

She lit her cigarette and thought about moving back up to the bar, decided instead to concentrate on the music, the big Sony speaker rigged up almost directly over her booth, and not the voices behind her. But the Alison Moyet disc she'd put on was ending, the last song over, and she could see Bunky making straight for the little stereo sandwiched in between the soft drink cooler and the coffee grinder. Bunky had recently developed a fondness for an old Johnny Cash album that bordered on the fanatic and stuck it in every chance he got.

"I mistrust that word," the woman said.

"Which word, Miriam?" one of the men asked. "Which word don't you trust?"

"Demon," the woman replied.

Daria shut her eyes, holding the first deep drag off the Marlboro like a drowning man's last, useless breath of air, wishing the smoke was something stronger than tobacco. Overhead, Johnny Cash began to sing, rumbling voice, broken glass and gravel and the time when she was seven, almost eight, and her father had driven her all the way to Memphis, just to see Graceland.

She opened her eyes and exhaled, forced the smoke out through her nostrils.

"God, Bunky, we have gotta talk," and she reached to stub out her cigarette, would finish it later, somewhere free of the song and the argument she'd tried not to overhear. But her hand froze halfway to the ashtray, possum on her grave shudder, and she felt suddenly lightheaded, not dizzy, but *light,* pulled loose, and the pale hairs on the backs of her arms prickled with goosebumps.

How long had it been since she'd thought about that trip, or anything else from that awful year?

You're just wasted, girl'o, that's all.

Too much Keith and too much Stiff Kitten, the better part of the night spent pretending that she wasn't pissed beyond words, pretending that what Theo had said wasn't the truth. Too much of that weary-ass Little Miss Martyr routine. And any way you sliced it, definitely way too much Bunky Tolbert.

Christ, you haven't even eaten anything tonight, have you? Just cigarettes and coffee and great big, greasy dollops of denial.

The smoke curling up from the fingertips of her right hand made a gauzy question mark in front of her face. And her hands were still shaking, dry wino jitters; the sense of dislocation had faded to the dullest gray unease.

And is that all it was, Dar? Malnutrition and caffeine, nerves and nicotine? Are you absolutely sure that's all it was?

Daria finished the cigarette while Johnny Cash sang about Folsom Prison, while the three behind her began to talk about the time, how late it'd gotten and how early they each had to be up in the morning. Slowly, the shakiness passed and she promised herself she'd grab one of the muffins or poppy-seed bagels in the pastry case before she went back to work.

Five minutes later when the Asian girl in the ratty army jacket walked through the door, she was still sitting there.

CHAPTER TWO

Niki

1.

One forty-five a.m. by the ghostgreen dashboard clock and Niki Ky's black Vega drifted across I-20 and rolled off the blacktop onto the narrow breakdown lane. The car had been driving badly since she'd left Georgia, crossed the state line into Alabama, and a mile or so before the lights of Birmingham had come into view, the temp gauge had begun to creep steadily, ominously, into the red. She'd stayed on the interstate, trying to keep one eye on the dash and one eye on the road, on the other travelers rushing past in the night, watching for the junction that would take her north. As she'd gotten her first clear glimpse of downtown, more tall buildings than she would have guessed, more of a city, the needle had swung quickly toward the "H"-side of the gauge and the oil light had flashed on. A second later the engine had died, no sputter or cough or ugly metal grind, just sudden, quiet nothing.

She turned off the ignition, cut the headlights, but left the flashers on, and for a time sat, slumped forward and forehead resting against the hard steering wheel plastic, the Pixies cassette she'd listened to since Atlanta still playing in her head. When she finally looked up, Niki caught her dark reflection in the rearview mirror, absolutely convinced for a moment that someone else's eyes were watching her from the glass. Her hair, which she'd kept shaved down almost to her scalp since high school, had started to grow out, spiky tufts more like pinfeathers and completely uncontrollable. The silver loops that pierced the entire rim of her right ear from lobe to helix caught the light of passing cars and glimmered like the scales of deep sea fish.

"Pretty mess," she said, and of course it wasn't the prettiest by a long shot, but it was bad enough. Broken down, maybe *badly* broken down this time, in a city that meant nothing more to her than a few black and white news clips from the sixties, fire hoses and snarling police dogs turned loose on crowds of teenagers and children and old men, starch white shirts and black faces.

And then the mirror filled up with headlights, too bright and she had to look away. Dim purple afterimages swam before her eyes. She blinked, wondering if it was the cops, hoping just this once that it would be cops, even a Birmingham cop. She reached for the glove compartment, for her license, fingers crossed against the chance they might ask to see the Vega's registration.

But when she slammed it shut and turned back to the window, the face peering in at her wasn't a cop, some lanternjawed good old boy instead. His thick fingertips tapped eagerly at the glass like it'd been their own idea. Niki paused, thought seriously about telling him she'd been driving all night, had only pulled over to rest for a while, that was all. How long would it be before a highway patrol car happened by, or anyone else bothered to stop? And the thought of setting out on foot in a strange city, *this* city, in the middle of the night, was even less attractive than the face at the window. She checked to be sure that her door was locked, then rolled the window down a cautious crack, barely enough to talk through.

"You havin' some car trouble?" he asked, and cold air and his breath, the sick-sweet reek of chewing tobacco or snuff, leaking in through the crack.

"Uh, yeah. I'm afraid I am."

"Well, I'll be glad to take a look at her, if you want."

The man looked like all the Boo Radleys of the world rolled into one jug-eared, unshaven package. *It still isn't too late,* familiar, worried voice that sounded like her mother, whisper inside her head, *It's not too late to tell him that someone's already gone for help, that the police . . .*

"Sure. Thanks," she said and smiled, nervous smile that she hoped looked genuine.

He smiled back, dirty row of crooked teeth, nodded and tugged at the brim of the grease-stained cap he was wearing.

"No problem, ma'am," he said.

"I think maybe I let the oil get too low and it overheated."

"That'd do it." He pulled a flashlight from the back pocket of his work pants and stepped around to the front of the Vega, fiddled beneath the grille for a moment, hands out of sight, until the hood popped up and all she could see was slick, black metal and the street lights overhead, the windshield reflected in the paint.

You should be home, the mother voice said. It said that a lot. *You should come home, Nicolan. Home, where it's safe.*

The man stepped back into view, the Vega's dipstick in one hand and the flashlight in his other, leaned in close to the window and held the stick up for her.

"See that, how the oil looks all brown and milky?"

The oil clinging to the stick was the color of café au lait, or almonds. Niki nodded.

"That means you got water in your oil. Prob'ly means you blew a head gasket."

Vague, sinking sensation in her stomach, bad news cranking up the gravity a notch or two, and she knew that very soon The Voice in her head would begin its carefully rehearsed I-told-you-so litany.

"That's bad, isn't it?" she asked him.

"Yeah," and he shrugged and switched the flashlight off, spit at the ground. "It's pretty bad. Wouldn't try to start her up again, if I was you."

"Fuck," Niki muttered. Behind her eyes, The Voice was busy asking why she hadn't considered this sort of thing before she'd chucked her old life like last week's fish heads. Why she never thought any further ahead these days than the end of her nose.

"Look," she said. "I'd really appreciate it if you'd call a wrecker for me when you get to a phone."

"No problem," he said again, staring down at the place where he'd spit. "But I'd be glad to give you a ride. There's a garage just off the highway over there," and he motioned toward the next exit, maybe a hundred yards ahead. "Friend of mine's a mechanic there, and they got a truck goes out twenty-four hours."

The Voice balked at the notion of her going *anywhere* with this guy. Niki fingered the little can of pepper spray attached to her key chain; a ride with Boo seemed like a sure way to wind up on next week's *America's Most Wanted* or *Unsolved Mysteries*.

" 'Course, they won't be nobody to have a look at your car 'til in the mornin'. But I guess you already figured that out."

"Yeah," she said, pressed the seat belt release with her thumb and slipped the keys from the ignition. The Voice was just a tired echo, mental tatters. It was all that remained of the old Niki Ky, the Niki Ky that had spent three years table dancing for tips in New Orleans' seedier strip clubs, lying about her age and waiting for some kind of life to find her.

She reached between the bucket seats and grabbed the big canvas gym bag nestled on the floorboard, melon pink canvas stuffed and bulging at the seams. Anything she had worth stealing was in there, along with plenty of other stuff that wasn't.

"You got a deal," she said, rolling up the window, opening the door and locking it behind her.

Outside the car, the cold had teeth, stinging wind that seemed unseasonably bitter. Niki saw the Ford pickup pulled in close behind the Vega, its front bumper tied on crooked with baling wire and a large set of deer antlers mounted for a hood ornament. She set the gym bag at her feet while she fumbled with the snaps on the baggy old army jacket.

When she was done, she held out her hand.

"I'm Niki Ky," she said.

He looked at Niki's hand warily, as if he'd been offered a suspicious cut of meat or some strange tool he didn't know how to use.

"You Chinese?"

"Vietnamese," Niki replied patiently, old routine like opening lines from vaudeville, starting to shiver.

"Vietnam, huh. My daddy, couple of my uncles, all fought in that war. One of my uncles got killed over there."

"I'm sorry," she said, and of course it was a stupid thing to say, but the wind was cutting into her, razor blades and Novocain, and she was still holding her hand out to him, even though her fingertips were going numb.

"Oh, that's all right. You pro'bly wasn't even born yet, and they sent the body home."

Niki's teeth had begun to chatter, clicking in her mouth like tiny, porcelain castanets. She looked longingly toward the waiting truck and tried to ignore the gun rack mounted in the cab's rear window, the two rifles resting there.

"My name's Wendel. Wendel Sayer. Pleased to meet you, Niki Ky." And Wendel smiled again, finally shook her hand before pointing at the truck. "That's my truck," he said.

"Wendel," she said, "I'm freezing my ass off."

"Oh," and he released her well-shaken hand, which she immediately jammed deep into one of the jacket's spacious pockets. "Well, then let's go find you that tow truck."

Before she followed Wendel to the truck, Niki double-checked the door, making certain that she'd locked it. The car was one of the few tangible links back to her old life, and lately, things had had a way of slipping away from her when she wasn't looking.

2.

Niki had been born two years after the fall of Saigon, twenty-three years after Eisenhower had agreed to fund and train South Vietnamese soldiers to fight the communists. Her parents among the lucky few, the handful of South Vietnamese evacuated along with American citizens. John and Nancy Ky had become Americans and immigrated to New Orleans, traded in tradition and their Vietnamese names, the horrors of their lives in Tayninh and Saigon for citizenship and a small tobacco shop on Magazine Street. They had named their only child Nicolan Jeane, would have named the son her father had wished for Nicolas. But Niki's birth had left her mother bedridden for more than a month, and the doctors had warned that another pregnancy would very likely kill her.

Neither of Niki's parents had ever made a habit of talking about their lives before New Orleans, had kept themselves apart from the city's tight-knit Vietnamese community. Always seemed to struggle to answer any questions Niki asked about their lives before America in as few words as possible, as if bad memories, bad times, had ears and could be summoned like demons. There had been letters, exotic stamps and picture postcards from halfway around the world, messages from faceless relatives written in the mysterious, beautiful alphabet that she had never learned to read. Her mother had kept these someplace secret, or maybe she'd just thrown them away. Niki had treasured her rare glimpses of this correspondence, would sometimes hold an envelope to her nose and lips, hoping for some whiff or faint taste of a world that must have been so much more marvelous than their boxy white and avocado-green house in the Metairie suburbs.

And when she'd been ten, just a few days past her tenth birthday, there had been a terrible storm off the Gulf. The ghost of a hurricane that had died at sea, and she'd awakened in the night, or the morning before dawn, and her mother had been sitting at the foot of her bed. Niki had lain very still, listening to the rain battering the roof, the wind dragging itself across and through everything. The room smelled like the menthols her mother had smoked for years, and she'd watched the

orange and glowing tip of the Salem, marker for her
mother's dim silhouette.

"Are you listening, Niki?" she'd asked, "The sky is
falling."

Niki had listened, had heard nothing but the storm,
and a garbage can rattling noisily somewhere behind the
house.

"No, Mother. It's just a storm. It's only rain and
wind."

"Yes," her mother had replied. "Of course, Niki."

The cigarette had glowed more intensely in the darkness and she hadn't heard her mother exhale over the
roar and wail of the storm.

"When I was a girl," her mother had said, "when I
was only a little older than you, Niki, I saw the sky fall
down to earth. I saw the stars fall down and burn the
world. I saw children . . ."

And then lightning had flashed so bright and violent
and her mother had seemed to wither in the electric
white glare, hardly alive in her flannel housecoat and
the lines on her face drawn like wounds. Off towards
the river, the thunder had rumbled contentedly to itself,
proud, throaty sound. And Niki had realized how tightly
her mother was squeezing her leg through the covers.

"It's okay, Mother," Niki had whispered, had tried to
sound like she believed what she was saying, but for
the first time she could remember, she'd been frightened of the night and one of the delta storms.

Her mother had said nothing else, had not moved from
where she sat at the foot of the bed, and Niki had eventually drifted back into uneasy dreams, sleep so shallow
that the sound of the thunder and the rain had come right
through. The next morning, her mother had said nothing,
had never brought it up, and Niki had known better. But
afterwards, on very stormy nights, she'd lain awake, and
sometimes she'd heard her mother moving around in the
kitchen, restless sounds, or the scuff of her slippers on
the hallway floor outside her door.

And years later, not long before she'd finally dropped
out of high school, she'd heard a song by R.E.M on the

radio, "Fall On Me," had bought the album even though she'd never particularly liked the band, and played that one track over and over again, thinking of her mother and that night and the storm. By that time, she'd read and seen enough to guess her mother's nightmares, had understood enough of jellied gasoline and mortars and hauntings to glimpse the bright edges of that insomnia. Finally, maybe twenty or thirty times through the song, picking the lyrics from the lush and tangled weave of voice and music, she'd put the record away and never listened to it again.

If New Orleans had taught Niki Ky nothing else, it had taught her the respect due to ghosts, proper respect for pain so deep it transcended flesh and blood and scarred time.

If her father had bad dreams, they'd never shown.

3.

Niki sat alone in the service station's lobby, part office, part convenience store, sat pinned beneath fluorescence glaring like noon sunshine on a hangover. The Thomas Pynchon novel she'd picked up at a secondhand bookstore before leaving Myrtle Beach lay open across her lap, its spine broken by the vicious way she tended to bend paperbacks double while she read. But she'd hardly glanced at the pages once in the last half hour, not since the tow truck had come back and deposited the Vega at one edge of the Texaco's wide, empty parking lot.

The driver was a heavyset black man named Milo, hair beginning to gray at the temples and his name stitched blue on his shirt. Milo had checked under the hood, shaken his head and wiped his hands with the same oily rag he'd used to clean the dipstick. His prognosis hadn't been any better than Wendel Sayer's, and worse, he'd brought up money.

"Exactly *how* much?" she'd asked cautiously, and Milo had shrugged and slammed the hood shut.

"Now, *that* all depends on whether you just got yourself

a blown gasket or a cracked cylinder head, or if maybe it's the engine block that's cracked. If it's just the head, we're talkin' five, maybe six hundred, but, if it's the block, well—"

"*Whoa,*" Niki had said, one hand up to stop him. "Thanks, but I really don't think I want to hear this right now."

Better to take the whole thing in one nasty dose later, when she'd know for sure just how bad things were.

Milo shrugged again.

"Hear it now or hear it later, it don't make no difference to your pocketbook and it sure don't make no difference to me."

Now Milo was sitting behind the counter, eating Fritos and watching *Green Acres,* Fred Ziffle and Arnold the Pig on a tiny black and white portable television. He chuckled softly to himself in time with the laugh track. Niki closed her book and slipped it back inside the gym bag. She was exhausted, every nerve scrubbed raw from the road, and her ass ached from sitting in the hard plastic chair. And it was pointless pretending her mind was on anything else but her dwindling cash reserves and the car.

And Danny. Always Danny, sooner or later.

She yawned, stretched her legs and arms, and felt the bloodless jab of pins and needles in her left foot. If she didn't get some serious caffeine, and get it soon, she was gonna crash.

"Excuse me," she said, and Milo, clearly annoyed and not ashamed to show it, looked glumly up at her from Hooterville and his noisy bag of corn chips. "Is there someplace near here where I could get a cup of coffee and something to eat?"

He pointed to the automatic coffee maker on the counter, to the racks of shrink-wrapped snack food; the pot was half-full, had probably been that way all night.

"Thanks, but I'm really picky about coffee." It came out shitty, but she'd forced down enough cups of the bitter sludge that passed for gas station coffee to know better. "I was hoping for a restaurant, or maybe a coffeehouse?"

Milo frowned, sighed.

"There's a Shoney's just down the street that way, and an all-night coffee place a couple of blocks over on Morris. But I recommend the Shoney's. Nobody much goes in that other place except fruits and weirdos." He stared at her then and she could feel the track of his eyes like disapproving lasers, their slow head-to-toe inventory.

" 'Course, I don't suppose some folks much mind that sort'a crowd," he said and turned back to the TV.

Without a word, Niki picked up her bag and pushed open the plate glass door. The jealous cold rushed around her instantly, but this time she didn't fight it. The chill felt good, felt cleaner, healthier, than the stale heat inside the station. Her breath came out in a white cloud that the wind picked apart, and she felt the fresh air working its way in through her lungs and throat, into her cells, burning like an icy shot of vodka. Waking her up, cooling the sudden anger.

Come home, Niki. Home where it's not so cold, but the mother voice wasn't really trying now, just muttering habit, easy enough to ignore. The important thing was not to let herself start thinking about the warm fall nights in the French Quarter, the heady smell of chicory coffee and hot beignets drifting from Café du Monde, the familiar faces and sounds of Jackson Square. The things she missed so much that sometimes she thought the pain of their absence would draw blood from her skin like the sweat of saints.

Niki stomped around on the concrete in her raggedy black hightops, stirring circulation, driving back the phantoms in her head, the threat of homesickness. On her way out of the Texaco's lot, she stopped and checked the Vega's doors one more time, then set off down the street in the direction Milo had pointed.

4.

Whenever Niki thought about the days immediately
after she'd run from New Orleans, run from Danny and
the things he'd confessed, the day she'd called home
from a motel room, his apartment but his sister picking
up the phone, it felt like a dream. As insubstantial, as
outside the normal flow of time and waking conscious-
ness. Better not to think about it at all, any more than
necessary.

She'd known Danny Boudreaux since her freshman
year of high school, hadn't started sleeping with him
until a couple of years ago, though; one summer night
after a rave, sweaty warehouse district chaos and both
of them fucked up on ecstasy but it hadn't been an
embarrassment the next morning. Had seemed natural,
something that should have happened, even though
Danny had always gone mainly for boys. He worked
drag at a couple of bars in the Quarter, was good enough
that sometimes he talked about going to Las Vegas and
making real money. Tall boy, trace of a Cajun accent
and wispy frail. A lot of foam rubber padding for his
shows so no one would see the way his hip bones jutted
beneath the sequins.

And then, late July and she'd met Danny for a beer at
Coop's after work, early Saturday morning and after
work for both of them, the bar crammed full of punks
and tourists. They'd gone back to his place on Ursu-
lines because it was closer, had raced sunrise across the
cobblestones, raced the stifling heat of morning, running sleepydrunk and laughing like a couple of tardy
vampires and before bed, cold cereal and cartoons. And
Danny had started talking.

Had dropped the bomb he'd carried all his life, waiting for the right moment or the right ear, or simply the
day he couldn't carry it any longer. More than drag, a
lot more than that, and she listened, stared silently down
at the Trix going soggy in her bowl while Scooby Doo
blared from Danny's television.

"I've been seeing a doctor," he said. "I started taking hormones a couple of months ago, Niki."

And when he was done there'd still been nothing for her to say, nothing to make it real enough to answer, and finally he'd broken the silence for her, asked, "Niki? Are you all right? I'm sorry . . ."

Not looking at him, speaking to the safe TV instead, black and white security, and she shrugged like it was no big shit, like he'd asked if she wanted to go to a movie tonight or if she wanted another cup of coffee. "I'm fucking wasted, Danny," she said. "We'll talk about it after I get some sleep, okay?"

"Yeah," and another apology she hadn't asked for before she'd lain awake beside him, staring at the summer day blazing away behind the curtains, one bright slice getting into the apartment. Concentrating on the clunking wet noises from his old air conditioner, the uneven rhythm of his breath until she was sure he was asleep and Danny Boudreaux always slept like the dead. And she'd gotten dressed, scrawled a note to leave beside the bed, *Danny, I have to figure this out. I just don't know. Love, Niki,* before she'd walked back to her apartment, sweatdrenched and sundazed by the time she reached the other end of Decatur Street.

She'd packed one bag and left the city on I-10, just driving, driving east and the radio and her tapes and towns that all ran together until she'd finally reached North Carolina sometime the next day. A room at a Motel 6 in Raleigh and she'd slept for twelve hours straight. Sleep that left her groggy and disoriented, guilt eating her like an ulcer, a coward to have run out on Danny like that, crazy driving all this way, and she'd called and his sister had answered the phone.

And after Niki hung up, easier just hanging up than trying to answer the questions, she'd sat on the stiff motel bed watching herself in the mirror across the room until the images of Danny were more than she could stand: stepping off the chair, whatever he'd used for a rope cutting into his skinny neck, his feet dangling like a pendulum above the floor. More than her head could

hold and she'd left Raleigh, driving northeast toward
the ocean, following something inside her, a primal inner compass, instinctual drive toward a mother older
and entirely more comforting than the nervous woman
who'd given her birth.

The Carolina countryside had slipped past like pages
in a pop-up picture book, the last fields and tobacco
barns giving way to pines and cypress stands, the first
hints of the vast swamplands that spread themselves out
a little further along. No more real than cardboard
cutouts, and the sun setting in her rearview mirror too
brilliant for anything but gaudy acrylic. Nothing real inside her head except the casual absurdity of his death,
her part in it, and for the first time in her life the tears
that had always seemed to flow so easily, had always
been there, eager to soothe any ache or loss, had refused
to come, and somehow, that had been the most frightening thing of all.

*Used 'em all up on trifling shit, and now there's noth-
ing left to cry.* Like something her mother or maybe a
schoolteacher had said a long time ago. Stop bawling or
someday you won't be able to cry, someone you love
will die and you won't ever be able to stop hurting. Stop
it, Niki, or your face will stick that way.

She'd fumbled through the scatter of cassettes and
empty plastic cases on the dashboard and front seat.
They were almost all ambient goth, darkwave driving
music, nothing she'd wanted to hear now, nothing hard
and sharp enough to drive away the storm, the whir like
locust wings behind her eyes. Finally, she'd lucked onto
a Jimi Hendrix compilation she'd dubbed as a Christmas present two years before and never given away;
the tape had kicked in halfway through "All Along the
Watchtower" and she'd turned up the volume until the
speakers had begun to whine and distort.

An hour after nightfall, dry-eyed and empty, Niki had
crossed the dark and brackish waters of the Alligator
River, secret black flowing beneath the causeway's
three-mile span. Beyond that, the road signs had history book names—Kitty Hawk, Nag's Head, Kill Devil

Hills—and the air roaring in through the open window had begun to smell salty.

For a while, then, there had only been more featureless night, far-off lights and occasional glimpses of the vast marshes stretching away on either side of the asphalt ribbon. Once, a fat raccoon had darted across the road and she'd almost run it down, had stomped the brakes and would have been dead if there'd been anyone behind her.

She'd reached another long bridge just as Hendrix had begun "The Wind Cries Mary"; a reflective green and silver sign had announced that she would be crossing Croatan Sound and that Roanoke Island waited for her on the other side. Niki wasn't a history buff, but she knew the legend of the Lost Colony, the English settlement that had completely vanished, nothing left behind except the word "CROATOAN" carved into the trunk of a tree. And there was a Harlan Ellison story with the same name, about alligators and mutant fetuses living in the sewers underneath New York City.

As the raven black Vega left the mainland behind and rushed toward the line of barrier islands and the cold Atlantic, she'd thought about what might hide itself at the blurry edges of her sight, and rolled up her window.

* * *

Niki had stopped for gas and a fifth of Jim Beam in the waterfront town of Manteo. Any maritime charm the town might still have had twenty, twenty-five years ago, had been long since smothered beneath a gaudy flood of vacationers and housing developments, white-washed seafood joints and video rental stores. She'd avoided the eyes of the old man who'd come out to pump for her, the disdainful stares from the old woman behind the cash register she'd guessed was his wife. She had paid with a twenty, and the old woman had snorted when Niki had told her that she could keep the change, had snorted but hadn't refused.

The highway crossed one more bridge, the last, and

the sodium-arc halo of Manteo had faded behind her as the dunes of the Outer Bank had risen up around the car, and she'd followed the single blinking eye of Bodie Lighthouse down to the sea. This time the darkness had felt less threatening, less like a hiding place for monsters and more like a shelter against the grinding weight inside. Maybe it was the moon, butter yellow and three-quarters full, just beginning to show above the sea oats, or maybe it was the ocean, so close she'd caught shimmering glimpses of it between the dunes.

Past the old lighthouse, there'd been a narrow, unpaved road leading away from the highway, packed sand and shells crushed under tires, and Niki drove slow until the road blended seamlessly into the beach. The tide had been in, and even over the blaring stereo, she heard the velvet crash of the breakers. She rolled the car to a stop a few feet from the waterline, shifted down from first into park and cut the motor, but left the stereo on, the headlights burning.

Well, what now, brown cow? Dumbass Danny Boudreaux thought, her mind speaking in his voice, something he said that had always made her cringe a little, and of course she'd had no idea *what* came next. The waves were pretty in the moonlight, and the sand silver below the stars, but there were no answers here, and no more comfort than could be found in loneliness anywhere. *Yeah, that's what I thought you'd say,* and she'd turned Jimi Hendrix down so that the surf had seemed to grow louder. Then Niki had opened the door, unlaced her tennis shoes and pulled them off her sockless feet, had set them out of sight in the passenger side floorboard, and stepped out onto the damp, nightcool sand. She'd eased the door shut, like whispering in a library, like someone might hear.

But there was no sign of anyone else, nothing but the lighthouse a mile or so to the south. No one to see or hear, no one to give a shit, and she'd tugged the smelly Speed Racer t-shirt off over her head and tossed it onto the hood of the Vega. The moon had flashed along the steel rings piercing both her nipples and Niki had stood, looking down at her small, firm breasts in the pale light. She'd had the piercings done almost two years ago on a dare, her birthday, and she and Danny wasted on rotgut champagne, and he'd said *I dare you,* that's all, *I dare you.*

She'd never been able to remember whether or not it had hurt much, if it had even hurt at all, could remember laughter and the piercer's latex hands, the commingled aromas of disinfectant and sandalwood incense, but not so much as a sting as the needle had passed through one areola and then the other.

I dare you.

Oh hell, Niki, I double *dare you.*

Niki seized the left ring, worked both index fingers through and forced it open, tearing skin and flesh, until the tiny hematite ball that locked it closed popped free and fell to the sand. And that pain she *had* felt, pain so fine and honest that it had taken her breath, had left her gasping the salt air in great, helpless mouthfuls. She held the ring up against the sky, caught the moon inside and clenched it tight in her bloodslicked hand.

"I fuckin' dare *you,* motherfucker!" each syllable punched into the blurring indigo sky, perfect blows driven by the blind red momentum of all the days and weeks and goddamned years, and the emptiness waiting at the end.

The first wave had broken apart around her ankles, foam and unexpected warmth, and she realized dimly that she was moving forward, the headlights throwing her long shadow ahead. Her hands moved to her right breast, lingered there, and the water had rushed hard against her knees, enough force to push her back a step. The next wave lifted her clear of the sand shifting beneath her feet and she heard her mother shouting from the beach, *Far enough, Niki, that's far enough.*

The spray splashed across her chest, spiced the fire spreading from her nipple. Her eyes were still dry.

"*Goddamn* you," but the fury had been lost, and her voice sounded papery thin and hollow. "You're gone and it's going to hurt forever."

Far enough now, Niki. Come back some.

A wave high enough to break over her head had driven her down, knees scraping bottom, and she'd come up coughing, spitting the ocean back into itself. Opened her eyes and she was facing back towards shore, blinking through borrowed tears into the glare of the Vega's headlights. Someone was standing in the black space between, someone small, watching her.

Come back some.

The next wave knocked her off her feet, and she had to dig her fingers into the sand to keep from being dragged further out by the undertow. Brief clarity, the illusion of clarity, fading with the pain, eclipsed by confusion and something that might have been fear if she'd cared enough to be afraid. And the silhouette in the headlights still there, although she'd expected it not to be.

Niki had tried to stand and another wave had slammed her forward, taken her another foot or two closer to the car and the shape in the light. And then a hand closed tightly around her own, a hand that felt firm and cold and terribly thin, and thin arms about her shoulders, hauling her gently back to the beach.

Niki tried to speak, had tried to say that she was all right, would be all right now, had only been able to gag and cough up more water, sea water and bile and the half-digested hamburger she'd barely remembered eating for lunch. Slowly, the arms released her and she'd sunk to her knees in the dry sand. The water burned coming up, seared her throat and nostrils.

"You were going to drown yourself," the girl said and Niki had slumped back against the car.

The girl had been so small, smaller even than Niki, so pale she seemed to glow softly, concentration camp skinny and dirty blonde hair ratted beyond anything a comb or brush would ever be able to undo. She'd worn a black dress, filthy plain cloth, torn and ragged, and would have stood out even among the Jackson Square goth crowd.

"You were going to drown yourself," the girl repeated, and it had almost sounded like an apology.

"*No,*" Niki croaked, before she started coughing again.

"It's all right," the girl had said, had reached out and brushed Niki's straggling bangs from her eyes. "The sea doesn't mind. I think it flatters her, mostly."

Niki closed her eyes, trying to untangle her racing pulse from what the girl was saying. Her nipple hurt like hell and her throat felt raw; her mouth tasted like puke and brine.

I wasn't trying to drown.

"My name is Jenny," the girl had said, "Jenny Dare."

"I was not—Christ—I wasn't trying to drown," and she hadn't known which sounded more ridiculous, her rasping voice or what she was saying out loud.

For a moment, Jenny Dare had said nothing else, just sat there in the sand, knees pulled close and her bare feet sticking out from under the tattered hem of her skirt, watching Niki with eyes the color of Wedgwood china.

"Jesus," Niki said, "I'm not—not a fucking suicide." There was blood in her mouth and she'd realized that she must have bitten her tongue or lip.

The corners of Jenny Dare's mouth turned down, faintest frown, her full lips the same color as her eyes.

"No," she'd said, finally. "No, I don't guess that you are. It isn't hard to drown, not if that's what you're after, so I guess you're not."

Then Niki had begun to shiver, sudden chills and fresh nausea, thought that maybe she was going to pass out, and those arms encircled her again, had pulled her close and held her. She tried to push away; there was something vaguely sexual about her bare breasts against this strange girl, and it frightened her. But she was too weak, too sick to do anything but give up and rest her head against Jenny Dare's bony shoulder, bury her face in the musty folds of the old dress, in the yellow-brown

hair that had smelled like autumn, like wood smoke and
frost.

Niki had wrapped her arms around Jenny Dare, returned the embrace and held on with what little strength
she had left.

"Shhhh . . ." the girl whispered, soothing dead leaf
sound, and she had stroked Niki's sand-flecked temples
and cheeks, the stubbly back of her neck. Her fingertips
slid across Niki's skin like an ointment, gelid cold that
bled heat. Warmth that soaked inside her.

In the car, the Hendrix tape had still been playing, cy-
cled back around to where it had begun, and Niki let the
living warmth and the singer's voice take her down.

* * *

Niki had dreamed of ships, wooden ships with tall pirate sails, and fishing boats, and gunmetal ships of war.
And Jenny Dare, watching silently, expectantly, as they
had passed in the night. And when she'd awakened,
when she'd been pulled slowly into purple-gray dawn
by the squawk and screech of gulls, she'd been alone
again.

* * *

Through the white scorch of July and into August,
Niki had worked her way south, never more than a few
miles at a time, sleeping in air conditioned motels during the day, wandering the dunes and beaches and getting drunk on bourbon after sundown. When she couldn't
sleep, when the alcohol had left her restless instead of
unconscious, she'd watched cable television or read
paperback horror novels until dark.

She'd gone as far as Savannah before she felt the
homesick tug of New Orleans and had turned back. But
the second time around, the roads and the marshy Carolina coastline had lost their comfort and she only made
it as far as Myrtle Beach. Niki had rented a room by the

week there and found a job stripping in a boardwalk
dive called The Palmetto Club; she slacked off the
booze, replacing the sweet amber numbness with the
ache of tired muscles and the adrenaline rush of performance.

And early in October, shortly after the first guarded
hints of cooler weather, the dreams of Danny Boudreaux like something in a butcher's window had become infrequent and finally stopped altogether, a long
and difficult fever breaking, leaving her free to face her
ghosts awake.

5.

"So why the hell did you stop in *Birmingham,*" the
girl said, the girl with hair like cherries who had surprised her, not only by knowing what a Cubano was,
but by actually knowing how to make one. Niki held
the demitasse to her nostrils, breathed in the rich steam
rising off the black, sweet coffee.

"You'd have to ask my car," Niki said. "My car must
have decided this looked like a good place to drop
dead."

The girl, whose name was Daria Parker, which made
Niki think of Dorothy Parker, smiled slightly. She was
taller than Niki, but hardly tall, and her face was too
angular to be called pretty, much too handsome to ever
be anything so simple or straightforward as pretty.

"Shit," she said. "I sure as hell know *I* could find a
better place to kick off."

Niki sipped at her Cubano, the warmth spreading
from her throat into her stomach, soothing away the
road ache and exhaustion like a reward for still being
alive. At least she'd found the coffeehouse, the only
thing that had been open on this odd street. She'd turned
the corner and at first the sight had been disorienting,
almost disquieting, the gaslights and cobblestones and
nothing open, planned anachronism, more of a Holly-
wood backlot than a street she'd have expected here.

"Okay, so why were you even driving *through* Birmingham?" Livid pink scars crisscrossed Daria's forearms, telltale barista tattoos, marking the careless and inevitable contact of soft flesh and the espresso machine's steam arm.

"Gee," Niki said, setting her cup down on the bar. "I must have missed the quarantine signs."

"The Chamber of Commerce keeps taking them down." And this time, there wasn't even the hint of a smile.

"Okay, I confess. I was just following directions," and she dug a crumpled, brightly colored brochure from one pocket of her jacket, smoothed it out flat on the bar. "SEE—Ave Maria Grotto!" it commanded, in bold black typeface on glossy blue, "Little Jerusalem—AN INSPIRATION AND WONDERMENT."

"You have got to be fucking kidding me," Daria said and she picked the brochure up off the bar

Niki shrugged. "Nope. I'm afraid it's the truth."

She'd found the brochure at the welcome station just across the state line, had grabbed a big handful from the display rack by the rest rooms and read through them while she'd sipped a styrofoam cup of coffee that had been free and had tasted like it. She had discarded brochures advertising places like DeSoto Caverns ("Underground Fairyland!") and Moundville ("Secrets of a Vanished Past!"). Ave Maria Grotto had been at the very bottom, last chance at direction, and she'd been hooked by the story of the Franciscan monk who'd spent his life creating a scale model of the holy city from bits of stone and trash.

"You must be one weird lady, Niki Ky," Daria said and tossed the brochure back onto the counter.

And Niki looked at it for a moment, trying to remember why she'd made that particular choice, why it had seemed important, or even interesting, at the time. She'd driven away from Myrtle Beach with only the vaguest sense of purpose, little more than the blind need to be moving again. Had danced her last shift at The Palmetto two nights before and given herself some time to sleep before she'd settled her bill with the motel and tossed the gym bag into the back of the Vega.

"So, you got a place to stay?"

Niki shrugged again, shook her head.

"I guess I haven't really thought about it," she said, "I guess I'm gonna have to find a room . . ."

"Or you could crash at my place for a few days, if you can deal with cockroaches and noisy neighbors."

"Are you *sure*?" The offer made her uncomfortable, made her automatically wary, and she wandered just when and where she'd gotten so goddamned paranoid. "I mean, a motel would do just fine."

"I have an entirely better class of roaches. And besides, it's not every day you get the chance to offer shelter to a wandering pilgrim."

"What?" Niki said, but then she remembered the brochure, the miniature temples pieced together from broken soft drink bottles and scrap metal, got the joke and laughed.

"Maybe you know some kinda a blessing for doomed musicians and bands going nowhere at the speed of light," Daria Parker said, and then someone was asking her for a steamed hazelnut soy milk and she rolled her eyes when the guy turned his back.

"One vegan pussy drink, coming up," she whispered to Niki and headed for the cooler.

Niki drank the last lukewarm sip of her Cubano, stared down at the few stray espresso grounds at the bottom of her cup. The feeling that things had slipped out of her hands, that she was no longer running the show, had been growing stronger and stronger since the ride to the Texaco station with Wendel Sayer; a helpless feeling too much like the way she'd felt after Danny's death and it made her want to run.

She'd gotten awfully good at running.

Niki left the money for her drink and a tip on the bar and found an empty booth. She set her bag on the seat next to her and took out the dogeared copy of *Gravity's Rainbow,* scrunched herself into the corner, and this time she made it through four pages before she dozed off. And when Daria woke her, gently shook her shoulder and whispered her name, the coffeehouse was empty and there was blue-gray dawn outside the steam-fogged windows.

CHAPTER THREE

Spyder

1.

Spyder stood out of sight, almost invisible in the dust-scented shadows, and watched Daria Parker, watched her as she gazed in at something in the window display. She knew Daria well enough that they spoke, nodded, exchanged smiles whenever Daria came in to buy hair color or used records or just to prowl around the shop. And of course she'd seen her on stage at Dr. Jekyll's, had sat and listened to her words and the steady hammer of her bass like a heart trapped inside the black box speakers. When the street lights came on, Daria looked over her shoulder and Spyder knew that she'd seen the cop car, knew she was leaving before she even turned away.

"What do you think *she* was looking at?" Byron said, and Spyder ignored him. He was still sitting on the wobbly-legged stool behind the register, chain-smoking cloves in the dark. Two hours ago, he'd stuck a New Order cassette in the tape deck and now "Bizarre Love Triangle" was coming around for the third or fourth time.

Daria walked away with her head down, guitar case swinging in her hand like a portable monolith, and the cops cruised slow, slink blue and white Ford past Weird Trappings.

"If you don't play something else," Spyder said, "I'm gonna make you eat that fucking tape."

"Like *what,* Spyder?" and without looking, without having to see, she knew the sour, impatient expression on Byron's face, the way his eyes narrowed and his lower lip pouted out like a wasp sting.

"*Anything* else," she said. She couldn't see Daria anymore, and the police had gone too; the cars out there now could be anyone. Spyder turned around and the big cardboard box was still sitting unopened on the floor, waiting right where she'd left it, only a few moments ago. The streetlights bled through the glass storefront, light pared, skinned down to its bones, and the shop was not nearly as dark as before.

Byron was rummaging through the shoe box of cassettes she kept beneath the cash register, making as much noise as he could, big, pissy Byron racket just for her. Spyder sat down beside the box, drew her razor-toothed carton cutter expertly, *schrunk*, over and through the shiny membrane of packing tape. Inside, wrapped safe within polyurethane, were dozens of rubber snakes and lizards. Gently, she pierced the topmost bag, then used both hands to rip it open wide and the rich smell of new car vinyl gushed up from the breach.

Plastic clatter across the room and Byron cursed.

Spyder reached inside, slipped her left hand smoothly between newly slashed lips and the air seemed much cooler, heavier, down there; she pulled something big out through the slit, molded scales and beady black eyes and a forked red tongue tasting the air.

Byron had put in her *Best of the Doors* tape and Jim Morrison crooned "Spanish Caravan" through the cheesy little off-brand speakers rigged up on the walls, one each in the four cobwebby corners of the shop. He knew she knew that he hated The Doors; he was just being snitty, pushing at buttons, pulling chains, seeing how much more she'd let him get away with. Byron was leaning over the counter, looking at her.

"God, that's ugly," he said. "What is it supposed to be? Some kind of alligator?"

"No," she replied. And Spyder read the shiny, gold paper tag to herself, gold and black tied around its neck with an elastic string. The African desert monitor, it said, *Varanus griseus*. She said the Latin aloud, and the syllables felt delicious on her tongue, like an incantation or eldritch password.

"What?" Byron asked, leaning a little further. "What did you say?"

Spyder set the monitor aside, hauled an identical twin from the box, one more and she had triplets. She tossed their empty bag away, deflated, transparent afterbirth, tore into the one underneath and found fifteen perfect red-eyed geckos. Digging deeper, she unearthed green iguanas with whiplash tails, a handful of coral snakes like deadly candystriped canes and a single six-foot Indian cobra, coiled snug inside its own wicker basket. Spyder stuffed the empty bags back into the box, tossed it in the general direction of the stockroom curtain.

"God, I hate this song," Byron said, almost a whisper, just loud enough for her to hear.

And she wheeled on him, no warning, threw one of the geckos hard and it bounced cleanly off the side of his head.

"Ow!" and Byron clutched at his ear like he was really hurt. "Christ, Spyder! Be a goddamned bitch, why don't you!"

"Do some work, buy something, or go home," she said.

"Jesus, Spyder. What the fuck's your damage?" and he smoothed at his hair by the faint reflection in the glass countertop, his face dimly superimposed on an assortment of bondage gear and bongs and clunky silver jewelry.

"Did you fuckin' forget to take your Prozac again this morning or what?"

Byron Langly, pushing, poking, a mean little boy, always surprised when the animal in the cage finally bites his fingers. Spyder closed her eyes, prayed to herself that this time he would back off.

"I mean it, Byron," and her voice was still calm, but she could hear the brittle edge that hadn't been there a minute before. "Go breathe someone else's air."

A mean and thickheaded child, no regard for signs hung in plain view, the signs posted for his own protection.

Byron took a deep drag on his cigarette, let the smoke

ooze like lazy ectoplasm from his nostrils. His tweezed
and painstakingly penciled eyebrows raised slightly,
and he cocked his head the smallest bit to one side,
twirled one finger absently into his black hair.

Pushing.

"I'm not kidding," and she was slipping past brittle
fast, slipping past the carefully constructed walls and
brick by brick control, the masonry box she kept her
mind in. A little more and things might start to spill out,
slosh ugly and acid over the top or leak hissing between
the cracks.

And he knew that.

Byron crushed his cigarette out in the big ceramic
ashtray on the counter, the ghost of a smile wrinkling
his red, rouged lips.

"I'm sorry," he said, purled in his silkiest honey-
voice, "I shouldn't have said that, Spyder."

"Please, Byron. Just go home now," and it shouldn't
have been so easy for him to get to her like that; Spyder
braced her hands flat against the floor, the smooth, cold
floor, and tried to remember if maybe she *had* forgotten
her meds that morning.

"But you're not mad at me?"

"No," she said, "Just please go."

"Sure, Spyder. If that's what you want. I'll see you tomorrow, okay?"

She didn't answer, stared down into her puddle of
creepy crawlies until she heard his footsteps, dramatic
sigh and then his footsteps and the cowbell over the
door jangled loudly after him. And she was alone in her
shop, except for the shadows and the stink of Byron's
cigarettes and the dead man singing through the stereo.

* * *

Four blocks from Weird Trappings, Byron stopped in
the shelter of an alley. He was not quite halfway home
to the cramped apartment he shared with a drag queen
named Billy (better known to her fans as the great Talulah Thunderpussy) and Billy's butt-ugly Pekinese. The

wind had picked up since he'd left the shop, had turned blustery and raw, and he'd forgotten his coat, the fine velveteen frock coat he'd rescued from a Southside estate sale, hanging useless on an old nail in Spyder's stockroom.

He cursed himself and took another step into the alley, deeper into the gloom nestled between the tall, old buildings, the walls on either side tattooed with spray paint tags and gang graffiti. He knew better, knew that he was safer if he kept to the main streets, the well lit sidewalks. And this particular alley was narrower than most, not even wide enough for a car. But he was *freezing*.

By now, Spyder had probably found his coat, was probably having herself a good old belly laugh at his expense. He imagined her standing alone in the stockroom, stuffywarm, cozy in her maze of boxes and brooms and junk, and Byron hugged himself tightly, shivered in his thin cotton blouse.

"Bitch," he whispered to the empty street, the alley, to Spyder snickering in his head, and wiped his runny nose on the back of his hand. A little of the maroon lipstick he always wore rubbed off onto his knuckles, smudgy dull smear the color of cranberry sauce. He glanced nervously over his shoulder into the dark, and realized that he couldn't see light from the other side, that the alleyway must dead-end instead of opening back out onto Morris.

A violent, sudden gust swept along First Avenue, air like ice water breath and Byron was forced even further from the useless comfort of the streetlight pooled yellow-white on the sidewalk. The wind dragged the rustling pages of a discarded newspaper past the alley and they were gone.

Just a couple more seconds, just until I can stop shaking so bad and get my . . .

Somewhere behind him, something moved; a dry and weighty *scritch, scritch, scritch* over asphalt and gravel and trash, the glass tinkle of an empty bottle disturbed.

And something else, something almost inaudible

beneath the rising wail and whistle of the wind, a sound like crackling autumn leaves or the guilty whisperings of children. A murmur and a sigh and the sharp, wet wheeze of breath drawn in quickly through clenched teeth.

Byron stepped out of the alley, three steps backwards and he was once again at the slicing mercy of the wind. But he did not run, knew at least enough to know that there was nothing to be gained by trying to run away, by wearing his fear like a gaudy gold cufflink on his sleeve.

And there was nothing in the alley, either, nothing but the empty, lightless space between two buildings, a few bottles left behind by winos, needles left by junkies. He made himself stand still and look, never mind the cold or the way his heart was pounding, pounding like it was ready to explode in a gory spray from his chest.

There ain't nothing under the bed, Byron. Nothing in the closet. See?

But he'd always told his mother, his grandmother, his big sister, that real monsters were fast, fast and much too smart to get caught when you turned on the light.

I'm not afraid of you, and although Byron thought he'd spoken, had expected to hear the words out loud, his lips had gone numb and there was no sound but the wind and the white noise backdrop of the city.

And from the alley, perfect silence.

Byron Langly turned and walked quickly away, not stopping once or even slowing down until it was to slide his key into the lock of his apartment door.

2.

Two-thirds up the side of Red Mountain, Spyder left the obstacle course of potholes and badly patched and repatched asphalt, pulled roughly into her narrow driveway. The turd-brown Celica coughed its oily exhaust against the cold, bald tires scrunching along the gravel furrow, haphazard excuse for a drive framed between tall, untended rows of holly and crape myrtle. Set far back from the last dim streetlight on Cullom Street, the house waited for her in its protective cocoon of dark, sheltered safe beneath the craggy limbs of water oaks and arthritic old pecans.

Dark windows like cheap sunglasses or the eyes of birds, and the long, dark front porch.

By the time she reached the door she was shivering, stood fumbling with her cluttered key ring, keys to Weird Trappings and its half-dozen display cases, some that fit locks that no longer existed and a few she'd picked up at yard sales and antique shops just because she'd liked how they looked or felt in her hands. The porch offered only the barest sanctuary from the wind; wild, junky confusion of debris, things tossed out and pushed to the back, forgotten except when she happened to trip over something or, much more rarely, when she discovered a use for some discarded this or that and reclaimed it. Deflated bicycle wheels and unidentifiable machinery, cogs and sprockets, an ancient Maytag washing machine she'd dragged out of the house years ago, now stuffed to overflowing with rags and garbage. The old Norton she'd bought meaning to fix up, had even gotten as far as breaking down the transmission one day late last spring.

She finally found the key that felt right, that had the right number of peaks and valleys of the proper heights and depths cut in the right order, held it tight in her trembling fingers and turned the dead bolt, opened the door and stepped into the murky warmth of the house.

And the house accepted her, slipped itself around her like a steaming bath and it hardly mattered that she'd closed the door; the house had its own meteorology, its own gentle system of fronts and pressure centers. Spyder stood very still as her eyes adjusted to the shadows and the darkness behind the shadows, letting the day slide off her like grime, breathing in the whispery dustiness of the little foyer. A few seconds more and she easily found the switch on the wall, the ornate iron switchplate cooler to the touch than the wallpaper skin, and flooded the room, the hall beyond, with soft white light.

Spyder blinked, squinted, dropped the brown paper grocery bag she'd carried from the car, bump to the floor, and one of the rubber monitor lizards tumbled out. It lay helpless on its back, legs in the air and "Made in China" molded into its smooth, cream-colored belly. She leaned down, set it on its feet, pointed the long snout and forever-extended tongue at the door. Then she made sure she'd reset the dead bolt and left the key ring dangling from the lock.

"Nothing personal," she said to the lizard.

Spyder checked the door again, rattled the sturdy knob, and followed the fleeing light down into the depths of the house.

Three days after Spyder's tenth birthday, her mother had died of uterine cancer. The irony had not been lost on her, that the creeping thing that had slowly devoured her mother from inside had begun in her womb, had grown itself there in secret like a seditious fetus. Her malignant, vindictive sibling, brother cancer, sister tumor. Her Aunt Margaret had kept Spyder out of school and together they had watched over her mother through the long last month. Spyder had washed her mother's piss and blood from the bed sheets, had measured out careful doses of the tea-shaded morphine elixir, had held her mother's head while she'd puked into the plastic garbage can that her aunt had moved from the kitchen.

And Trisha Baxter had left her daughter the rambling Victorian house at the nub end of Cullom Street, the house her grandfather had built and the only thing she owned worth leaving behind. Spyder's father had died years before, and her mother had kept them fed and clothed on what she'd made as a seamstress, that and the rare and grudging gifts from family members.

So, after the funeral, after the Bible verses and carnation stink, Spyder had been packed off to live in Pensacola, handed down to cousins that she'd never met.

And when she was thirteen she'd run away the first time, had been picked up by Florida state troopers, hitchhiking a few miles from the Alabama state line. Had finally spent a little time in juvie and no one had really bothered to argue when she turned sixteen and dropped out of school. No one had come after her when she'd bought the bus ticket back to Birmingham with her own money. She'd walked from the Greyhound depot downtown, dragging an old duffel bag behind her, military canvas crammed full of her ratty jeans and t-shirts and comic books like some gigantic, olive-drab sausage.

But her Aunt Margaret had rented out the house, *her* house, and the fat woman who'd answered the door hadn't even let Spyder come inside, had stood behind the latched screen, nervous, piggy eyes and children screaming over Saturday morning cartoons behind her. Had threatened to call the police when Spyder kicked the door and called the woman white trash. Spyder had dumped her clothes and junk out all over the front porch, had screamed obscenities while the terrified woman had frantically dialed the police and the children cheered from an open window. Finally, tired past exhausted, she'd sat down in the porch swing and waited quietly for the cops to come.

They'd put her in handcuffs and had agreed with the fat woman that she was probably on drugs.

Spyder had spent the next two months in the psycho ward at Cooper Green Hospital, courtesy her aunt and uncle's signatures, had lost entire weeks in a gooey tranq haze of Xanax and Amitriptyline, and once, after she'd punched an orderly, a needle full of Thorazine that had left her locked inside her useless body like a sentient corpse. But when they'd finally let her out, the fat woman and her children were gone, and her Aunt Margaret had handed over the keys and a savings account with the little money her mother had left and a third of what had come in from tenants over the years.

"You're on your own now, little lady," her aunt had

said and Spyder had looked her straight in the eyes and laughed.

"I always was," she'd said.

Most of her mother's things had been parceled out to relatives or given away to the Salvation Army, and Spyder had spent the first night alone in the empty house, listening to the hardwood and plaster voices, the familiar settling creaks and murmurs. Like her, the house had remembered, remembered her, remembered everything. In the last hour before dawn, she'd finally fallen asleep, nestled into a musty pallet of quilts and one of her Uncle Fred's mothball-scented sleeping bags.

And in the house where she'd been born, where her mother had been born and died, Spyder Baxter had dreamed.

Spyder was sitting at the kitchen table eating a cold Spam sandwich, washing it down with Buffalo Rock ginger ale, when the phone rang.

"Yeah," she barked into the receiver, gruff enough to put off anyone she didn't want to talk to anyhow, firemen selling charity tickets or salespeople wanting her to switch long-distance companies. She took another sip of the cola-colored soda; Spyder loved Buffalo Rock, maybe because it was hard to find outside Birmingham and seemed sort of old-fashioned, or maybe just because nobody else she'd ever met could stand to drink the stuff.

Nothing from the other end of the line for a second or two, and then Byron, his cultivated, slightly nasal Scarlett O'Hara drawl, affected so long that it had become as much a part of him as his ferrety eyes or his pretty, tapering hands.

"Spyder," he said quietly, but it came out more like "Spah'da," and she didn't answer, listened instead to the parking lot sounds in the background. There was no telephone in Byron's apartment, hadn't been since his roommate had run up a four-hundred-dollar phone bill calling the Psychic Friends Network and gay sex numbers. Byron had to walk half a block to a Shop-A-Snak to use a pay phone; she pictured him standing there, shivering in the freezing wind, thoroughly, righteously miserable. Spyder took another bite of Spam and chewed deliberately.

"I'm sorry, Spyder," and there was the faintest ash gray trace of regret in his voice, genuine regret, not the paper-doll remorse he usually tossed about like confetti.

Or maybe he was just getting better at the charade.

She swallowed, stared at the dirty venetian blinds covering the kitchen window.

"I said I was *sorry,* Spyder."

"I'm busy, Byron." She took a fresh slice of white bread, spread Blue Plate mayonnaise thick and added lots of pepper. A car horn blared through the receiver.

"You're just *eating,*" he said, indignant, and there was no question about his sincerity this time.

"Christ. Yeah, so I'm busy fucking eating, okay?" She sliced off a wedge of the spongy, pink meat, wrapped the bread around it.

"Just don't be pissed at me, Spyder. Please? Just don't be pissed anymore."

She laid the sandwich down on the table top, licked a dab of mayonnaise off her thumb.

"Jesus, Spyder. Will you please say *something*?"

"Stop sniveling, Byron."

Outside, a sudden gust of wind swept hard against the side of the house, wind that seemed to push itself slowly, painfully, against the old, paintflakey boards, pressing its insubstantial flanks against the windows.

"Spyder? Spyder, are you still there?"

The windows rattled and the wind thing slowly backed away, sighed itself roughly around the corners of the house and spread airflesh across the steeply pitched roof, over the cornices and gables. An icy draft leaked through the cracks in the window frame, winter breath oozing between glass and caulk and muntin.

"Spyder?"

"Yeah," and she could hear the sudden flatness in her own voice, the gloating satisfaction drained away now.

She closed her eyes and the world felt so thin, hammered down by the rumble and howl. Everything pressed into an onionskin moment, ready to tear and let the sagging, collapsing sky pour through.

The blaze of Heaven bleeding through, no matter how hard she squeezed her eyes shut.

"There was something in an alley, Spyder. On my way home," and part of her was listening to him, still hearing anyway, registering the fear it was probably tearing him apart to show.

"Just go home, Byron. Please, just go the hell on home before you catch pneumonia and die."

She didn't give him time to answer, cut him short and left the receiver lying off the hook on the table. Spyder finished her supper with her eyes closed.

This is the first time that Spyder's father made them spend the night down in the cellar. She isn't even Spyder yet, just plain old Lila Baxter. She's six, barely, and at the end of the summer she'll start first grade. Her hair is black and there's a filthy Band-aid on her left elbow where she fell off the swingset yesterday. She's sitting with her mother at the kitchen table and it's stickyhot July weather, dog day premonition, and still the supper is getting cold. The china bowl of butter beans and the greasy green tomatoes. She's reading a Dr. Seuss book her Grandma Baxter gave her a long time ago, and the pages have dirty fingerprint smudges and the cover's about to come off. She knows it by heart, can recite the words from beginning to end. Last winter, she had a black molly she named Sam-I-Am that died because she took it out of the water to watch it breathe.

She's thinking about Sam-I-Am, buried in a matchbox under her mother's roses, deep so the cats can't dig him up. She doesn't really have to read the words anymore, spends more time looking at the pictures.

The screen door slams shut (thwack), the way it does when she just lets it go, lets the spring snap it back. Her mother gets up, goes to the stove and takes the chicken out of the oven, is still standing there, peeling back the aluminum foil, when her father comes in. Her mother looks at him and frowns, wipes at a wisp of hair that's slipped loose from her ponytail and is sweatplastered to her forehead.

He stinks like work and whiskey (she wrinkles her nose), is still wearing his carpenter's apron, pockets with three-penny nails and roofing tacks and little canvas loops for screwdrivers and hammers. "Quikrete" stamped across the front in pale red. He goes to the sink and washes his hands, scrubs them and scrubs and scrubs with the sliver of Ivory soap, stares out the window, up at the sky.

"Is it looking stormy, Carl?" her mother asks, setting the chicken on the table, goes to the refrigerator for the watermelon pickles. "On the radio, they were calling for thunderstorms again."

And her father doesn't look away from the window above the sink, lathers with the soap again, rinses his hands and dries them on a dish towel.

"Maybe it'll cool things off some," her mother says, and sits down, starts spooning butter beans onto Lila's plate.

Her father stands at the sink a long time, after her and her mother have begun to eat. Lila puts *Green Eggs and Ham* on the floor beneath her chair because he doesn't allow books at the table. And he's still watching the sky.

"Come and eat, Carl, before everything gets cold."

He looks away from the window and slowly lays the towel across the edge of the sink. His eyes are bright and far away and look kind of scared. She stabs a butter bean and watches him while she chews it.

Her father takes big helpings of everything, moves slow, doesn't say anything or look at anyone. Takes two pieces of chicken at once, a drumstick and a breast, and doesn't eat a bite. There's no wind or thunder and it's still sunny outside and she wonders what her father was looking at in the sky.

He takes a pack of Chesterfields from his apron, lights one and stares at the food, untouched, on his plate. Her mother doesn't look angry anymore, worried, though, and a little scared maybe. She wipes fried chicken grease from her hands.

"Carl, is something wrong? Did something happen at work?"

He turns and stares at her, but his eyes are still not really there. And now Lila is scared, too.

"Carl?"

"I'm all finished, Momma," Lila says, although she's still very hungry.

Her mother looks at her plate.

"No you're not, Lila. You hardly ate a thing."

"But I'm full," and she pushes her chair *(scrunk)* away from the table.

"You sit still," and her mother is questioning her father again. He won't answer, smokes his cigarette, taps ashes into his hand.

"Momma, please, I really—"

"I said sit still, Lila." Her mother sounds very frightened now.

"Leave the girl alone, Trisha," and her father's voice is smooth, sleepy, whistles out of him the way air leaks out of a balloon. She imagines her father getting smaller and smaller, drawing in, until there's nothing left but an empty, wrinkled skin balloon draped over the back of the kitchen chair. "She said she was full."

She gets out of her seat, retrieves Dr. Seuss.

"Did someone get hurt on the job, today, Carl? Is that what happened? Oh god, was it Jess?"

Lila stands beside the table. Mr. Mouser is meowling and clawing at the screen to come in and she thinks that if it is going to storm, she should let him inside. But she wants to hear. People get hurt a lot on her father's jobs; sometimes they even get killed.

Mr. Mouser is climbing the screen door. If she turns around, he'll be hanging there like a big, furry bug.

"For pity's sake, Carl, *say* something. Tell me what's the matter."

And her father rubs his sunburned sandpaper cheeks with both hands, hides his face behind thick fingers, uneven, yellowed nails. And she realizes that he's crying, even though he's smiling when his hands fall, plop, on his lap. Shiny tears and a gray-black streak of cigarette ash.

"Lila, go outside and play." Her mother grabs a napkin and is wiping her father's face, and her father is smiling even more, showing all his tobacco-stained teeth in a huge Cheshire cat grin.

"What's wrong, Momma?"

"Right *now,* Lila."

And she's turning around, hugging the tattered book, and there's Mr. Mouser, claws and marmalade belly and dappled paw pads, clinging to the screen door and it seems very, very bright outside.

"Bad cat," she scolds, and now her father is sobbing. And he's laughing, also, and in her stomach something starts to wind itself up tight, like a rubber band. She thinks that maybe she'll barf up the butter beans. The screen swings open when she pushes it and Mr. Mouser is still hanging on, looking at her through the tiny wire squares.

"I can see angels," her father says.

She steps into the late afternoon heat. Closes the door carefully, pulls the cat loose one foot at a time.

"*Bad* Mouser. Bad, *bad* cat."

Lila sits down on the back steps, Dr. Seuss open to page one on her knees and strokes Mr. Mouser until he forgets about wanting inside and begins to purr in his loud, ragged tom cat voice.

Spyder swallowed the last bite of her second sandwich and opened her eyes. There was no globe on the kitchen light and the naked bulb jabbed needles at her. Somewhere, there *was* a globe, full of spare change, mostly nickels and pennies, left in a corner after the first time she blew the light, years and years ago. The globe was old, maybe as old as the house, frosted glass etched with a ring of grape leaves.

And it should be here to stop the light from hurting my eyes. It should be here to . . .

Spyder slammed her fist down hard on the table, hard

enough to hurt and snip at the voice in her head. The empty Buffalo Rock bottle jumped, fell to the floor. Rolled away into a dark place.

Get up, Spydie. Get up and do something easy, something normal.

/but she smells red, nasty cloying crimson, and gags, thinks that she's going to puke but/

She stood up too fast and knocked the chair over.

"No."

/and her voice smells like sour little crab apples and millipedes/

"I'm not going down tonight, I *won't* fucking go down tonight."

Spyder gathered up the supper stuff, the plate with the leftover chunk of Spam, the mayonnaise jar (screwed the lid down so tight it'd be a bitch to open next time), the dirty knife. She dropped the knife in the sink, put the Spam and mayo in the fridge. More careful than careful, paying perfect attention to each necessary step. Twist-tied the bread closed, set it on the countertop.

She fished the pop bottle out from under the table, ignored the dry scritching beneath the floorboards.

/ignores the red smell/

Spyder put the bottle in the trash, counting her footsteps. Got the noisy carton of crickets off the top of the relic Frigidaire and the styrofoam cup of mealy worms from inside. Carried them back to the sink and set the crickets down.

/but she's slipping now, for sure, and Dr. Lynxweiler is telling her to relax, ride it out, don't let it freak you out this once, Spyder, don't let it take you down/

There was something in an alley, Spyder, he'd said, and *On my way home.*

Spyder pulled the plastic top off the worms, stirred the sawdust inside with her finger to be sure they were still alive.

/she's in Alice time and crimson smells like the sound of starling wings/

She found a dead worm and washed it down the

drain. The others seemed healthy enough, just sluggish from the cold.

"It's all right, Spyder," she said and closed the mealies, picked up the crickets.

She turned off the light above the table and stood a minute in the darkness, fighting to anchor herself, to nail herself feet and hands and cold spike between her eyes, into *this* moment, clinging to the sound of the nervous crickets and the growling wind outside.

This is the first night that they waited in the cellar for the bombs to fall, for the trumpets and hurricane buzz of locust wings.

Her mother lights the oil lamp and warm orangeness floods the cellar, eclipsing the pale beam of her father's flashlight. The cellar smells like wet earth and mushrooms, sulfur from the match. There are rows of old boxes, cardboard and wooden crates, stacked high along the dirt walls. Sagging shelves crowded with forgotten mason jars and old newspapers. Rusty garden tools. She can see scraggly goblin fingers poking out of the dirt, knows they're only roots.

Her father is crazy drunk and her mother has finally stopped crying. They sit together, cast their three long shadows, and her father talks about the angels.

Her mother is crocheting, trying not to hear the things he's saying over and over again. A sweater out of green yarn from Woolworth's, and the yarn makes Lila think about the cats, Mr. Mouser and Sister and Little John, all locked outside at the end of the world. She set their supper on the back steps, asked her mother if cats went to Heaven and her mother too quickly told her yes, they go to Cat Heaven. But at least it's cool in the cellar, like air conditioning.

The shotgun across his lap and the big coffee table family Bible open to the last few pages. They sit inside a circle of salt and she watches her mother's lips, counting stitches with her. Her father reads out loud all the scary parts she's never heard.

When her mother says it's bedtime (How can she tell?

There are no clocks down here and she's missed television and hasn't even had her bath), she lies down on
one of the army cots. They smell like mildew and dust,
the blanket smells like mothballs, and she sneezes. She
wipes her nose on the back of her hand and her mother
doesn't even yell.

"Like a thief in the night," her father says, and after
she rolls over, he says it again. Her parents throw
monster movie shadows on the wall. She's never been
this afraid, not even in the tornado weather, but she
doesn't cry.

Lila stays awake as long as she can, fights the heavi-
ness dragging at her eyelids. Watches her father when
he gets up and paces the red dirt floor, never once stepping outside his circle. She counts sheep to stay awake.

And when she loses count, she dreams about blood in
the streets, and fire, and the sky as black as coal.

3.

At the end of the long hall, past the toilet and her
mother's old sewing room, a linen closet and the back
way into the room that had been her parents', Spyder's
bedroom was a shrine of glass and wax. A hundred
jars easy, fish tanks cracked or too leaky to hold water,
and everywhere candles, the only light she permitted
here. All the windows were nailed shut and painted
blind, two thick coats of flat Sears' black masking each
pane. She'd used a fine-tipped camel's hair brush to
trace the webs, not cartoon spider webs or the stylized
patterns tattooed on her skin, but painstaking reproduc-
tions copied from textbooks and photographs.

At first, after Florida and the nuthouse, she'd tried
sleeping in her mother's bedroom. It was so much bigger and it'd seemed a shame to waste, but she could always smell the deathbed stench and her dreams had
been even worse than usual. So she had crammed most
of her stuff into this narrow space at the very back of
the house, the room that had been hers as a child. Had
patched the drafty walls with spackling paste and wood

putty and used a staple gun to repair the peeling strips of wallpaper. Had tacked up the extra insulation of poster prints by Edvard Munch and H. R. Giger, Dali and Gustav Klimt.

Spyder lit a cinnamon-scented candle, closed and locked the door behind her. The crickets were making a fuss, and she shook the carton, stared through the wire mesh window set into the side ("Live Bait, Catch the Big'uns!"). Tiny bodies scrambling over each other, clinging to the sides, fidgeting antennae and hairtrigger legs.

"What do you little fucks know, huh?" And Spyder thumped the side of the carton, knocking some of the crickets over on their shiny brown backs. "You don't know shit, do you?"

She was starting to feel better by scant degrees, the whisper and shimmer at the borders beginning to ebb and fade. She'd double her Klonopin tonight, just to be safe, just to be sure things stayed that way till morning. But her room was almost as good as the meds, so absolutely her, nothing left to guard against. She could breathe here and let the vigilance fray, let the wariness begin to dissolve.

The candlelight glimmered dully off aquarium glass and old pickle jars. Behind the reflections, there was hungry movement, greedy patience. She no longer knew how many spiders she shared the room with, how many more, carefully pinned and labeled, were housed in the wooden museum cases stacked against the walls and hidden beneath the bed.

Spyder used the cinnamon candle to light a dozen others, passing the flame from wick to wick until the room was washed in the flickering glow. Then she plopped down on her squeaky mattress, a World War II army surplus hospital bed draped in an autumn-colored quilt. Her mother had made a lot of quilts, but her Aunt Margaret had most of them.

Her big Sony boom box sat on the floor, surrounded by neat towers of CD jewel cases. Spyder put on a Danielle Dax album, skipped ahead to her favorite track and turned up the volume far enough that she couldn't hear the insistent wind over the keyboards and guitars, the banshee vocals.

In the five-gallon tank on the little table beside the bed, Lurch and Tickler rustled about in their shredded newspaper. She'd bought the pair of Mexican red-legged tarantulas almost five years ago, a present to herself on the first anniversary of Weird Trappings' opening. Officially, red-legs were an endangered species, but she'd found these two with a local pet shop owner who'd claimed he'd gotten them from a breeder in Mississippi. More likely, through a black market connection in Mobile or New Orleans. Lurch and Tickler were both females; males of the species stopped eating when they reached adulthood, and promptly either fucked themselves to death or were eaten by females after mating.

Spyder opened the tank, let Tickler crawl cautiously into her palm. The chocolate and apricot spider was almost as wide as her hand. She stroked the stiff hairs on its back, gently pressed her cheek against Tickler's bristly abdomen.

"I'm gonna be okay," she whispered, pretending the tarantula could understand, and Tickler raised her frontmost left leg, seemed to caress the bridge of Spyder's nose.

Sometimes she imagined that the others watched, jealous of the affection she lavished on the red-legs, that the thousands of pinpoint black eyes glared at her through their plate-glass walls and longed for more than their suppers. But tonight she didn't think about them, focused only on the living weight of the tarantula and the glimmering candles. On the singer's voice, and the words and music.

An hour later, after she'd divided up the last of the crickets and mealies among the five tanks of black widows, after she'd rounded up Lurch and Tickler and traded Danielle Dax for Dead Can Dance, Spyder turned down the quilt and undressed.

Tomorrow morning, Byron would be waiting for her at the shop and she'd let him apologize again. And then she'd convince him that there'd been nothing waiting for him in that alley except a street crazy or maybe a stray dog.

She popped the safety caps off her scripts, dry swallowed two yellow and green Prozac capsules and two baby blue Klonopin. Blew out all but the candle closest to her bed. For a moment, she stood naked in the dim yellow light, admiring her strong body, the full firmness of her breasts, washboard flat stomach and the muscular line of her unshaven legs. The perfect tapestry of pain and ink covering her arms and shoulders.

Spyder lay down, covered herself with the mismatched sheets and her mother's patchwork, and watched the tarantulas stalk their dinners until she fell asleep. Toward dawn the dreams found her and she walked the blood streets under coal black skies.

CHAPTER FOUR

Yer Funeral

1.

Daria knows that she's dreaming, almost always knows, and so her dreams are like amusement park rides or tripping or movies of lives she might have led. And she knows that she is not seven, even though the world rushing past outside the Pontiac's open windows is too fresh, the sunlight and colors of the Mississippi countryside much too brilliant to have filtered through her twenty-four year old eyes. She knows that it's November and not the week before her eighth birthday at the end of May.

The warm breeze through the windows smells like new hay and cow shit, faint, syrupy hint of the honeysuckle tangled in the fences that divide pastureland from the henna ribbon of the unpaved road. Dust spins up off the tires and hangs like orange smoke in the morning air behind them; hard gravel nuggets pop and ping off the underbelly of the Pontiac.

"I have to go to the bathroom," she says, and her dad looks at her in the rearview mirror. "Not much further. You don't want to go in the ditch, do you?"

"I can wait," she says, isn't sure if she's telling the truth, not after two strawberry Nehi's from the styrofoam cooler in the backseat floorboard. She turns away from the window, back to the shoe box of crayola stumps and her big pad of manila drawing paper.

"Well, it's your call," he says from the front.

The paper is completely covered, crazy loops and swirls, figure-eights and broad smears from crayons skinned and rubbed furiously sideways. Psychedelic, her mother would say if she were here, or abstract, she would say, or impressionistic. A rainbow gutted, turned inside out, and she looks at the back of her dad's head, his hair dirty and almost to his shoulders now. There's nothing on the radio but country music stations and preaching stations and she doesn't know the words to any of these songs.

"There are some trees up there you could go behind."

"I said I can wait," she says again and picks all the broken pieces of black crayon out of the box, arranges them neatly on the seat beside her. With the largest, begins working across the page from the upper left corner, burying kaleidoscopic chaos beneath perfect, waxy black.

"I'm sorry," her dad says, and she bears down so hard that the crayon breaks again, crumbles into oily bits that she rubs into the paper with her thumb. Both her hands are stained, the sides of her palms, the tips of her fingers, smudged ocher and sky blue and salmon. Her thumb is the indefinite color of a bruise.

"You don't have to keep saying that," she says, older, tireder Daria voice speaking over whatever the child might have said, and he's staring at her from the rearview mirror, watching her through Keith Barry's pebble-polished eyes.

The crayon smears on her skin melt and run together, mercuric, drip off and splash the black, and now she'll have to use more black to hide them.

Something huge that coughs diesel smoke and hickory and rolls across the land on sinuous wheels like centipede legs rattles past the Pontiac, blocks out the sun for the instant before it's gone and she looks up, looks where it was, shining stitches in the red, red earth,

and "You go first," Keith whispers,

and uses the blade of his big pocket knife to pry away one of the rotten boards, weathered shimmery gray and splintery. The old wood mousesqueaks and pops free, rust-toothed nails flipped up to the cloudless spring sky.

Keith grins like a guilty weasel, folds his knife away

and the yawning dark slit where the board was sucks him inside the shack, the listing shack behind the store and gas station after she pissed, while her father talks nervous with the man who pumped their gas and wiped dead bugs from the windshield with his wet, blue rag.

"C'mon," he shouts back and she hears glass and grit scrunching beneath his shoes and it sounds like he's being chewed alive in there, ground up like a mouthful of raw hamburger. Mort hesitates, and *Maybe,* she thinks, *maybe he's thinking about being eaten, too.*

"Wait the hell up," Mort says and he's gone, leaving her alone in the sun and the sour stink of gasoline and the tall grass. More chewing footsteps, growing fainter, and she looks back, down Morris past the warehouses to the railroad, past the rusting water pump and the scrap metal heaped behind the gas station. She wants to call them back, call for her dad.

"Jesus Christ, Dar. Come the fuck on if you're comin'."

And then she squeezes herself through the gap in the wall, pushes between fear and the dry rot pine, out of the hot morning and into the cool, dustsmelly gloom. And the darkness *does* swallow her, takes her inside the whispery solitude of its velvet guts, the shack, the empty warehouse, makes it seem like there might never have been anything else. Except that the way back, the space of a single slat, blazes like the door to Heaven.

"Mort?" she whispers loud, the way she speaks at the library or a funeral parlor, and "Keith?"

Drifting back, then, from nowhere, from everywhere at once, "Over *here,* Dar. *Over here,*" and it might be Keith or Mort or anyone else. The darkness plays ventriloquist, throwing voices, bending sound, stealing words for its own.

"*Where?* I can't see you."

A long silence and finally something taunting like laughter or summer thunder way off and the voice shouts back, "Over *here!*"

Daria takes one uncertain step forward, crunching the gritty, invisible debris scattered across the floor beneath the rubber soles of her boots. Her eyes are beginning to adjust, slowest fade to fuzzy twilight, and she swallows, throat dry, dry mouth, and tastes the stale, dustbunny air. She remembers the big cooler sweating sweet condensation diamonds inside the Pontiac, the bottles of Coke and Nehi floating in its little arctic sea. And forces herself another step, two, three, moving haltingly now across a gray concrete plain littered with darker patches and the faint glint of broken glass. Streaky sunlight bleeds down through the roof, sieved through shadow, and by the time the dark finishes with it, it's nothing more than the pale ghost of the morning.

"Hey Dar! Look at this!"

"*What?* What is it?"

Up ahead of her, something falls over, startlingly loud, weighty metal crash and glass tinkle, and the sudden feathery rustle of wings high overhead.

"Holy *fuck,* Keith! Will you watch what the hell you're doing?"

And that laughter again, and the rustling, just swallows or pigeons, or bats.

"God, Dar, sometimes you can be such a goddamn pussy," Keith says, and now she knows the laughter is his, mean laugh, the way you laugh at sissies and fat kids and Carol Yancy when the school nurse found cooties in her hair.

Stop! she screams, *Stop it!* but just inside her head, the words just loud thoughts trapped inside her the way this darkness is contained inside the warehouse walls, within the walls of the shack that had seemed so much smaller from the outside.

Something touches her cheek, a tickling wisp of her hair or a cobweb, and she slaps at it.

"Lay off," Mort says, and then footsteps moving toward her.

"I can't see you . . ." but her voice trails off when the wispy thing brushes her face again. It isn't her hair. Some of it clings stubbornly to her fingers.

"Stay where you are," Mort says, or her father, "Stand still and I'll find you."

Hurry up, and she wishes that much had come out loud enough for someone to hear, but she's too busy swiping at the sticky wisps to try again.

"I can't see her, Keith. I can't see her anywhere."

Hurry.

"Dumb pussy bitch," Keith says. "Fuck her, Mort."

Stand still. Stand still and wait for him to find you. You're freaking yourself out, that's all.

It's just a fucking dream.

The footsteps seem to pass her by, dissolving back into the murk, each one a little farther away than the last.

And then the scurry of tiny legs, delicate across her upper lip, the bridge of her nose. And she gasps, loud drowning noise and sucks some of the clinging stuff into her mouth, her nostrils.

"Daria?!" and her dad sounds frightened, almost as much as she is. "Daria, where are you?"

She slaps at her face so hard it draws down violet stars, and there are others, all at once, moving rapidly up and down her arms, her bare legs, impatient as minute fingers drumming busy to themselves. One wriggles its way past the collar of her t-shirt, skitters along her spine, another over an eyelid. A hundred, a thousand legs dancing softly, crazily, and the webs like a living curtain all around her.

And finally she can scream, opens her mouth so wide and the sound tears itself out of her, sonic Velcro rip, leaves her throat raw and her ears ringing. When she tries to run, her feet tangle and she lands hard, the breath driven from surprised lungs in a loud whoosh, cutting off the second scream halfway through.

They are all over her then. Everywhere.

Strong hands on her shoulders and she can smell Mort, his omnipresent reek of pot smoke and sweat, before her father drags her out through the hole in the wall, back into the day, the blinding sun and the sky like a china plate. And then he sees the spiders, long-legged, yellow-brown hurrying things, and he screams too.

2.

Daria woke up, jerked violent from sleep, and lay very still, wrapped in dingy white sheets faintly damp from sweat and the steam hissing from the radiator across the room. An amber swatch of sunlight on the wall above her bed told her it was late, the last dregs of the afternoon, before she checked her wristwatch. She sat up slowly and leaned back against the plaster wall where a headboard should've been, wiped salty moisture from her face with both hands and stared at her unsteady palms and waited for the white noise, dreamshock, to pass, sluggish decompression bleeding her back into the world.

Niki Ky was still asleep on the floor beside the bed, curled into the old wool afghan and the Peanuts sheets washed so many times that Linus' blue blanket had gone gray. She only added to the disorientation, something else inexplicable, and Daria let her eyes wander the apartment, taking in safe familiarity, cataloging ratty furniture and the posters thumbtacked to the walls.

She'd never made a habit of bringing home strays; there were far too many of them on the streets, too many ways of charity going sour, no good deed unpunished, after all, and she was having trouble remembering what had been any different about Niki Ky.

Daria reached for her cigarettes, the half-empty pack lying on the fold-out card table she used for a nightstand. Her lighter was nowhere in sight, lost in the clutter of spare change and gum wrappers, snatches of song lyrics scribbled on fast-food napkins and scraps of notebook paper, weeks of accumulated pocket trash. She finally settled for a book of matches, one left behind the black cardboard cover stamped with the Fidgety Bean's gold logo, and when she struck it, the air smelled instantly of brimstone. She inhaled deeply; the Marlboro tasted good and helped to clear her head a little.

Clear away the cobwebs and . . .

She rubbed at the tender spot between her eyebrows, rough one-thumb excuse for a massage. Her sinuses ached, dull pressure and just enough pain to notice, as if the memories were a cancer swelling there behind her eyes. And if she rubbed hard enough, she might effect a remission.

Across the room, something bumped hard against the front door and she jumped, adrenaline jolt upright, a half-instant later recognized the probing scritch of a key.

"Motherfuck," she muttered, pushed sweatstiff crimson bangs from her face and pulled another hit off the cigarette.

The dead bolt clicked and the door opened and Claude shut it softly behind him, his cat-careful movement, so determined not to wake her that he hadn't noticed she was already awake.

"It's okay," she said, "I'm up," smoky cloud of words, and he smiled, held out a white deli bag for her to see.

"Then you can have breakfast with me," he said. "I got chocolate croissants . . ." and then he noticed Niki on the floor, only the spiky black top of her head and one leg showing from under her wad of covers.

"Well, she's definitely an improvement over Keith, but you shouldn't have made her sleep on the floor."

Daria transferred the cigarette to her lips and gave him the finger with both hands.

Niki mumbled something in her sleep and pulled the afghan completely over her head; both legs stuck out now, patient corpse feet waiting for their yellow toe tag. Claude just smiled that much wider and turned to the cramped kitchenette, one wall crammed with its gas stove and ancient Frigidaire, cracked and pitted formica and ruststained sink. He set the croissants on the countertop and opened the fridge door, took out the big Ball mason jar of coffee beans.

"She just needed a place to crash, that's all," Daria said around the Marlboro's filter. "And you're a pervert."

"Mmm-hmmm," he purred, and dumped three heaping scoops of the beans into their cheap little Regal grinder, held the button down with his thumb and the machine whirred its gritty racket. The noise of the grinder alone was enough to help some, drawing her further out of her

head, away from the dream that was already beginning to
blur and fade around the edges.

"Marry me," she said. "Please?"

"Darlin', you know I'm strictly mistress material," and
he opened the grinder, poured the fresh and fragrant
grounds into the drip basket of the Proctor-Silex Morning-
Maker. It had recently replaced Daria's battered old
Mr. Coffee, one of Claude's mysterious and welcomed
windfalls. Soon, the apartment would fill with the vel-
vety pungence of fine Colombian dark roast; Daria,
good Pavlovian pup, felt a gentle flush of saliva, cleans-
ing away the sticky taste of her uneasy sleep.

Niki moaned softly, sat up and blinked her dark eyes.

"What time is it?" she asked, groggy, slightest rasp, and
she squinted into the dazzling shaft coming in through the
apartment's only window, wide and smudgy sash looking
west. There were no curtains, no blinds, and the dirty
glass did little to mute the fiery November sunset.

Daria glanced at the digital clock radio on the card table. "Almost four," she said. "Three fifty-seven."

"Shit. I gotta see about my car."

Claude was taking mismatched mugs down from the
cabinet above the sink. He turned around, waved with
his free hand.

"Hi."

Niki blinked again. "Hi," she replied.

"Niki Ky," Daria said, "this is my roommate, Jobless
Claude. He's a pervert and a lay-about and an angel of
mercy. Jobless Claude, this here's Niki Ky. She's on her
way to find Jesus in Cullman County."

"Hi, Claude," Niki said.

"Cream and sugar?" he asked; he'd turned his back to
them again and was busy wiping at the inside of one of
the mugs with a gingham dish towel.

"Huh?"

"Cof-fee," Daria said, exaggerating syllables, slow
speak for the deaf or foreign or half-asleep.

"Oh. Yeah, sure," and then Niki added quickly, "Lots
of both."

"Good girl," and Claude, apparently satisfied that the

offending cup was clean, clean enough, went back to the Frigidaire, set a pink carton of half-and-half next to the row of mugs.

Daria stretched, toes and fingers pointing, offered Niki one of the Marlboros.

"No thanks. I don't smoke cigarettes."

Daria shrugged and dropped the pack back into the clutter.

The coffee maker gurgled, rheumy wet sound, and began to drain into the glass pot. When it had finished, Claude filled each cup, added generous spoonfuls of sugar to his and Niki's, fat dollops of cream; Daria's he left pure and black.

Niki rubbed her eyes, something little girl in the gesture, and covered her mouth when she yawned.

"Thanks again," she said, "for putting me up."

"No problem at all," and Daria sucked a final drag from her cigarette and stabbed it out in a large, cut-glass ashtray, oasis of butts and ash in the middle of the card table's chaos.

Caught there in the last glory of the day, Niki's skin seemed to radiate its own light, perfect silken complexion, balanced somewhere lustrous between almond and ginger. Daria knew her own skin was as unremarkable as her face, not pale enough for goth, despite her vampire's hours, but certainly no color to speak of. A few poorly placed freckles scattered beneath her eyes and she still got zits on the days before her periods. Niki was wearing a ratty Cure t-shirt she'd pulled out of her bubblegum colored gym bag, frayed sleeves cut off at the shoulders and the collar stretched shapeless and she *still* looked exotic.

Daria accepted the coffee Claude held out to her, white mug and the molecular formula for caffeine printed on one side. The handle had broken off a long time ago and so she held it cradled in both palms, which was really better anyway. The heat was almost painful, soaked quickly into her hands and flowed up her wrists. She closed her eyes and breathed the rich, slightly bitter steam, felt it working its way seductively into her aching sinuses.

"But you weren't born there," Claude said and Daria realized that she'd missed something. It didn't matter; Claude would entertain Niki Ky, had already moved in on her like a kitten with a fine, new toy. Claude would play the proper host while she brooded and sipped her scalding coffee.

"No," Niki said. "I was born in New Orleans."

"I have friends in the Quarter," he said, and Daria opened her eyes, stared across the brim of her mug at the giant poster of Billie Holiday hanging above her stereo. Lady Day watching over them like some beautiful, tragic madonna of heroin and the blues. Bee-stung pout in grainy black and white, enlarged too many times to retain integrity, resolution, black and white flowers in her hair. Eyes that let nothing in and gave nothing away. Claude had brought the poster home with him one night, had carefully mended a tear along the bottom edge with scotch tape, and she'd never found out where he'd gotten it.

It made her think of nothing now but Keith. Keith and his needles and his strong and certain fingers pulling music from the strings. From her.

"Since June," Niki said, half-sighed answer to a question Daria hadn't heard, and then, "But it seems like years, you know?"

This late, Keith had probably already made his connection, would have scored for the day and fixed. Was either laid up in his roachy little apartment or hanging out with the bums and punks and other junkies who used abandoned railroad cars, condemned and empty buildings, as shelter from the cold and cops. She held the mug to her lips, swallowed quick before the coffee had time to cool inside her mouth.

Another hour and Mort's shift at the machine shop would be over.

Claude laughed, soft boy laugh, almost as comforting as the coffee and she tried to let it all go for now, plenty of time later, the rest of her life, to worry about Keith

Barry and Stiff Kitten and the haunted places in her sleep. Her croissant sat neglected on an apple-green plastic saucer in front of her, pastry dusted with powdered sugar and cocoa and she didn't even remember him setting it on the bed.

"Does it bother you if people call you a stripper?"

"Christ, Claude, does it bother *you* when people call you a faggot?" and it didn't come out like a joke at all, sharp edges and acid where she thought she'd only intended to slip back into the conversation.

Claude was staring at her, his face gone stony hard and any surprise or hurt guarded safe behind a piercing what-the-hell-crawled-up-*your*-ass-and-died glare. *Good question, good fucking question.* Niki had looked away, quick glance down and picked at her own croissant, half-eaten and the gooey brown insides showing.

"No," she said. "It doesn't bother me. I am a stripper."

"I'm sorry," Daria said, meant it but there was no way to sound *enough* like she meant it.

"And that's *Mr.* Faggot to you," Claude said sternly, mock-severity that lifted the tension just barely enough that she could slip beneath his barbed wire gaze, could at least look away.

"I really do need to call about my car," Niki said. "I have no idea what time the garage closes."

"Yeah, sure," and Daria pointed at the clunky old rotary phone sitting on the floor next to one of the stereo speakers. "Help yourself."

Claude finished the last of his coffee, stood up, and walked back to the sink with his mug and saucer. Niki set her own dishes out of the way before she pushed aside the afghan and the Peanuts sheets, scooted across the floor to the phone. And again, Daria found herself watching, envying the subtle alliance of movement and unaffected elegance that made the simplest action seem graceful. She tried to imagine Niki Ky on some seedy, barroom stage, rehearsed bump and grind, bogus passion, through a haze of cigarette smoke and colored lights, but there were too many contradictions. All the strippers she'd met in Birmingham had big hair and nails like the talons of predatory birds, silicon tits and makeup caked like spackling paste. Drag queens without the sense of humor.

"The phone book's right over there," she said and pointed to a sloppy stack of magazines and comics by the bathroom door, "if you need to look the number up."

"They gave me a card." Niki was already digging through the pockets of her army jacket. "If I haven't lost it."

Daria sighed, looked at her wristwatch, and swung her legs over the side of the bed, bare feet flat against the chilly hardwood. Off toward the tracks, toward the other end of Morris and work, she heard the whistle of a freight train, desolate, empty sound, and she sat and listened to Niki arguing with the mechanic, Claude running water to wash dishes. And the steel wheels, razor wheels on steel rails, as the sun went down again.

3.

Daria had been nineteen when she'd fallen over backwards into her first band.

She was living in a Southside firetrap with a guy named Pablo, had worked day jobs flipping burgers and sold blotter acid on the side to keep a roof over their heads, Ramen noodles and Wild Irish Rose in their bellies. Their apartment had been on the topmost floor of a building that might still have been habitable when her grandmothers were her age. Rats as big as puppies and they'd slept with all the lights on to keep the roaches off the bed. When it rained, the roof was little better than a colander, rainwater seeping through a sagging foot of plaster and rotten lathe, pigeon shit and mold, before it dripped from the ceiling and streamed in murky rivulets down the walls.

Pablo had played bass for a band called Yer Funeral, three punker holdouts with identical Ramones haircuts who covered The Sex Pistols and The Clash and made everything sound like crap. The singer and guitarist, a painfully skinny cokehead named Jonesy McCabe, had lived in Manhattan in the early eighties and claimed to have given the ghost of Sid Vicious a blow job one Halloween. Carlton Hicks on drums, and they'd opened for marginally better bands on the local hardcore circuit, two or three shows a month and the rest of their time spent picking fights with rednecks and skinheads, fucking their girlfriends; counterfeit anarchists scrounging bedlam in the sunset days of Reagan's America.

Daria had never asked Pablo to teach her to play, had never had any particular interests in music or anything else creative. Sometimes she'd talked about college; she hadn't dropped out and her SAT scores had been decent enough, but there was never any money, never would be, and although there were loans, the thought of owing Uncle Sam twenty or thirty thousand for an undergrad degree had finally soured her on the idea. So she worked at McDonald's and Arby's and sold her cheap blotter, stamped with dancing rows of rainbow-colored Jerr-bears and so weak that even high school kids who still thought cigarettes were cool had trouble getting a trip off the stuff.

But the more bookings Yer Funeral managed to worm itself into, the more serious Pablo became about his music, and he'd actually begun to practice, hours spent sitting around their apartment rehearsing his bare-bone punk rhythms. And she'd learned that unless she paid attention, he ignored her altogether.

It had started as a joke, *yeah, Dar, let's see what you can do, let's hear what you got in there,* and Daria holding his silver Gibson while everyone laughed and made their punker boy pussy jokes. But there had never been a single moment of awkwardness. The instrument had seemed to belong in her hands, had almost seemed built for the span and stretch of her fingers, like something that should have been there all along.

And whenever Pablo was asleep or off screwing around with Jonesy and Carlton, she'd sat on their one chair and played, fuck the chords and notes, had listened hard to the bass lines on Pablo's pirate tapes and it was always so goddamned *obvious,* fingers here and here, then here, until she'd simply merged with the recordings. She had quickly discovered that the bass was capable of other sounds besides the all-the-way-up, tooth-grinding throb Pablo hammered out of the thing, sloppy attempts at discord that always dissolved into a noteless spew of ear-splitting low end noise as he got drunker and cranked the blue gain knob higher and higher.

Two weeks and she had figured out all of the songs in Yer Funeral's set list; so little variation in punker bass lines, anyway, almost everything on the bottom two strings. She'd deciphered most of the knobs on the cabinet and the bass itself, had grown puking sick of The Sex Pistols and The Ramones and The Clash, everything fuzzy and flat through Pablo's junker stereo, and she'd begun to just string notes together like popcorn or plastic beads. Pictured them as fat brown blocks of different shapes and sizes to be stacked any way she pleased. And Daria had realized that she was writing her own songs, things that might become songs, and she would shut her eyes and stand before the thumping rig, imagining the drums and guitars, the singer's wordless voice, all tied together with the warm chocolate rhythms she coaxed from the Gibson.

And then Pablo had smashed up his hand, had been drunk and fallen, tripped on a crack in the fucking *sidewalk* and tried to break his fall with his right hand. One week before Yer Funeral was supposed to open a big show, Battle of the Bands thing, and there were rumors that a scout from IRS would be coming down. When they'd gotten back from the emergency room, Jonesy had been waiting for them on the front steps of their apartment building, and when he'd seen Pablo's hand, ridiculous swollen fingers like splinted sausages and the shell of fresh, white plaster, he'd socked Pablo in the jaw and broken two front teeth.

Next day, after he'd heard that Jonesy was seriously looking for someone to replace him on a not-so-temporary basis, he'd volunteered Daria. She'd told him to fuck off, but he'd begged, and Jonesy had finally agreed to let her sit in on *one* practice. Yer Funeral had rehearsed in the garage of an abandoned Chevron station, concrete floors gritty oil-dark and darker pits where the hydraulic lifts had been. Pablo had sat alone in a shadowy corner, sucking beer and looking sullen and anxious; Jonesy and Carlton had exchanged doubtful smirks as she'd tuned and adjusted the strap to fit her shoulder.

Then Carlton had started off, no warning, three loud beats slammed from his foot drum before Jonesy leaped into the New York Dolls' "Chatterbox," spitting the words at the mike and his graceless fingers ripping madly at his guitar. Daria had only missed a beat or two, and by the time they reached Jonesy's solo, both drummer and singer were grinning. Daria had never looked up from the bass, never once taken her eyes off the strings, had chewed her lower lip until it bled, until the song had ended and Jonesy was laughing like a hyena and Carlton had kept repeating "Gawddammit, girl," over and over. Pablo hadn't said a word, had popped the cap off another bottle of Sterling and watched from his patch of gloom.

Daria had followed straight through Yer Funeral's entire borrowed repertoire, had ended with "Rockaway Beach" and her fingers had been numb, fingerprint whorls scraped raw and smooth. No breath left in her, gasping and her arms gone to slinkys, her sweat standing out on the garage floor around her feet, bright droplets and splatters unable to soak into the oil and antifreeze saturated cement. And Jonesy had slapped her on the back, big, stupid boy gesture of affection or camaraderie, fraternity, and then he'd hugged her tight and Pablo, drunk off his cheap beer and confusion, knowing that this whole thing was getting out of hand, blowing up in his face, but not sure why or how to stop the explosion, had mumbled something not entirely to himself.

Jonesy had asked him to speak up, come again, and Pablo had stood, slight reel and sway as he stepped toward them.

"What the hell difference does it make," he'd said,

had slurred. Jonesy and Carlton had looked back at him with blank faces, not following; Daria had kept her eyes on the grungy floor, on her rejected sweat and abused fingers.

"No freakin' scout wants to hear a cover band anyway, man. Punk's dead and you guys are pissin' up a goddamn rope." And then he'd staggered off to take a leak, to hunt down the toilet even though the station hadn't had water since it'd closed.

"Hey, fuck you, man," Carlton had shouted after him. "You fucking wanker. You're just pissed 'cause your old lady made you look like shit."

Pablo had ignored him, had disappeared through a darkened doorway (the door torn off long ago, propped useless somewhere nearby) into the darker lobby. A second later, he'd cursed, had given up his search for the toilet and they'd heard the metal through fabric *zrrrip,* the wet spatter of Pablo's piss on the lobby's tiles.

"Fuck him," Jonsey muttered as he'd lit a cigarette and stuffed his Zippo back into his shirt pocket. "That was some amazing shit, Dar."

Daria had wiped her face on the tail of her t-shirt, the clean, ocean smell of her sweat mixing with the lingering gasoline stench, hydrocarbon phantoms, and she'd finally smiled. She *had* been good, damn good, and more amazing, it had *felt* good. Had felt wild and alive and had consumed her, every fiber of her mind and body, in a way that not even the best of her infrequent orgasms had ever come close to doing. She'd been only dimly aware of a door slamming somewhere, the rust-bucket growl of Pablo's Impala outside the garage bay doors, the angry, hot spin of rubber on asphalt as he'd peeled out of the Chevron's parking lot into the night.

"Don't worry about it," Carlton had said, "He's bein' a jerk."

But she hadn't *cared* about Pablo, felt only the vaguest annoyance, disappointment that he could be so insecure, could act so petty. Her head was crammed too full of the Gibson's toothache throb, her senses clogged with the stinging numb of her fingertips, the delicious threat of cramp in her arms and shoulders and the small of her back, the heady smell of herself. And what she'd said next had spilled out like someone else's words, no thought, no consideration of consequence or her own possible inadequacies.

"If I wrote some songs, I mean, the lyrics, can you guys write the music?"

Jonesy and Carlton had looked at each other, slug slow comprehension, and then Jonesy had shaken his head.

"Forget it, Dar. Shit, even if I thought I could, there's not enough time."

"But would you *try,* Jonesy?" And that enthusiasm had felt strange coming from her mouth, alien vomit, shimmering silver and red in the amp-shocked garage air. "Would you at least give it a shot?"

"Why? We're good, right? *Twice* as good with you on Pablo's bass."

"Because Pablo's right, man," Carlton had said, grudging agreement, as he began to break down his kit. "He might be a jerk, but he's pro'bly right about nobody wantin' to hear a bunch of tired old covers."

"Just let me see what I can come up with," she'd said, had almost been begging and no idea why, and they'd agreed, Jonesy still shaking his head but agreeing anyway. Carlton had given her a ride home, and she'd looked for Pablo's car on the street, had looked without letting on that she was looking. But there'd been no sign of him, no sign inside that he'd been back by the apartment.

Daria had called in sick the next day, had lied to her jowly-fat asshole of a manager, something simple and contagious like the flu or a stomach virus. She'd coughed into the receiver, had ground her voice down to the croakiest wheeze, and of course he hadn't believed her. He handled his little legion of burger-flippers like an Egyptian foreman, building his pyramids from styrofoam and beef patties; but he couldn't prove she was slacking, would make it up by sticking her with all the shitty shifts for the next two weeks.

She'd found an old steno pad hiding on top of the

refrigerator, half the pages filled with phone numbers and doodles, games of hangman, the cardboard cover crusted with specks of cockroach poop. She'd used one of their two butter knives to scrape the cover relatively clean and had spent the next fifteen minutes looking for a pencil, or a pen that hadn't dried up.

Before nightfall, she'd finished her first song, "Iron Lung" scribbled like a prescription across the top of the page. Rambling and craggy and it hadn't felt anywhere near as good as the music had, had left only a dim sense of accomplishment and fingers smudged inky blue from the free-bleeding ballpoint pen. And the fear, almost certainty, that she'd been full of shit, that she should have kept her mouth shut, that Jonesy was gonna take one look at the words she'd scrawled and laugh in her face.

Before she'd gone to the bathroom sink to scrub the ink stains from her hands, to the boxy shower to scrub the previous night's sweatgrunge away, she'd stood a minute or two at the window, watching Sixteenth Avenue, pockmarked asphalt stripe up and down the side of Red Mountain. Pablo could be anywhere, drunk or just moping; he'd drag his ass home sooner or later. She should be used to his punker boy bullshit and posing, but the guilt was starting to get in around the bright, new edges of her excitement.

And she'd realized that what she was *really* beginning to fear wasn't that she might have driven something irreparable between her and Pablo, but the fact that the ecstasy and burn she'd felt with Jonesy and Carlton was temporary. That there would be only just so many fixes before Pablo's hand came out of that cast and she went back to being peripheral, hanger-on, the girlfriend who paid bills and sat, smoking and drinking beer in bar after identical murky bar, while the others took the stage.

But Pablo had stayed gone, three more days and her words had fitted seamlessly with the crude, growling melodies Jonsey had fashioned for them. It was darker stuff than the fuck-off-and-die anthems Yer Funeral had

always pushed. Darker and more urgent, and the thrill
that Daria had felt that first night had been nothing
compared to the rush that came from playing the new
songs, *her* songs. Her fingers had become more sure by
the minute, both of themselves and the strings, more
like remembering than learning. And she'd loved the
rawness of the lyrics, the way they rode high on the music, even if she'd still thought that Jonesy McCabe
sounded like a raccoon caught in a washing machine.

Saturday night had come around and still no Pablo,
no sign or word if he'd left town or gone to ground
somewhere. The excitement had begun to sour in her
stomach, intoxication curdled like old milk. They'd
been slated as the first of two opening acts, had sat back
in the shadows, staring out at the two or three hundred
people milling around inside the derelict Northside
warehouse.

"He ain't gonna show," Carlton had said, disgust and
nerves competing for his voice.

"Fuck him," Jonesy had replied. "Ain't that right,
Dar? *We're* the show now and tonight we're gonna kick
some ass."

Daria hadn't said anything, had scanned the scattered,
shifting sea of faces, and she'd known he was out there
somewhere. And that they weren't lovers anymore, that
she'd stolen something from him, and that, as far as
Pablo was concerned, she may as well have sliced off
his dick. She held his bass in her hands, sweatslicking
the instrument's long neck, and she'd wanted to call it
off, go back, but it'd already been too late. Because she
wanted *this* more, wanted this more than his cock between her legs or his body next to her in bed.

Someone had turned up the lights, gel bloodied red,
sunlight at the bottom of a shallow, red lake, and the
crowd had all but disappeared behind the glare. Jonesy
had put his arm around her shoulder, then, one-of-
the-boys-now embrace, and she'd stepped through the
stageside snarl of cables and Peavy amps.

The crowd had made a sound like some huge, mumbling beast, delight or dissent and a smattering of indif-

ferent applause. Someone had hurled a beer can and it had passed just inches from her face, drenching everything in foamy, malt-smelly stickiness.

"FUCK *YOU,* SHITHEADS!" Jonesy had howled into his mike, beer in his hair, dripping down his face, every muscle in his neck strained cord-taut. And *then* the crowd had come alive, big beast waking up, and *Blam, Blam, Blam,* three beats from Carlton and she'd taken her eyes off the hazy writhe and press of bodies at the edge of the stage, no room for anything but the business of her fingers.

A showy little riff from Jonesy, a little too showy, and then he'd hurtled her words into the steel-gray phallus of the microphone and the sound had poured out thick and sizzling around her, glorious wail and crash and backwash feedback.

Halfway through the first song, she'd tossed her head to one side, flipping hair from her eyes, had only looked away from the strings for a second but she'd seen him. Pablo, eyes like anthracite lumps of coal, face like weathered cemetery marble. One violently still point in the fury of the mosh pit.

"All you make me feel is depressed," Jonesy sang, *"I'm tired of toeing your line."*

Pablo had stepped forward, not the slightest change in his expression, his utter absence of expression; the slamming flesh had parted freely as he came, Charlton Heston dividing meat with zombie eyes.

"Let me out of this iron lung! I can fuckin' breathe on my own!"

He'd made it to the edge of the stage before Jonesy had noticed him, and there'd been no security down front, no security in the whole place except for one off-duty cop checking IDs at the door. And the door may as well have been a million miles away. Someone had turned on the strobes just then, and the red light had begun to pulse madly, arrhythmia flicker, as Pablo pulled himself up, pushed aside and between the monitors. He'd moved slow, and the lights had added the illusion of silent-film jerkiness.

Daria had taken one step back, her hands stumbling as the music came apart like a house of cards.

The crowd had shouted stupid encouragement, this new show as good as anything else, and Pablo hadn't even blinked when another beer can had bounced off the back of his head.

"Hey, man, we'll talk about this *after* the show," and Jonesy had laid one hand firmly on Pablo's shoulder, "okay, 'cause you're just gonna make an asshole outta yourself this way," but those emptydark eyes had stayed locked on Daria.

"Give it back to me," and everything that hadn't been in his gaze was coiled tight and hot inside those words. He'd held both hands out for the bass, his right still encased in dirty plaster, looking more like a zombie than ever, Frankenstein's vengeful monster come to collect his due.

"You don't even know these songs, man," and Jonesy had stepped away from his mike, had moved quickly to put himself between her and Pablo.

"It's mine and I *said* give it back to me, *you goddamn stinking bitch*," and Pablo had shrugged free of Jonesy's grip, had shoved him aside and lunged for the Gibson so fast that Daria hadn't had time to get out of his way. He'd grabbed the bass and yanked hard; the strap had held, but Daria stumbled, had lost her balance and gone down on her knees at his feet. The canvas strap had twisted up and under her chin, digging deep into her windpipe, cutting her breath off as it pulled her head around until she'd stared helplessly into Pablo's crotch. Her hands struggled to unhook the strap, desperate fingers still stinging from the last notes of the interrupted song.

Then Pablo had yanked again, harder than before, and Daria had heard her neck pop, had felt the nasty sensation of bone grinding cartilage. But the strap had come loose, had whipped free, and she'd crumpled, hands at her own violated throat, gasping the smoky air in reckless mouthfuls.

And Pablo had stood above her like some ax-wielding crazy in a slasher flick, the bass clutched by the graceful handle of its neck, the dull silver instrument washed metallic red in the strobes. He'd raised it slowly over his head, over hers, and then Jonesy had hit him hard from behind, sharp rabbit punch to the base of his skull, and he *should* have gone down and stayed down. Instead, he only stumbled and drove one hard shoe tip into Daria's left ear.

"FUCK OFF," he'd screamed, screamed high and shrill in a voice that had hardly sounded human, much less like Pablo. He'd swung the bass around fast and hard and nailed Jonesy square in the chest. Still wheezing, struggling to get enough air, Daria had clearly heard the wet snap of breaking bone, and Jonesy McCabe had sailed backwards, colliding in a noisy tangle with Carlton's drums. And then Carlton had tackled Pablo and they'd both disappeared over the side of the stage, swallowed immediately by the mad crush of bodies.

Daria had staggered to her knees again, and people had begun to back away from the stage, clearing out a small, irregular circle of the warehouse's concrete floor where Carlton was busy slamming his fists repeatedly into Pablo's face. The Gibson had lain a few feet away from them, trampled, broken, irrelevant.

She stood up, hands out cautious like a tightrope walker, purple-white blotches dancing in her eyes. Jonesy had lain in a limp heap, unconscious amid the jumble of brass cymbals and aluminum tripod stalks. Abruptly, the lights had stopped strobing, and she'd seen the dark trickle of blood at each corner of his mouth. For all she'd known, Pablo had killed him, and Carlton was in the process of killing Pablo. Because of her, because she'd tried to steal something that wasn't hers to take. Because for once in her grubby life something had felt right. Daria used the rig the bass had been plugged into to brace herself, had taken one step toward Jonesy.

And then the pain had gone off like a grenade lodged somewhere deep inside her skull, perfect agony filling in the place where her brain should have been, drowning body and mind in its searing electric gush. And the last thing she'd seen on the way down to merciful blackout was Carlton, climbing back onto the stage, nose squashed and bloodied grimace, and the shattered Gibson clasped triumphantly in one hand.

4.

Niki set the receiver back into its black cradle and sighed, loud exasperated sound, and Daria could see that she was really having to work at the half-smile, weak droop at the corners of her perfect lips.

"That bad?" she asked and Niki shrugged, stared down at her feet. Her toenails were painted a dark and pearly blue.

"Yeah," Niki said, "Or worse."

"Can they fix it?" Daria was sitting at the edge of the bed now, her own feet dangling over the side, not bare, but hidden inside tube socks with mismatched colored bands around the tops. Left, orange. Right, maroon.

"Yeah, if I want to hand over every penny I have."

"You should get a second opinion," Claude said from the kitchen sink; washing the breakfast dishes, three cups and three saucers and Ivory Liquid suds up to his elbows. "Most of those guys are crooked as the letter 'M.' "

"Yeah," Niki said, and then, "I don't know."

"Dar knows mechanics, don't you, Dar? The big guy that plays guitar for Vanilla Domination, and that other guy, the one who looks like Nick Cave, except not so ugly."

Daria was still looking down at her own feet, homely twins and a big hole in one heel so she could see the scar where she stepped on a broken 7-Up bottle last summer.

"Yeah, I'm sure I can find someone to take at look at it, if you want."

Niki stood and stretched, and Robert Smith, white

face, blackened eyes, fright-wig do, stared back at Daria from Niki's belly.

"Thanks, guys, but I'm afraid I'd only be delaying the inevitable. It's either my bank account or the junk-yard. I just have to decide which."

"It certainly couldn't hurt," Claude said, setting a coffee cup down to dry. "Just to be sure."

Niki shrugged again and then sniffed cautiously at one underarm, wrinkled her nose, and to Daria, even *that* seemed somehow graceful.

"God, I stink. Would it be okay if I used the shower?"

"Go right ahead," Daria said, and reached for another Marlboro, looking away before Niki Ky did anything else to make her feel awkward, dumpy, like a gorilla at charm school.

"You guys are wonderful," Niki said. "I just hope you don't get sick of me before I can get my ass back on the road," and she picked up the pink gym bag and stepped into the tiny bathroom, pulling the door shut behind her; Daria could hear her wrestling with the useless old lock.

"It hasn't worked since I've been here," Daria shouted, and, immediately, Niki stopped fumbling with the doorknob. A moment later, the rustyloud squeak of brass hot and cold water handles and the sudden, wet *shissh* of the shower head.

"Well," Claude said, fastidiously drying his hands with a checkered dishtowel. "I *still* say she's better than Keith."

Daria exhaled smoke through her nostrils, stared through the window at the fiery place in the sky where the sun had gone down.

"Just shut up, Claude."

She sat there until the sky was almost black, the deep indigo before true night, her cigarette smoked down to the filter and Niki still in the shower; trying not to think about Keith Barry or her father or the delicate itch of spider legs on naked skin. Unable to think of anything else.

CHAPTER FIVE

Robin

1.

The girl with absinthe hair, algae hair, slipped into her fishnets and fastened her garters to the elastic band around the top of the hose. Her doppelgänger in the big, gilt-framed mirror followed her every move, looking-glass girl who mocked her style and the nurtured pallor of her white skin. Sometimes Robin tried to outsmart her, misdirection, sleight of hand or foot or the slimmest parting of her lips. Nothing personal, but if the poor girl can't be more original, she has to expect a little flack, and Robin slid into the velvet skirt, mini-short, and her twin did the same, never missed a beat.

There was no hurry. She didn't have to meet Spyder and Byron at Dr. Jekyll's for two hours yet, and she was still horny, even after an hour in bed, masturbating with the plasticslick dildo and watching the pictures on her ceiling, the ones she painted there last summer, making this place safe: two ladders and plywood stretched between them, just like Michelangelo.

The hurricane swirl of clouds, black-and-blue as the swollen tummy of a thunderhead near the walls and the poppy red of Nagasaki at the eye, every shade of conflagration in between. Heaven spilling its fire and guts and the broken angels plunging, wings back and trailing starlight and feathers. And something terrible that she'd only suggested, watching from the still heart of the storm. The angels had skin like statues, eyes like sapphire and dusk, and between their legs the perfect alloy

of man and woman. Not sexless, but genitals that had
not yet been forced to take a side.

Ritual in pretended fresco, something against the
shadows.

The girl inside the mirror ran one pinkie through
the silver ring in Robin's navel, fresh piercing and the
wound still red at the edges, tugged gently, playfully.
Robin removed the blouse from its wire hanger, black
lace and no sleeves, crimson buttons like drops of stage
blood. The gloves were black, too, and lace, and they
hid the nubs of her fingernails, the cuticles chewed raw
and ragged.

Two knocks at her bedroom door, soft and hesitant,
and her mother speaking through the wood.

"Robin? Are you going out tonight, dear?"

"Yes, Mother," and the girl in the mirror stuck out her
tongue, bright and wet against lips rouged the color of
ash. Robin's teeth caught it, held it, supplicant flesh
squeezed helpless between her incisors.

"Your father's working late, and I'm having dinner
with Marjorie and Quentin. Don't forget to lock up, and
set the alarm when you leave."

Robin's teeth parted, and her tongue slipped grate-
fully back inside her mouth.

"Promise?"

"Yes," Robin said.

"Good girl," her mother said. "Have fun and drive
safe," like some fucking public service blurb, and
Robin turned her back on the mirror. Concentrated on
buttoning each sanguine button, on the retreating tattoo
of her mother's footsteps. Her mother played pretend,
pretend that Robin was still a child, pretend that her father was held up late over his blueprints and drafting
tools instead of his latest whore girlfriend. That her life
wasn't as hellish as everything else in the world, and
Robin didn't really give a shit as long they paid the bills
on her charge cards and didn't bitch about where she
spent her nights. Who she spent them with.

Robin sat down on one rumpled corner of the bed and
laced her feet tight into tall vinyl boots, icicle heels and

toes like fresh slices of midnight. The calm she'd felt only a minute before had dissolved completely, whatever dim sanctuary her room conferred violated by her mother's voice and brittle delusions, and now all she wanted was to escape. Put all the miles she could between herself and the neat suburban rows of brick and aluminum siding, pretty mortgaged cancers, and follow the interstate over the mountains, to Spyder and the honest desolation of the city.

But she'd wait a few more minutes, give her mother plenty of time to clear out. Robin lay back on the bed, the sheets that smelled like jasmine incense and clove cigarettes and her musty sex, and stared at the walls.

Walls her painstaking alchemy of acrylics and sponge dabbings had transformed into some impossible marble, simple sheetrock into ebony stone shot through with scarlet quartz veins. Four stark slabs supporting, framing, the tragic tableau overhead, the pillars of the world, and the walls were almost bare: only a giant Siouxsie and the Banshees poster above the headboard and a raccoon skull hanging snout down in the narrow space between her cluttered bookshelf and the new stereo her parents had given her for her last birthday.

"Nineteen," her mother had said, "Robin's so mature for just nineteen, don't you think so, Bill?" And her father had smiled, his eyes a hundred miles away.

She'd painted the door a single bottomless shade of glistening black, like hot tar or spilled oil, clinging absence of anything like light.

Robin listened, as patient as anything cornered, and when she finally heard the faint growl and clank of the automatic garage door, the softer purr of her mother's car backing out of the drive, she got up and opened the black door.

2.

This is where it started.

On an April night when thunderstorms had swept out of Mississippi, raking the world with lightning and the promise of tornadoes, and the city's civil defense sirens had howled shrill apocalypse. And Walter, who said he wanted to be a sailor and only pretended to be queer so nobody would think he was strange, had brought them a tiny bit of opium, black tar in Spyder's antique hookah, just like Gomez and Morticia. There was almost nothing that Walter could not secure, given time and the cash, no pill or herb or intoxicating powder too exotic that he didn't seem to have a source, somewhere.

Gawky Walter, rawboned and hair like a handful of dead mice, so hard in love with Robin that she always got to laughing if she looked at his eyes too long. He bought her company, Spyder's, Byron's, with drugs and clumsy, helpless charm.

And that night the storm and Bauhaus turned down low so they could still hear the thunder and the sizzling rain and sirens, and she'd nestled content and almost naked in Spyder's tattooed arms; waiting for her turn at the water pipe's brass mouthpiece. Listening to whatever Walter was saying, gathering his words inside her head: the book he was reading on the Holy Grail, having exhausted Jessie Weston and Roger Sherman Loomis, a book by Carl Jung's wife and the grail as vessel, the sword and the lance, grail as stone. She'd watched their candle-oranged faces: Walter's too excited; Byron, bored, but watching Spyder to see what she thought before he agreed or disagreed.

"And *these* angels, the *zwivelaere,* had wanted to preserve the original God-image," he said, "the *unity,* the divine inner opposites that were being torn apart by the war in Heaven."

"*Zwivelaere,*" the German had rolled easy and slow from Spyder's tongue. "What does that mean?" And then she'd taken the mouthpiece from him and filled her cheeks with the faintly sweet, acrid smoke, had leaned down and Robin parted her lips and accepted the kiss, taking Spyder's breath and the opium inside her, had closed her eyes and only exhaled when her lungs had finally begun to ache and the distant thrum in her ears, like the empty space between radio stations.

"The doubters," Walter answered, guarded awe in his voice like this was a secret, dangerous knowledge, and Spyder only nodded her head.

Robin had watched Spyder's slow eyes, eyes the gentle color of faded denim. Spyder almost never smoked anything but pot, routinely turned down the best acid and 'shrooms, but the opium was a treat too rare to allow her caution to interfere, her fear of the wild things and places in her head. Robin knew it was those parts of Spyder she loved most, the turbulence behind those pacific eyes, the part that Spyder locked away with her tranquilizers and antidepressants.

"The doubters hid the grail stone on the earth," Walter said, and she wished he would shut up. He rarely actually seemed to understand the books he read, arcane treatises on conspiracy and occult Christian orders; rattled endlessly in a desperate attempt to impress her, and so it had become a sort of a game: she fed his desperation by suggesting the most difficult texts and watched as he struggled, fixated on the obvious, the superficial skin of myth and history. Everything reduced to Tolkien-simple fantasy and the magic and deeper mystery lost on him.

She did not particularly dislike Walter, but she didn't love him the way Spyder did, either. Didn't see him as some integral part of the circle of her life.

The storm had rattled at the windows, wanting in, and she'd watched the water caught like glistening bugs in the screen wire behind the glass.

There was a longish pause in Walter's exposition, then, and Byron sighed loudly, got up from his seat on the spring-shot sofa to put a new CD on or a tape, cold molasses motion, and Walter had said, "I can get some buttons next week, if anyone's interested."

"Buttons?" Byron said. "What kind of 'buttons'?"

"Peyote," and the word had brought Robin drifting back from her velvet contemplation of the raindrops trapped inside the squares of wire, held fast by fate and their own surface tension.

"How much?" she'd asked him, and Walter looked lost for a second, shrugged.

"Randy said to get back to him about the price, but—"

"No, I mean how many *buttons* can you get?"

"Oh," and she'd seen his hot embarrassment, inordinate unease over nothing at all.

"Probably as much as we want," he'd said. "Why?"

" 'Cause I did peyote once when I lived down in Mobile, but I only got one button and it didn't do anything much but make me puke. You gotta eat a lot, like nine or ten buttons at least, if you're gonna get a good trip off it."

Byron had stopped fumbling through Spyder's CDs, clack-clack-clack of jewel cases against one another, and put on My Life With The Thrill Kill Kult's *Sexplosion,* skipped ahead to "Sex on Wheelz." The music drowned the storm, and Robin had to raise her voice to be heard.

"It would be worth it," she'd said, "*if* you could get enough."

"I heard that stuff tastes like shit." Byron had returned to the sofa, took his turn at the hookah.

"I'll see what I can do," and Walter had tried to sound matter-of-fact about it, sure of himself, but she'd heard the crisp uncertainty between his words, knew that the chances of his coming up with that much peyote were slim to none. Just another test, like Carlos Castenada and *Foucault's Pendulum.* Spyder had frowned down at her, sleepy brown eyes full of admonition and lazy passion.

A little while later, the last of the opium gone and she'd followed Spyder to the bedroom, leaving Walter and Byron alone in each other's company. Down the narrow hallway, past closed doors, into the dusty heart of the big house and the dark where she could hear the storm again.

* * *

Not the next week, or the week after, but early in May, Walter had shown up at Weird Trappings very late one afternoon, her and Spyder closing up the shop, planning to spend the whole night watching Dario Argento videos and screwing on the living room floor, and he'd stood on the far side of the counter while Spyder counted out the register. Had shifted, impatient dance, one foot to the other, occasionally looking back over his shoulder as if someone might be following him. Walter had set the book he was reading down on the smudgy glass countertop, a library copy of Charles Fort's *Lo!*, Robin's latest suggestion and his place marked about halfway through with a dirty pigeon feather. The book and a big Piggly Wiggly bag, grocery brown paper rolled closed at the top.

"I got them," he'd said, looking over his shoulder again, his eyes bright and proud and nervous.

"You got what, Walter?" Spyder asked, and then she'd lost count of the twenties and cursed him before she started over again.

"I got the *peyote*," he'd said, almost whispered, the last word squeezed down to a cautious hiss that had reminded Robin a little of Peter Lorre in *Casablanca* or *Arsenic and Old Lace*.

"No shit," and Robin had reached past Spyder and the cash drawer, had thought for a second that Walter was going to snatch the bag away from her. She'd unrolled the crumpled paper and in the shadows down at the bottom were three or four large Ziploc baggies, each filled with lumpy dark buttons of sun-dried peyote.

"Goddamn it, Walter," she'd said, and then Spyder, who'd given up trying to count the twenties, had taken the bag away from her, peered skeptically inside.

"Holy fuck," she'd whispered. "Where'd you get it all?"

Walter had smiled his tense half-smile, the dimpled corners of his mouth still drawn stubbornly down.

"Randy's got a connection somewhere out in Texas. It's legal for the Indians to grow it out there for religious purposes, but you have to be a member of this Indian church and have a lotta Indian blood to buy it."

"The Native American Church," Robin had said, remembering a book she'd read about the peyote religions, the state-licensed *peyoteros* who grew their sacred cactus, could legally sell it only to registered members of the NAC.

"A group of Oklahoma peyotists formed the Church in 1918 to protect their ceremonies from the Feds," and she hadn't missed the way that'd impressed him, took her full measure of delight from his futile admiration.

"Well, I told you I could get it," he'd said, and his unaccustomed smile had stretched wider, revealing a rare glimpse of uneven front teeth.

Spyder had continued to stare into the Piggly Wiggly bag, shaking her head slowly, mild, pleased disbelief on her white face.

"But what did all this cost?" she asked and he'd shrugged, "Not so much as you'd think. It's cheap shit, really. The Indians can get a thousand buttons for about a hundred and fifty bucks. Of course, Randy has to charge me a lot more than that, though. I got fifty buttons in there."

Spyder had handed the bag to Robin and gone back to counting the crumpled green bills.

"So, you guys want to call Byron and get fucked up tonight?" Walter asked, hopeful, fairly glowing with his little victory.

"No," Robin replied. "We're gonna do this right," and then she'd rolled the bag closed again.

3.

Or this is where it started, where it *really* started.

The night that Robin met Spyder Baxter. Still months to go before high school graduation, pomp and circumstance and her parents picking colleges for her like arranged marriages. Waiting around the civic center parking lot after the show, the Jim Rose Circus and Nine Inch Nails, as if something worth seeing might happen; one more in the smoky clot of bodies assembled around Tony's new Honda CRX. Warm Boone's Farm like soured Kool-Aid from a jug, and an amber bottle of Jack Daniel's making the rounds, too.

She'd sat in the open hatchback, too drunk to feel the cold night, Tony all over her, his rough hands and whiskey mouth, wanting inside. And she'd taken her turn at the jug and passed it on to someone else, another girl, nameless blonde from another school. The blonde girl was almost ready to spew and Robin had dimly hoped she'd at least go somewhere else to do it.

"There was a drive-by shooting here last week," someone said, and she'd blinked through the booze, trying to match the slurred voice to a face. "There's still broken glass all over that side of the street."

The other faces had oohed and ahhhed their suburban awe, and then Tony had pushed her down, kittensoft carpet against her skin and his stinking breath and new car smell slipping up her nose.

"Goddamn," and that had been Rick Reynolds, or one of the other varsity fucks. "Will you just get a load of *that*?" Laughter from the girls, then, egging him on, and he'd laughed too, husky, mean sound and she'd strained to see over Tony's shoulder.

"Goddamn faggot freak," Rick Reynolds said, and she'd seen the slight and pretty boy walking nervously past the group. He'd worn a woman's coat, big fake fur and leopard print with a high, turned-up collar, had held his head down, ostrich denial, misguided belief that if you don't look at the dog it won't bite you.

"Hey fag, you wanna show me some pussy?" and then Tony had pushed her back down, bruising shove and her t-shirt hiked up, his insistent hands working their way beneath her bra, relentless fingers across her rigid nipples.

"Aw shit, man, I just wanted to see some pussy," and the girls had laughed louder, caged bird cackle, loving the show, loving the threat and fear and their time on top.

"Get off me, Tony," Robin had said and then his mouth had covered hers, the probing gag of his tongue forestalling any further resistance, the rejections he wouldn't have to hear, wouldn't have to pretend he hadn't heard.

"I think he's gonna cry," someone said, not Rick but

one of the girls, and the zipper on her jeans parted as if by its own traitorous accord. Tony's hand had worked its way across her exposed belly, diamond serpent's head with five anxious fingers, slipped beneath the elastic band of her panties and tangled in her pubic hair.

"Oh, baby you want it," he said, "You *know* that you want it," and then she'd kneed him in the balls, had brought her leg up hard and fast and felt his nuts and his stiffened penis, still trapped inside his pants, all mashed helpless between her and his body.

"Well, you come back around if you change your mind, fag," Rick called after the boy and the girls laughing like nitrous hyenas while Tony's face had turned the same bright red as his new car. She'd wriggled out from under him, all the way out of the hatchback and into the cold, zipping up, straightening the rumpled mess he'd made of her clothes. And Tony held onto his crotch with both hands, leaned forward and spit curses at her like blinding venom. The others made a circle around her, just to see what had happened, she'd known that, but it felt like they were there to make sure she didn't get away.

"You goddamn *cunt!*" he'd hissed, and she could see the painsweat standing out on his forehead, the way he gritted his perfect white teeth together and forced the words through the spaces in between.

"I said '*no,*' Tony," she'd said, breathless, her voice too small and alone.

"Fuck you, cunt! *Goddammit!* I ought'a fucking hold you down and kick your fucking face in!"

"Christ, man, what'd she do to you?" Rick asked, and she knew he was standing just behind her, would be there if she turned to run.

"The bitch kicked me in the fucking nuts, you dumbfuck!"

"That's cold, Robin, that's real cold," Amy Edwards said and she'd sat down next to Tony in the hatch, all big-eyed concern and opportunist's reproach.

"*I told him 'no,'*" Robin said again, and then he lunged at her, cooing Amy thrown to one side, his sparkling hateful eyes, dog-snarled lips. His fist had landed once, big blow to her face like concrete and meat and a bag full of marbles.

No man had ever hit her, not even a spanking from her father; Robin staggered backwards, no one to catch her, and tripped, fell flat on her ass, the sharp parking-lot gravel unnoticed, her head too full of the suddenness and the force, the absoluteness of this violence. She'd sat there while the numbness in and around her right eye segued slowly into skin burn and bone ache, bright fire wherever he'd touched her. She was breathing fast and hard, and every time she exhaled there was a sticky warm spray of blood from her nose, red berry spatters down the front of her shirt.

"Christ, Tony," surprise and a whisper of fear in Rick Reynold's voice. "You busted her nose, man."

"I ought'a kick her fucking ass."

She'd tried to scramble out of his reach, scraped palms and the frantic heels of her Hush Puppy loafers slinging grit and dust, but there were legs like prison bars, legs that wouldn't step aside to let her through, faces that stared down in shock and disgust and something hungry like delight.

"She's not worth it, man," Rick stammered, and Robin had hung on those words, terrified, praying silently that Tony would see the obvious truth in them, that she *wasn't* worth it, wasn't worth the energy it would take to realize the bottomless fury in his eyes.

He'd stood over her, dangerous animal she'd never seen take off its mask, what big teeth you have, what big claws; big man, still holding his balls with one hand.

"Please, Tony," whimpered through the blood and snot and stinging salt tears, "I'm sorry. Please . . ."

"Fuck her, man," Rick said, creeping, oily desperation. "Let's just get the hell out of here."

"Yeah, whatever you say." And then, to her, "But baby, you better know that your life is *over.* The goddamn *niggers* won't even want you after I'm done talking."

He drew his foot back and she'd flinched, braced herself for the hard rubber toe of his sneaker, but he'd struck the ground instead and bits of the parking lot rained down in her hair, pelted her arms and face.

And lucky Amy Edwards had climbed into the candy apple CRX in her place, and the ring of drunken teenagers had broken up and wandered away to other cars and other bottles, and left her to the night and its consequences.

Twenty, thirty minutes later, and she was still sitting there, shivering and shielding her swelling nose with blood-smeared hands, trying to stop crying, when someone behind her had asked, "Are you gonna be okay?"

She'd turned around, and the pretty boy in the leopard coat had been there, and a girl with skin like milk and whiter dreadlocks haloed in the sodium arc glare. The girl wasn't wearing a coat, just a Hanes tank top and her bare arms were covered with silver-blue webs, spider webs like casting nets from the backs of her broad hands to her shoulders.

"Do you need us to take you to the hospital?" the girl with the tattoos asked, the white girl; beautiful, alabaster gorgon. And then another boy, not so pretty, something broken and wary in his lean face, had knelt beside her and wrapped a leather jacket around her.

"I think he broke her nose, Spyder," the boy told the white gorgon, and she'd knelt, too, made Robin move her hands and frowned. There was a small and perfect cruciform scar between the gorgon's eyes, softest rose against the snow, and it had almost seemed to glow when she leaned close to look at Robin's nose.

"Yeah, I guess you do," the gorgon said, and then they'd helped her stand and followed the pretty boy, haughty swish and fake fur, across the empty parking lot.

4.

Where the highway cut deep into Red Mountain, weathered gash down through its Paleozoic bones, shale and chert and iron ore ligaments, Robin switched her headlights on. The sun was gone, burned down to a molten sliver, orange-red streak in the western sky as she crested the mountain and started down into the wide valley below. The city twinkled and glittered in the fresh night, uneven cluster of electric light and the garish ribbons of I-65 and I-20.

She'd been concentrating on nothing but the cherry-red taillights of the eighteen wheeler in front of her, ignoring the oily flow of images that had begun to play behind her eyes, the memories past vivid that ate into her cool, her queen bitch deceit, like nail polish remover through styrofoam. She felt dim relief to see the city, to know that Spyder and Byron were so close now.

"Don't let it freak you out," Spyder would say, "They're only flashbacks. They can't hurt you." But Robin knew better, knew that Spyder knew even better than her.

Outside, it was getting colder, but she had the window down anyway; she hated to drive alone now, especially after dark, paced the Civic to keep up with the speeding patches of traffic. The heater was blowing full tilt, but her lips and ears and the tips of her fingers were still painfully cold, and her breath fogged like cigarette smoke. She leaned over and punched the eject button on the Civic's CD player and it whirred and spat out the P. J. Harvey disc she'd been listening to for the past twenty minutes. She'd begun to imagine, to suspect, that Polly Jean's jangling voice was mocking her own jangling nerves and she searched through the loose CDs in the passenger seat for anything calmer, found Sarah McLachlan's *Fumbling Towards Ecstasy* and loaded it into the empty tray.

In the last four or five straining seconds before the disc cued to the first track and the music began again, Robin clearly heard the quick, dry scritch across backseat vinyl, the weighty thump of something heavy falling to the floorboard directly behind her. But she did not jump or cry out, did not turn to see, but pressed the black toe of her boot to the accelerator and passed the truck, stayed even with its cab all the way to her exit.

5.

Three days spent piecing together the ceremony, blurred chain of days revisiting volumes on peyote religion and the general use of hallucinogens in shamanism; library tomb dust and Robin curled into a corner of Spyder's old sofa, the books scattered around her like fallen megaliths. Spyder had not dared to interrupt, to call her to the phone when her parents called, again and again, looking for her, or even to remind her that she'd forgotten to eat.

But the books contained only the smallest portion of what she was looking for, disappointing syntheses of the contaminations of Christian missions and older aboriginal ritual. The Ghost Dance, the Kiowa Half Moon Ceremony, and the Cross Fire Ceremony; revelations of the Creator's Road, the narrow way, old men's visions of the life of Christ and figures in the sky: celestial landmarks for the Spiritual Forces, the Moon, the Sun, Fire. Her head filling up and up until her temples ached with contradictory instructions and still, the keen awareness that none of these could be *their* ceremony, aching void, the certainty that *she* had to find it inside. Make it new, not so differently from what the Sioux and Caddo and Comanche had done, but a synthesis from inside herself, instead of bits and odd pieces cribbed from obscure ethnographies.

Through all this, Walter had hovered at the dim edges of her awareness, as if, found guilty of some crime, he was merely awaiting sentence, the ugly consequences of his indiscretion. Sometimes he sat across the room from her, alone and watching, and sometimes he paced anxiously through Spyder's house, impatient, barely comprehending her obsession and insistence on detail, on any ritual at all, for that matter. If he spoke, either Spyder or Byron was usually there to tell him to shut up, leave her alone, go home now, Walter.

And she'd known that they were all, even Spyder, just a little bit afraid of what she was setting in motion, of what she would soon ask them to do. These three, who had taken her in and shown her how to fill in the emptiness, had midwifed her rebirth from that suburban zombie hell; had shown her what they knew of darkness and light and the graying shades in between, of the power to be gained by living through death without first having to die. Grave-robbers and self-styled ghouls, cemetery children, daemon lovers, eaters of every opium and lotus, and now they were afraid, these three beyond fear or dread, and it gave Robin the slimmest satisfaction, that she could be so powerful and that she could, at last, give something back.

Four days after Walter had brought the grocery bag of peyote buttons to Weird Trappings, she'd finally called them all together, had given Byron a list of things they'd need and her Visa card, Spyder's car keys. And then she'd asked Spyder to find her something to eat, had soaked in a tub of hot, soapy water, rose-scented bath salts, while Spyder scrambled eggs and fried slices of baloney, brewed strong, black coffee in her noisy old percolator.

And Walter and Spyder had watched while she ate, stray cat ravenous after days of Cheetos and candy bars, and his eyes had seemed to follow every forkful from the plate to her mouth. But she was past being annoyed by Walter's gnawing adoration, too exhausted to object or care. When she'd finished, Spyder had rubbed her neck and shoulders, strong hands kneading away the kinks and knots, and they'd talked about other things until Byron had come back: a shipment of animal skulls that had come into the shop that morning, a documentary Walter had seen on cable about the Knights Templar.

It had been dark an hour when Byron returned, found them in the living room listening to Bach, and he'd sent Walter back out to the car for the bags while he'd bitched about a cashier at the supermarket who had looked at the credit card and wanted to know if *he* was Robin Elizabeth Ingalls.

"Did you get *everything* on the list?" she'd asked and he'd rolled his eyes.

"I'm not totally fucking incompetent."

"If I'd thought that you were, Byron, I'd have gone myself."

Revived by her bath and the food, by Spyder's gentle ministrations, she'd finally felt the first twinges of excitement, adrenaline promises and a tightness deep in her belly. When Walter came back in with the bags, she had him set them down on the floor and she prowled through them, one by one, checked their contents against the list in her head, and yes, Byron had found everything she'd asked for, the spices and salt, the paints and olive oil and two dozen white candles.

"Okay, Walter, if you'd please take this all down to the basement now . . ." and Spyder's eyes had gone wide, lightning swift passage of dread across her face before she'd turned suddenly away, and Robin had known that look, that special silver panic that rode piggyback on her madness. That flashed itself like a warning display, and she'd glanced at Byron and known that he'd seen it, too. Spyder walked away from them, stood by a window and stared out at the dark between them and the house next door.

"Spyder? What's wrong? Did I say something wrong?"

Nothing for a second, hearts beating and sluggish time, and then, "I don't want you to do this in the basement. Anywhere else is okay, Robin, but not the basement."

Robin had stared at Spyder's dim reflection in the window, Spyder reversed and so maybe that Spyder was sane, feeling her concern melting into annoyance, and anger not far enough behind.

"Why? What's wrong with the basement?"

"I don't want you to use it, that's all, okay? I just don't want you to use the basement."

Robin had taken one step closer, still some hope of defusing this, if she didn't get pissed, if Byron and Walter kept their mouths shut.

"It needs to be the basement, Spyder. I've worked this all out very precisely, and your basement is the only place I know that's even close to what we need."

In the window glass, Spyder's eyes were just shadows

beneath the ridge of her brow, her dark eyebrows, un-
readable smudges, and she didn't say anything.

"Come on. At least tell me why you don't want us to
use the basement for the ceremony—"

"I don't want you to use the basement. You can do
whatever you want in any other part of the house, okay?
But I don't want you to do this in the basement."

"You said that already," Byron mumbled, then, and
Robin had glared at him, dry ice and razors, had given
him a rough shove and silently mouthed *Shut the hell
up*; he'd sneered and given her his middle finger in
return.

"Just tell me *why*, Spyder, and maybe we can figure
something out . . ."

"No, Robin. There's nothing to figure out. I don't
want to do this in the basement. You'll have to think of
some other place."

The finality in Spyder's voice, the mulish resolution
and to her fleeting surprise, Robin had discovered that
this time she didn't really care if it was because Spyder
was sick, if she couldn't help these unpredictable barri-
ers and taboos. She loved Spyder and had always
walked on eggshells and china plates for her, had always been so careful, so mindful of the places and
things and words that you could never know were off
limits until you'd already stepped across the line.

"*Goddamn it,* Spyder! *Shit!*" Robin wheeled around
and Byron had flinched, maybe thinking she was going
to hit him that time. Instead, she'd stomped across the
floor and stood in the basket handle arch separating the
living room from the dining room that Spyder used as a
dumping ground for her hundreds or thousands of
books.

"There is no 'why' because there's no reason for us
not to perform the ceremony down there and you *know*
it. You're just freaking out over something and you
could at least tell me what the hell it is."

Spyder had not turned around, still stared through herself and the window, vacant and intent, but Robin noticed the way she'd begun rubbing her left hand against

her hip, her callused palm across ancient, ragged denim. As if her fingers had started to itch, as if there was a stain on her hand or her jeans, and Robin had know that Spyder didn't even know that she was doing it.

"It's my house, Robin."

"Oh *please,* don't give me that shit. Just tell me why the hell we shouldn't use the basement and I'll shut up about it. But I want a reason, Spyder."

Robin had glanced at Byron, at Walter still standing there holding the bulging brown bags in his arms; both of them nervous, frightened, caught in the middle and as if she could read their minds, scrape the thoughts off the gray folds of their brains: *This is not the way it works, Robin,* and *Don't push* and *It doesn't matter, it doesn't matter near enough for this.*

"Please, Spyder . . ." she said. "All I want is a reason."

Then Walter had set the bags down again, both of them on the coffee table, and rammed his hands deep in his pockets.

"Maybe we should just forget about it, Robin," he said. "Wouldn't it be better if we just forgot about it? I didn't really care that much any—"

"Shut up, Walter," and Spyder had sounded like the still and quiet before a summer storm, the voiceless threat in the eyes of something wild. And she'd turned away from the window and crossed the room to stand in front of Robin; her left hand rubbing furiously at her jeans and the fingers of her right kneading the puckered cross between her eyes, the scarred flesh that turned scarlet when she was upset or angry.

"You do whatever you want," she'd said, poisonous calm between each word, "if it's so important to you. Do it and get it over with and then get out of my house."

"Christ, Spyder. Jesus. Won't you even *try* to tell me why you're afraid?"

But Spyder had already stepped past her, had kicked over a towering stack of paperbacks on her way to the darkened hall, scattering dust and silverfish and brittle, yellowed pages. Robin had stared down at the jumbled collage of faded covers, a painting by Frazetta of a sword-wielding woman with impossible breasts, something dead and scaly at her feet, Stephen King and Robert Heinlein and Ray Bradbury. Knowing how badly she'd fucked this up, knowing that Spyder might never let her take back these things she'd said. And knowing that without her, the ceremony would be flawed, not hollow but not whole, either.

"Well?" Byron had asked, some time later, long enough that her legs had begun to ache from standing in the same position. She'd kept her eyes on the floor, the tumbledown fantasies.

"Take the bags down to the basement, now, Walter," she'd said, and he hadn't waited for her to tell him a third time.

6.

Later, what Robin had remembered of the ceremony and the basement was like pages torn apart and hastily Scotch-taped together again by a blind woman, pages illuminated with needles and metallic inks and black words that she was glad had all but lost their meanings.

She'd remembered the preparations, Walter hefting open the trapdoor in the hallway floor and the cool air rising from the darkness, acrid-sweet stench of dust and earth and mildew. No light but their candles, and her feet uncertain on the steep and narrow stairs down, wood that creaked, cried, beneath her bare feet and the dust against her skin had felt like velvet. Velvet that clung to the soles of her feet, and her lungs had filled up with the basement air like drowning waters. And Walter had closed the trapdoor behind them.

While she'd traced her lines on the red dirt, Walter had dug a very small pit in the center of the floor, rusty garden spade breaking through the stubborn crust packed down by almost a century. Byron had stood quiet and alone, smoking his cloves, throwing candlelight shadows like craggy people, pen-and-ink shadows for Mr. Poe, Roderick Usher gone down to crazy Madeline. Everyone trying not to think about Spyder and thinking of absolutely nothing else.

She had laid the signs in Morton's salt and Crayola tempera, had driven the twenty-four white candles into hard ground, markers of wax and fire in places that mattered.

And when she'd finished and the basement glowed soft and flickering orange, the dark driven back into cracks and corners and the spaces between floorboards overhead, she popped the lid off the little can of Sterno from one of Byron's bags, struck a kitchen match and set the flaming can at the bottom of Walter's shallow pit.

"Take off your clothes," she remembered having said that, and the looks on their faces, Byron's exasperation and Walter trying not to look at her while he'd stripped. And then they'd sat in a circle around the Sterno fire, faint chemical heat against their faces and the circle incomplete, missing one, the one that mattered most of all. Walter had handed her the crumpled bag of peyote buttons and she'd taken the first one, had bitten into the bitter, rubbery flesh and gagged. But she had swallowed, and swallowed another bite, and there'd been lukewarm bottles of mineral water to calm her stomach. They'd passed the bag around, counterclockwise, each of them taking their turn again and again, chewing slowly and drinking water and not talking, until the nausea had found them and Robin had set the bag aside.

She had sprinkled salt and rosemary, nutmeg and mace, above the fire.

"I'm going to puke," Walter said, rolling, seasick voice and, *"No,"* she'd said firmly, "Not yet. Hang on as long as you can." And he had, but that hadn't been much longer. "Please," he'd whispered, sweat on all their faces, slack eyes, sweat on their naked bodies, and she'd only nodded. He'd crawled quickly away and emptied his stomach somewhere in the maze she'd drawn. Byron had gone next, before Walter had even finished his loud retching; and Robin last; had waited so long that she'd only made it three or four feet away from the fire before she'd thrown up the pulpy stew of chewed peyote, bile and Perrier, the half-digested meal Spyder had cooked for her, and sat coughing, staring through watering eyes at the candle she'd drowned in vomit.

One at a time, they'd gone back to sit around the scrape in the earth and the Sterno and Robin had taken Walter's hand on her right, Byron's on her left, held on tight, little-girl-on-a-carnival-ride grip. And Byron had taken Walter's hand, and the warmth that had settled over her, peace inside and deeper peace than she'd ever known or imagined. And she'd begun to speak, knowing that it was time, had clutched at the strict words she'd laid out as scrupulously as the designs drawn on the floor, the candles, the pinches of spice and salt. But the world was raveling, taking itself apart, and the words had run from her like scurrying black beetles. She'd squeezed their hands harder, so terrified and so completely beyond fear that she'd never be afraid again.

Later, she had remembered that Byron had begun to cry, joy and sadness, and that the wings of the angels that rose from the candle flames blazed and trailed razor night, obsidian shards that sliced her eyes, that cut her lips.

And that when the dry and whispering things had begun to dig themselves from the walls, claws like Walter's spade and the scrambling legs that glistened and drew blood from the shimmering air, that she'd finally closed her eyes.

And the sound of thunder, and Spyder laughing, far away.

7.

In the world above, Spyder had come out of her room and stared for a long time at the trapdoor, silently watching its paper cut edges and the tarnished brass handle, handle borrowed from a chifforobe drawer, bolted there by her father after the old pine hand grip had broken off years and years and years before. No sound rose up through the floor, no evidence that any-

one was down there, no proof that they'd left her behind. She wiped at her dry eyes and walked over to
stand directly on top of the trapdoor; the wood had
sagged slightly beneath her weight.

She went without you, her father chattered in her ear,
from inside her ear, *You see that, don't you? They all
went without you, and here you thought you were the
big magic . . .*

"Shut up," she'd whispered, whispered the way she
had learned to whisper so no one else would hear, so no
one would ask, *Who you talkin' to, Spyder? Who you
think you're talkin' to?* and she'd chewed at her upper
lip, toyed with a ragged bit of skin.

*Did you think they couldn't do this without you, Lila?
Did you think that little green-haired whore of yours
wasn't wicked enough to do this witchy shit on her own?*

"Shut up," and her teeth had ground through flesh,
salty warm blood in her mouth like chocolate melting
on her tongue.

They don't need you.

"*Shut up!*" and she covered her ears with both hands,
useless, knowing that his voice wasn't getting in that way.

"*You* don't know, you don't know shit!"

She's taking them away from you, Lila. I know that.

"*SHUT UP!*" and then she'd thrown herself hard
against a wall, so hard that the plaster had dented and
cracked. "*SHUT UP, SHUT UP, SHUT UP!*"

Dull smack of her shoulder against the wall, again
and again, meat thud tattoo, and the cracks had spread
like the patterns on her arms until she'd punched a hole
through and plaster dust had silted to the floor like flour
snow. Dark smear of herself down the wounded, white
wall. And she'd known he wasn't wrong. That her father
had eyes to see through the lies she told herself, the lies
that Robin had been telling her.

Spyder had gone to the kitchen, found a claw hammer
and the pickle jar full of different-sized nails beneath
the sink, two-penny, ten-penny, and all the time him
muttering in her skull, Bible verses and his own crimson

prophecies. When she'd opened her mouth to answer the questions he put to her, his voice came out, red and gristle spew of dead man words that she couldn't stop. She'd poured the nails out across the hall floor, rusty iron scatter, picking them up at random and sinking one after another into the hardwood, crazy angles, but enough of them piercing both the trapdoor and the floor. All the way around, stitching them in, while jumbled gospel and condemnation dribbled from her lips.

When she'd finished, Spyder pushed and dragged the big steamer trunk from her mother's room, great-grandmother heirloom, had used it to cover the smashed and crooked nail heads, the basement door, passage down to all her hells. And then she'd climbed on top, had crouched there, predator's huddle, and through her mouth, her father had howled his Armageddon songs.

* * *

When Spyder woke up, curled next to the trunk, there'd been watery light, dawning shades of gray and ivory, shining from the dining room and through the smudgy little window at the other end of the hall. She did not remember having fallen asleep, ached everywhere at once and when she sat up her back and neck and shoulders had hurt so badly that she'd had to lay right back down.

There was no one but herself inside her head, and she'd lain still and thankfully alone, her cheek pressed against the cool, smooth wood, wax and varnish, left ear against the floor. And at first, the scritching sounds had meant nothing to her, the faint sobbing like lost children, another part of the house and nothing more; she'd listened, squinting as the light through the dirty window had brightened toward morning.

And then, "Spyder?", but the voice was too small and broken to have been real, to have been anything but an echo of an echo of something she'd forgotten.

"Spyder, please . . ."

The sun had seeped into the hall and, by slow degrees, the night washed back over her: that they had all gone down to the basement without her, Robin and the peyote and her idiot ceremony; that the voices had come, her father's jibes and eager barbs, her father's paranoia and zealot's fear.

"Please . . . please, Spyder."

She sat up, ignoring the pain, the tilting dizziness it tried to force on her, and stared at the trunk, the banged and dented edges of the trapdoor and stray nails scattered everywhere like vicious pick-up sticks. Something under the floor thumped twice and was quiet.

"Robin?" and her throat hurt, strep raw; she tried to swallow, but her mouth had gone cottony and dry.

No sound from beneath the trunk, beneath the basement door nailed shut, no sound anywhere but her heart and a mockingbird squawking loudly in borrowed voices somewhere outside.

She'd tried to wrestle the trunk aside, but there was no strength at all in her right arm, dislocated bones and sickening pain, the black threat of unconsciousness, and so she'd had to use her feet to push it out of the way. But then there were the nails, dozens of them and she'd looked around desperately for the hammer, had finally found it hiding on the other side of the trunk.

"I'm opening it," she croaked, over and over again, protective mantra against what she'd done, "I'm opening it."

A lot of the heads were sunk too deep for the claw end of the hammer to get at, pocked, circular wounds in the floor where she'd buried them. With her good hand, Spyder pulled and wrenched loose the ones she could reach, nail after bent and crooked nail squeaking free of the wood.

When she finished at least half the nails were still firmly, smugly, in place; she tugged at the chifforobe handle and the boards creaked and buckled, made pirate ship sounds, and she was able to get her hand under one corner of the trapdoor, able to force it open a few inches and see the blackness beneath.

When Robin's fingers scrambled out, lunged through

the narrow opening, Spyder had almost screamed. Nails split and torn down to bloodied quick, blood caked maroon and the ugly color of raisins.

"Move your fingers," she'd grunted, struggling not to let the door slip shut again, imagined her hand and Robin's trapped together in the squeezing crack, their blood mingling and dripping down into the darkness. *"Move your fingers."*

Robin strained desperately toward the light leaking into the basement.

"I said move your goddamned fingers!"

The fingers pulled themselves back slow, one-at-a-time retreat like the heads or tentacles of some frightened sea thing. When they were all gone, Spyder had eased her own hand out, let the trapdoor snap closed again, and someone on the other side had screamed, wild and terrified animal sound, impossible to tell who it might have been.

Breathless and lost in the empty space gouged by the scream, Spyder bent low, prayer bow, her mouth almost touching the drying stain where Robin's fingers had groped only seconds before.

"Listen to me," she said, speaking too loud, too fast, "There's a crowbar out on the porch. I've got to go and get it so I can pry this open."

"Don't leave me . . ." and that had been Robin, something shattered using Robin's tongue, Robin's vocal chords.

"I'm coming right back, I swear, I'm coming right the fuck back, okay?"

There was no answer and she hadn't waited for one.

* * *

She'd found the crowbar wedged tight between the old washing machine and the house, and she'd had to work it back and forth for three or four minutes before it had finally pulled free, unexpected, and she'd staggered backwards, had almost lost her balance and fallen onto a heap of rusted motorcycle parts. The morning was

clear and warm, bright Alabama morning, spring fading
into summer, and for a moment she'd stood there, holding the crowbar out in front of her like a weapon from a
martial arts movie.

Her car sat in the driveway, right where Byron had
parked it the night before.

You could just go, and she'd had no idea whose ghost
had said that, which lips had whispered behind her eyes,
but not her father's. He'd never tell her to leave the
house, and not her mother, either. She'd let the arm drop
to her side, the crowbar clunking against the junk at
her feet.

The Celica's keys were lying on top of her television,
and *You could just go,* the voice said again, *They'd only
be getting what they deserve.* And this time she'd recognized it as her own, no one to blame for these
thoughts but herself.

*You could drive away and just keep driving . . .
wouldn't ever have to come back here.*

Pretending that she hadn't heard, that she hadn't seen
the clean blue sky through the leaves of the pecans and
water oaks, Spyder had lifted the crowbar again and
stepped back inside the waiting house.

8.

After the sky had closed again, Robin cradled the
hand the light had touched and given back against her
chest, blessed thing, still glowing faintly at the lightless
summit of the world where she and Byron had climbed.
Mountain or tower of splinters, ladder hung above the
pit and void and he was pressed into the firmament,
whispering his name again and again like it had power
against the ribs of the night, like he would forget it and
be no one and nothing if he ever stopped.

"Spyder . . ." she said, but the sky had closed and
they were alone, inside each other but outside themselves, and the wet edges of the hole wanted them back,
wanted them to slide screaming back into its roiling,

muddy belly. She thought that she'd given it Walter, thought that she'd seen his eyes wide at the end like frying eggs and glass slippers, dragged away, and that should have been enough.

Byron slid his arm around her again, hung around her neck like dry bones and wire, dried flowers and the ragged jewelry of martyrs. She held him close to her, his naked flesh as cold as sidewalk concrete beneath ice; her hand brushed across the gashes in his back and he screamed again, twin and running sores from acromion to spine that wept hourglass sand and the memory of wings. Her own back burned, bled sand and regret from its own deep, unhealing wounds.

Behind them, the fire had stopped falling from Heaven, the dim red afterglow a million miles or years below, and there was nothing left in the World but the two of them and the skittering things, the bristle-haired things with their crowns of oildrop eyes. And the Preacher, the man with the Book and skin that fit too tight. When He'd come for them, long strides across the earth and the skitterers dropping off his clothes, she'd begged Byron to tear her wings off, so that they would be as black as the night, as invisible. So that they would be nothing He could see or want. They'd hung their wings like trophies from the walls of razor wire, wreaths or trophies of feather and fire and withering sinew.

And they'd left Walter, too, somewhere at the edge, on his knees, tearing madly at himself, and the World had shaken as He came.

She had reached out and touched the Dome of Heaven, tore again at its closed eyelids with her ruined hands. Behind them, the skitterers were getting braver, jabbering murmurs and she'd heard their legs like sharpened pencils, the hairbrush scrape of their bodies against one another.

"Undo me. Swallow me," Byron whispered. "Don't let them take me."

And then the sky, its single blazing eye, had ripped open wide, steel lashes tearing loose like jutting teeth and the night had rushed back down toward the hole, catching the skitterers in its undertow rush and dragging them back to where Preacher picked his teeth and waited. Her hand and the white serpents around Her white face, and the white nimbus of flame around Her head. Robin's hand in Hers and they'd been hauled into the light.

9.

Still three blocks from the club, Dr. Jekyll's and its melting pot mix of punks and slackers, queers and skins and goths, lookie-look rednecks and wannabes; Robin pulled into an empty parking lot and dug around in the glove compartment until she found the right prescription bottle. The name on the label was her mother's, an old script for Halcion that she'd lifted from her parents' medicine cabinet and exhausted months ago, half-filled now with the Lortab and carnation Demerol and powder-blue ten milligram Valium that she bought from her connections. She dumped a few of the pills out in her palm, pastel scatter like Easter candy, picked out one of the Valium and dry swallowed it.

Too bad the pills never worked fast enough, or long enough, anymore, never managed to do much more than soften the edges of the things that came looking for her, the things that scampered and hummed, the things that only Spyder could send skulking back to the grayer parts of her brain.

Spyder, like a nursery rhyme or prayer, dim words from her mother's lips when she was very small and the night light had only seemed like a way for the monsters to see her better: "From ghoulies and ghosties . . .

And long leggity beasties . . ."

Robin slumped back against the bucket seat and willed herself to relax, buying time until the Valium kicked in. She focused on the staggered pattern of bricks in a warehouse wall across the wide parking lot, a hundred rectangular shades between red and brown and black caught in the Civic's headlights. Bricks laid before her parents had been born, when her grandparents had been children, maybe. The engine was still running, faint and soothing metal purr of fans and pistons, and Sarah McLachlan sighed like gravel and rain from the stereo.

The shadow slipped across the wall, blackened mercury, gangling arms or legs and so sudden that it was gone before she'd even jumped; she sat up straight and stared, unblinking, across the hood, the empty space between the car and the wall and the unbroken shafts of her headlights.

. . . and long leggity beasties . . .

And then the pain between her shoulders, the shearing fire that left her breathless and wanting to puke, and she yanked the Civic out of park, never taking her eyes off the wall, not daring to glance into the rearview mirror, as the tires squealed and she backed out into the street.

CHAPTER SIX

Keith

1.

The sun down an hour, first long hour of cold, and Keith Barry sat on one end of the old loading platform; no trains on these tracks now, just the rotten boards and brick and concrete crumbling down to grit and dust, the barrel that the bums and junkies kept their stingy little fire inside. He sat with Anthony Jones and his banged-up Honer harmonica and they'd been playing Tom Waits and Leadbelly for the rambling empty stretch of railyard, dry, whispering weeds between the ties and broken glass and a stripped pickup burned to a red-brown cicada shell. Keith plucked his pawn shop twelve-string and Anthony Jones's harp cried like all the ghost whistles of all the trains that would never rumble past this platform again.

"Almighty Christ," Long Joey muttered, Long Joey who stood in the crunchy gravel ballast and stomped his feet like someone trying to make wine from breakfast cereal. "Too damn cold for November. We *all* gonna have blue balls by Thanksgiving."

The last chords of "Gun Street Girl" and then Keith laid the guitar down beside him, although Anthony let a few more notes straggle from the instrument pressed to his dark lips. Keith took a big swallow from the half-empty pint of cheap rye whiskey and handed the bottle to Long Joey.

"Maybe this'll put a little spark back in them," and Joey grinned his crackhead smile and accepted the bottle in his shaky hands. "Just don't drop it, okay? Drop it and I'll have to kick your ass."

Anthony finished his solo and wiped the harmonica on a flannel sleeve. "And then you give it here, L. J."

Keith had been at the platform since late afternoon, since he'd made his connection, cooked and fixed in the men's room of the Jack's Hamburgers on Second Avenue. He carried the twelve-string in a case so beat up that it stayed together only by the sticky grace of a roll or two worth of duct tape and some copper wire he'd strung through the holes where the hinges used to be. He also kept his works in the case, hidden inside a compartment intended for picks and capos; Keith never used a pick, relied instead on his sure and callused fingers. He had enough stuff left for one more fix, tucked safely inside his left boot.

There were twelve or thirteen men on the platform tonight, most of them huddled around the flickering barrel, but he was the only one into junk. Most of them were winos or dirtbag crackheads, street addicts too far down the food chain to even have house fees. They bought their bits of rock from the cruisers who pushed from their cars. Every now and then he caught the caustic stink of someone's pipe over the smell of piss and booze and burning wood.

Long Joey passed the bottle to Anthony, noticeably emptier for its time in his hands, and then he started stomping his feet again, pulling hard at his earlobes. Long Joey was a puller and sometimes his ears were raw and caked with dried blood. He liked to talk, but never talked about anything but crack and the women he either imagined or lied about having fucked.

"I *told* this bitch L. J. don't put no jimmie cap on his dick, but she just kept on whining about the big A, so I finally slapped her around until she shut the hell up."

"And you just took you some pussy, ain't that right, L. J.?" and Anthony grinned and winked at Keith.

"Goddamn right. *Goddamn* right."

Anthony passed the bottle back to Keith, just enough

left for one more round; the rye felt warm burning down
his throat, settling in his belly.

"You still seein' that pretty little girl with the fire
engine hair?" Anthony asked and for a second Keith
was too busy looking through the neck of the bottle,
strange and useless telescope that looked out on nowhere, to answer.

"Yeah," he said at last. "Yeah, I guess so."

"You *guess* so? What's with that, you *guess* so?"

When Anthony Jones talked, he waved the Honer in
the cold air like a conductor's wand.

"You either down with that red-headed lady or you
ain't. There ain't no in-betweenin' pussy."

"Man, I had me some fine white pussy last week . . ."
L. J. started and Anthony cut him off with a knifeblade
glance, stabbed the harmonica at his heart.

"Why don't you shut the hell up for a little while?"

"You think I'm lyin'? You think I gotta lie 'bout get-
tin' white bitch pussy?"

"I think I'm tired of listening to you talk trash."

And L. J. looked offended and hurt, pulled hard at his
right earlobe and wandered off, mumbling to himself.

"That nigger can't even get hisself a skeezer these
days," and Anthony laughed and stared off towards the
darkened windows of the Eagle Syrup plant. This side
of town was a wasteland of empty warehouses and
abandoned factories, a prelude to the miles of derelict
steel mills further west.

"I just can't seem to stay out of the shit house with
Daria these days."

Anthony Jones didn't make any sign he'd heard, still
gazing across the tracks and the street at the ridiculous
giant honey jar perched atop the roof of the syrup plant.

"That her name?" he asked. "Daria?"

"Yeah, man, that's her name."

"She the same girl that's in that band with you?"

"Yeah. Shit, she *is* the band. She's gonna dump me
and find someone else to play guitar for her. She
ought'a fuckin' dump me."

"Man, you just down on yourself tonight, that's all,"

and then he looked quickly down at his feet, scuffed shoes from one of the missions, rubbed at his eyes. "You got gold in them fingers."

Keith held his hands out, stared into his palms like he could read his past or future in the lines etched there.

"She takes a load of shit, man."

"I hear you," Anthony said. "I do hear you. Had me a good woman long time ago. Some pretty little babies, too."

Keith passed the almost empty bottle back to him and picked up his guitar again, ran his fingers once across the strings and started tuning, gently twisting each rusted peg in his magic fingers. And Anthony Jones drained the last of the whiskey before he hurled the useless bottle at the darkness that lay like sleeping dogs between the platform and the syrup plant.

2.

Niki Ky had finally found a place to sit in the back of the van, a plastic milk crate covered over with a warped piece of plywood. The crate was mostly full of cords and cables, rubber black coaxial serpents that stuck out through the checkerboard holes in the sides and bit at her legs every time the van hit a bump or rut or pothole. At least they hadn't gone directly down Morris from Daria's place, hadn't jounced over all those goddamned cobblestones. The rear of the van was sectioned off with a sagging barrier of chainlink fence, soldered and bolted into place and there was more junk back there. Niki thought briefly about scooting the crate closer to the wire, close enough that she could hook her fingers through the diamond spaces and hold on.

"There, Mort. Turn right there," Daria ordered, pointed one insistent finger at a side street. She was sitting on a huge, red Sears Craftsman tool chest behind the driver's side, straddling it, hanging onto the back of Mort's seat. The tools inside the chest clanked and clattered, and Niki imagined that it was the sound of her bones and teeth and kidneys.

Mort missed the turn and Daria slammed her fist into the back of his headrest.

"*Goddammit*, Mort! Are you fucking deaf?"

"There's no left turn there, Dar—"

"Did you see any fuckin' cops?! Who would've given a shit? *Huh?*"

"Why don't you calm down," Theo said, and Niki saw the fire jump like lightning in Daria's eyes.

"Why don't *you* stay the hell out of this?" she said, almost snarled, and Niki wished again that she had stayed back at the apartment with Claude and his Ella Fitzgerald tapes, his comforting coffee and conversation.

"*Hey,* will the *both* of you just shut the hell up and let me drive?" Mort growled, no patience infinite and Niki could tell he'd had enough.

She had just stepped out of the shower when the phone rang, was still standing naked and dripping in the steam, drying herself with a thin, not-quite-white towel that had once belonged to a Holiday Inn. Someone who'd heard from someone else that Daria's boyfriend had been in a fight, had gotten himself cut up and might be dead. Dying, at the very least.

A minute or two later, the towel wrapped tightly around her and "It might just be a false alarm," she'd said, trying her best to sound hopeful, reassuring, starting to feel awkward and misplaced.

"You don't know Keith," Daria had said, pulling her boots on and not bothering with the ratty laces.

"Which makes you a very lucky girl," Claude said and had turned quickly away, shielding himself from the hot recrimination in Daria's eyes.

"Put on some clothes if you're coming," Daria had said and Niki thought maybe it would be rude to say no thank you, I'll stay right here. Rude, or dangerous.

"Okay, look, you can turn left at the next light, on 17th, and circle back around . . ."

Niki tried to shut out Daria's frantic commands, shut her eyes and then immediately opened them again, not wanting to make car sickness any more likely than it already was; puking would do absolutely nothing to improve the van's all but palpable funk, reek of ancient sweat and cigarette smoke, oil and the sweet and sour hint of rotting food. She hung onto the edges of her plywood raft, and rode the wave.

* * *

After they'd checked two titty bars and a park full of bums and monuments to dead civil rights leaders, Daria had finally thought to call the hospitals. Niki and Theo sat in the van while Daria and Mort fed precious quarters into a pay phone and argued with emergency room nurses.

"God, I hate that asshole," Theo said.

Niki, who'd decided she was better off just staying in the floor after having been twice bounced off the milk crate, shifted her stiff and aching butt, rubbed her freezing hands together. Obviously, the van had no heater.

"You mean Daria?" she asked.

"No, not Dar. Keith-fucking-Barry," Theo answered too quickly, pulled the cheesy, flamingo-pink polyester and velvet tux jacket she was wearing tighter around her shoulders. "Dar's a doll, when she's not chasing after that fucker's junky prick."

"Oh," Niki said, knowing nothing else to say.

An uncomfortable and silent five minutes later and Mort and Daria were climbing back inside, driver's door popping open and banging closed again, the sliding side door complaining viciously on its rusted tracks. Night rushed into the van, soaking Niki in chill air and the colder glare of the streetlights.

"So?"

" 'So' *what,* Theo?" Daria said, reclaiming her seat on the tool chest.

"*So* is he dead or what?"

Mort sighed, pulled off his baseball cap and ran fingers through his hair.

"No one named Keith Barry has been admitted to any of the ERs tonight," he said and put his cap back on, the bill turned around backwards so Niki could read the red, white and blue STP patch stitched on the front. He slapped his big hands together loudly. "And there are no John Does that fit his description. We checked the city morgue, too."

"This is bullshit," Theo muttered and lit a cigarette.

"We should check out that house in Ensley," Daria said, ignoring her. "The one with all the windows painted yellow."

"Christ, Daria," Mort hissed and slumped over the steering wheel, already defeated before he'd even begun to object. "I do not want to go wandering around that part of town after dark."

"I wouldn't want to go wandering around that part of town in broad fucking daylight, Mort, but what's your fucking point? I'm not just gonna sit around on my ass and wait for the cops to call."

"I've had enough of this crap," Theo said and blew a cloud of smoke against the cracked inside of the windshield. "You guys can let me out downtown. And Niki, I'd advise you to come with me."

Niki felt helpless, lost, flashing back on her years of powerlessness and lingering indecision. None of this had anything to do with her, but she felt caught anyway, stretched suddenly between Daria and Theo like the rope in a particularly nasty tug-of-war match. And of course the advantage went to Daria, Daria who had taken her in and given her a place to sleep, a bath.

"Uh, I guess I'll just stay with you guys," she said, speaking to Daria, who frowned and stared down at the bare metal floor between her boots.

"Yeah, well, whatever," Theo said. "It's your ass."

"What's the deal with this place, anyway?" Niki asked, certain that she didn't really want to know. "What sort of house is it?"

"A crackhouse," Mort said and started the van. "It's just a goddamned crackhouse."

* * *

After they'd left Theo, and she'd asked Niki, you sure, are you absolutely sure you don't want to come back to my place?, Mort drove west and Daria took Theo's seat; Niki sat on the floor and watched the street-lights become dimmer and further apart, wider pools of night between them. Downtown surrendering to the first belt of decay, neighborhoods wilted and gone to ugly, cancerous fallow. She didn't know this city, was becoming increasingly disoriented as the oasis of tall buildings slipped behind them. Daria had stopped talking, had stopped pointing and now she sat smoking, staring intently out her window at things Niki couldn't see.

Niki glimpsed the incongruously bright facade of a Burger King over Mort's shoulder and then he turned, pulled the Ford Econoline up to the curb.

"Man, I can't believe the cops haven't shut this fucker down," he said, reaching beneath his seat for something Niki couldn't quite make out, something black and heavy slipped quickly inside his coat.

Daria slid the side door open for Niki and she stepped out onto the sickly brown patch of grass between the street and the sidewalk. The house had once been something grand, Victorian gingerbread and dormer windows, a disintegrating cupola perched on the high, gabled roof. And every window hidden behind irregular sheets of plywood, all painted the same neon shade of canary yellow.

"It certainly isn't inconspicuous, is it?" Niki said as Daria slammed the sliding door shut behind her.

"It doesn't have to be," she said, stepping past Niki, heading up the walk to the long front porch. "The cops are all too busy hassling hookers and queers. They don't get out this way very often," Daria was walking fast, purposeful steps and words more purposeful; Mort had to jog to catch up with her.

"Might be bad for their health," she said.

Up the crumbling stoop, five steps, and now Niki could see the swirling graffiti tangle laid thick across almost every available surface, tags and gang warnings, spray can pasta, the universal language of urban tribes. She recognized some of the stuff from the Quarter, crude 8-ball placa and dollar signs to show all this territory was controlled by Crips and Disciples.

Daria hammered on the front door, hard fist against flaking wood; Mort stood just behind her, struggling to look calm and cool, obviously neither, trying to keep an eye on every corner and shadow. The only response from the darkened house was the steady, muffled *thump-thump-thump* of rap, and Daria pounded the door again, used both fists this time.

"*Hey!*" she shouted, howled, hands cupped around her mouth to make a megaphone. "Open the goddamn door or I'm gonna call the cops!"

"Come on, Dar . . ." Mort whispered, urgent, but she'd already started kicking at the door. It shuddered in its frame with every blow from her Doc Martens.

The scrabbling, clicking sounds of locks turning, chain sliding back, and the door opened an inch or two. The face pressed into the crack was backlit and featureless in the glare of yellow incandescent light, leaking like pus or urine from the house.

"*What the hell do you want, bitch?*" the face hissed, voice worn raw and gravelly, female voice, old as someone's grandmother.

"I'm looking for somebody," Daria said, slipping the toe of her boot into the crack between door and jamb.

"Well, you're lookin' in the wrong place," the woman said, glancing down at Daria's intruding foot.

"He's been here before."

"Well he *ain't* here *now!*"

"Then let me in and I'll see for myself."

The woman opened the door an inch wider and Niki caught a glimpse of her burning eyes, eyes like the pit of famine's stomach, and the long, uneven keloid scar beneath her right eye, proud flesh like melted plastic.

"Look, white girl. If you keep shootin' off your mouth and makin' all this noise, Mr. Wilson's gonna hear you and he ain't as tolerant as me."

Mort's big hand on Daria's shoulder then, and Niki

could see that he was almost ready to drag her from the porch, kicking and screaming and squeezing his balls if that was the only way back to the van.

"He's not here, Dar. Let's go," he said.

"She might be lying," Daria said, as if the woman wasn't standing there, as if she couldn't hear.

"Girl, you think tonight's a good time to die or you just stupid?"

Behind the woman, down the half-glimpsed throat of pissy light and wallpaper peeling in long skin strips, someone shouted, "Who the hell is it, Tabs?!"

The woman stared at them, at Daria, with her starvation eyes and after a moment she yelled back, without turning around, yelled, "Goddamn Jehovah's-fuckin' Witnesses!"

And the other voice, male boom and rumble, "At night?! Well, tell 'em to go the fuck away!"

"You heard the man," she said. "He won't say it that nice again."

"*Now,* Dar," and Mort *was* hauling her backwards, Niki sidestepping quickly to get out of their way.

The door slammed shut and the house was as dark and sealed away from the rest of the universe as it had been before. Daria pulled free of Mort and almost tumbled ass-first down the steps.

"What the hell did you think you were doing, Mort?" she demanded, looking back at the closed door.

"Trying to stop you from getting us all killed."

"You're so full of shit!"

A red and listing Plymouth crammed full of teenagers, black boys in sunglasses and black knit caps cruised shark-slow past the van, big white van beached like a lunatic's whale there against the curb.

"Can we just *please* get the hell out of here?" Niki asked, heard the fear and exasperation wrestling between her words, fussing over the tattered rags of her resolve.

"We're already on our way," Mort said and headed for the Ford. Niki, painfully uncertain, waited for Daria, who stood for one moment more, with fists clenched, staring back at the scarred and defiant house.

3.

The first time that Keith had seen Daria, had laid eyes on her, back when the junk still felt like gold and Dr. Jekyll's was still The Cave. Barely six months since he'd had that last and grandest fight with Sarah and she'd driven off alone to find her own gilded peace pressed between rails and spinning steel wheels. Without her voice and her fraying scraps of sanity, the weak but vital gravity of her center, Stiff Kitten had come apart, had disintegrated and left him alone with his needles and veins. He'd still picked up occasional solo sets for the money and beer, and Mort had been there, Mort and his sticks and his foot keeping all the time Keith had left. But he'd refused to play the old songs, covered shit by just about anyone else, especially Tom Waits because he figured he couldn't do the vocals much harm.

And then he'd walked into The Cave one night, needing a fix and not a copper penny in his jeans, no credit, hoping that he could wheedle a few drafts out of the skinny albino kid who tended bar on Wednesday nights. And a band had been setting up on the stage, no one he recognized. It had taken him fifteen minutes to sweet-talk one lousy beer, watery Bud in a plastic cup and then he'd sat, sick and alone in a corner booth, watched past empty tables and wobbly handrails at the steep edge of the pit, across the black moat (dance floor for Techno Tuesdays and mosh pit hell the rest of the week).

Her hair had been the dirtiest sort of blonde back then, and he'd watched her unpack her bass, had tried to remember the name he'd seen on the marquee as he'd come in, red plastic letters that had meant nothing. Wednesday nights were always dead and there was no one to watch her, no one but him and the bartender with his pink eyes and cornsilk hair. She'd finished tuning and looked toward him, but he was hidden by shadows and the glare of the lights; she'd shaded her eyes with one hand and, to the geeky boy with his too-new guitar and tie-dyed Sonic Youth t-shirt, had said, "Okay, guys. Standing room only tonight." The geeky boy had laughed and Keith scrunched down deeper into the shadows, had felt like a hungry cockroach, sipping his shitty beer and watching someone laying out a feast from his kitchen crack.

And then the songs had come one right after the other, no introductions or titles or stupid banter between the singer and her guitarist or drummer. Just her words and her aching voice, like stained glass, beautiful and shattered sound fused together with solder, frozen lead seams binding the deepest reds and clearest cobalt blues.

He'd finished his shitty beer and for a while there had been only the empty cup, worried between his jonesing fingers. At some point the albino kid had brought him another, even though he hadn't asked, but he'd hardly noticed. Had hardly even thought of the pain worming about in every cell of his body, no room for anything but the nameless girl and her nameless songs, nameless band behind and around her like electric bishops.

A few people straggled in towards the end, goth queers who sat near him in the back and talked loud enough to hear themselves over the music. He'd leaned over to them in the white space between songs, before the very last, and "Why don't you guys just listen," he'd said. A fat girl with so much eyeliner she'd looked like a gluttonous raccoon had sneered at him and they'd all started talking again.

"Stupid fuckers . . ." he'd grunted, but they'd ignored him, too infatuated with the patter of their own voices to be bothered by the world.

The last song had been more amazing than all the rest together.

Afterwards, he'd slipped unnoticed into the sour hall behind the stage that led back to the dressing room, the ten-by-four closet where a thousand bands had sweated and smoked and scribbled cryptic messages to each other on the swimming-pool blue walls. Had brushed at his crazy hair with his hands and tried to rub the cloudiness from his eyes. They'd all been there, packed in tight with their instruments and b.o., the singer sitting on the floor, putting Band-Aids the phony color of mannequin flesh on her fingers.

He'd still been trying to think of something to say, when she'd looked up and seen him and her eyes had gone big and her mouth had dropped open a little ways.

"Hi," he'd said, one clumsy word.

"Hi," she'd said, that voice so much different when she spoke, but still the *same* voice. "You're Keith Barry, aren't you? You used to play with Stiff Kitten."

"Uh, yeah . . ."

"Wow," the Sonic Youth boy said, springing up from a rusty folding chair, hand out like a karate chop. "You guys were fucking killer, man."

"Uh, yeah, thanks . . ." and Keith wanted to be somewhere else, out front sipping his charity beer, looking at the empty place where she'd stood on the stage.

"Whatever happened to that chick that sang for you guys, man? God, she was cool."

"A train ran over her," Keith said, no emotion left in the words, and the boy's camera grin had drooped and faded away, the offered hand hanging uncertain between them. The girl on the floor frowned up at him and he'd sat back down on the scabby chair.

"Can I, uh, can I talk to you?" Keith had asked her then, pointing at the girl with one hand and pulling nervously at the collar of his shirt with the other.

"Sure," she'd said, getting up, the final Band-Aid wrapped around her right index finger.

And then they'd been walking back down the hall, had paused at the steps that led up to the stage, the way back, and she'd leaned against the wall, thumbs hooked into the pockets of her jeans.

"I'm sorry about Sherman," she said and looked back the way they'd come. "He isn't a dork on purpose, not usually."

"No problem," he'd said and then, "Do you guys have a name?"

"You got a cigarette?" she asked and he'd fumbled at his pockets, but had come back with nothing but an empty pack and a few dry crumbs of tobacco.

"Thanks anyway. Ecstatic Wreck, but that's just until we think of something better."

"That's a pretty cool name," and he was trying not to show the jitters, the way his hands shook and the cold sweat, wishing his fucking junk-starved body would let him be for five lousy minutes.

"I played with some other guys for a while, but they joined the army," she said. "Tonight was our first show."

"Well," he said. "I just wanted to tell you you're goddamn good. Better than that."

"Thanks," she said, embarrassed, he could tell. "That means a lot."

"You want to maybe get a beer or go for a walk or something?"

She'd shaken her head and his stomach had begun to roll again. "Sorry. That'd be cool, but I have plans already."

"Maybe another time, then," he'd said.

"Definitely."

They'd shaken hands, his damp and hers so dry, and she'd started back towards the dressing room. He was up the first two steps, two to go, hoping he'd make the toilet before he puked the beer back up, when he stopped and called after her.

"Oh, hey, what's your name?" and she'd said, "Daria Parker," without even turning around.

* * *

It had been two weeks before Ecstatic Wreck played again, another Wednesday night at The Cave, and this time he'd fixed and worn a cleaner shirt, and he'd dragged Mort along with him. There had been more people, word of mouth and he'd seen some fliers stapled up around town, pink paper and black letters. They'd sat in the same booth, because the best sound was way back there and this time Mort had bought him cold, long-necked bottles of Old Milwaukee.

The same songs in a different order, and between every one Keith had reached across the table and poked Mort in the shoulder.

"What did I *tell* you, man? What the hell did I tell you?" and Mort had nodded his head.

"I know what you're thinking, Keith."

"What? What the hell am I thinking, then?"

"Your guitar's still in hock, man, and don't tell me it ain't, 'cause I saw it this morning hanging in the window at Liggotti's."

Keith had taken another hit off his beer and watched the stage while she adjusted the strap on her bass.

"She's already got a band," Mort said, "And they're too good for you to go bustin' up."

"*She's* good," Keith said. "They're just there because she wants them there."

"Shit, for all I know you're just horny . . ."

"Man, I haven't been horny in a month of Sundays," Keith had said, knowing there was so much more truth in that statement than his admission of a junky's impotence. Daria had played her black Fender like hot midnight, her voice a chorus of hoarse and growling angels, and Keith's hands had felt empty, lonely for his strings, for the first time since Sarah's funeral.

* * *

"I'd be a shit," she'd said, "if I just walked out on them like that."

Keith frowned, sighed and slumped back into the booth. Mort was busy shredding a napkin.

They'd been talking for an hour, talking in tight little circles, figure-eights, mobius conversations, and Mort was almost no help at all. Keith knew that he wanted it just as much, wanted to play again, to plug himself into Daria Parker's wild energy.

"They're not the ones you should be worrying about," he said and lit another cigarette.

"They're my friends . . ."

"Sure, they're your friends. But you *know* that they're nowhere near as good as you are, right? You've admitted that much already."

And then Daria Parker had looked at him, had nailed him to that moment and the back of the booth with her green eyes like flawed emeralds and she'd said, "Yeah, I said that. But I also know that your arm's got a habit."

"Whoopee-shit," he'd said, feeling the old anger start to rise, not wanting to see its face. "I guess that makes you Sherlock-fucking-Holmes."

"That sort of thing doesn't stay secret in a town like this. All I'm sayin' is, I want to know if it's something you got a handle on, or if it's got you. You're asking me to ditch some really good guys. I think I have a right to ask."

"You some kinda saint?" And Keith knew how close he was to blowing it, blowing it like a cheap hustler, but the words were too close to the surface to push back down. "I had a lot of nasty shit the last few months . . ."

"Just answer her, Keith," and that was only the half of what Mort was saying; the rest was there in his face, coiled like twine and baling wire.

Keith took a long drag off his Lucky and let the smoke out slowly through his nostrils; the haze made it easier for him to match her cut-glass scrutiny. *Blink, fucker, and she's got your number.*

"Yeah," he'd said, cool and calm as well-water. "It's under control, okay? I just need to get back to work. It's not a problem."

And she'd nodded, slow, wary nod, and finished her beer.

"I'm gonna think about this for a couple of days," and the beer bottle had thunked back down onto the table in front of her, glass the color of honey from wildflowers and amber beads of sweat.

"Hey, that's fair. I'm not asking you to make a decision right this minute."

"I just gotta think about it, that's all."

"You got my number at the shop," Mort had said and

offered her his hand as she slipped out of the booth. "Thanks, Daria," he said when she shook it.

"You won't be sorry," Keith said, as if the deal was as good as done, adding the smoldering butt of his cigarette to the overflowing ashtray.

"We'll see," she'd said, quick half-smile, and walked away into the night outside The Cave.

* * *

Mort caught up with him three days later, found him in front of Liggotti's Pawn and Fine Jewelry, staring in at his guitar like a child looking in at candy he'll never taste or toys he'll never have the chance to break.

"She said yes," and Keith had put one hand against the storefront glass, leaning closer. "She called me this afternoon and said yes. Just give her a few days to break the news to her band. They have a gig next Wednesday and she doesn't want to leave them hanging."

"I knew she'd say yes," Keith whispered, smiling, feeling something warm spreading through his soul that wasn't junk, and he'd said, "So, you gonna lend me the money to get her out of there?"

He'd waited almost a minute for Mort's reply, sixty seconds full of traffic and dry wind between buildings.

"No, man. I'm just gonna let you get up there and play with dick."

Keith had grinned and stepped back, away from the window filled with musical instruments and typewriters and portable televisions, all indentured for a few bucks and a yellow hock slip. He'd been standing watch over the Gibson for days, had been threatened with the cops twice by old man Liggotti and the Korean woman who worked for him, threats of jail if he didn't stop standing around staring through their window all day.

"I'll have to go by the teller machine first," Mort said, and Keith had lingered only a moment longer before following him across the street to the white van.

4.

Sometime after ten, the van bumped across a railroad (another railroad, this city seemed shot through with them like varicose veins) and left the road, rocking over uneven ground, gravel and bigger rocks, rolled to a stop a few feet away from what looked to Niki like it might once have been a loading ramp for the empty factories and warehouses. Her ass ached, the small of her back, the place she imagined her kidneys to be, and she had to piss.

The platform was dark, too far from the streetlights, nothing but a dull red glow from a barrel and that surrounded by shivering men in ragged clothes, freezing scarecrows or tramps.

"That goddamn son-of-a-bitch," Daria said, relief and furious anger, and she slammed her fist hard against the sun-cracked vinyl dashboard, jumped out of the van and Niki could hear her Docs crunching toward the platform.

No one bothered letting her out this time; Mort swore and killed the engine, got out and followed Daria. So Niki was left alone to wrestle with the rust-cranky handle of the sliding door. By the time she caught up with them, Daria had climbed up onto the platform, hands on her sturdy hips, leaning down to yell at someone sitting on the concrete edge. It had to be Keith, guitar across his lap like a disobedient child, not dressed for the weather and she could tell he'd be a tall man when he stood. It was too dark to see his face and he was looking down besides, past his dangling legs, at the ground where broken bottle glass glittered faintly.

Mort stood a few feet away from her, helpless watcher.

"Do you have any fucking idea where all we've been out looking for your ass tonight?" Daria hissed and then she kicked an empty beer can; the can flew high, end over tumbling end like a football or grenade, and clattered to the ground somewhere out in the darkness.

The figure did not move, did not shift its wide shoulders or tilt its head toward its accuser.

"Why the hell d'you do that?" he asked. "I've been right here all evening. Mort knows to look for me here."

"Christ!" the swear spit like crackerdry crumbs, and Daria turned, paced to the other side of the platform and stood staring out across the tracks. The bums watched from the safety of their barrel fire.

"I got a phone call that you'd been in a fight," she said. "That somebody had cut your guts out over a bad deal."

He shrugged and shook his head.

"Who said a fool thing like that?" he murmured, so low his bear's voice was almost lost in the wind.

"What the hell difference does *that* make, Keith? *Huh?*"

"Because some people will say anything, Dar. You gotta know who to believe and who's just full of shit."

Muffled laughter from the glowing ring of bums and junkys, and one of them said, "That's some *fine* white bitch ass, all right, Mr. Barry. Yessiree . . ."

"L. J., why don't you just shut the hell up," Keith said, but Daria had already turned on them, had taken a step toward the huddled circle of orange-brown faces and warming palms; Niki felt Mort tense in the dark beside her.

"Man, you're only gonna piss her off more than she already is."

"I ain't tryin' to disrespect your lady," said the man with arms like twigs and a face like a hungry weasel, all guilty innocence. "I'm just payin' her some due, that's all."

"Shut up, L. J.," another of the men growled.

"You just gotta be properly respectful of fine white pussy like that, that all I'm *sayin'*. That's *all* I'm sayin'."

Niki took a step closer to Mort, felt her hand on his arm before she knew she'd put it there.

A howl like metal past fatigue, the point where stress becomes shear, and Daria rushed the men, moved howling her steel gash howl across the platform, and most of them had time to jump out of the way before she reached the barrel. Except for the one they had called L. J., who stood like a shabby rabbit in blinding headlights.

Daria kicked high and her right boot connected with the rim of the barrel; it lifted a little ways off the concrete, short flight before gravity took it back and it tipped over, spraying embers and ash, showering the paralyzed L. J. in the sizzling rain, dumping its little inferno at his feet.

"FUCK OFF!" she screamed, vague word shapes pounded from the howl, and L. J. dove off the side of the platform, yelping and cursing, stomping his feet and slapping madly at his clothes. Some of the other men moved in cautiously to help put him out.

And from the smoking barrel litter Daria seized a charred stub of wood, broken fruit crate slat, held it high like a burning tomahawk and turned back to Keith Barry. He stood up slow, moving as if invisible lead hung from his limbs, one hand out like a traffic cop or safety guard, the guitar hanging limp from the other. Upright, he was at least a foot and a half taller than Daria.

"Man, you have got to get a grip on yourself," and Niki kept waiting for him to flinch, take a step backward, for Mort to intercede. But no one moved.

"You listen to me, Keith Barry," she said, "I am sick and goddamn tired of this shit."

"Mort. You better tell her to back off, man."

"We have a show *tomorrow* night at Jekyll's, Keith, and you *will* be there and you *will* be as straight as you are still capable of being. Are you listening to me?"

She held the brand a little higher, bright cinders dripping to the concrete at her feet.

"What the hell is your *problem* . . ."

"I *said,* you *will* be there. All you have to do is say, 'Yes, Dar, I'll be there and, no, I *won't* be too fucked up to even take a piss.'"

"Mort?" he said, the name uttered like a prayer, deliverance expected.

But Mort was insensible granite beside Niki, immovable.

"Last chance," Daria said. "You gonna be there or not?

'Cause if you're not, I have absolutely no reason not to go ahead and shove this board up your ass right now."

"Tell the woman you're gonna be there, asshole," said the man who'd told L. J. to shut up.

"Yeah," Keith said, and Niki felt a little of the white-blue tension, crackling threat, drain out of the air. "You *know* I'm gonna fucking be there."

"And you're gonna be straight," she said.

"Yeah, straight," and he sat back down, the guitar held out like a shield of wood and strings. "I ain't gonna fuck up this show."

Daria sighed, seemed to let out a breath she might have held a hundred years, dropped the glowing slat and ground it out with the toe of her boot. Niki felt herself breathing again, pulled her hand back from Mort's flannel shoulder.

"Sound check's at eight o'clock," she said, "Don't be late." And she stepped past him, then, down from the platform without looking back.

"Come on," she said as she passed Niki and Mort, "This place smells like rat piss."

CHAPTER SEVEN

Stiff Kitten and How
Shrikes Fly

1.

This end of Morris, down past the parking decks and The Peanut Depot and the loft apartments that rent for small fortunes and have neon sculptures in their windows. Where the cobblestones are more uneven and the warehouses are still warehouses, caverns of bulk and shadow that feed the ass-ends of trucks all day long and whisper rat feet patters at night. Where the tracks are closer and the trains rattle windows. Past Daria's building, where no one bothers with the broken glass or weeds that grow through asphalt and concrete, the kudzu that seems to grow from nowhere and creeps like mutant hungry ivy. Dr. Jekyll's, brick front washed matte black and one door the color of something royal or orchids that could grow underground. The old marquee that sags dangerously, although this never was a theater; another warehouse once, before the seventies, before the sixties and maybe before that. Crooked red letters, plastic messages that no one can read after dark, that fall off if a strong wind blows.

Daria and the guys were already inside and Niki had spent the last hour down the street in The Fidgety Bean with Theo, waiting out sound check, watching the cold night through steamy windows, bright clouds, orange with city light, rushing by overhead, drinking a cubano and then another. Too much caffeine, even for her, and Theo talking like she'd just discovered her tongue.

Now she followed Theo along the sidewalk, half a step behind and hurrying to keep up.

"It's a great place to hear shitty punk bands," Theo explained. "And really shitty hard-core bands. And drink shitty beer. If you want rock and roll, you go to The Nick, and if you want thirtysomething pop crap, you go to Louie Louie's. If you want to hear techno or industrial, there's The Funhole, just across the tracks," and she pointed.

They huddled together in the doorway, no shelter from the November wind but their own bodies, while a boy with three silver rings in his lower lip checked the band's guest list for their names.

"Come on, Jethro. You fuckin' know I'm on there," Theo said, her teeth beginning to chatter so that there were little hitches between her syllables. They had both begun to shiver, the coffee a fond and dimming memory.

"I know *you*," he said. "But I don't know her."

"Niki Ky . . . N-i-k-i K-y," she said. "Come *on* man, I'm freezing my titties off out here."

"You should have to sit on this stool for a few hours . . ." and he tapped down the list, name after name, with the eraser of a nubby yellow pencil.

"And *you* should have to suck on the drippy end of my fuckstick . . ."

"*Here* it is. Niki Ky," and he drew a graphite slash through her name. "Show me your wrists, ladies."

The rubber stamp left a fizzing green beaker on Niki's skin, and she let Theo lead the way in, into air so suddenly warm and smoky she thought at first that she might not be able to breathe this new atmosphere. Almost impenetrable haze of cigarette smoke and the damp and sour reek of spilled beer underneath, almost masking the fainter, more exotic hints of pot and piss and puke. The sound system was blaring drums and meat-grinder guitar, something like Soundgarden, minus any trace of rhythm or melody or talent. Across a sea of heads and shoulders, Niki caught a glimpse of Daria, doppelgänger much too tall for Daria, waving, and Theo took her hand and pulled her through the crowd.

Daria was standing up in one of the burgundy red naugahyde booths and Mort was sitting across from her, nursing a Miller High Life.

"I don't suppose you saw Keith out there anywhere?" Daria asked, shouted to be heard above the carnival din of music and voices. Theo shook her head and slid in next to Mort. He put one arm around her and kissed her cheek.

"Sit down," Daria said to Niki, leaning close, and she obeyed. Mort reached across the table and shook her hand.

"Good to see you're still with us," he said. "After last night, I thought maybe you'd head for higher ground."

"What the hell *is* that shit?" Theo sneered, one finger pointing up at Heaven or the speakers overhead.

"Bites the big one, don't it?" and Mort finished his beer and laid the bottle on its side, began to roll it back and forth with his free hand.

"That," Daria shouted, "is Bogdiscuit."

"The opening band?"

"The *missing* opening band."

"Last seen in Lubbock, dropped off the screen somewhere in the wilds of Mississippi," Mort added.

"Which means *we* have to go on forty-five minutes early and play *two* sets." Daria was still standing, her Docs sunk deep into the duct tape-patched and cigarette-scarred upholstery, still scanning the crowd for some sign of Keith.

Mort sighed and bumped the beer bottle against one corner of a glass ashtray. "But at least we've all been spared the live-and-in-your-face Bogdiscuit experience."

"This is plenty bad enough," Theo said. She laid her lunch box purse on the table, opened it and began to rummage through the junk inside.

Niki tried not to notice Daria looming over her like a vulture, or the way she kept sliding toward the gravity well of those boots pressed into the springshot booth. Instead, she watched the crowd, the sandshift of flesh and fabric, pretending she was also looking for the tall guitarist. But really she was just taking in these faces, same faces as New Orleans or Charleston or anywhere else she'd sat in crowded bars. A lot of the faces were clearly too young to be here, fake IDs or bribes or stamped hands licked wet again and pressed together, and for a second that passed like the lead-blue shades of sunrise, she felt homesick.

And then, across the room and tobacco veil, the Bogdiscuit tortured space, she saw the girl with white dreds, punk dyke attitude scrawled on her white skin and another girl with hair as unreal as Daria's snuggled under one arm. Six or seven kids were crowded into the big, semicircular booth with them, the white haired girl at their center.

Niki leaned across the table, not taking her eyes off the velvet clot of goths, whispered loud to Theo, "Who is *that*?" Indicated who she meant with one hitchhiker's jab of her thumb toward the crowded back booth.

Theo looked up from the cluttered depths of her purse, lipstick tubes and tampon applicators and a Pink Power Ranger action figure, followed Niki's thumb.

They all looked like underagers, ubiquitous black and glamorous dowdy. Robert Smith clown white and crimson lips, bruise-dark eyes.

"Oh," Theo said, quick, dismissive wave of one hand and eyes back down to the purse, "That's Spyder Baxter, holding court over her shrikes."

"Shrikes?" Niki asked, and Mort chuckled. He'd stopped rolling the Miller bottle, bread dough kneading the tabletop, was now busy making spitballs from his cocktail napkin and flicking them over Daria's head. She hadn't noticed, or if she had, chose to ignore him. They sailed by, just inches above her scarlet hair and stuck to the black plastic Christmas tree set up behind the booth, decorated with big rubber bugs and Barbie doll parts.

"That's what Theo calls our local death-rockers."

And Niki nodded, though she'd always hated that

label, death-rockers, more reminiscent of heavy metal, headbanger crap than anything goth.

"You wouldn't think a chickenshit city like this would have so many of them," Theo said, found what she was looking for, a worn and creased emery board.

Niki had treasured the dark children who congregated in Jackson Square, who haunted the narrow back streets of the Quarter, the same white faces and black lace pouts as these, the same midnight hair. These could be the *same* children, she thought, transplanted like exotic hothouse vegetation, identities as blurred as their genders. Seeing them here only seemed to redouble her homesickness, the vertigo sense of being misplaced herself, a refugee.

One boy stood apart from the others, better dressed than the rest. Bell-bottomed stretch pants and a wide, white belt, puffy white shirt with balloon sleeves and a lace jabot that looked purple from where she sat. He stood with his back to the others, staring out into the crowd with vacant intensity, back straight, as alert and detached as a bodyguard. They made eye contact and she looked quickly away, back to Theo.

"Why don't you like goths?" she asked.

"Well, let's see now," Theo answered without pausing from her furious work on a hangnail. "They're shallow and vain and whiny . . ." She stopped filing, held the nail closer to her face for inspection. " . . . pretentious drama queens with bad taste in clothes and worse taste in music. How's that?"

"Oh," Niki replied, a sound soft and hard at the same time, and suddenly she was much too tired from the hours of listening quietly to Theo Babyock's diva prattle, too tired to care if she pissed off Daria by picking a fight.

"HEY! ASSWIPE!" Daria screamed over her head, then, and there was Keith Barry, pulling free of the throng, blotting out her view of Spyder Baxter. His head was shaved closer than the night before and his dull eyes squinted through the smoke and shadows, recognition rising as slow as the sun on a cloudy morning. He towed some blonde chick behind him like a little red wagon, Aqua Net teased bangs and trailer park makeup.

"Key-*rist* on a boat," Theo hissed, having entirely missed the brief flash of anger on Niki's face, "what the hell did he scrape *her* out from under?"

Daria scowled down at them, "At least he's learning how to come when called."

"I'm not even gonna *think* about touching that one," Theo said, dropped the emery board back into her purse and snapped it shut.

Keith pushed his way to the booth, icebreaker through sweaty flesh and t-shirt shoulders.

"Hey," he said, barked the word like a stoned pit bull. "I want you guys to meet Tammi, here." And he stepped to one side so she could stand next to him.

"Tammi with an '*i*,' " the blonde girl said, voice as perkystiff as her hair, lipstick smeared and obviously very drunk; Niki looked down at her hands, embarrassed flush, feeling the tension like lightning-charged air crackling dry against her skin.

"Well, *I'm* simply thrilled," Theo said, bouncing-ball parody of Tammi's drawl, and offered the girl her hand. "Hows about you, Dar? Ain't you simply thrilled, too?"

Daria, almost as tall as Keith from where she stood, nodded but kept her eyes on him.

"You guys go on back, Mort," she said, checking the time by her big, ugly wristwatch, deceiving calm. "We'll be there in a few minutes," and Mort, always happy to miss the next messy installment in this soap opera, pushed Theo out of the booth.

"Oh damn," Theo said, mocking eyes doe wide. "Just when I was about to ask Tammi where she finds that simply *marvi* shade of eye shadow—"

"Just shut up and keep walking," Mort said and they were gone, one step toward the stage and swallowed immediately in the press.

"What's *her* problem?" Tammi asked and Niki cringed, wishing Keith wasn't blocking her escape from the booth, that she could have followed Mort and Theo backstage.

"Do you think you can make it through the fucking set?" Daria asked, Tammi completely ignored.

Keith rubbed his shabby goatee, looked down at Tammi and grinned, slow turn back to Daria.

"You think I'm too fucked up to play, don't you?"

No reply from Daria, her original question not brushed aside, and Niki felt herself sagging deeper into the naugahyde, wished she could melt and slip liquid from her seat, pool unnoticed beneath the table.

"I'm cool, Dar," he said. "I'm fine. So lay off, okay?"

"Yeah," Daria answered. "Whatever you say, Keith. Just don't screw this show up," and then, to Niki, "You gonna stick around?"

"Oh yeah, sure . . ." Niki said, leaned way back so Daria could step over; her Docs left two deep prints in the shiny red upholstery, scars that would heal themselves as slowly as rising dough. Daria's ass almost brushed Niki's face, faded and threadbare denim that smelled of coffee and ancient cigarette smoke.

"Cool," Daria said. "Save us the booth." Keith moved aside and she hopped down. "The sound's good from here."

And she slipped away. Keith lingered a moment longer, still rubbing at his chin, before he finally released Tammi's long-nailed hand, nails as pink as bubblegum pearls, and without another word, followed Daria.

"Is it okay if I sit with you?" Tammi asked, and Niki shrugged, wondering what Theo would have said, what Daria wouldn't have had to say.

"Thanks," Tammi slurred cheerfully and sat down. "You know, I went to high school with a Japanese girl."

"Really?" Niki sighed, half-smiled through her gritted teeth.

"Yes ma'am," Tammi replied eagerly. "She said she was born in that city we dropped the nuclear bomb on."

"Which one?" Niki asked and glanced longingly back, past the girl's puzzled face, at Spyder's corner, towards the goths and the boy standing watch over them, but someone had already turned the house lights down, and there was only shadow.

2.

Because she was Spyder, they came to her, to sit near her and breathe in the air she breathed out. They brought her the meager precious offerings of their company, their fragile faces painted like gentle death to hide the real scars and pain. She wasn't sure what she had to offer them, but accepted that it was something that they needed, something that soothed or at least distracted, and they never seemed to take anything away.

Robin pressed tighter against her, as if that were possible, and Spyder knew how much she enjoyed the masked envy of the others, these who could come as close as a seat or standing room at her booth on Saturday night, but never any closer.

Walter was sitting on her left, and Byron standing point like a pretty gargoyle, or just keeping his distance, distant now since Thursday evening in the shop. He'd stayed away on Friday, hardly a word to her since he'd called her house afterwards, and she thought that maybe he'd flinched when she kissed his cheek earlier in the evening. She'd said nothing more to him about what he had or had not seen in the alley, knew he wouldn't listen to her anyhow.

The terrible grunge that seemed to have been playing most of the night ended abruptly, middle of a song and even over the rambling voice of the crowd, the silence seemed profound. "Thank god *that's* over," said the boy sitting next to Robin, black *Sandman* t-shirt and tonight he was calling himself Tristan. Spyder nodded her head and the lights were going down lower, pumping new life into the shadows; more darkness to hide within and at her table she felt nervous bodies relax a fraction. Except for Byron.

You're losing him, she thought and shoved the thought quickly back the way it had come.

The stage lights came up and Spyder buried her face in

Robin's jasmine-scented hair, kissed her throat. Tonight, she'd come for more than the usual self-conscious and jealous attentions, had come knowing that Daria Parker and Stiff Kitten were playing, a month or more since she'd seem them last. Daria had not come back to Weird Trappings on Friday as she'd hoped, had hoped for no reason she'd been able to recognize. Except that Daria had been getting into her dreams lately, sometimes looked down on her from high places while Spyder walked the Armageddon streets. More than once, Spyder had looked up and there she'd been, her face pressed against window glass, hair like the blood that filled the gutters and gurgled down storm drains. Silent judgment in her eyes.

"I heard this band really sucks," Tristan said, risking brave opinion; Robin leaned over and whispered something into his ear. He bit his lower lip, then, and shrugged, looked sheepishly away.

"Well, the girl who said that's a dweeb anyway," and he was quiet. Robin smiled, wicked mean grin, and Spyder kissed her on the forehead.

The band entered from a door poorly hidden behind the stage, taking their places on the rough platform of plywood and railroad ties: drummer first, skinny stick man whose name she always forgot, and then the towering guitarist and Daria last of all. She wore her bass like an albatross or something deadly from an old Buck Rogers film. Spyder sipped at her watery gin and lime, the one drink she'd allow herself all night, savoring the pine sap or turpentine bite of the liquor.

The band opened gently with a cover of The Velvet Underground's "There She Goes Again," spooky lilt and punched up just a little, but still as much a lie, as much an act of misdirection, as the hushed moments before a tornado. Last verse and Byron turned and she caught him looking at her, his face more than its usual pinched, and he looked immediately away again.

Yeah, you're losing him, and she took a bigger sip from her drink, pretending it wasn't true, watching Stiff Kitten across the writhing dark of Dr. Jekyll's. The spotlights stabbed down from the cramped balcony, borrowing definition from the smoke, blue and red, too much like something toward the end of any one of her nightmares.

Only if you let *him go.*

Daria Parker was building a mournful, droning bridge with her strings, segueing into their own "Imperfect." Spyder knew the titles to a few of the songs because she'd bought their demo tape a few months back, five tracks and a grainy, black-and-white photocopied snapshot for the cover, snapshot of a very run-over cat.

Up there, her lips pressed to the microphone, muscle-taut fingers locked in their brutal tarantism, Daria drove her words like nails. And Spyder tried not to think about anything else, nothing but the sneer and tremble of Daria's lips and words.

"*'I always meant, always meant to open up,' my skin starts to tear, my skin starts to tear, my skin starts to tear . . .*"

Down in the pit, bodies slammed together, meat stones pounding themselves for some sympathetic spark, some uglier echo or answer, and from where Spyder sat, the moshers looked more like the condemned souls from a Gustave Dorré illustration for Dante.

"*. . . and what's inside pours itself out, pours itself out, ink into your arms.*"

Daria wheeled suddenly away from the mike, yielding to the guitarist, set her back to the crowd and played now to black building block stacks of amps. Under the gels, Keith Barry's red Fender looked bruised, damaged by his hurried, certain hands. He was left-handed and played left-handed, and Spyder always felt like she was watching him through a mirror, reversed. Then Daria was back, managing to sound bitter and innocent in the same conflicting instant. Daria, mike stand pushed forward and teetering on the edge of the stage, head bowed, leaning out over the damned, leaning into herself. Her hair, washed red-violet in the lights, ripe plum tangle and spray of sweat, whipped side to side, her face a blurred snarl.

"You see there's nothing else left for you in there, nothing that you'd want to fuck, nothing you could steal . . ."

Her fingers released the steel strings, drawing sudden silence from the bass, and Keith Barry and the drummer were on their own for the last furious, rushing beats. At the end, after the end, the fading whine of the guitarist's final, angry chord, alone for the brief and empty space before the applause. And Robin's hand, like a hungry child's, at Spyder's breast.

3.

"It doesn't snow down here, does it?" Theo asked, hugging herself tight, stomping her feet loudly on the sidewalk.

"I don't know," answered Niki and Theo nodded her head.

"I keep forgetting you're not from around here either."

Niki looked up at the low sky, the baby aspirin clouds hanging closer than before the show, pearly and swollen with reflected city light.

"Well, *I* think it's gonna snow," Theo said.

They were waiting for Keith, who was supposed to be bringing the van around, had been waiting for almost ten minutes now, for Mort and Daria still inside the club. Shivering caryatids bracketing what Niki supposed you'd call the stage door, standing guard over the amps and cases of sound equipment stacked up beside the curb. This door was wider and the same black as the wall, no handle on the outside so it would be almost invisible when closed.

"I've never really seen snow," Niki said.

In the big parking lot across the street, there were still people lingering around cars, stalling, wringing the last dregs from a Saturday night already gone well over to Sunday morning. Smoking and getting sick drunk on cheap wine and beer. The back edge of the lot ran all the way to the railroad tracks and Niki noticed a few of the goths there, clustered around an old brown car, Spyder

Baxter sitting on the hood, still the center of their attention. And the green-haired girl so close she could pass
for a Siamese twin.

"Come *on,* guys . . ." and the door swung immediately open, as if Theo had commanded it, open sesame,
but really just Daria kicking the door wide, trying to
brace it open with one shoulder. Niki caught it, held it
open while Theo hugged herself and Daria and Mort
wrestled the last of the equipment through.

"So, where the hell is he?" and Daria still sounded
every bit the queen bitch, but Niki could feel how much
of her tension had drained away during the show,
through the show. Up there, she'd slipped around the
diffusion somehow, wrapped herself in soothing rhythm
and feedback, electricity and discord sedation. She wore
a fresh Band-Aid on her right index finger and her hair
was plastered flat, dried sweat from two long sets and
the beer that someone down front had drenched her with
halfway through the last song.

"First guess don't count, right?" and Theo laughed,
only half to herself, began to whistle the chorus of "Let
It Snow." Niki was amazed; Theo even managed to
whistle sarcastically.

"Fuck," resigned and weary moan from Daria and she
helped Mort roll the clumsy-big flight case the last couple of feet to wait with everything else, one wheel missing and so it tipped and wobbled like a drunken
monolith. Mort had painted the band's undead mascot
on one side of the scraped and dented black box in his
most careful acrylic. The zombie kitten leered hungrily
at Niki, broken fangs, one eye rolled back in its rotting
skull, the other dangling by gooey optic nerves.

"Shit, it's *cold* out here," Mort said, pulling Theo
close to cop what little body heat she might have to
spare.

"That's cause it's gonna snow, dumbass," she said
and Niki let the door slam shut, sealing them all outside.

Mort grumbled something rude and unintelligible
through his steaming breath. And then, one thunder
crack backfire, shotgun loud in the brittle air and Niki

jumped, felt her heart lurch and skip inside her chest. The van rumbled around the corner of Dr. Jekyll's, pulled out of the side lot and bounced down onto the cobblestones, cough and blat of a muffler shot like a coal miner's lungs. Keith pulled in too close and the right front wheel scrunched against the curb; the wind caught white puffs of the Ford's exhaust, blew acrid warm and choking gusts into their faces. The van idled and Keith stepped around the side, unlocked the rear doors and opened them like the wings of a giant, albino scarab.

"Okay, boys and girls. Time to feed the shitmobile," Mort said, mock glee, and Niki stepped back, out of the way, feeling useless and uncertain, feeling outside. They moved like this chore, too, had been choreographed and rehearsed, performed a thousand times, as practiced as their music. They filled the caged-in back of the van while she watched, attentive, just in case someone asked for her help.

When they were done, Keith bummed a cigarette from Mort, bummed a light, spoke around the Camel's filter, "Did y'all settle up with Bert?"

"Oh yeah. And he said we could have the second week in December if we wanted it. Dar has your split."

"You mean you got *cash* out of him?"

"Twenty-five each," Daria said. "Don't spend it all in one place."

From across the street, the gravelly, coarse rumble of male laughter, threatening and primal as the warning growl in a bad dog's throat; Keith turned to see and Niki followed his gray eyes. Back to where the goths had gathered around Spyder and the cruddy brown car. Except now there were three big guys, almost everyone else had gone, and Spyder sat alone on the hood, head down as if she were praying or straining under an invisible weight.

"Assholes," Keith muttered. "Christ, I hate those fuckers," and Niki heard the threat there, too.

Daria had opened the panel door, crouched inside, almost out of the wind, trying to tease a spark from her lighter. She glanced up at Niki. "What's he talking about?"

"Some guys're messin' with Spyder and the shrikes," Mort said.

"Skins?" asked Daria, and the lighter flickered, framing her face for a yellow-orange instant before the flame guttered and died again.

"Nah," Mort answered. "Just some assholes."

"Well, *you* stay the hell out of it, Keith," Daria said. "You hear me?"

"Yeah, Dar. I hear you."

The laughter again, smug and hateful chuckle, and whatever the guy closest to Spyder said was spoken almost loud enough for Niki to hear. Spyder raised her head slowly and Niki imagined she could clearly see the anger glistening in her eyes. The guy leaned closer, seemed to whisper something in her ear and his friends sniggered.

"I fucking *mean* it, man." Daria gave up on the lighter, exasperated, tossed it out of the van and disposable pink plastic clattered across the pavement. "We don't need you getting your ass kicked tonight by a pack of bulletheads."

But Keith was already moving, quick around the driver's side, the door jerked open and he pulled a dented aluminum baseball bat from behind the seat, black tape strapped around the handle.

"There he goes," Theo said, both hands up, helpless, furious gesture, and Niki knew this was something else practiced, something else played over and over, something else she had no part in.

"Stop him, Mort!"

"Oh yeah, right. Fuck you, Dar. *You* stop him."

"Goddammit," and Daria was out of the van and running to catch up with Keith. Niki hadn't even seen her reach for the tire iron that she held clutched in both hands, close to her chest, as she ran.

"Jesus Christ, why don't we just call the cops?" Theo pleaded, "This one time, Mort, why don't we *please just call the fucking cops*?" and she sat down on the curb, kicked at Daria's dead and discarded lighter.

Yeah, Niki wanted to say. *Good idea.*

Mort sighed, loud and vaporous sound, his face helpless as Theo's, almost as fed up.

"You guys just wait here, okay."

"No, Mort. It is *not* okay," Theo spat back. "Goddamn it. One night you're gonna get killed playing Mr. Third Musketeer and it is not fucking okay . . ." but he had already gone, chasing Keith and Daria through overlapping pools of streetlight.

4.

When the three jocks showed up, Spyder had been thinking about bed and the flowersweaty smell of Robin's naked body, contentedly enduring the idiot argument between Tristan and a chubby girl named Darlene over whether The Sisters of Mercy were better pre- or post-*Vision Thing,* with or without Patricia Morrison. Most of the evening's earlier doubts had faded, dimmed almost to irrelevant mist, and she'd been about to tell them both that they sounded like comic book fanboys, fussing over which superhero had the lamest sidekick or the biggest dick.

And now these three in matching green and gold UAB baseball jackets, haircuts like a lawn mown too close to the earth and eyes full of piggy stupid trouble.

"See, Tony? Man, I *told* you there were dykes over here," the tallest said, blonde hair and Nazi-blue eyes.

Tristan and Darlene shut up and stepped out of their way. In the Celica, Byron and Walter paused in their own affairs, Byron up front alone and Walter in the backseat with a boy dressed like a deb from Hell's cotillion; Spyder could feel their uneasiness seeping sticky cold through the windshield.

"Goddamn," said the jock named Tony, and Spyder felt Robin shudder, then, saw the frightened recognition on her face. "I guess that you were right, man."

The third guy, shorter and chunkier than his buddies, didn't say anything, laughed and spit tobacco juice into a McDonald's cup.

"All kinda freaks hang out down here," the first guy said. "Half the time, you can't tell the fuckin' girls from the boys."

"That was original," Spyder said, speaking through the sudden playground memories of adrenaline and shame, and she felt Robin tense, maybe start to push away. "Did your daddy teach you that one before or after he taught you how to suck his cock?"

Shortest perfect silence, and then the guy took one step closer, "*What* did you say?" Surprise and disbelief and hardly any room left for the anger bubbling up between his words.

"You heard me. Bet your daddy told you if you acted like an asshole, nobody would know how much you liked his dick."

And his friends laughed, stinging loud belly laughs.

"Digger, man, you gonna let this freak talk to you like that?" said the guy with the half-full McDonald's cup and he laughed again.

"Let's just go," Robin said, her voice too shaky, like they'd never had to listen to this shit before. "I know one of these guys. They're not worth it," and she did pull free of Spyder's embrace, slipped off the hood to the blacktop.

"What's the matter, little girl? Don't you think your bigmouth lesbo girlfriend here can take care of you?" Digger asked, but Robin was already opening the passenger side, getting in beside Byron and locking the door behind her.

"Why don't you just leave us alone," Spyder said, confused, more hurt by Robin's retreat than anything these creeps could say,

"Is that it, lesbo? Think maybe you can talk like a man but afraid you can't fight like one?" And he leaned close, whispered loud so everyone could hear. "Bet you sure as hell can't fuck like one."

Chunky gales of laughter from the other two and Spyder stared down at the scuffed toes of her boots.

"I don't know 'bout that, Digger," Tony said. "Bet she's got one of them plastic strap-on jobs."

"Is that true, lesbo?" and he leaned close enough that Spyder could smell him, sweat and sour alcohol, after-shave and sweet wintergreen snuff. "You got yourself a strap-on dick, lesbo? You fuck that weird little bitch with a big, hard strap-on dick?"

"Back off . . ." Spyder said, final useless warning murmured just for this one asshole, knowing that he wouldn't, that this had already gone too far for either of them to simply back out now.

"Does it feel good, lesbo?" sneered Digger. "Does it make you feel like a *man?*"

"Digger, you are just too fine," said Tony and slapped Digger on the back.

And then Spyder reached up, circled his neck with her strong arms, leather and the inky webs hidden underneath, and pulled him down, the cactus stubble on his cheek scraping at her smooth, white skin.

"Let me show you how it feels, motherfucker," and she opened her mouth very, very wide.

5.

Daria ran all the way across the street, across the wide parking lot, never more than a few steps behind Keith and her heart banging away like it meant to kill her. She screamed out his name one time, wasted curse or warning, but the wind was growing stronger, raw and living without flesh or bone, and it had snatched her voice away in its icing fingers. And by the time she caught up with him, it was already too late to stay out of the bad shit going down around the rustyguts Toyota, had probably been too late all along.

Keith had seized one of the bubbas by the collar of his jacket and was towing him backwards, away from the car. The guy backpedaled and flailed the air with his arms, mad, pin-wheeling arms, spilled the syrupy dark contents of the cup he was holding and lost his balance anyway, landed on his ass. His face was livid red, competing startled and pissed and embarrassed hues of scarlet, and when he started to get up, Daria kicked him in the ribs and he sat back down.

She looked up and there was Spyder, still sitting on the hood of her car and one of the guys bending down over her. Both her arms were locked firmly about his neck, her tattooed hands shimmering oily in the mercury vapor light. Her mouth was pressed viciously against his left cheek, grinding; it looked like she was kissing him.

"Keith, wait a goddamn minute . . ."

But he'd already shoved the second bubba out of the way, grabbed the one leaning over Spyder by one broad shoulder and yanked hard; Spyder let go and the guy stumbled, almost fell as he spun around to face Keith, clutching his jaw. Blood oozed black and wet from between his fingers, rouged Spyder's chin and grinning lips.

"She *bit* me!" he said, squawked, his face going sickly pale in the yellow parking lot glare. "The dyke *bit* my fuckin' face!"

"Get out of here, man," Keith growled, tightening his grip on the bat, testing its familiar weight like he was stepping up to the plate for a fastball.

"Fuck you, buddy, she bit a hole in my *face*."

"And I'm gonna knock your head off if you don't get the hell away from her. *Now.*"

Daria moved in closer to Keith, nerves sizzling like bad wiring behind old walls, but she kept her eyes on the guy on the ground and the one Keith had pushed aside, the one holding a liquor bottle wrapped conspicuously in a brown paper bag.

"Oh yeah," she whispered. "This is some mighty nice shit you've gotten us in tonight, Keith. Extra *special* shitty."

Sudden footsteps, heavy and coming up fast behind them, but she didn't have to turn around to know they belonged to Mort. A second more and he was standing next to her, wrapping her in his welcome reek of drummer-sweat.

"Tony, the bitch chewed up my face!"

"Don't worry, Digger," said the bubba with the liquor bottle, his eyes locked firmly on Keith's bat. "We're gonna mess her freak ass up real good."

"Last chance, brother," Keith said, smiled as he spoke, and Daria knew that he'd be disappointed if the guy did back down now, the days of empty black rage that would follow. She braced herself, glad for the weight of the tire iron, gladder for Mort at her side.

"Last chance."

"Screw you, fucker. The bitch probably gave me fuckin' AIDS—"

Spyder shrieked, a piercing and guttural cry like night birds or barbarian soldiers, rocked back and drove the heels of both her boots into Digger's kidneys, pushing him stumbling towards Keith. He howled, fresh pain and surprise, and threw a desperate, sloppy right at Keith's head; Keith ducked the blow effortlessly, side-stepped and swung his silver bat, connecting hard with the guy's right arm. Daria heard clearly the muffled *thwump,* the sick wet snap of living bone, and Bubba Digger crumbled to the pavement.

Bubba Tony took a single, hesitant step in Keith's di-rection and Daria heard the steel soft click of Mort's knife, the big, folding lockblade he carried for cutting electrical tape and splicing cable. Tony saw the knife and stopped, free hand disappearing into his jacket, returning a second later with a snubby little handgun.

"Screw this," he said and aimed the .32 at Keith with one unsteady hand. "Screw *all* this shit."

The car coughed suddenly awake, then, whined and hacking roar from its reluctant engine, and Daria no-ticed Byron Langly for the first time, crouched intense behind the steering wheel, bright panic glittering in his eyes as he tried to wrestle the car into first gear. The Celica lurched forward and Spyder groped frantically for handholds that weren't there, pitched sideways into the windshield. Bubba Tony yelped, tried too late to jump clear before he was knocked sprawling to the ground. His bottle smashed loudly against the asphalt and the gun skittered out of reach, spinning butt over glistening black muzzle.

Spyder managed to hang on a second or two longer, hands spread flat for traction against smooth metal and smoother glass. Then the car bounced violently over a speed bump and she was tossed clear, rolled like a stunt man in a TV cop show. The Celica squealed and screeched out of the parking lot, fishtailing and burning precious rubber from bald tires, missing the van by inches.

And nothing else for a long moment, then, time like caramel and cooling wax, nothing but Digger sobbing incoherent threats and curses, and the sound of Spyder's Toyota, the flight of the shrikes, fading into the distance.

"Jesus," whispered Mort and Daria realized that she'd been holding her breath, breathed out and inhaled deeply and the air tasted like car exhaust and spilled whiskey.

* * *

The sound that tore itself from Spyder's mouth dragged Robin immediately back down to the dreams, the creeping things that had followed her back from the peyote, up from the pit of Spyder's basement. The angry screech of denied retribution, raging shadows and nightshade teeth, and she covered her ears, squeezed her eyes shut, not wanting any more of this, not understanding how everything had gone so wrong so fast.

"Open your door, Byron," Walter said. "We gotta help her." And when Byron didn't move, didn't say a word, Walter kicked the back of his seat. "I *said* open the goddamn door!"

Robin was busy trying to make safe pictures in the imperfect darkness behind her eyelids, trying not to

believe that one of those neanderthal fucks was the
same Tony Falleta that she'd happily let maul and screw
her once upon a time, the same asshole that had tried to
rape her the night Spyder and Byron and Walter had
taken her home with them. She tried to see herself back
inside Dr. Jekyll's, making fun of the wannabes and
them not even bright enough to know. Still sitting safe
in Spyder's arms, two hits of ecstasy burning in her
brain. Back in Spyder's bedroom, the silent, watchful
tanks and web-painted windows safe as a church and
their flesh bleeding sweat and reassurance and the
smells of sex.

"Byron, *open the fucking door!*"

The words that Spyder knew that had made sense of
all her terrors, whispered like a private talisman in her
ear and the warm tangle of sheets and fuzzy blankets.

"Open the fucking door!"

"Don't you see it?" and Byron had sounded so small
and alone, so far away, that she'd had to open her eyes.

"Can't you *see*?"

And she *did* see it, the blackness unfolding itself from
inside Spyder like her body was only a shoddy cocoon,
the needle-tipped legs opening, stretching wide as the
night, wide as the boundless emptiness that Robin had
summoned to poison them all.

And then she saw the gun in Tony's shaking, coward's hand and Byron started the car.

The scream from the parking lot had left a gooseflesh
rash on Niki's arms and Theo was swearing, trying to
get the van to start. Keith had left the van idling, but
Theo had killed the motor when she'd shifted out of
neutral and had forgotten to keep her foot pressed
firmly on the clutch.

"Fuck, fuck, fuck . . ." She turned the key and the van
jerked and sputtered and was quiet again.

"I think you flooded it," Niki said, sounding almost as
useless as she felt, looking past Theo, through the
driver's side window. She followed the silver arc of the

baseball bat in Keith's hands, strange scythe, and the big redneck kneeled at his feet.

"It's not flooded. It's just a worthless piece of shit," and that time it turned over, half-hearted piston taunt, and almost caught.

But then the brown car jumped, seemed to spring forward like a hungry, pouncing animal, and the white-haired girl tumbled into the windshield. The front bumper caught the only one of the rednecks still standing, knocking him down, as the car swerved past the triad of Stiff Kitten. Halfway across the parking lot, the white-haired girl lost her grip on the hood or windshield and was tossed off, rag doll rolled a few feet and lay very still.

Niki gasped, grabbed Theo's arm; for a second she was sure the Toyota was going to plow straight into the van, but at the last possible moment the driver cut the wheel sharply to the left and the car squealed past, only inches to spare, vanished up Morris in a fog of its own exhaust. As they had passed, she'd caught a hurried glimpse of the faces inside, fear rigid and gaudy as cheap Halloween masks.

And then the van made a painful grinding sound deep in its internal combustion belly, backfired again, and rattled violently to life. Theo cursed and wrenched the gear shift into first, bumped over the curb and into the parking lot. Another three seconds and they were pulling up alongside Mort and Daria.

"Thank god for the cavalry," Mort said, closing his knife and putting it into his back pocket. "Better late than never."

Keith was squatted down beside the guy the car had clipped, prodded him with one end of the bat.

"Is he dead?" Mort asked and Keith shook his head, "Nah. He's breathing," and he looked back at the first guy he'd put down, still sitting on his butt, holding his ribs.

"Better call your buddies here an ambulance," and he picked up the revolver, flipped open the chamber and dumped the bullets out into his palm. He threw the gun into the tall weeds by the railroad tracks, pocketed the five cartridges.

"What about Spyder?" Daria asked, sliding the van's side door open as Niki climbed down from the passenger seat.

Spyder was lying on her back a few feet away, eyes open, staring blankly up at the clouds. Keith walked over and waved a hand in front of her face.

"Hey. Spyder. Are you dead?" he said and Niki saw the white-haired girl's lips move, but couldn't make out what she said.

"Spyder says she ain't dead yet, Dar."

Spyder tried to sit up and Keith helped her to her feet. Niki ran over to them, gladly seizing any chance to do something besides stand around gawking; she slipped one arm around Spyder and helped her towards the van.

"I can walk," Spyder said, but Niki helped her anyway.

"C'mon, guys. Move your pokey butts," Theo yelled. "I think Bert called the cops," and immediately she was answered by the not-distant-enough wail of sirens.

"I'm just surprised *you* didn't do it for him," Mort said, climbing into the cab beside her.

"It's snowing," Spyder said as Niki guided her past the pug snout of the van and she looked up into the city bright sky, felt the snow an instant before she saw it, huge, sticky flakes spiraling lazily down like Walt Disney fairies.

Spyder opened her mouth, bloodsmear-ringed like smudged lipstick or the candy apple halo around a little girl's mouth, and caught a single flake on her outstretched tongue. It lingered there a moment, ice water crystal on pink flesh, before it melted and Spyder swallowed what was left.

And Niki shivered as something warm and sharp passed through her, there and gone again almost before she even had time to recognize it, something she hadn't felt since the last time she'd seen Danny Boudreaux in the French Quarter, five months and a thousand years before. And they stood there, her and the white-haired girl, in the space between the beams of the van's headlights, watching the snow fall, until Theo finally honked the horn.

CHAPTER EIGHT

String Theory

1.

Byron was driving like an idiot, ignoring red lights and stop signs. From the backseat, Walter was cursing him, cursing himself for not having forced Byron to let him out of the car, for not having done something to help Spyder.

"She's dead," he said, finality and icing despair. "Yeah, god, *you* know she's dead. *You* killed her, Byron. You fucking killed Spyder."

The porcelain boy he'd been making out with sat very quiet, wide scared eyes, waiting to see exactly what he'd gotten himself into and how he was going to get himself back out again. Robin kept her eyes off the road, watched the beautiful, frightened boy reflected in her outside mirror, his black Betty Page wig and magenta lips. And the snow, falling down on them like manna.

"Just shut up," Byron said. "Just shut the hell up."

He raced through another red light and Robin heard tires squeal, desperate hot scream, horns blaring like pissed-off harpies and they were speeding south along a street she felt sure she'd seen a thousand times but couldn't begin to recognize.

"She's not dead," he said.

"How the hell do you know that, Byron? *Fuck.* How the hell do you know?" and he punched the driver's seat headrest.

"You didn't *see* it?"

"Man, I didn't see shit, except for you running over Spyder with her own goddamn car."

"Well, you just ask Robin, then. Robin saw. She knows . . ."

But she said nothing, watched the snow and the buildings slipping past as downtown turned into Southside and everything was powdered soft and sugar-white. What she had seen, what she thought she had seen, and all the things she had or had not seen since that night in the basement, crept behind her eyes, interceding, keeping themselves between the world and her mind. The things that left shadows but never showed themselves, that passed between her and lights, lamps and headlights and candles. The watchers, the skitterers, that had come up, been *sent* up, after them.

"Tell him," Byron said, begging her now, pleading for her soothing concurrence, her damning corroboration. "For god's sake, Robin, tell him you saw it, too."

"Why?" she whispered, softer sound even than the snow, "He knows what you're talking about."

"No!" and Walter punched the back of Byron's seat again. "I do *not* know what the fuck either of you are talking about!"

"You were down there the longest," she said. "Spyder had to go down after you."

"Fuck you, fuck you both," he said and this time Walter struck the little backseat window, hard enough that Robin was surprised it hadn't broken. "You killed her, man. You're both crazy and you killed her, Byron." But all the fury was draining away, something in his soul lanced and his voice was suddenly as brittle as brown October leaves.

"I want out," the porcelain boy said. "Just stop the car here and I'll get out."

Byron glanced uncertainly at the rearview mirror, as if he'd forgotten all about the boy, as if he'd never known he was back there.

"I'm not gonna tell anyone anything, I promise. Just let me out and I swear I won't say a thing to anyone."

"You didn't see it either?" Byron asked him.

"Please," the boy said, "Please let me out," and Robin could almost feel his fear and confusion like needles or a wire brush against her skin, knew that he'd be crying soon.

"Stop the goddamn car and let him the hell out, Byron," she said.

Byron pulled over at the next light, green for go but there was no one behind them; Robin opened her door and stepped out into the storm, her shoes making their shallow mark in the snow. She had to pull the little release lever before the seat popped forward, catapult quick, and the porcelain boy could climb out of the backseat.

"I didn't see anything," he told her, eyes wet, rouged cheeks already redder from the cold.

"I know," she said, "This doesn't have anything to do with you," and he walked quickly away, as quickly as he could without his black patent pumps sliding on the slippery sidewalk. She watched him for a moment, wet snowflakes gathering in her hair, sticking to her face, already missing Spyder.

2.

Walter had been the last one out of the basement, the one that Spyder had gone down for herself, while Robin and Byron had sat naked and filthy in the morning-filled hall, still clutching tight to one another. Robin had cried, had pleaded with her not to leave them alone, not to step through the protecting floor into the hungry black.

"That's what He wants," she said, not meaning Walter, meaning Preacher Man and His red book.

"Robin, I can't just leave him down there," and she'd been sucked down through the gaping trapdoor hole.

"*No!*" she'd wailed. "Oh please god Spyder, no," and she'd tried to scramble across the floor after her, but Byron hadn't let her go, had held on, held her back.

And what had seemed like a long, long time later, Spyder had brought him back to them. Walter, his pale and hairless chest, his legs, scraped and gouged, his face caked with red basement dirt and maroon-brown streaks of his own blood. Spyder had whispered something in his ear and he'd sat down next to Robin and Byron, both hands crooked like arthritis claws and cradled close to his body. Robin had wanted to pull him to her, lock him up safe in her embrace with Byron, but his eyes, unblinking, full of nothing, had scared her too much to even touch him.

"It's gonna be all right now," Spyder said and she was crying too, silent tears shiny beneath her eyes.

And then something had reached up out of the dark, two jointed legs or arms raised cautious from the trapdoor, probing, testing the bright, warm air; night bristling hairs, quills and chitin barbs. Robin screamed, had pointed at the hole as Spyder turned and stood staring. The appendages had rasped and tapped anxiously at the floor and a third rose straight from the center and unfolded like a knife, felt its way eagerly along the wall.

"*What?*" Spyder had asked her. " What is it? There's nothing there."

"Oh Jesus, they're still coming," Byron had whimpered, "They're still coming," and he'd pushed flat against the wall at his back as if he could squeeze through. So Robin had known that he saw it too, that Spyder must see it and was only trying not to scare them. When the tip end of the fourth leg appeared and she'd screamed again, and Byron had started screaming too, Spyder lifted the trapdoor with the toe of her boot, wood studded with a hundred nails like slanting needle teeth, rising, falling, and the thing had pulled itself back through just as the door had slammed closed.

And then she had pushed the old trunk over on top of the trapdoor.

"See?" she'd said. "Now you're safe. Nothing's gonna get out of there now." She'd gone away for just a moment, had disappeared into her bedroom and Robin's eyes had drifted back to the trapdoor, the trunk like the stone that sealed the tomb. But Spyder had come right back, carrying one of her prescription bottles; she'd opened it and pretty blue pills had poured out into her palm. She'd made them each swallow one, had to force Walter's past his lips and far back on his tongue.

And then she'd led them all down the hallway to the big bathroom and its lion-footed cast iron tub, white enamel and sparkling warm water and the calming smell of soap.

3.

Sitting in the diner, faded sunflower walls and plastic yellow booths, the stink of pork fat and waffles and other people's cigarettes. Walter held his head in both hands as if it had grown too heavy for his shoulders, his spine. Robin across from him, sipping the sour diner coffee, close to Byron, as if they'd chosen sides; Walter the puppy loyalist and her and Byron somehow turned traitorous, coconspirators in an accidental *coup d'état*.

Outside, the snow was still coming down, half an inch or more on the ground already and falling so hard that she could see no farther out the plate glass window than the first row of cars in the parking lot.

"We should just go back," Walter said again.

"I'm fucking tired of hearing that shit, Walter, so can it, okay?" Byron folded and unfolded a paper napkin, making and unmaking a sloppy origami bat for the umpteenth time. His own coffee sat untouched, cold and black.

"I'm just saying it still might not be too late, not if we go back now."

"Too late for *what,* Wally? Huh?" Byron said, loud enough that the waitress looked up from her pencil, pad, and scribbles.

"You mean it might not be too late to watch them loading that cracker's corpse into a body bag? Might not be too late to catch the pretty lights on top of the ambulance? Or how about this one, Wally: it might not be too goddamn late to spend a little time in the Birmingham jail, getting fucked up the ass every time you bend over?"

Robin flinched, and Walter looked at them for the first time in ten, fifteen minutes, his eyes rimmed puffy red and irises seething with onionskin layers of hurt and fear and anger, palm print impressions framing his face like the tailfeathers of kindergarten turkeys.

"You cold-hearted son of a bitch," he said. "You don't even care if she's dead or not, do you? You're just worried about yourself. You're just worried about having to explain this mess to the cops."

"Frankly, Walter, I think jail's about the *last* thing I should be worrying about right now, don't you?" and Byron pulled the wings off his napkin bat and let its torso flutter to the tabletop.

"What is that supposed to mean?"

"You know what he means, Walter," she said and looked back out at the snow, the candyland world without sharp edges. "You can pretend all you want, but you're still just as much a part of this as we are, as much as Spyder."

"She lied to us," Byron said. "She lied to us and the whole thing is just a trap."

"You two just don't get it, do you? The game is fucking *over,* okay? This shit is for real."

Robin closed her eyes, feeling the x still burning inside her, her stomach and muscles tight from the strychnine and everything that had gone wrong in the last hour.

"What did you see down there, Walter?" she asked without opening her eyes. "What did you see in the basement? What did you dream about before Spyder made the dream catcher?"

"Robin, we were just fucked up. We were tripping our fucking balls off. We didn't see anything real, nothing that wasn't in our heads all along."

"That's horseshit," Byron said, rolling his dismembered bat into a wad and sinking it in his glass of ice water. "And you know it and you're just too big a pussy to admit it."

"You never believed any of the story," Robin said, not a question, a revelation, maybe, and she opened her eyes, turned slowly away from the window to face Walter; he winced, looked quickly back down at his hands.

"I know you guys aren't this stupid," he said. "It was just a bad trip and all that other stuff was just something Spyder made up to try and make us sleep better."

"You're a liar," she said, Robin, her voice more bitter than the coffee. "You think maybe it'll all go away if you say it never happened. That you'll stop seeing the shadows if you say they're not there."

"Robin, I haven't seen *jack shit,* okay? I'm telling you the truth. I haven't seen jack-fucking-shit."

"I don't believe you," Robin said.

"That's not my goddamn problem."

Short silence then, and Byron tapping impatient black nails against formica.

"So, you're not even going with us?" he asked, finally. "You won't even do that much?"

"We're in enough trouble already without breaking into Spyder's house."

"It wouldn't *be* breaking in," Byron said. "Robin has a key. You know she has a key, Walter," and without asking permission, he grabbed for her purse, chrome cut and bolted into a tiny coffin with a handle and latch and a purple velvet ankh on the lid; she let him take it, let him in.

"We have to protect the dream catcher," Byron said as he dug through the junk in her purse, dumped everything out on the table and there was her key ring, more goth kitsch, a plastic spine and pelvis.

"I'm sorry," Walter said and left his mouth open like there was more, but he couldn't find the words.

"She used your hair, too," Robin said, but now she was looking at the storm again, frantic blur, falling ice white sky, but not at Walter or the mess of her things Byron had spilled on the table. If they didn't leave soon, they'd be spending the night in the diner, or walking.

"I'm sorry," he said again, no more meaning than the first time, a little more regret, and she could hear the bright jingle of her keys, Byron holding them up for Walter like something he'd be helpless to refuse.

"I'm going back," he said. "Maybe I can explain . . ."

"Then to hell with you," and Byron picked up one of the glasses of ice water the waitress had set down in front of them, obligatory courtesy, never mind the weather, and dashed it in Walter's face. Walter gasped at the cold, the surprise, and she still looked at the snow, the softening shadows between the cars, perfect shadow canvas.

"I'm sorry," Walter said, last time, third time the charm, and slid out of the booth, dripping, pocket-wrinkled dollar dropped on the table for his coffee. "Please be careful," he said and *"Please."*

"Fuck off," Byron hissed and then Walter was gone, the diner door jangling shut like a phantom cow and they sat very alone in the booth, each waiting for the other to speak, waiting for whatever came next.

4.

"Before the World, there was a war in Heaven," and then Spyder had stopped, had gripped Robin's hand tighter and looked into all their eyes at once. Three pairs to her one, bright six to her pale two.

They'd all come back to her, after staying away for days and days, back to the house, with their nightmares and the lanky things they thought they saw during the day tagging along behind. Robin and Byron had sobbed out every detail, had told her all the things about the basement that at first they'd kept back, the burning things that Preacher Man had said. Walter had sat apart from them at the kitchen table, looking nervously from window to nightblack window. And Spyder, quietly watching them and listening and watching too the secret, jagged places inside herself.

She hadn't told them the truth, or what she'd suspected might be the truth. Instead, she had held her lover's hand hard so Robin's fingertips had gone white and she'd given them a lie so perfect and pretty she'd have died to make it true. Had prayed to the darkness in her head that the words would be enough to save them, to bring them all the way back to her.

The way she'd always kept herself alive.

"And after the angels had fallen," she'd said, "there were a few who hid themselves where the World would be. And they were made into the World, stitched into the fabric so tight that it took them a million or a billion years to find their way out again. They slipped out without God seeing them, when volcanoes erupted or the rocks wore away into canyons or when caverns fell in and made sinkholes.

"But they knew that God was still looking for them, because they'd stolen things from Heaven, things they didn't think could ever be trusted to Him again. And they'd hidden them deep inside the earth during their captivity, had found . . ."

"This is total bullshit," Walter had whispered, watching the bushes that pressed themselves against screen and glass, switching twigs and restless green leaves.

"Shut up, shut up, shut up," and Robin had whirled around at him, spitting the words out between teeth clenched and lips snarled back, rabid, furious warning that she had to hear what was being said and she might hurt him if he pissed Spyder off and she quit talking.

But Spyder had only pulled her closer, Robin and the kitchen chair *scrunk* across the old linoleum, fresh scuff marks on the checkerboard squares and she'd pressed Robin's tearslicky face against her chest, hadn't even looked at Walter.

"They'd stolen important things," she said. "Very important things. Treasures.

"They thought they'd put them places that even He would never find them. But they were wrong, and He sent His lieutenants and angel captains down to bring them back. And to kill the thieves."

Outside, something had padded quickly by, hurried feet below the window's sill and Walter had jumped, wiped sweat from his forehead. "Goddamn dogs," he'd said. "Doesn't *anyone* around here keep their fucking dog on a leash?"

Spyder had looked up at the window for a moment, and then she'd continued.

"Some of the exiled angels, although they weren't really angels anymore because God had taken away their wings and made them all mortal, mortal enough that they'd grow old and finally die someday, some of them got away and took a few of the treasures with them, spent thousands and thousands of years running from the loyal angels that hunted them down one by one. Until there were only three or four, and the only treasure they had left was a stone . . ."

"That's just the stuff *I* told you," Walter said, almost as much contempt now as fear, cheated, lost emotion like whiskey stink on his voice. "The stuff from that fucking book that Robin told me to read. You're not even making this up yourself . . ."

And Byron had lunged at him, reached across the table, knocking over everything, ketchup bottle and hot pepper sauce and a dusty dry vase of dead roses. Had seized Walter by the collar of his Misfits t-shirt and slammed him down hard against the metal tabletop, held his head pressed down with both hands while the red bottle of ketchup rolled over the edge and broke on the floor.

"It doesn't matter," Byron said, loud and male and not sounding much like anyone he'd ever been before. Each syllable a lead weight from his lips. "It doesn't fucking matter *where* she knows it from," and then he'd smacked Walter's head against the table again.

"Byron, turn him loose, *now*," and when she'd said that, Byron had looked at Spyder like he'd forgotten precisely who she was.

"Make him shut up," he said.

"He's not gonna say anything else. He's just scared too. Turn him loose."

And he had, had slowly let Walter stand up, Walter almost a foot taller than Byron but the blood running from his busted lips and nose anyway. He'd sat back down in his chair, not a curse or a threat, one hand held over his wounded face.

"Don't stop," Robin whispered, desperation like dirty oil, and "Please don't stop, Spyder."

She'd waited only as long as it took for Byron to sink back into his own chair, only as long as she dared.

"Please . . ."

"The only part of the treasure left was a stone," and a pause, maybe a sort of challenge to Walter, but he'd been watching the windows again, his own blood in his hands.

"A beautiful blue-gray stone full of God's most beautiful and terrible secrets. And they knew that they'd been wrong, that there was no way for them to hide themselves or the stone much longer. Instead, they found a way to take it apart and put it back together again inside themselves. But they knew that still wasn't enough, so they found men and women and fucked them, seduced them or just raped them, and that passed the things in the stone into innocent human beings that they didn't believe He would ever hurt to take back his secrets."

"But they were wrong, weren't they?" Byron asked, asked like he already knew the answer, had known it all his life.

"Yeah," she said. "They were wrong. The people that carried the things from the stone inside them disappeared from the World one by one, but some of them had children first, and their children had children, and little bits and pieces got away after all."

They were hanging on her words, then, even Walter, salvation in these lies, waiting just beyond the last thing she'd said. And Spyder had strained to see the fetal lies in front of her, curled slippery as moss-hairy stones almost invisible under rushing water, shitty stepping-stones, but the only path she had to give them.

"These bits and pieces were passed along generation to generation, getting smaller and smaller all the time, spread out further and further. Getting harder and harder for the angels to track down, the angels and the things that hunted for them, the things that God made especially to be able to smell out those special people that looked human but really were part stone and part secrets and part something that had once been angel."

"Oh," Robin said. *"Oh."* She'd almost stopped crying, her face still pressed urgent between Spyder's breasts, her ear to Spyder's wet drumbeat heart.

"People like us," Byron said. "That's what you're saying, isn't it, Spyder?"

But she hadn't wanted to say that part, to take them that last deceitful step, had known that if she left just one or two seconds empty, they'd do it for themselves.

"And what we did down in the basement," he said, catching on so fast, as if he could follow inside her head and pick her thoughts like shiny, scarlet berries.

"We didn't mean to, but we got their attention, didn't we? That thing that Robin keeps calling Preacher Man, that's one of the angels, isn't it? And the other things, the shadows we keep seeing, those are what it uses to hunt down the . . ."

A gentle, keening sound like something alive tearing itself in two and Walter had pushed his chair back from the table then, slow and calculated movement, stood up and walked away into the house alone.

Spyder had ached to call him back, ached to take this all back, take back the nails she'd driven through the trapdoor, the damning permission she'd given that had sent Robin and Byron and Walter down there to begin with. Better if she'd just lost them then, lost them clean.

"Oh god," each word barely a sigh, soft murmurs to her chest. "Oh god, Spyder. How do we stop them from finding us? How will we make them leave us alone?"

"They're using our dreams to find us," Byron said. "They're changing our dreams."

Robin had sat up, eyes watery-red and puffy, wiped her nose roughly on the back of her hand like a child, and she'd said "A dream catcher. We have to make a dream catcher, Spyder. Like the Objibwas made to keep away evil spirits that caused nightmares, to trap them in the webs . . ."

And then she'd touched Spyder's arm, one finger tracing the silver-blue tattoos, inkscar patterns, and Robin had begun to cry all over again, but this time there had been as much hope and relief as fear, and she'd held Spyder and Spyder had held her, too.

5.

At the end of the road, the house waited for them, crouched way down in its blanket of snow and bare tree limbs like an alley cat. They'd left the Celica blocks away, abandoned where the bald tires had finally lost traction for the last time and they'd slid gracefully, dream smooth loss of control and direction, into a line of sugar-coated garbage cans. Their feet ached from the melted snow that had seeped into their shoes, lungs ached almost as much from the cold air and the extra effort required not to fall on their asses every time they took a step up the icysteep slope.

Spyder never bothered with the porch light, had always told Robin that it only attracted burglars, and past the pool of this last streetlight there was only the glow that had gathered underneath the storm, creamy champagne light filtered so soft and kind it played with the eyes. Brighter back there away from the street than it should have been, but no comfort in the illumination.

The snow falling around them, on them, made a crisp sound, like rice paper crumpled slowly in dry hands or small and padded paws on dead leaves.

"We can't back out," she said, "not now," before Byron had a chance to say that maybe Walter had been right, after all, maybe they *shouldn't* be here and the cushioned world muffled her voice, magnified it at the same time, made it as wrong as the light.

"We can't back out now."

Lightning then, a dull and greenish flash trapped in the low clouds, unearthly, and thunder wrapped tight in velvet before the crackling boom of a transformer blowing somewhere, sympathetic chaos, echoed across the mountain. The street light flickered, dimmed, and died.

Byron said nothing, stepped silent past the withered scraggle of oleander and honeysuckle that framed the crooked walk to Spyder's front door, cracked and weed-crowded flagstones lost now beneath the equalizing snow. And she followed as silent, her boots where his had gone before, pockmarking the perfect, white mantle.

Spyder's house had never seemed anything but welcoming, the one sure sanctuary from her parents and the whole shitty world; even that first time she'd come back after the peyote and the basement horrors, even then, through all her dread, it had seemed to welcome her back, to want her inside where Spyder and the old walls could shield her safe. Tonight it wasn't friendly, sat gathering drifts on the tarshingle pitch of its roof, dark windows staring straight through them with vicious indifference.

Robin counted their steps to the porch, twenty, twenty-five, counted to keep herself from thinking about what they were about to do, what they'd already done; what might be pursuing them across the yard or waiting for them inside the house, watching, hungry and pleased with itself, from any or all of the stark blind windows. Thirty-five, forty-three and they were standing amid the garbage and porch junk. Looking back the way they'd come, the arrow-straight scar of footprints disfiguring the snow, incriminating for however long it took the storm to fill them in again.

Then there'll be no way to tell we were ever even here, and that should have been a comfort.

"Hurry," Byron whispered, shivering, whispered like there was someone to overhear, and she realized that he was waiting on her now; for a moment, terrifying and optimistic seconds, she thought that maybe she'd left the keys in her purse, tucked beneath the passenger seat. She reached inside a pocket of her jacket, reluctant hand, anxious fingers, and there they were, right where she'd put them before she and Byron had even left the diner. Pocket lint and prescription bottle and the familiar weight of the key ring, the gently arched bridge of vertebrae connecting the plastic triumvirate of ilium and pubis and ischium at one end with the four keys at the other. And from the corner of her left eye, something quick and no real shape at all, slipping across the snow, crossing the space between pecan and oak before she could turn to see.

"What?" Byron's voice like stickpins, and *"What is it?"*

She put the key ring in his hand without turning her back on the yard. The snow between the tall trees was smooth and sparkled faintly, no sign at all that there'd been anything there but her imagination, nerves and the x or a trick of the weirdass light.

"Just open the door," she said.

"Which one," and she could hear the keys jingling in his hands, could hear the scratch of key metal on lock metal as he tried the wrong one. Another wrong one after that.

"I don't know which one it *is*," he said, and there it was again, no fleeting, peripheral glimpse this time, the lingering impression that something was hunched down behind the trunk of the water oak, something *almost* narrow enough to hide itself behind the bole.

"Open the fucking door, Byron. Open it *now*," and she flashed back to Walter, two hours before, the same words, the same desperate, useless insistence.

"*I am trying,* goddammit, so please just shut the hell up," and the last key slid in cocksmooth and the dead bolt clicked back, gunshot loud. A sudden gust tossed the naked limbs like puppet arms and legs, set every shadow dancing, perfect diversion and Robin turned and pushed, shoved Byron through the half-opened door, out of one cold and into another drier arctic, certain that something rushed liquid smooth toward them across the yard on jointed, spindle legs. She slammed the door behind her, turned the bolt in the same frantic motion, and they both heard it, both *thought* they heard it: the softest thump against the other side of the door, the ragged, heavy breath, panting dog sound, and then nothing at all but the wind.

"What . . ." he started to ask, his sweatcool palm finding hers; she shook her head, stepped back from the door.

"Nothing," she said. "Nothing at all."

She felt along the wall until she found the old iron switch plate, switches for the porch and foyer and flipped both up, but the dark stayed put, no electricity, the lines down from wind or the weight of icicles, more likely that last transformer explosion.

"The power's out," she said and Byron's grip tightened around her hand.

"I can't see for shit," he said.

"It isn't that dark, pussy," and it wasn't, really, her eyes just beginning to adjust and there was enough pale light spilling in through the opaque rectangle of glass set high up on the door that she could see a little ways down the hall, could make out the darker entrance to the living room on her left, the closed door to the front bedroom on her right.

The room where Trisha Baxter had died and Spyder stored the junk there wasn't space for on the porch.

"Do you have your lighter?" and she heard the cloth rustle as Byron rummaged through the pockets of his frock coat.

"Yeah, it's right here."

"Then we can light candles," and she led him by the hand, little brother tow, deeper into Spyder's house.

6.

They had sat together on Spyder's bed, surrounded by the glint of aquarium glass and the web-painted windows, and watched Spyder make the dream catcher by the soothing light of rose and cinnamon-scented candles. Had all gone out together to the wild backyard night, even Walter, and Spyder had cut a green and slender branch from one of the crape myrtle bushes. Back inside the house, she'd used her pocket knife to strip away the twigs and leaves, had left the cuttings in a sap sticky scatter on the kitchen floor.

And with the same knife, tiny thing but razor sharp, she'd taken locks of their hair. Robin's first, emerald in the candlelight, then Byron's, dyed jet black and slick as mink, and Walter next, dirty, unwashed tortoiseshell. Had saved her own for last, sliced colorless strands from a place near her right temple where one of the dreads was coming loose. And then she'd laid each lock out on the quilt, four fraying streaks against the cotton patchwork.

She had bent the branch carefully while they watched (all but Walter, who'd pretended to read from a thick book on fossil arachnids while she worked), bowed pliant wood into a perfect hoop, near perfect mandala six or seven inches in diameter, and tied it closed with white nylon kite twine from a box beneath the bathroom sink. And then she picked up the pocket knife again, brass handle and stainless steel gleam, had passed the blade slowly through the flame of the red votive candle burning on the table beside Lurch and Tickler's tank.

Spyder cut herself in the soft bend of one elbow, had drawn the cooling blade quick across her skin, severing tattooed lines and the vein hiding beneath. Dabbed her fingers in the wound and slicked the hoop with her blood.

And no one had said anything, not one word while she wove their hair with certain, patient fingers, tied the concentric rings and irregularly spaced radial lines running from rim to hub.

"It's just a simple orb web," when she'd finished, almost dawn, and Spyder had pointed to the design on one of the windows, "A snare, like garden spiders make."

Last of all, she'd used more of the twine to tie a couple of musty, old mockingbird feathers to the rim.

Robin had held it while Spyder stood and stretched, wiped at her jeans and a few stray hairs sifted to the floor.

"Now, we put it someplace safe," she'd said, and had taken the dream catcher from Robin, lifted the lid off one of the bigger tanks, twenty-five gallons of air, mostly, a few sticks and rocks strewn across the bottom. Robin didn't have to read the sloppy writing on the yellowed strip of masking tape stuck to one corner of the tank, didn't have to know the correct pronunciation of *Latrodectus geomstricus* to understand: the shiny black bodies like living vinyl, crimson hour-glass bellies. Spyder brushed several clinging forms from the underside of the lid with her bare fingers, mother-voice whispered to calm them, the widows, Robin, Byron half asleep on Robin's shoulder, Walter still staring at the pages of his book. She slipped the dream catcher inside and replaced the lid, weighted it down with a lump of shale.

"Nothing's gonna fuck with it in there," she said, and Robin, "We're safe now?"

"Yeah," she'd lied. "Yeah. Everything's gonna be fine now. No more nightmares." And after she'd blown out the candles, they'd followed her back out to the kitchen.

7.

"It's still closed," Byron said, hushed awe and relief, and she wanted to hit him. Standing close together in the hall, flickering candlelight on their faces and the wallpaper, hot wax dripping onto her fingers. Of course it was closed, the basement door, hidden underneath the moldy old Turkish carpet she and Spyder had found cheap at a junk shop months ago, had beaten with brooms but still there was as much crud as color to the thing. But she didn't hit him, because she'd been afraid, too, afraid for no sane reason that the carpet would be rolled back and the trapdoor would be open. So she made him go first this time, held his hand and they stayed close to the wall until they were past the spot, until they were standing at Spyder's bedroom door. It was closed, always closed whether she was in there or somewhere else.

"Did you hear something?"

But she was already turning the brass cold knob, the metal like dry ice in her hand, and it took everything she had, nothing left over for Byron or anything else. Even through the fear, the thickening hum behind her eyes, she felt like a thief, like a rapist; Spyder had always asked them here, had always trusted them . . .

So she made herself remember what she'd seen in the parking lot outside Dr. Jekyll's and she opened the door.

"There," he said. "Something on the roof."

Robin stepped across the threshold and Byron lingered behind for a moment, looking up at the high ceiling like an idiot. She set her candle down on a tall and listing stack of magazines on Spyder's dresser, *The Web* and *Blue Blood* and *Propaganda;* wax-scabbed hand, maroon blobs like some bizarre skin disease. Picked them off and stood staring at the utility shelf that sagged against one wall, held most of the old aquariums and jars, the only one that mattered, biggest tank on the center shelf.

"Hurry," Byron said, so she knew he wasn't going to do it, should have known that all along. Robin crossed the room alone, laid her hand on the rock that held the plywood lid in place. Inside, she could see the dream catcher leaning forward against the glass, matted in funnel silk and here and there, a few of the spiders hanging like black and poison berries.

"Do you remember what Spyder said about the widows?" she asked him, set the ash-colored stone on the next tank over, smaller tank and nothing in there but harmless wolf spiders.

"What did she say?"

"That black widows aren't aggressive. That they hardly ever bite people."

"Oh. Yeah, yeah," and he almost sounded like he did remember, but she could tell he was just playing the game, knew that Byron never paid attention when Spyder talked about her bugs.

"That's what she said, that they're very shy, and usually nobody ever gets bitten unless they fuck up, like, if they step on a widow or lay their hand on one so there's no way for it to escape."

She lifted the lid slow, and at least there was enough light from their candles that she could see there was nothing clinging to the underside of the board.

"You practically have to *make* them bite you."

"Be careful, Robin," he said, "Please be careful," but she was already slipping her hand between the aluminum rim of the tank and the wood, her fingers already inside.

"And even if you do get bitten," she whispered, words so far away, like someone else's and her heart too fast, head too light, "Hardly anyone ever dies."

Her hand in past the wrist now and the dry crape myrtle pinched gently between thumb and index finger; one of the widows dangled only an inch from her thumbnail, hung from green strands of her own hair twisted together with ivory strands of Spyder's. When she tugged cautiously at the dream catcher, it scuttled away to safety.

"See?" she said. "There's nothing to be afraid of."

And then, the sound, like a sack of bones and Coca-Cola bottles rolling along the roof, like scrambling legs or marching pry-bars, and she closed her hand tight around the dream catcher and pulled, ripping apart the shrouding webs, scattering black bodies. The shelf creaked loud, groaned and swayed toward her, precarious balance undone, and Byron screamed, something she couldn't make out, nothing that could ever have possibly mattered anyway, before the wall of glass and metal and a thousand tiny lives crashed down upon her.

He did not leave her lying there, wrestled her limp and bleeding body from the glittering tangle that had been Spyder's menagerie. Not because he was brave or because he loved her, but because he was more afraid of being alone, much more frightened of the sounds outside the painted windows than he could ever be of the pin-prick of venom fangs. Had hauled her from the wreckage and into the hallway, towing her under the arms because he couldn't pick her up. Sobbing and his face a wet smear of sweat and tears and snot and ruined eyeliner; angry red welts rising on her face and hands, a jagged gash across her forehead that had peeled back enough scalp that he caught a sickening glimpse of skull through all the blood. And one of the widows, snarled in her hair and he stomped it, ground it beneath the toe of his boot until it was unrecognizable pulp.

"Robin, don't be dead, don't be dead, please don't be fucking dead," repeated like a mantra, something holy or unholy with power against the night and the storm and whatever he could hear moving about on the roof, scritching beneath the floor.

He dragged her roughly across the rug, wouldn't allow himself to consider the trapdoor or what wanted out, but her boots snagged on the carpet and pulled it back, like the flap of skin above her eyebrows.

"Come on, Robin, remember what she said? Remember what Spyder said? You just fucking told me, remember?"

Robin's head lolled back on her neck like a broken toy, eyes half open to scleral whites and he knew she was still alive, still breathing, because of the air bubbling out through the blood clogging her nose.

"Hardly anyone ever dies, Robin. Hardly anyone ever dies."

Through the laughing, vindicated house and back into the cold, the razor wind so much worse than when they'd gone in and the snow falling so hard and fast, pelting him with its touch like needles and feathers. It had swallowed the world, mercifully swallowed the house as soon as they were halfway across the front yard. But Byron didn't stop until they reached the street, a thousand miles from the porch, until they were all the way off Spyder's property and all the way across the street, a meandering, Robin-wide swath plowed through the snow.

And then he collapsed, slumped and gasping against the curb, no air left in his lungs and his muscles aching in ways he'd never hurt before. Robin sprawled at his feet, the blood from her face almost black on the snow, the places where the widows had bitten her turning dark, bruise livid. He lay there, hearing the snow and his heart and listening for anything else, anything at all, until the dizziness and nausea had passed and he'd stopped wheezing.

"Robin?" and her eyes fluttered, half-mast lids and no recognition, so he slapped her cheek softly and spoke louder. "I have to get help. I have to find someone to call an ambulance."

She coughed once, and a little glob of bubblegum pink foam rolled past her lower lip, slid down her chin.

"*Robin.*"

She opened her eyes for him, then, lost, glazed eyes, and she began to shiver violently.

"See what I see?" she said, words around clacking teeth, a voice like Robin's broken and put back together wrong, full of pain and wonder. She was looking past him, back toward the house, "In the trees, like grinning foxes."

And the goosebumps on the back of his neck, prickling his arms, skin that felt watched, kept him from turning around to look for himself.

"I have to go get help, Robin," he said, pulled off his coat and covered her with it. "I have to go get help right now."

"Yeah," she said, detached and blurred. "Yeah, Byron. Don't leave me, okay."

I have to leave you, he started to say, *I can't find help unless I leave you,* but there were branches snapping behind him and so he stood instead, and walked away from her as quickly as he could.

8.

Halfway across town, the city crippled, already shutting down before the storm, Walter stood alone in the empty parking lot opposite Dr. Jekyll's. The snow swirled down through the arc lights and stuck to his hair, melted against his face.

He'd walked part of the way from the diner, freezing and his clothes soaked through from the glass of water Byron had thrown at him, had finally hitched a ride with a woman inching cautiously along in her Jeep. She'd been wearing freedom rings and had talked too much, nervous chatter about the weather, what they were saying on the radio: blizzard conditions expected, the worst winter storm to hit the southeast in more than a century. She'd let him out in the short tunnel just before Morris, where 19th Street ducked beneath the railroad, had asked him twice if he was sure he had a place to go. The warmth from the Jeep had clung to him for only a second or two before the wind rushing through the tunnel had ripped it away.

And the parking lot was as deserted as the streets.

Nothing he could do, no way to even know what had happened.

He shivered and stared across the tracks, the uneven lights, black pockets here and there where the lines were down. Looked for the exact place where Spyder's house would be, but the mountain was just a black smudge against the sky. No way to tell, exactly, so he turned, fingers crossed that the Fidgety Bean would still be open, that he wouldn't have to try to walk all the way home through the storm and the night. And then movement or the fleeting impression of form, quickest glimpse from the corner of one eye, something stretched too long across the snow and too tall across brick. He tried to turn fast enough to catch it there, finally, more sick of the dread than afraid, better to be damned and sure than to spend another night jumping at shadows.

But there was nothing to see but the storm, the wind making a silvery dust devil with the snow, and he pulled his damp clothes tighter around bony shoulders and walked away fast toward the coffee shop.

CHAPTER NINE

Paperweight

1.

They went to Keith's, because Daria was afraid the cops would spot the van if they stayed anywhere on Morris. A single room a few blocks away, three flights up the carcass of an old office building. His uncle owned the place and was letting Keith live there rent-free, dodging zoning ordinances by pretending he only worked there nights as security. When Keith switched the lights on, they buzzed like drunken wasps, half-hearted fluorescence that made them all look like hung-over zombies.

"Oh Keith," Theo crooned, sarcasm thick as old honey. "I do *love* what you've done with the place!"

They all followed him inside, Niki and Spyder last, stepped into the room, stark and ugly and soulless, almost as cold as the night outside. Nappy gray-green carpet, water-stained ceiling and walls, big holes punched through the sheetrock in a dozen places, exposing pink insulation and two-by-fours. Unfurnished, except for a scary-looking mattress in one corner and two metal folding chairs, three bulgy cardboard boxes stuffed with dirty clothes.

"What do you call this, anyway? Late Bosnian refugee?"

"Theo, why don't you just shut the hell up?" and Daria turned around and punched her once, hard, in the shoulder.

Theo flinched and dropped her purse, the flamingo-pink plastic Barbie lunch box, bump to the floor; it popped open and everything inside spilled out onto the sallow carpet.

"Christ, Dar! Fuck *you!*" and she looked to Mort for defense.

"Just lay off for a little while," he said, frown deepening, exhaustion and weary annoyance in his eyes and voice. "You know it's not gonna kill you."

"Christ," Theo hissed, "You're all a bunch of crazy fucking assholes," rubbing her arm, as she kneeled and began scooping everything back into her purse.

Daria and Niki helped Spyder to one of the chairs. She was limping, still bleeding some from a deep gash above her left eye; dried and congealed blood caked her dreads, crusted and sticky maroon masking the left side of her face.

"It looks a lot worse than it is, probably," Keith said again, seventh or eighth time since the parking lot. And for the seventh or eighth time, Spyder nodded, sluggish agreement.

"Can we at least turn the heat up a little?" Niki asked. Spyder had started to shiver, and Niki wondered if she could be going into shock, wondered if she could have lost that much blood, if maybe she was also bleeding somewhere inside.

"Would gladly," Keith said, dull and jovial grin, "if there was any." But he pulled a lemon-yellow sleeping bag off the scary mattress and handed it to Niki; there was a dark smear down one side that she hoped was only motor oil.

"Thanks, man," Spyder mumbled around her swelling lips.

"Don't mention it," and he shrugged once, walked back to the mattress and sat down.

Niki unzipped the sleeping bag, wrapped it around Spyder's black leather shoulders.

"Thanks," Spyder mumbled.

"We should have taken her to a hospital," Niki said and Keith shrugged again.

"Hey, man, it was her call," and he pulled a pint of Thunderbird from beneath one corner of the mattress, unscrewed the cap and drank deeply from the green bottle.

And there was nothing else for Niki to say. In the van, Mort had asked Spyder if she wanted a doctor, if they should just drive straight to the UAB emergency room, and Spyder had flatly refused, had insisted she was fine. So Theo had driven them here, instead, had parked the van in the narrow alley around back, had hidden it poorly behind a big blue Dumpster.

Keith offered the bottle to Mort and he accepted.

"Man, you're as happy about that whole stupid mess as a pig in piss-warm mud," Mort said, tilted the bottle of wine at the ceiling and traded a little air for its sweet buzz.

"Did you see the look on that dumb fucker's face?" and Keith stopped unlacing his boots, twisted his own face into a grotesque and exaggerated mask of anger and surprise, chuckled. "You really laid some heavy juju on that asshole, Spydie. Put the *bite* on him," and he took the bottle back from Mort, half-empty now, half-full. Spyder smiled weakly, wan and guarded pride beneath the clotting scars of battle.

"And you got your ass-kicking fix for a few days, didn't you?" Daria said, vacant reproach, from the room's only window where she stood alone, watching the snow falling outside.

"Just doin' my part to keep the lady with the scales honest, babe."

Niki sighed loudly, loud to derail the conversation, loud enough to get everyone's attention.

"Is there at least someplace I can get some water to clean the blood off her face?" And she could hear the tightness wound around her words, hoped that she sounded as fed up as she felt.

"Down the hall," Daria said. "There's a john down the hall. Jesus, it's really coming *down* out there."

"I guess a washcloth or a towel would be too much to hope for," Niki said.

"I've got a handkerchief." Theo had stuffed everything back into her purse, sat on the ugly carpet beneath a tattered Nirvana poster stuck up with tacks; someone had drawn graceful angel wings, black magic marker plumage from Kurt Cobain's shoulder blades, a cheesy halo over his head. Theo found the handkerchief, actually clean except for a couple of lipstick smudges, and tossed it to Niki.

Niki tucked the sleeping bag tighter around Spyder and went alone to find the john.

* * *

The sickly light from Keith's room petered out on her about halfway down the long hall, and at the very end, a door she couldn't see and the richer blackness of the stairwell dropping away on her right. The sort of darkness that begins to move, writhes, if you stare at it too long or too hard. She pushed the door open, felt along the wall until she found the switch. More shitty light.

Tiny closet of cracked tile and yellowed walls, the faint smell of disinfectant and the thicker smell of piss. Two stalls without doors and a dented and empty paper towel dispenser. Niki went to the sink, turned the knob marked "H," waited to see if the water would ever get warm. Her reflection in the cracked mirror over the sink stared back at her, disheveled, wind-chapped cheeks bright in the white-green light. She looked at least as misplaced, as ineffectual, as she felt. Her round face lost in the ruins behind her, broken into glassy pie slices that converged between her tired eyes. She noticed a spot of something dark at one corner of her mouth: a streak of grease from the van, or dirt or . . .

Blood. Spyder's blood.

Niki grabbed for the handkerchief, soppy cold, and scrubbed at the stain, and then shame at her horror, that there might be something in Spyder's blood more dangerous than her own. She dropped the white cloth, plop, back into the rust-stained sink.

The water isn't ever going to get warm, Niki, not tonight, her pecan shell eyes said from the broken looking glass, eyes that looked suddenly older than the smooth

face they were plugged into, the eyes of someone who
ought to know better than to have ever wondered if the
water was going to get warm.

What happened back there, Niki?, remembering that
moment in the parking lot back at Dr. Jekyll's, something there and then gone again, but something left behind, too. And suddenly the cold in the little rest room
seemed to press at her, deep-sea pressure, liquid cold,
and she gasped.

A whisper somewhere behind her, from the stalls or
the hall outside or right into her ear, something dreamed,
maybe, and forgotten on purpose, "It isn't hard to drown,
not if that's what you're after . . ."

Niki turned off the faucet, quick twist and the water
stopped flowing, squeezed out the handkerchief; she
left the light in the rest room burning and hurried back
to Keith's apartment.

* * *

Spyder didn't flinch when Niki touched the wet
handkerchief to the cut on her forehead. It was deep
enough to need stitches; Niki was afraid that if she
rubbed too hard at the dried blood, she'd see bone
underneath. She dabbed, gentle as she could, and fresh
blood welled up along the half-moon slash, ugly loose
flap of meat as wide as her thumb.

"I'm sorry," she said. "I know that's gotta hurt."

"Yeah," Spyder said, soft chuckle, "Like a motherfucker."

Now Keith and Daria were together on the mattress,
Mort on the floor next to them, the Thunderbird just
about gone. Theo had picked through the boxes of
clothing, had come up with a couple of raggedy flannel
shirts and a ridiculous-looking toboggan cap, Play-Doh
blue with a huge lavender pom-pom sewn on top. She'd
jammed the cap on over her fallen pompadour, wrapped
the shirts around her double-breasted polyester jacket
and sat back down under the Nirvana poster.

"You'd be a lot warmer over here," Mort had said,

had patted the floor beside him, and she'd told him to go fuck himself, that she'd have been warmer in her own goddamn apartment.

Niki had barely begun, and already the handkerchief was filthy crimson and she was just smearing the same blood and grime around and around. She considered going back to the restroom, rinsing it out and starting over again, but the thought of another stroll down that hallway made her shiver, the thought of her reflection in that fractured mirror. Instead, she tried wiping it clean on the carpet, silently dared Keith to object; he didn't, of course.

"You don't have to do this," Spyder said quietly.

"I just wish you'd let us take you to a doctor."

Now there was a bloody splotch on the carpet and the handkerchief was still a useless mess. Niki looked around the room, spotted a crumpled Taco Bell bag nearby.

"Just a second," she said, and yes, there were paper napkins inside, only one grease-stained from the half-eaten and mummified burrito hidden at the bottom. And there were at least a dozen other fast food bags scattered around the room. She dampened a corner of the napkin with her tongue, dry paper taste and hint of refried beans, forcing herself not to think too much about germs, infection passed either way. Wiped at the crust between Spyder's eyebrows.

"*Now* we're in business," she said and smiled.

The scabby blood peeled away like old paint, and there was the scar, uneven cruciform, white and faded pucker but still perfectly recognizable for what it was.

Niki did not mean to pause, or stare, or allow the small gasp past her lips.

"Wow," Spyder said, more curiosity than concern. "Is it *that* bad?" And she raised her fingers and touched the spot between her eyebrows.

"Oh," she said, and nothing then, for a moment, as her fingertips moved over the scar, as if she were reading an old note to herself in Braille, private significance in the raised flesh.

"That," she said. "I guess I should have warned you. It's real old."

"But how," Niki began, stopped herself, knew she'd already done something, enough, wrong.

"I was a little kid," as if that explained anything, everything, and Spyder continued rubbing her fingers over the spot as if maybe she hadn't thought of it in years, fingers rediscovering the intersecting ribbons of scar tissue.

"I'm sorry," Niki said, shivering, thinking again how terribly cold it was in the "apartment," not wanting to think about the cross sliced into Spyder's forehead.

"I was a little kid," Spyder said again, smiled this time, sheepish it's-no-big-whup smile. And outside something big and noisy, a garbage truck maybe, growled along the slickening street.

"Most of the time I just forget about it."

Niki said nothing, wet a clean corner of the napkin, and began scrubbing the blood from Spyder's cheeks.

When the wine was gone, Daria had turned off the lights, curled up with Keith on the bare mattress. Mort was still sitting beside them, slumped against the wall, head back and mouth open, snoring. Id, ego, and super-ego of Stiff Kitten, drunk and unconscious and, as far as Niki Ky could tell, content with the world. Theo had drifted off into her own fitful sleep beneath Kurt Cobain's protective glare, anything but content.

Niki had managed to get the worst of the blood off Spyder's face, found a handful of bruises and scrapes. When Spyder had complained that the metal chair was freezing her ass, first sign of complaint and really more of an observation, they'd sat together on the floor. Huddled together in the window-framed square of light, watching the snow. They talked, quiet talk so they wouldn't wake anyone: Niki telling the story of her trip from the Carolinas, the death of the Vega and how she'd met Daria, and then, Spyder telling Niki about her tattoos and Weird Trappings.

This is what it would be like to live inside one of those

winter paperweight things, Niki thought, picturing the Christmas flurry of fake snow and water, trying to listen to what Spyder was saying. *Someone picks up your whole little world and shakes the holy fuck out of it and then you just sit there in your plastic cottage and watch the fallout.*

She sneezed, then, loud and wet spray, and Spyder wrapped the sleeping bag around them both. It smelled only slightly less than Spyder herself, but the hoarded body heat, the shelter from a thousand drafts, was almost irresistible. And the snow was coming down harder, if there'd been any change at all in the storm in the last hour. Clumpy white flakes pelting the window, reducing the view of the building next door, grainy brickwork and fire-escape zigzag.

Niki yawned, growing even groggier in the sudden warmth.

"Sleepy?" Spyder asked, and Niki thought maybe she heard disappointment, disappointment or guarded alarm.

Niki shook her head, *no, not at all,* but then she yawned again.

"Maybe just a little," she said, and "You too?"

"No. I can't sleep without my meds."

Something else Niki wouldn't ask about, not now, better to watch the snow, wait and see if perhaps things would explain themselves further along.

"I didn't know I wouldn't be going home tonight," Spyder said.

Niki nodded, looked over at Keith and Daria, twined in one another's arms and legs, Mort alone.

"Hell's slumber party," she said.

"Yeah," and Spyder shut her eyes a moment, opened them very slowly, drawn out, predatory blink.

And through her weariness, Niki was amazed that she felt this comfortable so close to Spyder, someone she'd never even seen just a few hours earlier. More than an absence of discomfort, the pit-of-her-stomach homesickness all but faded away, the dread gone with it, mostly. She felt something like safe, something like peace. And she thought again about whatever they'd exchanged in the parking lot, whatever she might have *imagined* they'd exchanged; frightened at the possibility of it having been real, cautioning herself that it might have been nothing at all. Contradiction all around.

"You must be pretty pissed," she said, praying her voice wouldn't break the spell, the calm inside, "Your friends running out on you that way."

Spyder closed her eyes again, and Niki marveled at her eyelashes, so black after her white hair, long and delicate. Spyder frowned, eyes still closed.

"That was just Byron," she said, and Niki remembered the terrified face behind the wheel of the Toyota, the boy in his velvet frock coat that she'd watched across Dr. Jekyll's. "He does that kinda shit. It doesn't *mean* anything," so much stress on that last part before she opened her eyes again.

"You don't count on Byron in a fight, that's all. I guess he just freaked out."

"You're not mad at him?"

And the frown softened, a little of the tension in her face melting away.

"When I catch up with him, I'm gonna kick his skinny faggot ass all the way into next week."

"Oh," Niki said, and it was still there, that sense of *rightness*, something she'd experienced so seldom that it felt like borrowed clothes.

"But what I *really* want to know is why Joe Cool over there stuck his neck out for me tonight."

Niki glanced at the mattress again, at Keith Barry, one arm slung protectively or possessively around Daria.

"I think maybe he just likes to fight," she said.

"Crazy fucking junky. I thought he hated my guts."

And then Niki turned and looked at Spyder's eyes, eyes like marble the faintest shade of blue, palest steel, that divine wound between them, and Spyder gave her another long, animal blink. And then Niki kissed her. Clumsy kiss, too fast and their noses bumping, urgent and too much force, but Spyder did not pull away, opened her mouth and Niki's tongue slipped between her teeth, explored cheekflesh and teeth and tongue. Spyder laid one hand against Niki's face, stubby fingers cold from the chill and Niki opened her eyes, pulled away. She was breathing too hard, too fast, her heart stumbling, missing beats in her chest.

She'd never kissed a girl before, had kissed no one for what seemed like a very long time. Not since that last morning with Danny; immediate guilt and Niki pushed his memory away again. Spyder smiled at her, brushed the coarse tips of those fingers across her lips and chin.

"I'm sorry," Niki said, feeling the warm rush of blood to her face.

"Don't be *sorry*," Spyder said. "It's okay. But I do have a girlfriend already."

"I shouldn't have," Niki said and she felt dizzy, the madness and violence of the night and then this, and the snow outside the window playing Caligari tricks with her head. Her exhaustion swimming upstream against the adrenaline flash, gathering itself like the drift piling up on the windowsill. And Spyder still getting in through her nostrils, the leather muskiness and old sweat, stale smoke and something else, sweet and sharp, that might have been Old Spice cologne, her father's smell.

She shut her eyes, discovering the retinal burn-in of the window and the storm where she'd expected nothing. And then Spyder was talking, words as soft as the worn tapestry of her smells.

"Niki, do you remember when they'd announce on the news that there was a twenty or thirty-percent chance of snow, just flurries, you know? But you'd be too excited to sleep because maybe there wouldn't be school the next day? It was nuts, 'cause it *never* fucking snows on school nights.

"But you'd stay up all night anyway, all goddamn night, and of course morning would come and there wouldn't be any snow, and it didn't matter that you'd hadn't slept a wink. You still had to get your ass out from under the covers and go to school anyway. Remember how cheated you felt?"

"It doesn't snow in New Orleans," Niki said. "It just rains a lot."

"Oh," Spyder said. "That makes sense," and Niki thought, *Yeah, Old Spice,* the white bottle in her father's hand, a spot of white shaving cream behind one ear.

"I think I'm too sleepy to talk anymore, Spyder," she said, "I'm sorry," and Spyder didn't answer, hugged her closer inside Keith's skanky sleeping bag. Niki listened to the wind and the pattering sound of the snowfall and later, when she opened her eyes, Spyder was asleep.

2.

Spyder doesn't know she's fallen asleep, never knows, so there's never even that small distance from the rage and his voice and the things that move back there in the corners of the cellar, where the lamp can't reach.

He raves, opens his rough hand and pours red earth and she presses her face against moldy army cot canvas; her mother's footsteps overhead, heels on the kitchen floor boards, like hopscotch tap dancing and there's no comfort at all in the dust that sifts down and settles in her open eyes.

The angels are crawling on the walls, pus dripping from the tips of their blackbird feathers and raw things hung around their necks, things that used to have skin and writhe.

"Why do you think they haven't taken me?" her father wants to know, always wants to know that (and she doesn't *know*), and his baggy Top Dollar work pants keep falling down, funny, and that

"Answer me *that,* Lila! Why won't they take me?"

is really funny and horrible and it whips back and forth, back and forth, like maybe it wants to tear itself loose from his crotch and come millipede slithering across the dirt floor after her.

Her mother laughs upstairs and she can hear television voices, too.

She wants to scream, scream that she doesn't know, she doesn't fucking know, swear she'd tell him if she did, so he could go. But the dust from his hand fills her mouth, spills over the sides, past lips and chin, gets into her ears, her eyes.

"Goddamn you, Lila," he says, lips trembling and sweat on his face, glistening slick in the orange light, glistening like the slug trails and shit the angels leave on the cellar walls.

"*You* make them keep me here, you make them come and watch and laugh and leave. All fly away to Glory without me."

The dust is sliding down her throat, filling her up, making her his choking hourglass.

"You don't have the sign," he says and points, presses his finger so hard against her forehead she thinks it'll punch on through. "I look at your face and the sign's not there, so they *can't* take you, Lila, so they won't take *me,* either."

His dust is the World, the binding world, the soil that binds and holds her like roots and the coils of worms, beetle legs, will hold her to the World forever.

"You're a damned and sinful freak, keeping me here, keeping your mother here," he howls, the man become a storm of flesh and blood, righteous and his lightning is taking it all apart; the angels titter and clap their fingerless hands for him, hang from the ceiling and drip drip drip.

The razor blade gleams in the lamplight, kerosene light on stainless steel and he holds it close to her face, presses a corner of the blade to her forehead and recites their names. Slices in and draws the razor down

longitude

and the angels are twisting, shriek and rust engine chatter, fishhook teeth gnashing, dripping,

as he pulls the razor out and begins again, second cut, across

latitude.

The blood runs into her eyes, mixes with the dust and burns like saltwater.

"There," he says, cautious satisfaction, waiting for their approval. But the angels have gone, have slipped back into the walls and he's still here. She thinks she can hear their wings far away, wind fluttering kites stretched too tight over balsa frail skeletons, the way the kids laugh on the bus to school when they see what he's done to her.

And he's still here.

Niki Ky sits next to her, holds her hand; cold air through the bus window as it bounces over railroad tracks, and Niki points at the gray lead clouds hanging low over the city, tells her that if it snows, maybe they can go home early.

Her father has crawled away from her cot, sobs in a dark corner, shadow hidden, and blames her, blames the bitch he married and his bitch-freak daughter.

And Robin walks past her across the cellar, doesn't stop when Spyder calls her name, Robin and the tenpenny nails like rusted porcupine quills bristling from her skin, crimson wrists and ankles and then she's gone, swallowed by the unforgiving, hungry earth.

"Is she the one? The one you said you loved?" Niki asks, and Spyder can only nod, too full of dust to speak.

And then there is perfect and absolute blackness, country midnight, and she thinks, *This is new. This wasn't here before.* "Before when?" Niki says with Robin's voice, Niki an empty universe away. Spyder reaches out, strokes the tangible, rubbery nowhere and nothing and never that wraps her in kindly amoeba folds. Knows that it has come from her, out of her, excreted like sweat or piss or shit, puke or dark menstrual blood.

Her skin itches and goose bumps as big as pencil erasers, and papery crumbling noises from her guts.

Pain that is everywhere and means everything and she welcomes it with open arms.

At the edge, her edges, at the quivering lips of the concealing, living dark, a single blazing shaft of impossible white, adamantine light singeing the ebon membrane,

("Spyder," Niki says, "I'm sorry. I shouldn't have done that . . .") the whiskery little hairs. She smells wood smoke and ash and burning tires.

And with hands that feel gloved, rubber gloves too small and tight to contain her, she pulls the slit in the starless night closed, and is alone, without Robin or Byron or Walter, without Niki Ky. Without him.

Sometime before dawn and the cold and the ache in Spyder's neck and shoulders woke her; she'd fallen asleep sitting up, hunched over, Niki Ky propped against her. No particular expression on Niki's sleeping face, peace, maybe, maybe the face of someone who didn't have nightmares. Not something Spyder would recognize. But no tension in her lips or brows, no frantic REM flutter beneath her eyelids. Spyder watched the snow still falling outside, drift and swirl and she wondered if it was true that no two flakes were ever the same.

Didn't it hurt?, just the memory of a question Niki had asked about her tattoos, but so loud and clear that for a moment Spyder thought maybe she was awake, too, and Spyder's fingers went to the scar between her eyes, as if that's what Niki had meant, instead. And the dream rolling back over her, weightless feather crush, the part she *hadn't* told Niki, and the truth about the tattoos. Never mind the details, all the business she'd volunteered about ink and the sound of the artist's silver gun, time and money and aftercare. Fact but nothing true, and she stared unblinking at the storm.

After she'd come home from Florida, but years before Weird Trappings, before Robin, before Byron and Walter, and the dreams had been so bad she couldn't sleep at all, not even with the pills; after sundown she walked the streets and sat alone in all-night diners and empty parks. Talked to herself and bums, the street lunatics, other people too crazy to sleep, and there had been a woman with a rusty red wagon loaded full of rags and Coke cans and newspapers. A madwoman named Mary Ellen, and one night Spyder sitting alone under a dogwood, crying because she was so tired and too fucking scared to even close her eyes. She'd bought a pack of Remington razor blades at a drugstore and sat beneath the tree, one of the blades out and pressed against her wrist. Felt her pulse through the stainless steel and just a little more pressure would have been enough, but she was too scared for that, also, and she'd kneaded the scar between her eyes, as if it might be rubbed away like dirt.

"Hey there, you," and Mary Ellen sitting on a bench nearby, watching, and she must have been sitting there all along, but had kept very quiet so Spyder wouldn't notice. "Fuck off, Ellen," Spyder muttered, "I don't want to talk to anyone tonight." But Mary Ellen hadn't fucked off, had left her bench and come to sit in the grass with Spyder, dragging the squeaky wagon behind her.

"It's okay," she said. "I won't try to stop you. I *know* what that feels like, when you got some bleeding to do and they stop you and sew you up like a hole in a sock," and she'd shown Spyder her wrists, then, bony bag-lady wrists and the crisscross of scars there.

"But ain't nothing wrong with having some company, Lila."

"Does it hurt?" Spyder asked her and Mary Ellen had shrugged, nodded her head. " 'Course it hurts. Shit, yeah, it *hurts,* but only for a little while. It's not so bad after a little while." And she'd taken something out of the heap in her wagon, handed it to Spyder: an old pickle jar, kosher dill spears, but half the label torn away.

"I got you something," she said.

"I don't need a jar," Spyder said and Mary Ellen frowned, "No, damn it. Not the *jar. Inside* the jar." And Spyder had held the pickle jar up so the closest street-light shone in through the smudged glass.

"Found her out back of the Woolworth's, under a box, under a *big* motherfucking box, and I didn't mean to listen. I don't *talk* to bugs, but she knew your name," and there, inside the jar, a huge black widow spider and Spyder's mouth suddenly so dry, too dry to speak. "She said you might have forgotten her, Lila, said once upon a *time* she had a hundred black sisters and they saved a princess from a troll or an evil magician . . ."

"Thank you, Mary Ellen," she'd said and Ellen had stopped talking and smiled. Smiled her brown-toothed smile and hugged herself. "Yeah," she said. "Yeah, that's cool, Lila. Anytime. I find lost stuff *all* the time."

And Spyder had gone home, left her razor blades under the dogwood tree with Mary Ellen and walked back up the mountain to Cullom Street with her gift; it didn't matter that she wasn't crazy enough to hear the voices Mary Ellen heard. She had her own, and the next day she'd taken the bus across town, carried the widow hidden down in her knapsack, a new and smaller jar with some newspaper crumpled inside. She'd shown the tattooist the drawings she'd worked on for hours, colored pencils on the brown back of a grocery bag. "Just like that," she'd said, pointing, and the money from her savings and she'd had all the time it would take.

The salvation ink bleeding beneath her skin, beautiful scar to stand against all the other scars, the one on her face and the scars past counting in her head.

Outside, the wind gusted and the white flakes buffeted the window of Keith's apartment. Niki Ky made a soft sound in her sleep, like something a word might leave behind, and Spyder held her and watched the snow until she could stop remembering.

3.

In the morning, gray only a few shades lighter than the night, Niki was awakened by the sound of water, the distinctive spatter of boypiss on porcelain. While they'd slept, Spyder had moved closer, had gripped Niki's right hand so tight that the fingers had gone stiff and numb. She looked around the room, Daria alone now on the mattress and Mort lying on his side, still snoring. Theo in a cattight ball of strange and mismatched fabrics on the other side of the room, but no sign of Keith. Down the hall, a toilet flushed and then footsteps, and he strode through the doorway, twice as rumpled as the night before. Carnation splotches beneath his hard eyes, rubbing his big hands together.

"Mornin'," he said. "You looked out the window yet?"

Niki glanced at the snow heaped on the sill, perfect cross-section of the drift that had grown as high during the night as gravity would allow.

"No," she said. "Is it deep?"

"Ass-high to a Watusi Indian chief," he said and rubbed at those raw eyes.

"What time is it?" Niki asked and he shrugged, hell-if-I-know-or-care shrug. On the mattress, Daria opened her eyes, grumbled something indecipherable and shut them again, covered her head with the pillow.

Keith yawned loudly, lion yawn, and went to one of the holes punched through the sheetrock, reached inside and pulled out what looked to Niki like a leather shaving kit. He sat down against the wall, the hole gaping like a toothless mouth above his head, his dirty hair.

"Daria says your folks are from Vietnam," he said and unzipped the little case. "North or South?"

"Yeah," Niki answered, and "South. My mother was born in Saigon. My father is from Tayninh."

"Vi-et-nam," Keith Barry said, drawing out the word slow, syllable by syllable, his heavy southern drawl making the name something new. And he took a small baggie of white powder from the case, poured a tiny bit into a tarnished spoon, twist-tied the bag shut again with a rubber band. Mixed a little of his spit with the powder.

"Yeah, my dad was there right at the start of that war," he said, and began to heat the underside of the spoon with a disposable lighter. Niki had never actually watched anyone shoot up before, tried not to stare, tried not to seem rude by looking away.

"He was Army, two tours," and after the powder had turned a dark and bubbling liquid, he wrapped a green-and-yellow bungee cord tight around his bicep, thumped hard at his forearm with one index finger while the heroin cooled. "Took a bullet at Nhatrang during the Tet Offensive."

"I don't know where that is," Niki said, and flinched inside when he took the needle from the case, old-fashioned-looking glass syringe that he had to screw the needle onto.

"Shit. Neither do I. Just one of those places he used to talk about, that's all it means to me."

Keith drew the heroin carefully, carefully, every drop in through the needle, tapped the syringe and pushed out the air bubbles. He set the needle against his skin, skin scarred with tracks like a pox, needle aimed away from Niki, toward his heart.

"He used to talk about the war a lot. Had a medal and everything 'cause he got a foot blown off."

And he pricked the skin, shifted his thumb slightly, easing the pressure on the plunger; Niki clearly saw the dark flow of his blood back into the syringe, billow darker than crimson in the shadowy apartment before he injected. When the syringe was empty, he slipped the needle out, removed the bungee cord. Closed his eyes and inhaled loudly.

"It doesn't hurt?" Niki asked him.

Nothing for a moment and then he exhaled, slow.

"Babe, it only hurts when the well runs dry," he smiled, and for just a second looked so much younger, so much more vulnerable, more than a fucked-up junky rushing after his wake-up fix. And she could almost see in him what Daria might see, glimpse of something that Niki had heard in his music the night before, someone he kept safe and out of sight.

"It only hurts when it ain't there."

And she thought of the things she'd read, secondhand life, William Burroughs and something about Billie Holiday. And how little any of it meant, how she understood that she'd never understand, unless she let the needle kiss her own skin one day, and another day after that, until the junk became as much a part of her as air or water or the blood in her veins.

"Most of this kit was my dad's, too," Keith said, and

when he saw the surprise on Niki's face he laughed. "No shit. They sent him back short a foot, but he had that fucking medal and a hell of a morphine habit."

And then neither of them said anything for a while, just the wind outside talking to itself, and Keith stared past her out the window.

"Should we wake them up?" she asked, finally.

"Sure," he said. "Bunch'a lazy-ass motherfuckers."

"And then what?" Niki asked and Keith grinned.

"Bet you never built a snowman, New Orleans girl."

"No," she said. "I never did."

After the icebox of the building, the cold outside wasn't such a shock, except when the wind gusted, came roaring at them around the corner of a building, up a deserted street, sluiced through garbage-can alleyways. A wind that made Niki think of places she'd never been, Chicago wind, Manhattan wind, wind that flayed without bothering to peel back skin and muscle first, that cut straight through no matter how many layers of clothes.

There'd been no hope for the van, half-buried by the dumpster, so they'd all borrowed layers from Keith's rag-pile boxes, set out on foot, and when they passed the smoked glass window of a shoe-shine and repair shop, Niki thought they looked like the shambling survivors of some Arctic apocalypse, ice not fire, Robert Frost's second choice. Tube socks for gloves, flannel like the hides of plaid antelope, and Niki had found a second pair of jeans, Levi's that would have been huge on Keith or Mort, cinched around her waist with an old extension cord the color of a neon-orange warning.

They built their skinny snowman on the sidewalk outside the Compass Bank on 20th Street, just a little taller than Niki and Daria, three uneven tiers and he listed a little to the right. Mort found limestone gravel for the eyes, an old windshield-wiper blade for an industrial Cyrano, snapped sticks off a frozen shrub for twiggy arms.

"Ugly fucker," Keith said, and then he'd made the snowman a bifurcated dick with another twig.

"You are so sick," Theo said and so he smacked her in the back of the head with a snowball big around as a grapefruit. The one she lobbed back at him was only half as big, packed harder; it missed Keith altogether and caught Daria right between the eyes. Keith started laughing so hard that he had to sit down, holding his stomach, sinking up to his waist in the snow.

"Fuck you, asshole," and she'd found some wetter snow in the gutter, muddy snow, and a few seconds later she'd nailed him and Keith was spitting and coughing, still laughing so hard he couldn't talk.

Spyder had sat down beside the bulbous lower tier of the snowman, had pulled out his stick-dick and was busy using it to trace swirling lines in the snow crust. Niki joined her, sat as close as she dared, remembering the awkward kiss the night before, still just as confused, still just as attracted. The designs Spyder drew in the snow reminded Niki of aboriginal rock paintings, or sloppy paisley.

"Are you okay?" she asked, and Spyder looked up too fast, clear she hadn't even noticed Niki until she'd spoken. The cut over her eye was red, red against her wind-pink face.

"Um," she said. "Yeah, but I should go home now."

"Do you think Byron will be there, and Robin?"

"Maybe," she said, and in the street, Theo and Daria had paired off against Mort and Keith, and they cursed and laughed and shrieked as the snow flew like shot from fairy cannons.

"Look like fun?" Niki asked Spyder and Spyder only shrugged; she'd refused any extra clothes, except a pair of socks for her hands, a hole in one so her left pinkie stuck out the side. Her jacket stood out, contrast like a hole in the day.

"I don't know," she said.

"There is something else I've always wanted to do," Niki said. A missile intended for Theo sailed over their heads, then, hit the snowman instead and sprayed them both with crystalline shrapnel. And she stood, found a patch of snow they hadn't messed up yet with foot-prints, and lay down.

"What are you doing?" Spyder asked, turning to see, face scrunched into a James Dean squint.

"Just watch," Niki said. "When I was a little girl, I read about kids doing this, in those *Little House* books or somewhere."

And then Niki began to move her arms up and down, legs scissoring open and closed again, displacing snow, plowing it aside. And then she stood, shaking and brushing away the white powder before it could melt and soak through.

"It's a snow angel," she said, proud that it had come out looking just like she remembered the pictures, and Spyder only stared, said nothing, eyes intense like she was trying to solve a puzzle, an optical illusion.

"See," Niki prompted, "Those are the wings . . ."

Spyder got up, started off down the street with-out them.

"Hey, where are you going?"

"Home," Spyder called back. "I have to go home now."

"Well, wait," and by then Keith and Daria had no-ticed, although Mort and Theo were still busy pummel-ing one another.

"Where's she goin'?" Keith asked and Daria shook her head, asked "Where's Spyder going, Niki?"

"Just come on, guys," and Niki was already running to catch up, what passed for running in the snow halfway to her knees. The street rose steeply here, last hill before the mountain, and she was out of breath after only three or four lumbering steps.

"Wait!" she called after Spyder, "I can't walk that fast," her voice so loud and small in the cold air and no sign that Spyder had even heard, trudging ahead as if there were no one left on earth but her.

At the top of the hill, Niki stopped, lungs aching, teeth aching from the cold, legs filled with lactic acid knives, sweatsoaked underneath her clothes and Keith's.

And Spyder still ten or twenty yards ahead, the others
still twenty or thirty behind. She looked north, back
toward downtown, the frozen city paralyzed, cocooned
after the storm. Not a car on the roads, hardly anyone
else on the sidewalks. The shouts of other people blocks
away and everything too white under the low and racing
clouds. The wind up here was worse, tore at her clothes,
stung her face and made her ears hurt.

Hands on her knees and bent double like she was
puking, Niki waited on Daria and the rest.

Two blocks west, they caught up with Spyder, finally,
but only because she'd paused to knock snow off the
soles of her Docs, slam one foot and then the other
against a telephone pole.

"You're gonna have a heart attack," Niki wheezed,
"or a stroke or something if you don't slow down,"
coming up behind Spyder, startling her again although
she'd made noise on purpose so she wouldn't. There
were little snotcicles dangling from each of Spyder's
nostrils, her face like a boiled crab from the wind and
exertion and the cut on her forehead had opened again,
fresh blood trickling into her eye.

"This is *not* a fucking forced march," Daria said;
Mort was actually holding Theo up now.

Spyder only looked at them uncomprehendingly,
blank disregard, went back to kicking the telephone
pole, black rubber against creosote pine.

"*Man,*" Keith gasped, leaned against convenient
chain link, steel division between sidewalk and a smothered church parking lot. "Man, *why* are we chasin' this
crazy bitch, anyway?" Another pause, another gasp, and
"That's what I'd like someone to tell me."

"I can make it fine from here," Spyder said, examin-
ing the bottom of one boot. The hard-packed snow
she'd kicked off lay all around her feet, molded like
weird albino waffles.

Niki ignored her. "Because she could have a concus-
sion for all we know. We at least need to see she gets
home all right."

"Christ," Mort panted. "She's in better shape than I am. Look, she's not even outta breath! Christ."

"How do you know if you're freezing to death?" Theo whimpered from his side.

"We can at least get some coffee," Daria said, "Just one fucking cup of coffee," and Niki asked, "Where?" then noticed a diner across the street, a Steak and Egg Kitchen squeezed in between an apartment building and a Pizza Hut. The Pizza Hut was dark, but inside the Steak and Egg, the lights were on.

"Yeah," Theo wheezed. "*Please?* I can't feel my tongue."

Niki looked at Spyder, unfathomable urgency burning as cold as frostbite in her eyes, unearthly eyes, and Spyder turned away from her, gazed past and through trees and street signs and houses, at the frosted mountain, half-hidden now in the heavy clouds.

"This ain't up for debate," Daria said. "If you want *me* along, you'll wait until after I get some coffee and catch my fucking breath."

"Spyder?" And Niki risked one hand on the back of Spyder's jacket, leather wet with melted snow, leathery skin as impenetrable as the girl wrapped inside.

"Yeah," she said, looked back at Niki and her eyes had changed, the strange silver fire only smoldering ash like dread or regret and nothing much there but exhaustion. "Some coffee would be good."

"Thank fuck," Theo muttered, and they followed Daria across the empty, icy street.

* * *

The diner was too warm, stifling after the cold, and the grease-haunted air smelled and tasted like all the deep fat ever fried, ghosts of a million sausages, a hundred million eggs. The place looked smaller from the inside and there was only one other customer, an old and grizzled man at the counter, slurping his coffee noisily from a saucer. They all piled into the booth furthest from the door, scrunched in together: Keith, Daria, and Mort on one side, Niki, Spyder and Theo on the other. A sleepy-looking woman wearing too much makeup took their order, six cups of coffee, a bowl of grits and a side of toast for Mort and Theo.

"We'll eat it fast, okay?" Mort had said when Niki had started to protest.

The coffee came immediately, black and bitter but fresh, very hot, almost not as bad as Niki had expected. She waited her turn as the sugar was passed around the table, the sweating cream decanter. She folded her hands around the cup to catch the heat, soak it all through her palms and into her bones. Burned her mouth on the first sip, was still blowing at her coffee, when a thin black boy brought the food, grease-stained apron and bones too big but his face was smooth and pretty, eyebrows plucked and arched and his long hair oiled and tied back in an elaborate bun. A single tear tattooed at one corner of his left eye.

"Hey there, Spyder," he said, setting down the steaming bowl of grits, garish yellow margarine pat dissolving on top, and the toast cut into four neat and crusty wedges. Niki had known too many drag queens not to clock him, not to catch the significant flourishes of body and voice, the dozen subtle and flamboyant giveaways. Not to be reminded of Danny.

Spyder glanced up from her own coffee, the cup she hadn't even touched, surprise and recognition, some new unease wrinkling her face.

"Oh," Spyder said and a nervous half-attempt at a smile. "Billy. I didn't know you were working here."

"Just 'til Christmas," he said. "Gotta make me some Santa Claus money, you know. 'Cause the cheap faggots that been comin' out to see Talulah these days ain't been tipping for shit, honey."

"Yeah," Spyder said.

Billy lingered, serving tray balanced one-handed, head cocked coyly and both dark eyes on Spyder.

"Ain't you even gonna introduce me to your friends, Spyder? Oh, except you, girl," and he jabbed a thumb at Theo, "I *already* know you."

"Yeah," Spyder said, pointing at each of them as she spoke, "That's Daria Parker, and that's Keith and that's Mort. Their band plays at Dr. Jekyll's . . ."

"Spyder, you *know* I stay away from them punk rock places," Billy said and to Stiff Kitten, "Nothin' personal, but you got to be careful. And there ain't too much careful these days."

"And this is Niki," Spyder finished. "This is Billy. He does shows at 21 and some other places."

"Some other places too scary to mention in polite company, she means," Billy said and smiled, warm and honest smile. "By the way, Spyder, when Miss Thing come dragging her ass in last night, well, this morning, actually, she was a *mess*."

Spyder's hand bumped her cup and a little coffee sloshed over the brim and onto the table. "What do you mean, Billy?" she asked.

"I mean, she was absolutely freaked, child. Like she just spent the whole last week on pink hearts and nose-candy. Went and locked herself in her room and I ain't seen or heard a peep outta Miss Byron since."

"I'm sorry," Spyder said, almost shoved Theo into the floor as she climbed out of the booth. "I have to go home."

"Spyder," Niki started, "If you'll wait just a second," but Spyder spun around, cut her off with those eyes, bright new flames in there.

"No, Niki, I'm sorry but I have to go home and I have to go home *now*."

And she pushed roughly past Billy, then, and was gone, down the narrow aisle between booths and matching burgundy stools, and the door jingled shut behind her.

Halfway across the Steak and Egg's parking lot and she slipped, one boot skating on the ice hiding slick beneath the snow and she almost fell. But there was no time left to be cautious, no time for Niki Ky shouting somewhere behind her, had been no time left all morning, all night and she'd been too dazed to understand, not listening, even in her nightmares; that they would go to her house, *into* her house, that Byron might be so afraid that he'd try to steal the dream catcher. Destroy it or squirrel it away someplace where she'd never find it, and so Spyder kept moving, left the pavement as soon as she could and stalked across lawns and vacant lots where the footing was a little surer, where the frozen grass and weeds crunched like glass underfoot.

And it wasn't the fairy tale lies she'd told them that scared her, that made her almost too afraid of what she'd find waiting at the end of Cullom Street to keep moving, not her father or the angels that had never stopped coming anyway, hunting her through sleep and the grinding days. None of them had ever suspected, not even Walter who hadn't believed any of it for a second, that the talisman could be one thing to them, protection, and something entirely different to her. Insurance, binding them together, like a wedding band, stronger than gold or silver because it had been made of them. Robin had almost torn it all apart, and she had patched it back together with wood and blood and strands of their hair.

The rat-toothed cold gnawed at her body, inside and out, playing sidekick to the crushing weight in her head. Together, they would pull her down and leave her broken and alone, lost in impossible white, suffocating. If she was weak, if she let them. So she made a picture of Robin in her mind, beloved symbol for all she stood to lose, and stepped around the pain.

They left Mort and Theo in the diner, resolutely eating their breakfast and talking to Billy. Would have left Keith, too tired of chasing after Spyder's crazy ass to care, he'd said, but Daria had pulled him out of the booth anyway, two dollar bills tossed on the table and she'd pushed him grumbling out the door. By the time they reached the parking lot, Spyder was already past the Pizza Hut, coal smudge on linen. Niki stopped, shouted for her wait until her throat hurt.

"She doesn't even give a shit, Dar," Keith said, "Spyder Baxter doesn't need any help finding her way back home," and Daria looked at Niki, waiting for an answer, a reason why this still had anything to do with them.

"She didn't ask for your help last night, either," Niki said and Keith shook his head. "Yeah, well, but right now she ain't about to get her butt kicked."

"He's right," Daria said, as if maybe it was a little painful to admit. "She acts like this sometimes, Niki. She has problems, you know?"

"She's scared fucking shitless," Niki said, watching Spyder getting smaller in the distance, listening to the wind, lonely wail like mourners in the bare tree limbs. "That's all I know, Daria. And I just want to make sure she gets home okay."

Daria hesitated, glanced back at the warmth and shelter of the diner, up at the sky hanging purple and almost low enough to touch.

"Come on, then," sighed resignation, was already two or three steps past Niki, hauling Keith by the arm again. "I don't even know where the bitch lives and if we keep standing around talking about it, we're gonna lose her."

"Thanks," Niki said, taking long strides to catch up.

4.

A long way off, still, but Niki could see the yellow crime tape fluttering in the wind. Familiar enough thing to know the words by heart, *Crime Scene—Do Not Cross,* a hundred different murders or burglaries in the Quarter, suspicious fires and that happy-bright plastic stretched across a doorway or burned-out window. But waiting for them, there at the top of Cullom Street, tied tight between two old trees, it had never looked more like a warning.

Halfway up the mountain and the snow had begun again, nothing like the night before, but hard enough that it intensified the impression that she was tramping through some fairyland or Ice Age waste and she was starting to feel sick, ill from the cold and exhaustion, had been plagued for the last five minutes with the idea that there was someone else walking with them, someone visible just at the corner of her vision. She'd turn to see, expecting Mort, or maybe Theo, and there was never anyone but Keith, face red and pissed off, cursing her and Spyder and the storm, Daria the same. And now, there was the police tape.

Part of her wanted to sit down in the snow and cry, cry until this was over. That part she thought she'd left behind, thought she'd shed forever like a bad skin, but instead Niki kept walking, ignoring the new cold leading her stomach, dread and everything that tape might mean. Ignoring how tired she was and the urgent little voice inside that begged her to see this had nothing to do with her, begged her to walk away from it all, while there was still time.

Spyder paused at the barrier of tape and Niki thought then that she would wait, that they would catch up at last, and then she vanished into the shadows beneath the trees; when they finally reached the yellow tape, there was nothing waiting for them but Spyder's footprints. She hadn't crossed the line, had gone through a hedge and around.

"Okay," air gasped and Keith's words slipped in between, "What . . . the hell's . . . going on . . . now?"

"Cops," Daria said, and Niki could only nod, point at the dark house set back away from the road and more of the yellow tape strung like garland around the porch, ripped loose and dangling at the front door.

The Radley house, she thought, *It's the goddamned Radley house.* Spyder's tracks and nothing else, lonesome scar across the snow, all traces of whatever might have happened in the night erased, buried, by the storm.

Hey, Boo? Wanna come out and play? and then the sound, the hurting, furious wail from the open door, broken sound, and Niki ran, fell once and hit her knee against something sharp hiding beneath the snow, got up and kept running. Until she'd ducked beneath the tape and was through the door, the house wrapping its musty shell around her, and in here, the sound was almost more than she could stand.

Howl from her dreams, civil defense siren wail and the sound that came from her when she opened her sleeping mouth to answer them. The sound, remembered, that had kept her mother awake on muggy suburban nights. The sound of the sky falling at the end of the world.

"Spyder!" she screamed, and *"Spyder! Where are you?!"*, but the house ate her voice alive, digested the words whole and added them to the sound, and the sudden smash and tinkle of breaking glass.

Niki rushed from room to room, hardly a thing noticed but the smell of old dust and the way the wail grew louder the further she went, past a kitchen and down a hall with peeling paper and the ghosts of missing pictures hanging on the walls.

The last room, very last place she looked, a tall black utility shelf pulled over and the glass ankle deep, tiny bodies like drops of ink amid the wreckage, scarlet warnings on countless bellies. With one arm, Spyder cradled something against her chest, something small that Niki couldn't see, and with her free hand she punched out window after window, windows painted black and spider-webbed with white paint and impossible care. And now the wail was changing, plunging octaves, an endless growl as Spyder drove her fist through another pane, shattered another perfect web, and the weak sun through the holes glistened on her bloody knuckles.

"Stop it!" Niki screamed and was crunching through the glass, scrambling across the bed to Spyder on the other side.

But Spyder pushed her easily away with the bloody hand, shoved her back down onto the bed and into the aqaurium glass biting at her thick clothes. And the growling was warping into words, pain and rage across Spyder's lips and enough like words that Niki could understand them.

"I have to let them out," she said. *"All of them. I have to let them out. Houses catch things."*

And she turned away, and another window burst,

blackened shards traded for the storm swirling in through half a dozen empty frames.

"Houses catch things, Niki."

Niki wrestled her way free of the razor tangle on the bed, gashed her palm in the process and Keith's dirty tube sock was immediately soaked a deep and ugly crimson. She grabbed Spyder again, soppy, bloody sock firm on one leather shoulder and spun her completely around, almost all the strength left, aimed the punch the way she'd been taught years and years ago, thumb safe outside so it wouldn't break.

And as her fist connected with Spyder's jaw, she saw the limp and lifeless things Spyder held close against her chest, like she might protect them, even now.

Daria had chased Niki across Spyder's scraggly, snow-covered front yard, Keith never more than a couple of his long strides behind her, had followed melting tracks through the house to Spyder's bedroom. The fallen shelf and glass everywhere, a purer, meaner version of the ice outside, broken windows and the snow getting in, flakes drifting and settling comfortably into the chaos. And on the other side of the bed, crouched in the narrow space between mattress and wall, Niki and Spyder.

"Shit . . ." Keith whispered and Daria took one step into the room, the crunch beneath her boots like something she almost remembered from a nightmare, and then she stopped when Niki held up one bloody, sock-covered hand. There was a new sound where the terrible wailing had been, softer sound and somehow worse for that. It took Daria a moment to realize that it was the sound of Spyder crying.

She took a step closer to the bed, ignoring Niki, and Spyder turned her head away, pressed one cheek hard against the wall and Daria noticed a trickle of blood from the corner of her mouth, like maybe she'd bitten her lip or tongue.

"Oh," Spyder said. "Oh, fuck them. Fuck them. Fuck them."

"Who did this, Spyder?" Daria asked, but Niki only shook her head, shrugged, and Spyder pressed her face to the wall that much harder, ground it back and forth against the old wallpaper.

"Fuck them forever," she whispered. "Fuck them until the fucking end of time."

Behind Daria, Keith muttered, started to follow her into the room, his boots louder, heavy boy feet, until she stopped him with her eyes. He sighed loud, sagged inside his rags, and *Whatever,* silent from his lips.

"They don't know," Spyder said, "They have no *fucking* idea what they've done," and then she was crying again, crying too hard to say anything else. But she held something out for Daria to see, stroked sienna fur and orange stripes as if she held a kitten, and it took Daria a second to recognize the crushed thing in her hands, no, *two* things crushed together. Two huge tarantulas, sticky, bristling mess, some legs missing and others hanging over the sides of her palms and Spyder held them out and up, like an offering, like a surrender or a promise.

And then the voice, dry paper voice of an old, old woman, straining to be heard, floating through the cold, still house and Daria jumped, almost screamed.

"Lila?" the woman called. "Lila? Are you home, dear?" and a faint knock on wood.

Daria turned around, "Keith, will you go see who that is?" but the hall behind her was empty and over the sound of Spyder's sobs, she could hear him walking away, the rhythm of his boots on the floor, tracing his way back through the house.

* * *

The whole fucking thing was giving him the creeps, and if nobody asked him soon, Keith was just about ready to tell them anyway. And that look in Daria's eyes, colder than the goddamn blizzard, like he had no business even being alive, much less any chance that he could help. Because he had a dick. Well, she knew where she could stick her this-is-a-girl-thing bullshit.

The old woman sounded like a ghost, pathetic phantom, confused and lost and frightened, urgent. Keith was halfway across the living room, could see the pale light from the open front door leaking from the foyer when something snagged at his pants leg and he stumbled, almost tripped and fell sprawling on Spyder's junk-cluttered coffee table.

"*Goddammit . . .*" and he reached down, thought for a moment he felt strong cord or nylon fishing line, like a tripwire, probably Spyder's dumbfuck idea of a burglar alarm. Before he cut his fingers on nothing he could see, nothing there at all, nothing strung to snare intruding feet, and he pulled his hand back as the same taunt nothing gently brushed his forehead, cut him across the bridge of his nose.

"Lila, honey? Is that you?"

"Just a minute," he shouted, slapping at the empty air, and for an instant, a noise drier than the old woman's grating voice, almost too high or far away for him to hear, rustling around him, sand and bones and autumn leaves. Then he was staggering into the foyer and there was only the old woman, waiting in the doorway like a storybook witch. Incredible, frizzy mane of hair as stark as the snow behind her, no coat and a dirtystiff blue dress, torn stockings above her black galoshes. Dark, distrustful eyes and her frown setting like concrete.

"Who are you?" she demanded, took a step back and Keith tried wiping the blood off his nose, but that hand was bleeding even worse and he felt the wet smear across his face.

"I said, *who are you?*"

"Uh," and he tried wiping the blood on his jeans, "Uh, I'm a friend of Spyder's."

"Where's Lila?" the witch demanded. "I have to talk to Lila right *now.*"

"She's, uh, right back there," and he jabbed a thumb at the shadows over one shoulder. "In her room, I think."

"I have to speak to Lila right *now,* young man."

"Yeah," he said, and the fresh cuts were stinging, the one across his nose making his eyes water. "I'll go get her."

"You gonna leave me standing here to catch my death?"

The cuts stung like alcohol or iodine, like salt rubbed into the wounds.

"No," he said, "Of course not. Come on in," and she crept past him, hugging close to the wall, as much distance between them as she could keep, just in case.

"Terrible business," the witch said, shaking her head, "Terrible," her shaggy, tousled white hair. "And you know, I might have fallen and broken my hip coming up that hill. I could have broken my neck. But I promised the police I'd be here to tell Lila what happened," and then Keith shouted for Daria, because he felt suddenly ill and dizzy, the world pressing its callused thumbs at his temples like a hangover or a bad fix, and he couldn't imagine making it all the way back to Spyder's bedroom.

"Daria! There's someone out here to see Spyder!"

"Oh!" the witch said, eyes round and hands clamped over her ears. "Oh, please don't shout so."

"Sorry," he said, and made it out onto the porch before he had to sit down. The fresh air helped a little, drove back the claustrophobia, washed soothing cool across the cuts on his hand and face. He sat on the steps, top step clean of snow or ice, head down, waiting for the sick, spinning sensation to pass.

"Terrible business," the witch muttered again somewhere behind him; despite the clouds, it was too bright out here, too much white and he squinted at his feet, old shoes like the old woman's leathery skin.

He heard Daria, now, questions in her voice and the witch answering them, and he looked up, slow and his eyes shielded from the murky day.

"They found her laying right out there in the street," the witch said, and he heard her just as clearly as if she were standing next to him, heard a sharp breath drawn and then the day seemed to brighten around him and he risked looking up through the branches, looking up for the sun breaking through the clouds.

"Someone called," the witch said. "There wasn't nothing they could do, though."

The sky was still as overcast as it had been all morning, scraping its insubstantial violet belly across the mountaintop. So he looked away from it, counted the braid of footprints in the snow, five separate sets, coming together and splitting apart again, all except his own, the biggest, apart from the rest. He could count each individual print, each a pool of gloom now as the air shimmered and grew bright around him.

"You shouldn't a had to hear it this way, Lila," the witch said, the old woman who looked like a witch and his footsteps looked like a trail of giant and moldy bread crumbs in the snow. *So we can find our way back,* he thought, *so we don't get lost in the woods.*

And then Spyder screamed and the air crackled, electric tendrils pricking at his skin and hair, ozone stench or burst fluorescent bulbs, and the sky flashed like a hundred thousand cameras snapping the same shot at the same instant, like a film he'd seen once about Hiroshima and this was just before the fireball and the mushroom cloud. And riding on the light, a brassy trumpet blare or simple thunder.

"Spyder . . ." and that was Niki Ky, pretty Niki Ky from New Orleans.

He barely felt Spyder pushing him aside as she rushed down the steps, barreling headlong into the darkness left behind after the flash, wanted to say something to her; a warning, or that he'd cut himself on her goddamn booby-trap, but she was screaming too loud to hear him and the cuts were sizzling.

Niki followed Spyder, across the sepia snow, between colorless trees, negative world and he closed his eyes, called out for Daria, called her name as loud as he could, over and over until she was beside him, until she was close enough that he could put his arms around her.

"I'm here," she said. "I'm right here, Keith."

He opened his eyes and it was all just snow again, all just clouds, just Niki and Spyder kneeling in the street and Daria's green and saving eyes.

"Spyder's girlfriend's dead," she said, and "Christ, what a mess," and she let him hold her.

PART II

Ecdysis

"I'm gonna kill you in my sleep
Hold a pillow over my face until you die,"
                                   "Su(in)cide"
                                   Stiff Kitten

CHAPTER TEN

Heaven, Hell,
and Purgatory

1.

And a week later:
   After Niki and Spyder had been taken from the
house on Cullom Street in a noisy ambulance with snow
chains on its tires;
   After Spyder had spent six nights in the psych ward at
Cooper Green, no one in to see her but Niki and a
psychiatrist and the nurses in their squeaky white nurse
shoes, paper cups of pills;
   After Niki's hand had been stitched, twelve silken
loops across her palm, lifeline, heartline, soulline severed and the rift pulled neatly, deceptively, closed
again;
   After the police had asked everyone their urgent police
questions and there'd been no answers good enough to
satisfy them, and no one had found Byron Langely yet;
   After Daria and Keith and Mort and Theo had each
gone back to their respective routines, day or night jobs;
Daria to the healing smell of roasting coffee beans,
Keith to the needle and spoon, Mort to his crankshafts
and busted transmissions, all three to Stiff Kitten, and
Theo left somewhere around the edges.
   A warm front, lighter air washed up from the Gulf
had melted almost all the snow, just scabby white
patches left behind, hiding in places the sun rarely or
never reached. Spyder went home and Niki went with
her, Niki's one bag retrieved from Daria's apartment
and she'd left Daria's extra key with Jobless Claude, a
few more things from the Vega she couldn't afford to

have fixed, couldn't even afford to think about and so it was parked out back behind the service station to wait.

Consequence and fading shock.

False bottom in a treacherous box of shattered glass and spider legs.

Daria and Keith began to have nightmares that left them wide awake and coldsweating in their beds, dreams they never mentioned to one another, never talked about; the white-haired old woman who'd always lived next door to Spyder had a heart attack, three o'clock in the morning the night after Spyder came home and they took her away in an ambulance, too.

* * *

Papers signed and the doctor looking over the rim of her expensive spectacles, skeptical narrow eyes, telling Niki again when Spyder should take which pill, Mellaril and she couldn't ever remember what the other was called, which hours and how important it was that she not skip a dose; the Suicide Crisis Line and other numbers scrawled on a pale pink page from a gummed memo pad and pressed, sticky, into Niki's hand. Keep these, like they could protect her, could protect Spyder, like holy beads or dashboard saints, keep these close.

Spyder never asked Niki to stay with her and Niki never asked if it was what Spyder wanted. Unspoken, unagreed, Niki had visited her in the hospital every day, had brought her candy bars she didn't eat and comics she didn't read, and when it was time for Spyder to go home, she paid their cab fare back to Cullom Street. Spyder stared out the smudgy window of the cab, no words, her face so blank, so calm it still frightened Niki, nothing in those eyes but the cold reflection of the buildings and winter-bundled people and the other cars they passed on the streets, nothing getting in, nothing out. She worried at the white plastic ID bracelet the nurses hadn't bothered to remove.

Short ride and then Niki counting out a five and ones

to the driver, the stingy tip, and Spyder stood staring at the house waiting patient for them under its naked mourning veil of pecan branches. The cabby turned around in Spyder's driveway, spitting a little gravel, like maybe he was anxious to leave them, spooky, silent Spyder or the solemn house, or maybe he just had another place to be.

"It isn't true," Spyder said, cloudy speech still slurred from her new medication, "What they say, about things being smaller when you grow up. It's the same size it ever was . . ." and the last word fading like a radio turned down too low to hear. They stood in the wind and afternoon blurring into twilight, Niki waiting, starting to shiver.

Until finally, "Let's go inside now, okay?" she said, "Get the heat on," and Spyder nodded, blinked and maybe there was the faintest ghost of a frown; at least that was something, communication and the hint of emotion. Niki carried her gym bag and the paper grocery sack with Spyder's few things up the walk, Spyder a step or two behind her, and the house took them back.

* * *

There was no talking Spyder out of sealing off her bedroom, though Niki tried, something Spyder had to do that had nothing to do with practicality or sentiment, something Niki could see might as well be a matter of life and death. Spyder would not even step across the threshold into the mess, but Niki managed to persuade her to board up the windows first, that much at least, before she nailed the door shut, allowed Niki to retrieve some things from the room. The portable stereo and the CDs, some clothes and a few posters and the glass cases that had not been shattered, protected beneath the bed. Niki felt like she was plundering an odd museum after a war, salvaging treasures, precious bits and pieces of old exhibitions, from the rubble before bulldozers and wrecking balls leveled the treacherous ruin.

Spyder found plywood somewhere, gray and warped with age and what water and cold, heat and mildew, could do to wood, and while Niki picked through the glass and metal, shuddered when she had to brush aside another black widow corpse or some species she didn't recognize, Spyder hammered and the walls rattled. It made Niki think of Amontillado, doomed Fortunato watching as stone after stone was lifted into place, and for a moment, she wanted to turn and run from the house, escape, as if this might be her last chance; instead, she lifted the last case of spiders pinned and labeled and carried it out into the hallway, stacked it with the rest. There were Mason jars and tanks that had not been broken, filled with torn and neglected webs and tiny things curled in on themselves, nestled in transparent corners or dangling like minute suicides; Niki left them, to be buried along with the rest, everything Spyder was burying at once in this mass grave, dead pets and memories she couldn't stand.

When Spyder had finished with the windows, Niki watched as she mixed epoxy and smeared the honey-colored goo along the top and sides and bottom edges of the door, made sure the glue filled the old lock and the newer latch bolt before she shut the door for the last time. And then fifty-seven three-penny nails before Niki lost count, and last of all, more of the gray, bowed plywood nailed over the door, hiding it away completely.

"I'll paint the boards, later," Spyder said, "To match the walls."

And then she turned and stared at the neat stacks Niki had made of her belongings. While Spyder had been working, she'd seemed more alert, more *alive,* than Niki had seen her since the night of the storm. But now that life, driving urgency and purpose, was draining away, quick withdrawal and slack-faced again, the face that Niki had come to think of as a mask woven of shock and the antipsychotics. A mask growing out of Spyder's flesh and so hard to fight through; now Spyder was exhausted and the mask was back, shadowing the girl inside. What she'd had to do was finished and now she could stop fighting the pain and the drugs.

And then Spyder stooped down, something held up so Niki could see. And yeah, Niki remembered picking that free of the glass, a dream catcher; had thought it might be something Spyder cared about. A couple of the strands that made its wood-framed web had broken, and Spyder began to laugh, soft chuckle at first, but then louder and Niki saw the tears at the corners of her eyes. For a while, Spyder just laughed and cried and then, when she was done, she used her hammer to pin the dream catcher to the plywood she'd nailed over the bedroom door.

* * *

Robin's funeral was something else that had come and gone, of course, had slipped past unannounced, like the snow's incremental exit. Spyder hadn't said a word to Niki about it, nothing else about Robin, for that matter. Niki had found an obituary in the *Post-Herald* and clipped it, not knowing if Spyder would ever want it or not, but had thought she should anyway.

And then, their first night back and Niki too tired to notice how hard the floor was through the quilts and blankets she'd spread out for them on the living room floor, the phone had begun to ring.

"I'll get it," she volunteered, reluctant to break their embrace, to leave the sweaty safe smell of Spyder, but Spyder was already up, already on her way to the kitchen. Niki lay still, listening, but nothing else from Spyder after "Hello" and "Yeah." Just her medusa silhouette in the kitchen doorway, construction paper cutout framed and backlit with dim moonlight through the windows. Spyder saying nothing, standing perfectly still, as Niki's heart beat like a slow second hand, five minutes, ten minutes, and Niki got up.

"Who is it, Spyder?" she asked, feeling like it was none of her business, hoping Spyder would tell her so.

234 _Caitlín R. Kiernan_

But Spyder said nothing, held the receiver pressed to her ear and stared into the dark kitchen.

"Spyder," and the house so quiet that Niki could hear the angry voice on the other end of the line, speaking hard and fast and she reached out and took the phone from Spyder, no resistance.

"Hello?" Niki said, and the voice paused a moment and then, "Who are _you?_"

"A friend of Spyder's," Niki said. Freed of the weight of the phone and the voice flowing through it like acid, Spyder sank into one of the kitchen chairs and laid her head against the tabletop.

"Yeah, I bet you are," the voice said, a man, maybe drunk, from the way he talked, and Niki trying to sound brave and strong, "Tell me who you are or I'm going to hang up," firm, watching Spyder at the table.

"Robin's father," he said. "And what the fuck difference does it make to you? I guess you're her replacement, though, aren't you?"

"I'm sorry about your daughter," Niki said, straining for calm. "I'm going to hang up now."

"Don't you _dare_ fucking hang up on me, goddammit. I'm not . . ." and Niki set the receiver back in its cradle on the wall. Within seconds, the phone was ringing again, shrill and angry as the man's voice had been, and she followed the wire to the jack above the baseboard, an old style she couldn't simply disconnect, the wire disappearing into a metal plate.

"Make it stop now," Spyder whispered, so low Niki almost didn't hear her over the ringing. "Please, Niki."

Niki grasped the cord, wrapped it tight around her hand and tugged once, hard but not hard enough, jerked again and the wire snapped free of the wall, the phone silenced in midshriek.

"Thank you," Spyder said, and Niki looked down at the severed phone cord dangling from her hand.

"I didn't kill her, Niki. I wasn't even here," Spyder said, "I was with you," and Niki dropped the cord to the floor. "I know," she said, nothing else she could imagine saying that wouldn't sound trite or stupid, and led Spyder back to their pallet.

* * *

After breakfast, fried slices of Spam and scrambled eggs, Spyder's so runny they were hardly cooked at all, Niki's like India rubber nuggets. Blueberry Pop-tarts and Coke. Niki busy with the dirty dishes and Spyder reading a comic at the table.

"Do you want to live here?" Spyder asked, and Niki stopped drying the dish, one of Spyder's multitude of mismatched china plates. Plate back into the sudsy water sink and she laid the dish towel aside, stood with her back still turned to Spyder.

"I haven't really thought about it," she lied. "I didn't think you should be alone right now, that's all."

"That's all?" Spyder asked and Niki stared out the dirty kitchen window, steamed over and the tangled backyard soft-filtered, tall grass winter brown and untended shrubs blurred together between the trees.

"No," she said, "that's not all."

"Oh. Yeah. I didn't think so," and Niki had no idea what came next, what her line was, *how* to say what she thought she *wanted* to say. Terrified of the words themselves, saying something she might want to take back, have no choice but to deny further along, time-release lie. She'd been going somewhere, a long time ago now it seemed, wild flight west and maybe she could have lost herself and the sorrow somewhere uncluttered, deserts or prairies, all sky and clean wind; someplace with a Spanish name, Los Angeles or San Francisco, maybe, and now she was *here,* instead, with Spyder Baxter. Birmingham, Ala-fucking-bama and she hadn't even made it as far west as New Orleans.

What'cha gonna do, Niki?

"I'm not an easy person to live with, bein' crazy and all," Spyder said. "That's why Robin never moved in with me, you know?" and that was the first time she'd said the dead girl's name since they'd kneeled together in the pelting snow and Spyder had screamed it over and over again at the falling sky while Niki held onto her.

Gonna keep running?

"But if you want to, you know, if you want to, I'd like that, Niki. I just want you to know I'd like that a lot. And it ain't 'cause I need nobody to take care of me, or just because I don't want to be alone."

Grab this brass ring, Niki, because there might not be another. Or. Let this distract you and you may never know . . . More than that, though. Irony like an evil joke she was playing on herself, that she'd run from Danny partly because she hadn't been able to imagine herself with a woman, knee-jerk repulsion. Other reasons, but that one so damning huge. And now Spyder, vicious edification, fairy tale punchline too brutal not to be real.

"I'm not afraid of being alone . . ." Spyder almost whispered.

"I am," Niki said, not turning around, had to say this fast before she chickened out. "I would very much like to stay with you for a while Spyder," and the sex they'd had the night before, furious and gentle, and the doubt like hungry maggots. But it was out. She'd said it, had decided, and behind her Spyder breathed in loudly.

"That's good," she said. "I was gonna miss you."

* * *

The new bedroom would be the room that had been Spyder's parents' and then just her mother's, the room where Trisha Baxter had died. It had been Niki's idea, and she didn't know, like Robin and the basement, and Spyder had surprised and frightened herself by saying yes, yes Niki, that's a good idea. It was much bigger than her old room, crammed full of boxes and crap, most of which she could just set out on the curb for the garbage men. Old newspapers and clothes, magazine bundles and broken furniture, an old television that didn't work. They could get a bed from the Salvation Army or the thrift stores, import stuff from other parts of the crowded house.

And then Spyder had Niki drive her downtown and she made a sign from poster board and a squeaky purple Magic Marker, masking-taped it to the window of Weird Trappings—"Closed Until Further Notice"—had shown Niki around the shop, picked out a few things to take back to Cullom Street with her.

It was Niki's idea to go to the Fidgety Bean afterwards, wanting to keep Spyder out a little longer, wanting to see Daria and be out herself. Spyder shrugged and nodded yes.

"I don't drink coffee," she said.

"Not ever?" Niki asked, incredulous, and suddenly she was thinking about Danny, first time in days, Danny whose love of coffee had bordered on the religious. She pushed his ghost away, reached out and held Spyder's warm hand as they squeezed down an incredibly narrow alley to Morris.

"It always makes my stomach hurt. Makes me nauseous, sometimes. Big-time handicap for a member of the caffeine generation, I guess."

And then the alley opened, released them to the cobblestone street and they were under the dreary sky again. Three doors down to the Bean and Niki changed the subject, talked about going thrifting for a bed, tomorrow perhaps, and maybe a new lamp, too.

Early afternoon and the coffeehouse was almost empty, nobody but a rumpled wad of slackers in the back smoking and talking too loud. Niki sat down at the bar before she saw Daria, bleary-eyed and a big coffee stain down the front of her little red apron. She smiled, genuine glad-to-see you smile, and put down the tray of glasses she'd been carrying. Spyder took the stool next to Niki, stared out through her dreads.

"Hi there, stranger," Daria said and hugged Niki across the bar and a cautious "How you doin', Spyder?"

"Okay," Spyder said, and turned her attention to a jar of chocolate biscotti. "I want one of those," she said.

"Sure," and Daria reached beneath the counter for metal tongs, the lid off the jar and then a big piece of the biscotti on a napkin sitting in front of Spyder. "You gonna want some coffee with that, right?"

"I never drink coffee," Spyder said again.

"Makes her barf," Niki added.

"How about some hot chocolate or tea?" But Spyder shook her head and then she took a loud, crunchy bite.

"Christ, Spyder," Daria said. "You're gonna break a tooth or something."

Spyder smiled and there were cocoa-colored crumbs on her lips.

"And *you* want a cubano, right?" to Niki and she thought about it, looked at the long list of exotic coffee drinks chalked up behind Daria, neon chalk rainbow on dusty slate.

"Yeah," she said, "Sure, and I want you to make Spyder an almond milk."

When Spyder started to protest, Daria held one finger to her lips, shhhhh, "I promise, it won't make you barf. Just steamed milk and a shot of almond syrup. Unless you'd rather have hazelnut or caramel, or vanilla," and Daria pointed to a row of tall bottles behind her, lurid shades of Torani syrups and Spyder looked at Niki.

"Almond's fine," she said, mumbled around her second noisy mouthful of biscotti.

"Coming right up, ladies," Daria said and turned her back, went to work with coffee grounds and sugar, almond syrup and the shiny silver Lavazza machine.

"So," and Niki wasn't looking at Spyder, speaking to her but watching the kids at the back table. "How'd you get the shop going, anyway?"

Spyder wiped her mouth with the napkin, picked up stray crumbs from the polished countertop, each one pressed down until it stuck to her fingertip and then transferred them to her tongue.

"A friend helped me," she said.

"But didn't you have to get a loan from a bank or something?"

"No," Spyder said. "I tried, to start with, but nobody's gonna give *me* a loan, Niki. I had a friend."

And Niki was looking at her now, soft smile on her Asian lips, held Spyder's hand again.

"A friend who loaned you the money?"

"No, a friend that died and gave me the money," she said and Niki's smile faded a little.

"I'm sorry," she said. "That your friend died, I mean."

"Yeah. He died from AIDS, long time ago. The only goth drag queen this city ever had, Lamia Martyr, and he could look just like Siouxsie Sioux, except you never called him a drag queen. You had to call him a 'performance artist' or a 'female illusionist' or he'd get pissed off at you. Andy hated to be called a drag queen."

Too close, sick irony or coincidence, and Niki hoped nothing showed on her face, and "You guys were real close?" she said.

"Yeah, I guess," and Spyder released Niki's hand, laid both hers palm-up on the counter, empty offering to no one and nothing in particular. "We hung out at Rushton Park when I was still a kid, you know, hanging out on Highland with the hustlers and runaways. It was nice, in the summer.

"Andy didn't hustle, though. He had money, money his mom had left him when she died. Just enough to keep him going until he started getting sick . . ." and she paused, looked up at the ceiling, ornate plaster molded and painted a green so deep it was almost black.

"Andy's mom was great. She knew he was queer and all, that he'd gotten AIDS, but she was still great. She used to cook us these big-ass Sunday dinners, used to let him bring home street kids on cold nights and shit. It's unfucking believable, Niki, that anyone ever gets parents that cool, you know?"

"Yeah," Niki said, and how many months now since she'd seen her own mother and father, anyway? She'd called her mother twice from motel rooms, just to let them know she was okay, never stayed on the line long enough that home could sneak its way through the connection and find her.

"Anyway, he left me a whole bunch of money when

he died, enough to start Weird Trappings and keep it going a while . . .

"I stayed with him, you know, at the end. He went blind finally and toxo got his brain. But he'd made me promise that I wouldn't let him die alone, and he didn't."

Niki swallowed and wanted to hold Spyder, but instead her eyes wandered away, afraid: Daria noisily steaming milk, an old photograph of a trolley car on the wall, finally down to her lap. Anything but beautiful, unfathomable Spyder, simple as a single thread knotted over and over and suddenly too much to grasp, like particle physics or her own mortality. And then Daria was setting their drinks on the bar, Niki's in a crystal demitasse, pitch black and a perfect skim of créma on top, Spyder's in a tall glass and the color of a quadroon's skin.

"Hey, you guys okay?" she said and Niki nodded, but Spyder only looked out at the street, wrapped her tattooed hands around the warm glass. "Christ, it's this fucking depressing-ass music," and Niki noticed it for the first time, blues she didn't recognize. Could tell from Daria's eyes that she knew it had nothing to do with the music, but she changed the CD anyhow. Exchanged the blues for Joan Jett and one of the kids in the back stood up and yelled, "All *right*! Goddamn right!"

"Thanks," Niki said.

"No problem. Listen, how'd you guys like to come to our show this weekend? We're part of this big deal at Dante's Saturday night, in Atlanta. Three or four bands and someone from Atlantic is supposed to be there, so I'm fucking freaked, you know? It'd be *really* cool if you guys could come. I'll put you on the guest list."

"I don't know," Spyder said.

"Maybe you could ride up in the van with us if you wanted," and Niki couldn't tell if Daria was just trying to help, give them something do, another excuse to get Spyder out of the house, or if she really wanted them along. Or both, perhaps.

"We'll think about it and let you know, okay?" Niki said and sipped her cubano, sweet and scalding. Spyder hadn't even tried her almond milk, just held onto the glass and stared out the window at the gray street.

"Sure," Daria said. "Just let me know if you wanna go. Look, I gotta go check on the roaster, but I'll be right back."

And when she was gone, Niki took another sip of her coffee, glanced out the window, through THE FID-GETY BEAN painted careful and the letters two feet tall, words running backwards from this side of the glass.

"What you looking at?"

"Nothing," Spyder said. "I thought I saw someone I knew, that's all. But it was someone else."

And then she tasted her milk and left Niki to stare at the street by herself.

* * *

He *knew* that she had seen him, that she had caught him watching her, frozen, too afraid to move, and Byron Langly walked quickly, shoes too loud (like she might hear), clothes too black (like she might see); finally stood out of the wind in one of the alleys that led up to First Avenue and Weird Trappings. His heart too fast, breathless, bright fear and adrenaline ache, muscles knotting like a bad dose of ecstasy or acid and now the strych was working on him.

He had not been back to his apartment in days, not since Billy said the cops had been by asking about him and maybe he should lay low for a while, and then Billy had mentioned seeing Spyder at the Steak and Egg, said he'd talked to her the day before, day after the night Byron had left Robin lying in the snow, bleeding and poisoned and helpless against the skitterers. But he had called the ambulance, right, he *hadn't* abandoned her? He'd hunted a pay phone through that fucking, blinding storm and he'd called 911, even though he'd wanted to run straight home, even though his hands and face were numb and he'd kept catching glimpses and skulking hints from the corners of his watering eyes.

"*She* left in a hurry," Billy had said, "Like that girl's ass was on the way to a fire or some shit," and then they'd both seen the thing creeping toward him across Billy's yellow and green candy-striped coffee table, eight busy legs and its body like a black pearl.

Billy had run to find the can of Raid he kept under the sink to kill cockroaches, but Byron had smashed it beneath a heavy ashtray, could see the widow's ruined body pressed between cut glass and painted wood, its life and deadly juices and a little movement left in its legs. So he'd ground the ashtray hard against the table, scratching the lacquered finish, had put all his weight on the damned thing until Billy had grabbed his shoulders. And then he'd sat on the sofa, crying again, holding the ashtray like a shield, cigarette butts and ash spilled all over his lap, parts of the spider stuck to the glass and the rest smeared on the table.

And he'd left the apartment and he hadn't been back. Walked the streets like a bum and lingered outside Weird Trappings, keeping track of the dark inside, living off coffee and cigarettes and junk food from the gas stations and convenience stores, sugar and salt and caffeine. Sleeping in doorways and almost freezing to death, trying not to see himself reflected in the windows he walked past.

Maybe, if he could find Walter, they could figure something out. But Walter hadn't answered his phone and no one had seen him in days. And everything twisting inside kept telling him to run, get a bus ticket to Atlanta, people there he could stay with for a while, people who wouldn't ask too many questions.

But he couldn't run, did not know why, if he was too afraid or not scared enough, but he couldn't. Could only wait.

When his heart had slowed, exhausted beat, and the fear faded to the steady background white noise it'd been for a week, he moved on.

2.

Finally, Niki had talked Spyder into going to the show, but only by agreeing that they'd take the Celica instead of riding along in the van. That way, they could leave when they wanted, which seemed important to Spyder, that she not feel trapped, restrained, by Stiff Kitten's itinerary, by whatever plans Daria and the band might have. That she could leave if and when she wanted to.

"No problem with the car going that far?" and Spyder had said no, that she drove to Atlanta and even as far as Athens sometimes, once all the way to New Orleans and it had only overheated a couple of times.

So Niki had called Daria and on Saturday afternoon, almost twilight, they met the band around back of a store that sold baby stuff. Keith and Daria were loading the van, instruments and the big rolling flight cases, amps, Theo sitting in the front seat, filing her nails and listening to a Lemonheads tape.

"You're gonna run down the battery again," Mort said and she rolled her eyes and turned the volume up.

Jobless Claude was there too, watching them lug their crap out of the practice space upstairs, Baby Heaven he called it, smoking Camels and complaining about Theo's taste in music.

When they were done, Keith locked the rear doors. Mort had been tinkering with something under the hood, cursed once when he bumped his head.

"Are you finished fucking around up there?" Daria shouted and he grunted some sort of affirmation, slammed the hood closed and the whole van shuddered.

"If we don't throw a rod this trip, it's gonna be a god-damn miracle, Dar."

Daria ignored him, dire oracle of grease and socket wrenches, turned instead to Spyder and Niki. "Hey, do you guys mind if Claude rides up with you? It'd make a lot more room in the shitmobile."

And Niki didn't think to ask Spyder, "Sure," she said, "That's cool," and Spyder only shrugged.

"I don't eat much," Claude said and laughed, clean laugh that made Niki feel more at ease than she'd felt in days, in weeks, maybe.

"Well, look. You guys just follow, but if we get separated, you've got the directions I gave you, right? Dante's isn't hard to find."

"I know where it is," Spyder said, "I've been there," not helpful or reassuring, more like someone had said, *Spyder, honey, you couldn't find your way around Atlanta with a road map, a compass, and an Indian guide,* and Niki began to wonder just how bad an idea this had been.

"We'll be fine," she said, and Daria hugged her, nodded, and they were all piling into the van, Mort sliding the side door shut and the last one in.

"And turn off that crap," Niki plainly heard, Daria speaking loud over Evan Dando and "Mrs. Robinson."

A few minutes later, Claude stuffed into the backseat and talking excitedly about the time he'd seen The Sugarcubes at Dante's, and Spyder ignoring him, slipping a Joy Division tape into the deck. Niki started the car, driving because Spyder wasn't supposed to on the Mellaril, and they followed the white van through the city toward the interstate.

* * *

Absolutely no danger of losing the van, of not keeping up, even in Spyder's grumbling Toyota. Niki followed close behind the Ford, maybe too close, but Spyder's silence was making her nervous. When she could read the stickers plastered all over the back doors of the van, entirely covering its bumper, she would back off. Catching whiffs of the Econoline's dark exhaust through the window Spyder kept cracked despite the cold outside, burning oil up there for sure; she wondered if Mort was right and they'd all end up stranded somewhere, middle of nowhere, between Birmingham and Atlanta.

On their way out of town, she'd noticed the spot

where the Vega had broken down, how long ago had that been now, almost three weeks? Better part of a month, then, and how could it have possibly been that long? And at the same time, the feeling that it must have been much longer, must have been months since that night.

"Why'd you get those tattoos," Claude asked Spyder, asked like a ghost from the dark backseat, "It must have hurt."

"I don't feel like talking," Spyder said, "I'm getting a headache." She turned up the stereo and Claude was silent for a while.

And the miles rolled by, distance marked off in reflective yellow paint and the changing of cassette tapes.

They crossed the state line, welcome to Georgia and a peach on the sign that made Niki think of a big pink butt, and she was getting too close to the van again, could read "Picasso Trigger Sodomized My Honor Student" and "Five-Eight," "WHPK Chicago" and "My Other Car Is A Penis." She relaxed, lifted her foot off the accelerator a little and backed off.

And the miles rolled by.

* * *

A long time ago, turn of the century or before, Dante's had been a grain mill, a place for grinding kernels of wheat and corn and barley into flour. Rough-hewn chunks of native stone, glinting mica schist, and huge pine beams. And after that had sat empty for years, decades, until someone had opened the club, had taken advantage of the mill's layout, three main levels, for its theme. In the shadow of skyscrapers, shadows of a New South of steel and glass, it sprawled like a Civil War fortress, framed in asphalt and train tracks and tendrils of strangling kudzu. *Divina Commedia* in wrought iron hung above the doorway and loops of razor wire strung around, past the booth where IDs were checked or tickets for shows were taken, where different colored plastic bands were fastened tight around wrists to prove whether or not you were old enough to buy booze.

Mort pulled the van into the circular drive out front, gravel pinging under the tires and red mud hardened to clay red crust, while Niki parked the Celica in a pay lot across the street. Two dollars to the kid at the gate and she paid it herself, locked the doors and they walked together across streetlit blacktop, the parking lot already half-full, kids hanging around or heading for Dante's to get in the line forming outside the ticket booth. Mostly punkers and goths, club kids, a few suburban casuals. Niki and Spyder reached the van and Keith was already opening the Econoline's rear end. Claude had stopped to talk to someone that he knew. A couple of equally battered vans parked close by, one old Winnebago that looked like a prop from a Mad Max film; the other bands, four on the bill in all.

They were all listed on the fluorescent white marquee hung high on one wall, black plastic letters from top to bottom, order of appearance reversed, of course. The headliner was a funk-punk-industrial fusion band Niki had heard on the radio once or twice, Shard, thought they might have a video out. Then Stiff Kitten, second string so third to play. The two bottom, then, TranSister, a local riot grrrl group, and last of all, something called Seven Deadlies.

"Why don't you guys go on in," Daria said. "There's no sense in you standing out here freezing while we load in."

"We could help," and Niki felt Spyder's impatience just fine without having to see her face; swelling, burring, silent disapproval like something solid as the old mill.

"We can handle it just fine. Just tell the guy at the box office you're on Stiff Kitten's guest list and you won't have to stand in line."

"Well, if you're sure . . ."

"Hey, girl'o, we are three buff motherfuckers," Daria said and flexed her biceps like Mr. Charles Atlas, her scrawnyhard arms hidden underneath her coat, anyway. "We can handle this shit just fine."

And so they went to the box office, Claude catching up with them, and a guy with three steel rings through his left eyebrow and a violet goatee checked their IDs against sheets of paper on a clipboard, checked them off one after the other: Niki, Claude, and Spyder last and he complimented the tattoos on the backs of her hands, disappearing up and inside the cuffs of her leather jacket.

"Yeah. Thanks," Spyder said. All three got Day-Glo orange bracelets and a stamp on one hand that left behind nothing they could see. Then they bypassed the long line of shivering faces waiting for nine o'clock to come, foggy breathers, passed under the wrought iron sign into a short passage with an uneven dirt floor; must and the same bare stone walls seemed to go up forever, the ceiling lost somewhere high overhead.

On the right, a rough arch and the sense of vast space beyond, swallowing depth and dark lit only by incandescent lightning and black-light strobes, flashes that revealed empty cages hung, lasers that stabbed crimson shafts through a roiling haze of glycerine smoke. Some of the smoke drifted into the bright hall, hesitant tendrils out of their element. A huge gargoyle the color of shit squatted on one side of the arch, warty plaster haunches and a spiked, leather dog collar around its neck, the collar fastened to a chain bolted to the wall. In there, the DJ already warming up for the night and the smoke shimmered and the dusty floor ached with the twining, remixed passion of synthesizers and drum machines.

And above the door, of course, another heavy iron sign on its rusted chains, one word burned through the metal, meaning in the emptiness left within the raw edges of acetylene cuts. *Inferno,* and Claude said, "Hell," and jabbed a thumb at a smaller archway to their left and another sign, this one a plank of dark wood, wood sculpted like muscle, straining shoulder and gritted teeth, empty eyes and *Purgatorio* carved there, hung on oily-looking ropes. The heavy wooden doors to Purgatory were closed and padlocked.

"They do special shit in there," he told Niki. "Fetish night and things like that."

At the end of the passage there was more wrought iron, a spiral staircase winding up and up and a long-haired boy, blonde and Niki thought he looked like a misplaced surfer, California tan in Georgia November.

Claude presented his hand, palm down, and surfer boy ran some sort of scanner across it, neon blue light and ANGEL stamped right there on Claude's skin. Niki next and the same secret message revealed, and then he reached for Spyder's hand, but she had backed away, stared, eyes wide and her mouth the slightest bit open, gazing into her tattoos.

"What's wrong, Spyder?" Niki said, soft voice, calming voice. "Is something wrong?" and surfer boy looked annoyed, sighed loud. Claude was already halfway up the stairs, noisy clanging shoes; he stopped and waited, looked down at them and whatever was happening.

"I don't want that on my hand," she said. Niki looked at Spyder's face, cheeks *too* pale, the cruciform scar between her eyes angry pink and Niki understood, *click,* like revelation or an impossible math problem that you've sweated over and then it just makes sense.

"Are you going up or not, ladies?" surfer boy said and waved his glowing scanner at them like a magic wand. "In or out, one way or another."

"Just a second," Niki said and smiled, wanted to kick him instead.

"I've got to wash it off," but Niki wrapped Spyder's hand up in hers, held it tight.

"It's just ink," she said quietly, "That's all. We'll wash it off as soon we get upstairs, I swear. We'll find a rest room and wash it off."

And she led Spyder past the cruel, unveiling light and they followed Claude up the winding stairway, around and up and around and up, to the landing above. And the third sign set above the third arch, chisel-scarred marble and *Paradiso,* like the punch line to a dirty joke.

"Where's a rest room?" Niki asked, and Claude pointed into the shadows on one side of the landing.

"Right over there," he said, confusion and worry thickening his voice. "You gonna be all right, Spyder?"

"She'll be fine," Niki said, smiling, nodding, trying to sound like she believed it. "You go on in and we'll catch up, okay?"

Spyder had begun to dry scrub the back of her hand hard against her jeans.

"Come on," Niki said, and Claude watched them step free of the dazzling light spilling out of Heaven and disappear into the gloomy spot where the women's room was. After a few seconds, he went in without them.

* * *

They'd emptied the van, everything lugged clank and crash up the black stairs, black carpet and black walls and two narrow flights up to Heaven's back door. Each branded with garish orange stickers by the security goon guarding the door, Gabriel or Michael in a muscle shirt and nothing on his face but pure and frosty ennui, and the stickers read DANTE'S, "Stiff Kitten" and the date scrawled underneath with a smeary black Sharpie.

Then the goon had grumbled that they had one too many guests on the list, only three allowed for the second band, not four. And so Mort and Keith had told him Theo was their harmonica player. The goon had shaken his head, no dice, and so Theo had begun to dig through her purse.

"It's in here somewhere, really," but she'd found nothing but a dented old kazoo, and he'd said what the hell and given her a sticker, anyway, had stamped their four left hands. And then they'd found out the sound man was going to be late and Theo had broken a nail and spent fifteen minutes bitching about it. Three dressing rooms behind the stage and only the one for the headliner had a heater.

As typical a load-in as they could have asked for.

Keith was sitting alone in a total loss of an arm chair, sandwiched between his guitar and the wobbly flight case with Mort's drums inside, and Mort and Theo had gone to find Niki and Spyder and Claude.

He looked sick, and not just junk sick; Daria knew that look well enough. She lit a cigarette and handed it to him.

"Thanks," he said and held her hand.

"You gonna make it?" and he didn't answer, drew smoke deep into his lungs and rubbed at his stubbly cheeks.

"Can't sleep," he said and the smoke rushed back out again. "Not a wink in three goddamned nights," and she looked at the red welt across the bridge of his nose, angry red of infection, remembered the cuts from that morning at Spyder's and never any explanation for how they'd gotten there.

"Bad dreams?" and she wanted to look over her shoulder, then, maybe even wanted to take back the words before he could answer her. But Keith looked at her and laughed, took another drag off the cigarette and blew two streams of smoke from his nostrils. Nothing in his gray eyes she could read.

"I think Cephus's been selling me bad shit, that's all," and the moment had passed them by, opportunity missed and no shared confession, no accounting of the horrors that had dogged her sleep for a week blurted out before she could stop herself. No release, no sense of relief afterwards. Only more dread, another weight to carry alone, and regret that the heroin had gotten between them again.

"I'm gonna have to stop buying from that jerkoff before he kills me."

And she gripped his hand tighter, chewed at her lower lip as she read the graffiti, the writing on the dingy dressing room wall.

"Tonight's the night," she said, to him or just to herself, *wanted* it to be for him but couldn't be sure if he was even listening. "We're gonna knock that rep on her ass, and she'll be talking deal before we can get off the stage."

"Yeah," Keith said, surprising her, and when he rubbed at the cut on his nose a single drop of pus the color of custard welled up, beaded, and he wiped it away.

"Tonight's the night," he said.

* * *

The rest room was freezing, nothing on the blue door but a "W" slashed into the paint and so much cold inside it was hard to breathe. No hot water and Spyder was still scrubbing at the spot where he'd stamped her hand with "ANGEL" in invisible ink, had scrubbed it raw already, strange red under the tattoos, and Niki knew that soon it would be bleeding.

"It's gone," she said. "You've washed it off, Spyder."

"How do you know?" vicious eyes answering Niki from the mirror, vicious tone. "How the hell can you tell? There's no way to know if it's still there or not. You couldn't fucking see it to start with, so how are you supposed to know if it's gone?"

"It was just ink, Spyder. And ink comes off with soap and water. *That's* how the hell I know."

But Spyder pressed more of the candy pink soap powder from the dispenser over the sink and began to lather her hands again.

"You *don't* know," she said, "You don't know shit."

And Niki grabbed Spyder's hands, slippery wet and living art, got her around the wrists and held on. Skin like ice from the water and Spyder howled and tried to pull free.

"What don't I know, huh? That your father was a fucking lunatic and cut your face up when you were a kid? That you *think* this has something to do with that?"

"Let go of me," Spyder said, hissed, and Niki clearly heard the threat, the danger wrapping those four words like acid and broken glass. But she didn't let go.

"What don't I know, Spyder? What don't I know?"

Spyder shoved hard and Niki was stumbling backwards,

collided with a wall and her breath whooshed out between her teeth. Her head hit the metal paper towel holder and she almost blacked out, almost let go.

No, she tried to say, *No way until you tell me,* but there was no air, nothing but pain in her chest and head, nothing to drive the words.

And something else, something glistening in the air like fishing line or piano wire, not there a few seconds before and now crisscrossing everywhere, everything, strung through the air like taut and silver tinsel, draping the black stalls and collecting in drifts on the floor. And then Spyder body-slammed her against the wall again.

Silk like spun razors, like steel and slicing thread.

Niki gasped, fish gasp, useless attempt to breathe, and released Spyder's left hand, tangled her fingers in dreads and sidestepped before she smacked Spyder's forehead into the wall. And then they were both falling, sinking to their knees, Niki's arms wrapped tight around Spyder, Spyder sobbing loud and jagged and blood on her face again. What Niki might have seen hanging in the air a second before was gone, had never been there, nothing now but the weak light above the sink and the sounds of the water still gurgling from the tap and Spyder sobbing like a broken child.

Niki struggled to fill her lungs again.

"You're not fucking chasing me away," she croaked, finally. "Not like that."

Something settled lightly on her neck, weightless presence and nettle sting, and Niki absently brushed it away, fought for another precious mouthful of oxygen and the stink of piss and toilet deodorizers.

"You're going to tell me and then I'm going to understand."

Through her tears, Spyder said only one thing, over and over again, a name, and it wasn't Niki's.

* * *

Heaven was a single long room, cavernous rectangle of naked stone walls on three sides and the fourth painted with a mural of blue sky and cottonwhite clouds, hardwood floor and the rafters overhead. The bar at one end and the stage way off at the other, two or three times as big as the stage at Dr. Jekyll's; Spyder and Niki sat with Claude and Theo on rickety bar stools, watching the show over all the heads and waving arms. Spyder couldn't drink alcohol, because of her medication, and so they both nursed flat Cokes in plastic cups while Theo and Claude drank cough-syrup colored mixtures of cranberry juice and vodka.

Niki's head still hurt and Spyder had an ugly goose-egg bump on her forehead, a little cut that had bled like something serious; they could both have concussions, she kept thinking, or worse. Niki told Claude she'd slipped on a wet spot on the bathroom floor and when Spyder tried to catch her, they'd both fallen.

"I didn't used to be such a klutz," and Spyder had looked the other way.

"Maybe you could sue," he'd said, not helpful at all, and Niki shrugged and nodded. "Maybe so," she'd said.

Seven Deadlies turned out to be goth, eight white-faced boys and girls in gauzy black, guitars and drums and a cello, creepysoft renditions of "House of the Rising Sun" and a couple of Leonard Cohen songs before they'd drifted on to louder, ragged rock, but everything covers.

"Wake up, dead babies," Theo sneered in a thrumming quiet space between songs. "It can't be 1985 for*ever*."

TranSister was earsplitting grrrl grunge-metal that trebled the pain in Niki's head, each song separated from the last only by the grace of the singer's mike-shouted obscenities and diatribes against punker boys and pro-lifers. Halfway through their set, she unzipped her jeans and pulled out a two-foot rubber dildo and let it hang there between her legs, swinging like an eager-shy elephant's trunk while she gyrated to the guitarist's grind and wail.

And all Theo had said between two sips of her red drink was, "These chicks have issues," and she and Claude had laughed.

3.

Daria stood in the darkness behind the stage, counting seconds and clutching her bass like something blessed, talisman or fetish, teddy bear or lover or crucifix, waiting as TranSister thrashed their way through an encore. Keith was right behind her, smoking, comforting presence despite himself, and Mort, drumming nervously along with the band, his sticks on the black wall.

And none of this seemed as important as it should, she knew, hadn't since that morning on Cullom Street, the morning they'd taken Spyder home; the urgency, her scalding ambition that permitted precedence to nothing and no one, was slipping away, deserting her when she needed it most. The fire that she'd used to keep them all in line, working and dreaming and creeping steadily toward this point, this opportunity or one like it.

It was nothing she could explain, even if she'd tried, to herself or anyone else, no more than she could explain why she'd started jumping at shadows, why she'd bought a night-light (Donald Duck in his blue sailor's hat) and slept with it burning. When she slept.

Her stomach made a sound like air in old plumbing.

Stiff Kitten was the second band, so they'd gotten one free plate of supper each, greasy yellow rice and stale tortillas, dry black beans and drier strips of chicken, from the kitchen behind the bar. The headliners got as much as they wanted, and the two bottom bands were left to fend for themselves. Daria, Keith, and Mort had carried their sagging plates and cans of Coca-Cola and 7-Up back to the freezing dressing room and eaten with plastic forks. No conversation, and when Mort flicked a bean at the back of Keith's head and it stuck there like a rabbit pellet, Keith had only wiped it away and gone back to his own food.

The sound guy had shown up, finally, half an hour late and everyone looking at their watches and grumbling. They'd waited backstage, bundled and shivering, while the headliner finished its check and then they'd taken the stage, taking direction through the monitors.

"Gimme one," the sound guy said, so they'd played a few chords of "Imperfect" and Daria couldn't hear anything but Mort's kick drum. Keith broke a string, hadn't had another and he'd begged one off Shard's guitarist.

The last cascade of drums and the crowd and the vocalist for TranSister sneered something through the mike, one last taunt or jibe, before the lights went down. And instruments revolved, bands revolved, and she was climbing the four steps up onto the stage, second time tonight but this time for real. This time the crowd surging against the stage and maybe seven or eight security guys between them and the mosh pit, and somewhere out there, Niki Ky and Spyder and Claude, and the Atlantic rep. Daria adjusted her mike stand and looked around, Mort sitting down behind his kit, Keith seeing nothing now but his guitar. And then she looked down at her feet, ratty shoes and the set list taped to matte black plywood.

"It's gonna be good," Keith whispered, leaning close, surprising her again. "It's gonna be killer." And he kissed her on the top of the head.

The lights, then, and fresh applause, blue and red gels making violet. *Lights of Heaven,* she thought and stepped up to the microphone, just one word, "Thanks," breathed through the black windscreen, before Keith stepped in with the first chords of "Gunmetal Blues," Mort following softly on his snare and Charleston cymbal. Her fingers, third voice, steady heartbeat behind it all.

* * *

This was one of his songs. Not that they weren't *all* part him, varying degrees of him and Daria, but this one was *his,* picked out one afternoon when Daria had the flu and they had canceled practice. So he'd fixed and sat alone in Baby Heaven, just loving the feel of his fingers on the strings, just glad there was this one thing that was his, this one thing that was so right, so pure, it was almost stronger than the junk, almost clean enough to redeem. The sky outside had been the color of the music in his head, the low clouds moving out before thunder and lightning and he was the rain. He'd played it for Daria, wanting her to add some words, but she'd shaken her head and he'd seen the tears straining in her eyes, holding back, shaken her head and when she could speak, she'd said, *no, no Keith, it's right—just like this—I'd only fuck it up.* So he'd shown her the bass lines in his head and it had stayed his song.

Following the notes where he knew they'd lead, letting Daria and Mort tag along and the restless bodies stretching out before them, almost lost in the glare. But he was doing it for himself, no deception there, not like it was any better now than that day on an old sofa in their loft above Storkland, or a hundred times he'd sat on the street and picked it out for Anthony Jones or L. J. or anyone who cared to listen. Just for himself.

Eyes shut almost to the end, not wanting distraction, not needing encouragement. But there were a few bars right at the close that were tricky, a little teasing trap he'd made for himself, so he had to stay alert or trip over his own big fingers on the way out, and he opened his eyes, watching the bruised light, the darkness on the other side of the spots and up there something moved. Something hanging upside down, and at first, well, it *had* to be one of the stupid fuckers from the pit who had somehow made it up into the rafters, maybe a boost on the shoulders of his buddies and he *might* have managed to pull himself up. It moved again, hauling itself closer, easier to see now, dangling head down, bony-long neck twisting around for a better view of the stage, of him, and those eyes, one after another, black and wet and lidless, running round and round its bristling head.

His fingers stumbled, missed and feedback whined through the amps.

Or that was the sound it made when it opened its mouth, shifted its bulk and began to drip, leak, onto the upturned faces and outstretched hands. Leak slicker and blacker than oil, and Daria had stopped playing and Mort had stopped playing. Both of them staring at him; he knew they didn't see it, knew they wouldn't, even if

he pointed and the crowd was howling, pissed and starting to throw crap at them.

"Keith?" Daria said. She wasn't even angry yet,
sounded confused, scared maybe, and he shrugged, tried
to smile and make himself look back at his guitar, the
strings and "Sorry, man," he said, but he could hear it
moving around, wire brush on old wood and raw meat
and he couldn't even begin to remember where to put his
fingers.

A painful twinge across the bridge of his nose, his ankle, the syrupy *smell* of cold air, and Keith could feel
the sweat on his face, under his clothes, like he hadn't
fixed. Daria's lips moved without letting go of any
sound, *what's wrong,* and he knew this performance was
everything to her and that he was fucking it up, *what's
wrong, Keith,* might have already fucked it up. Because
there was no telling what Cephus Lee was using to cut
his smack these days, no telling what he'd shot into his
arm in the toilet down the hall from the dressing room,
and someone in the crowd threw a beer bottle and it ex-
ploded like an amberglass grenade at Daria's feet. Two
of the big security guys tackled him and he was gone,
and Daria turned away, one last look at those eyes full
of panic and disgust fermenting in her green irises, disgust for him.

Scritch, and he tried to find his way out of the crackling silence, *scritch,* crackling around him like the air
had that morning at Spyder's, kept his eyes on the
strings, his fingers, the play list at his feet. Another beer
bottle sailed past, hit the wall behind Mort and Bud-
weiser shrapnel rained down around them.

"Will you give us a fucking break?" she growled into
her mike, and the crowd growled back.

The next song on the list . . . the list in Daria's handwriting, precious scrawl she'd photocopied at Kinko's,
three copies and the masking tape beginning to curl
where it didn't want to stick to the stage . . . the next
song was "Su(in)cide" and he fumbled at the first few
chords, nothing in the whole goddamn world but his
hands and his guitar and Daria's list.

Behind him, Mort began to follow, cautious three-quarter cadence, but Daria was too busy yelling at someone and it didn't matter, because his fingers felt like he was trying to play the Gibson with yellow Playtex gloves on and the cut across his face stung so badly that his eyes had begun to water.

And one oilwet splat, then, one drop from somewhere directly overhead, and he watched the stain as it spread, bloomed, and *whatever you do, man, just don't fucking look up, just don't fucking look up, 'cause you already know* and he stepped back from the sheet of paper taped to the stage, the acid stain, and *you already know and there ain't no point in seeing.*

Then she was in his face, right foot planted squarely on the ruined photocopy and the stain still spreading beneath the sole of her Doc, right in his face and her eyes were as green as summer and he loved her almost as much as his music.

"Get the hell off the stage," she said. "Just get the hell off the stage."

* * *

Behind the crowd, Niki saw Keith falter and the song ended, nothing now but fading echo whine, static strips and tatters of sound. And she saw the way Spyder flinched, familiar confusion in her blue eyes that said something else was going wrong and she was there so it had to be her fault, somehow had to be her fault. It made Niki mad, mad that anyone, sane or crazy, could blame themselves for every goddamn thing that happened.

Wouldn't be projecting just a little tonight, would we, Niki? and no, she answered herself firmly, no, we wouldn't.

"Oh," Theo said, "this is just fucking wonderful," and she gave Keith the finger, obviously not caring that he couldn't see her from the stage. Like she *had* seen, Daria, through the mike, " . . . you give us a fucking break?" and even way back at the bar, the crash of the beer bottle right over Mort's head.

"Christ," and Theo was gone, slipped away and into the crowd, heatseeker, and Niki rubbed unconsciously at the faint and lingering sting on her neck, hairline welt that had risen on her throat.

Then Daria was saying something to Keith, shoved him, and Stiff Kitten was leaving the stage, sulking away from the hail of boos and catcalls and flying beer bottles. Daria looked back once, everything but her face swallowed in the shadows behind the amps, but she was too far away for Niki to read expression or intent, anything.

"Come on," Claude said, then, "Maybe we can at least stop them from killing him."

"We'll wait here," Spyder said, stirring at her Coke with one finger, not looking at anything, and Niki didn't argue.

* * *

Out of the spotlight heat and down the black hall to the dressing room, pulled deeper and deeper into the cold by the gravity of Daria, the furious wake of her. His skin felt sunburned, flashburned, and his nose hurt, and the place beneath his eyes, like the time when he was ten and he'd snorted green Kool-Aid on a dare. He followed her, because anyone would have and he knew she hadn't seen anything hanging above the crowd, hanging there above his head.

The light in the dressing room made him squint and he sat down, him and his guitar and Mort must have stopped to talk to the manager because it was just him and Daria. She had stopped in the doorway, lit a cigarette and didn't look at him.

"I'm not gonna ask what happened out there, Keith. I know what happened."

"Yeah," he said, and she just shook her head then, drew gray smoke and exhaled.

"You're a fucking mess. Just look at your face in the goddamn mirror. We can't count on you."

He didn't look in the mirror behind him, but when he

touched the place where his face ached, his hand came away wet, ginger alloy of pus and blood; he wiped his fingers on the couch and Daria flicked her half-smoked cigarette away into the dark, cold hall, little comet of sparks arcing away into space.

"You're out, man," she said, "Out of the band, out of my life." Keith sighed and ran his fingers through his hair, no surprise, nothing he hadn't known was coming, but it hurt anyway, hurt too much for him to respond. And then Mort was filling up the doorway, red cheeks and he didn't even glance at Keith. "I'm doing what I can, Dar, but this dude's really steamed," and she nodded and he was gone again.

She lit another cigarette.

"I can't sleep," he said. "I just can't sleep anymore, not since . . ." and she nailed him silent with her eyes, stabbed two fingers and her cigarette at his chest, "You're a fucking *junky,* Keith. Period. You are a goddamn fucking worthless ass junky bum and I'm tired of listening to your bullshit excuses. We can't count on you and it is *over.*"

Outside the doorway, the darkness shifted, but it was only Theo, bristling like a terrier on speed, wanting a piece of him, too, a big, juicy piece, and Daria told her to fuck off and get in line, take a number.

"You're a real fuck-up," Theo said to him anyway, "You make me sick," and left before Daria told her to.

"This is such a goddamn waste," Daria said, that sound in her voice that meant she'd cry if she could.

"I can't sleep anymore," he said again, because he had to say something, because he could handle the junk and she knew it. "Just tell me you're not having nightmares, too," and the anger getting into his voice past the pain and loss and self-loathing, and she stared at him, smoky question mark curling above her fingers.

"Yeah, Keith, I have nightmares. Is it any fucking wonder I have nightmares? Everything we've worked our asses off for just crashed and burned out there."

"And it's my goddamned fault! Yeah. I know, Daria, I know," and he stood up so fast he almost hit his head on the low ceiling, the Gibson clasped in both hands like his baseball bat before a fight and it smashed against the concrete wall, spinning plexiglass volume and tone control knobs, bent vibrato arm whizzing by an inch from Daria's face. Busted black pickguard and the neck cracked loud and snapped off the body of the guitar. He held it out to her, the whole thing bound together now by nothing but the strings, steel and nylon ligaments binding broken bone, dropped it at her feet.

"I'm sorry," he said, fury spent so fast and a shudder through him at the sight of the damage, the ruin, part of himself dead and in a heap on the floor. She didn't say anything, just stared at the shattered guitar and now there were tears, swelling and escaping the corners of her eyes, bleeding down her face, wet streaks over the shock.

He pushed his way around her, out into the hall, the darkness waiting for him, confident, and there was Mort, like a blockade, Theo right behind him.

"Hey, where are you going? Don't you think we've got some talking . . ."

"You know I owe you everything, man," Keith said, "I owe you and I'm never gonna make that up, so you need to just get the hell out of my way now."

Mort hesitated, long enough to read the rest of it in Keith's gray eyes, the threat and regret, before he stepped aside, one arm protectively around Theo, and let him go.

CHAPTER ELEVEN

Loose Threads

1.

Word of mouth, questions whispered and answers, and so Byron knew that Spyder and her new girlfriend had gone to a show in Atlanta. That the house was empty—no, the house was never *empty*, but she wasn't there and he might not ever get another chance. Knew he only had so much time left, his time slipping away like the crimson sand through the Wicked Witch's hourglass. And the days and nights had become worse than his fear of the house, of whatever lay coiled underneath, what he and Robin and Walter had awakened like stupid, noisy children. Worse than his fear of whatever guarded Spyder and kept tabs on him, too. The eye-corner lurkers, the dream haunters, and it was better to go and be done with it. One way or another, be done with it.

He'd tried to find Walter for days but no one had seen him, no one knew anything or at least they weren't willing to tell him, if they did. He could hardly blame them, the way he looked, like a fucking street person, the way he smelled, because he was afraid to go home long enough to shower and change his clothes. His eyes the worst, because he could never sleep for more than ten or fifteen minutes at a time before he snapped wide-awake and sweating. Anyway, Walter had probably left the city, run off somewhere safe (if anywhere was safe) and left him alone, the way he'd let them go to the house alone, the night of the storm and the beginning of the end of the world.

He'd waited until after dark, drinking cup after bitter cup of coffee at the Steak and Egg because Billy would fill his cup for free, would slip him a danish or a slice of apple pie. He took pink hearts with his coffee and waited until there was no day left in the sky, no moon up yet, either. Just Venus and a couple of stars, the sky so clear and indigo tonight.

"You should go home," Billy had said, soft concern, honest pity, filling his coffee cup again, and Byron had nodded his head, as if he was agreeing. And so Billy had said, "Promise me you'll go home and get some rest tonight, Byron. A bath and a shave would make you feel so much better. Just promise me you'll at least do that, okay?" And Byron had nodded again, because it was easier and made Billy smile cautiously and go back to work.

But instead he followed the duskstained streets up Red Mountain, house by house, toward Cullom Street. Except he'd learned *something,* and this time he wouldn't be walking up to the front door, bold and dumb, no way. This time he took 16th Avenue, instead, and finally left the street, blocks from Spyder's house, traded asphalt for the dry cereal crunch of fallen leaves beneath his shoes, twig snap, and the naked craggy trees reaching for him all around. Safer this way, because he could hear *them* better, always just out of sight, but their erector-set legs as loud as his feet in the woods. He could tell the skitterers were trying to keep in step with him, to cover their pursuit in the sound of his own footsteps, but there were too many legs, too many needle hairs to scrape against tree bark, leather bellies dragged, raked along, and Byron kept speeding up and slowing down, walking tightrope on fallen logs when he could.

Slowly making his way up the mountain, rough angle that he guessed would take him close to Spyder's overgrown backyard. The cold air made his chest ache, aching legs, but he kept moving, stumbling over chert and sandstone boulders like scabs sticking up through the leaf mould, bits of bone showing through the forest's decay. And the dark as thick as the frigid air, until

the moon slipped up over the ridge and bled its satin
light through the trees, three quarters full so he could
see, could see that he'd wandered past the house and
would have to double back.

He stood still and stared down, between the trees and
briars, at the roof of Spyder's house. Off to his left,
something big moved fast, crawling forward three or
four quick feet before it stopped and was silent, too.

"I *know* you're out there," he said, loud enough so
anyone could hear, and turned around, nothing there, of
course, but he spoke into the woods anyway, because he
knew they heard him, spoke slow and certain words and
the rust-jagged edge of ephedrine and exhaustion and
anger in his voice.

"Why don't you just come on if you want me? Are
you afraid? Are you fuckers afraid of me?" and he
laughed at the skitterers, not an act, really laughed at
them, skulking back there out of sight like cockroaches.

"Maybe you *can't* stop me. Is that it? Maybe you
can't do anything but creep around and watch."

And he took a step downhill, toward the house and
heard the nervous whispers and drought rustle of their
bodies all around him in the dark.

"Does Spyder keep you guys on that fucking short a
leash?" and he laughed louder, laughed like a lunatic
and then he was crying again before he could stop himself, cackling and crying and he took another step; their
legs punched through the ground eight times, sixteen
times, twenty-four times. Thirty-two, and Byron stooped,
found a rock and hurled it into the night. He never heard
it hit the ground.

"I'm right, aren't I?" Urgent words spit at the skitterers, and "You're all bark and no goddamn bite. You
made Robin hurt herself, got us so fucking scared she
pulled that shelf over on top of herself and the goddamn
widows and the snow did the rest *for* you."

And then he was running, headlong pell-mell rush,
jumping deadfall tumbles and ripping his face and
hands in blackberry thicket briars. Feet almost tangling,
ankles almost twisting, balance nothing but accident

and the roof of Spyder's house rising up to meet him. A hundred yards left, now, a hundred yards at most, and he almost whacked his forehead on a low sycamore limb as big around as his leg. Ducked at the last minute, the last minute before he hit something else, something that was and wasn't there and it wrapped around him, tripped him but held him up, let him stumble three or four steps more before it began to slice into his flesh, slice through cloth and skin like garroting wire, and slicing, drew him backwards.

He screamed and kicked, thrashed his legs, tore at nothing he could see, could only feel because it was cutting him apart, sinking into him. Gauzy silver hints like the moonlight, or only the reflection of the moon off something wet and razor sharp that had no color of its own.

"Spyder! Spyder, oh god get it off me Spyder please," and the scrunch and scritch of them all coming for him through the trees, through the leaves, slipping between the trees and out of the corners of his eyes so that finally he could see them. Calling his dare, calling his bluff, and drinking him in with eyes like Spyder's that weren't Spyder's eyes. As many eyes as the night, and a second before the silk cut through his throat, sprayed fever-warm blood and left him mute and gasping, Byron felt his feet leave the ground and he dangled like an angel or a fly without wings.

2.

Putting the old mill behind him and its casual three-tiered judgments, Keith walked west, walked toward downtown Atlanta and away from far-off morning. Away from Daria. Headful of ashes and simmering hate for no one but himself, plenty of room left for regret, and he didn't know the name of this street, didn't know where that alley led, and that was good, that was how it felt inside, exactly. Anonymous brick and cinder block like his soul and the expression on Daria's face when he'd smashed his guitar. Like she hadn't already done the honor, like *he'd* hurt *her* by making her decision final, irrevocable, her one wish on the monkey's paw and he'd sealed it tight.

Spaces between streetlamp pools and the eyes that watched him suspiciously from black faces, the sound of his boots on concrete cold and hard as the cast of her mouth.

He shivered, zipped his jacket closed and kept moving; turning here, crossing empty chainlinked lots of cracked and potholed asphalt, broken glass, junky little white mousie in the maze—big hollow man striding under the moon and sodium-arc suns. Hey man, give me a buck, man, and he stopped to look at the ragpile that had spoken from a doorway, nailshut doorway and glass painted red. Something human in there, or just something alive, empty Thunderbird bottle in one claw like a lifeline and he found two dollars in his pocket, held the bills out and the ragpile snatched them away and mumbled bitter and thankless to itself.

You go down, and down, thinking there's not a bottom, and Keith looked past the ghetto ruin at the shining new towers, clean light up there, windwhistling Heaven up there and ragpile wino Hell down here, down and down, and this time she wasn't gonna be there to haul him back to himself, back to Purgatory. One more alley and it was a dead end, Dumpsters and the crap that had tumbled out of them, shitclogged cul-de-sac in the city's guts. Keith followed the alley all the way back, kicked a stiff, daysdead pigeon out of his way and sat down in the trash.

Absolutely untogether, Mr. Barry, and just an hour before he'd been somewhere else, someone else, a mile away and the burn and eager need of all those bodies stretched out before him like a banquet, and Daria there beside him. Now, just the knowledge that things might have gone different.

If we hadn't followed Spyder home, and he knew that was true, that it wasn't the H this time. Rushing to the door and that damn old lady, whatever he'd touched, whatever had touched him. Something bad left lying around and his big feet had tangled in it. Too cold to shiver anymore, Keith closed his eyes and tried to think about nothing but the night before, sleeping over at Daria's place and her in his arms, radiator warmth and their hard bodies straining against the things held between them, sex and the musky safe smell of her. And afterwards, sleepless, he'd read from a book about Vietnam and thought about Niki Ky while Daria slept, had spent more time listening to the smooth chest rise and fall of her breathing than following the pages.

The lines on her face, the wrinkled place between her eyebrows betraying her nightmares, and he'd put an arm around her, as if he could drive them off, or at least keep her company down there.

He had enough junk left for one more fix, and two dilaudid he'd scored a week ago and been holding back. Without opening his eyes, he fished a prescription bottle from one pocket and dry-swallowed the dilaudids, tossed the empty plastic bottle away. And smelled something, damp dried stench, jasmine and roadkill, dusty basement air and the cold rot smell of something left too long in a refrigerator. Wind swept down the alley, wind that went straight through his clothes and he was shivering again; wind and the puke smell of all that fucking garbage and he tucked his face down inside his jacket, a little warm air in there and just his own rank, familiar sweat stink.

Something bad that cut if you weren't careful where you stepped, as mindless, pointless and mean as barbed wire wrapped around his ankles and trailing after him. And what he hadn't said to Daria, bright dream of the hole torn in a spider's web, and whatever had escaped dying anyway, writhing in grass, silk-tangled wings and never mind that the fucking spider hadn't even wanted it in the first place.

"Please," she said, voice so close, voice that seemed to spring and then roll back on itself, reverb, and he opened his eyes, nothing but the empty alley leading back to the empty street. A prickling rash of chill bumps on the back of his neck, kid fear, and he yelled at the nothing, fuck off, go the fuck away, I don't have any more goddamn money. But he watched the shadows of the Dumpsters, the space between the high brick walls. And she said, "Please, wake me up . . ."

"Fuck off, I said," and a panel truck rumbled noisy past the other end of the alley and was gone.

Keith unzipped his jacket, bleeding all his warmth away into the night, felt for the comforting bulge of his kit, tucked safely into an inside pocket, his rosary, trinity of spoon and powder and syringe.

"It's a dream," the girl said, same voice, same papery wasp-nest voice, and there was a knife in that pocket, too, just a little pocket knife but he took it out and held it clasped in the sweating palm of his hand.

Something scuttled from one shadow to another, too dark for him to see, just the impression of mass and movement and he tried to open the knife, but his fingers were sweaty, too, and it was hard to get a grip on the blade.

"It's just a dream," and the knife popped open, useless blade he used for cutting his nails, for splicing cable. The scuttling sound again, closer, " . . . wake me up."

He wanted to stand, leave the voice and the rancid smell, what all this meant or didn't mean, and she said, "Please . . ." before one leg like a giant's beetle-shelled finger reached slowly out of the dark, jointed leg and hairs more like quills and another, then, testing the paler darkness that surrounded him. Keith wanted to close his eyes, but he watched as she came, all that was left of her and what there was now, instead. Enough of her face in there that he knew, the way he knew the pain in that one green eye, swollen and helpless contrast to the others, her new eyes, bulging, all-seeing pools of pitch and the stingy hours before dawn. The eye and the voice and the tufts of green hair.

Her lips there between the furred vise jaws, the needle-hooked fangs, lips cracked and this was worse than anything from the dreams, worse than the thing hanging, dripping, from the rafters of Heaven.

"I want to go home," it said, she said, too-pink lips, raw, and clumsy mandibles, and now the air was full of drifting threads, gossamer falling around him, settling everywhere like spun sugar or glass, cotton candy or angel-hair. The world growing too bright and thin around him, before the flash. The strands burned his skin and the ground sizzled and smoked where they landed.

"It's worse," she said, "over here," perfect, beautiful sadness and inched backwards into the shadows, leaving something glistening wet and sludgy behind. Keith Barry shut his eyes, as the sparkling silk rained down like Christmas, and he tried to find the memory of Daria's face through the acid filling his veins and hold it as the world dissolved around him.

3.

From Birmingham to Nashville, Nashville to Louisville and on to Indianapolis, buses and interchangeable bus stations, and Walter had no idea where he was going, hardly why. Less money left every day and no direction, no solution but this movement that solved nothing, and nothing inside but dread and terror pushing him further and further from that spot on the earth where Spyder's house sat festering in his head. Sometime Sunday morning, and he waited for the connection to Chicago, only half-awake in the molded blue plastic chair and his ass hurting, watching the faces around him, the eyes with their own simpler worries. Worries in the real world, solid world, not the insane things, what he didn't believe and could no longer deny.

At the Greyhound counter, a greasy-looking woman in a Pennzoil windbreaker was arguing with the clerk, something he couldn't hear, but something to watch anyway, her lips moving and the sneer on her face, white-trash contempt, the annoyed disinterest in the clerk's eyes, and sleep moved silently up behind him . . .

* * *

. . . and it's always the same, always Walter lost in those hours or minutes or days before Spyder comes down from the brilliant, burning hills to take him home, to lead him back to the World. And always that sudden sense of aloneness, severed cord, broken chain, knowing that Robin and Byron are free, that they've slipped away, escaped, and he's still cowering in the sulfur rubble on the edge of the Pit. He wants to be happy, to cheer, because they're gone, like Dorothy to the Scarecrow and the Tin Woodsman and the Cowardly Lion, *they got away, they got away*; Preacher Man knows at once and He roars so loud the world rumbles and the pit rips wider, devours more of this place that is no place at all. The powderglass ground beneath his feet tilts and is turning, accelerating counterclockwise spiral down and down and the Pit yawns and belches, grinds its granite teeth.

And Preacher Man fills up the roiling floor joist sky, spreads His scrawny hard sermon arms as wide as that and the book is a blazing red sun bleeding out his voice. Ugly black things cling to His hands and face, biting things and Walter is on hands and bloody knees now, clambering for any hold, crawling as the earth shivers and goes powdery. And he remembers his wings, his beautiful charcoal wings, mockingbird boy, and that's why Preacher Man hates him, isn't it, and he tries to stand, spreads them wide, but the raining fire has scorched them raw, ragged feather scorch, and Preacher Man laughs and laughs and laughs.

"Come back with me," Spyder says, her hands around his wrists and Preacher Man looming over her shoulder. "It's gonna be all right now, Walter," but the world turns, water down a drain, down that mouth, and the earth tremoring so he can't even stand up.

"Help," he says, every time, and every time she smiles, soft and secret Spyder smile, nods and puts her arms around him so that Preacher Man howls and claws the sagging sky belly until it bleeds; the sour rain sticks to them like pine sap, turning the powdered ground to tar. "He won't let me leave, Spyder. He knows what I've seen, what I know . . ."

And she turns and stares up and into His face, like there's nothing to fear in those eyes, nothing that can pick her apart, strew her flesh to the winds and singe the bones, and she says, "He's not part of this," and "You can't have him." And the tattoos on her arms writhe electric blue loaded gun threat and now Preacher Man is not laughing. Now He takes a step backwards, puts the Pit between them, His protector, and His face is a rictus of rage and pain, and He is fury.

"Lila," He says, "What you've done to me, you'll burn in Hell forever." Voice of thunder and mountains splitting to spill molten bile. "What you've done to me, you'll burn until the end of Time."

And the blue fire flows from her, crackling static cage that He won't touch, and she's pulling Walter from the muck, hauling him across the shattered plains, days and days across the foothills with Preacher Man howling her damnation, her sentence, but Spyder doesn't look at Him again, ignores His promises. Drags Walter over the pus-seething caleche and stones that shriek like dying rabbits, stands between him and the rubbing-alcohol wind that whips up dust phantoms and throws burning tumbleweeds.

"Close your eyes, Walter," she says again and again, and at the end he does, because the long-legged things are so close, and he knows the climb's too steep, that he's too tired and she's too exhausted and their jaws drip the shearing sound of harvest . . .

. . . and he jerked awake, hard like hitting a wall, and the fat dude sitting across from him was staring. Walter wiped cold, oily sweat from his face, and the fat dude whispered, "Hey, buddy, if you need a fix, and you sure as hell *look* like you need a fix . . ." Walter shook his head, stumbled to his feet, and the basement hell was still more real than the predawn fluorescent glare of the bus station. He made it to the men's rest room, to a sink before he puked, sprayed half-digested McDonald's and coffee, heaved again and again until his insides cramped and ached, but his head was starting to clear and at least there was no one else in there to see.

He ran cold water in the next sink over, cold water in clean porcelain and splashed his face. Shivered and the roll of his stomach, braced himself, but it passed and he rubbed more of the gurgling water across his face. Looked up into the mirror and the long, bristling legs were draped limply over the door and sides of the stall just behind him. Every detail clear in the hateful light and something dripping onto the filthy tile underneath. The air smelled like cleanser and vomit and rot. Walter whirled around, so fast and him still dizzy so he almost fell and there was nothing there. Four silver stalls and no one and nothing in any of them.

"Christ!" he screamed, slammed the doors open one after the other, commodes and toilet paper dispensers and bus station shitter graffiti.

And the door opened and the fat man was staring at the sinkful of barfed-up cheeseburger and fries, shaking his head, "It's good shit, man, and you *are* hurtin'. I ain't no goddamn DEA man . . ." but Walter pushed past him and out the door, across the terminal to the Greyhound counter where the clerk glanced up at him from his receipts and claim slips. "Are you all right, Mister?" he said, reaching for the phone, "I can call you a doctor if you need a doctor."

Walter shook his head, trying to see through tears, the schedule behind the man's head and he dug his ticket out of his jacket pocket, laid it on the counter. "No," he said, "I just want to exchange this. Can I do that? Can I exchange this ticket for one to Birmingham?"

"It's cool with me, man," the clerk said, and took the old ticket to Chicago away.

4.

And the white-haired old woman who had always lived just across a kudzu patch, downhill and next door to Spyder, next door to Lila and her parents, to Spyder's grandparents before that: the old woman who'd lived there nearly sixty years, in the rambling big house her husband built in 1934, before he went away to Europe to be killed by the Nazis and buried in France: the old woman who spent her life alone, because she could never refill that empty place in her heart or soul, alone and watching the world fall apart around her: who had always kept her eyes open.

She woke up in the hospital-quiet hour before sunrise, same time she'd awakened every morning for decades, never mind the pills, the medication they gave her to keep her calm and make her sleep. She woke and the moment of disorientation stretched, fog in her head after the dream and this was not her bedroom, not her things around her. The strange ceiling and tubes leading from her arm and nose up to IV bottles and bags, wires to the glow of the machine that told her that her heart hadn't stopped, not yet, that made soft green peaks and valleys of her old pulse. In seventy-seven years, how many times does a heart beat? and she remembered where she was and remembered the squeezing pain in her chest and sighed, closed her papery-thin eyelids for a moment. But it was all still there when she opened them again, and her memories.

"For the love of Pete, what were you *doing* in the backyard that time of night?" her niece had asked, middle-aged woman who tried to look younger, "What were you doing out in the cold in your gown and slippers with that old shotgun in the first place?" Had asked her that question again and again, and always the old woman told her that she'd heard the possums or raccoons in her garbage again, or maybe it was dogs, she'd said. Shameful, people letting their dogs run loose and getting into the trash, strewing it all over, and it's shameful and her niece kept making that puppy sad face which meant she was thinking about nursing homes again.

Why were you out there? and for an answer she stared at the dark curtains, the dark places in the corners of the hospital room. Knew she wouldn't tell the truth, not about the shadows at her bedroom window or the sounds that had come out of the phone when she'd tried to call the police.

"It's a wonder you're not dead," her niece had said and yes, she'd answered, you get this old and it's always a wonder you're not dead.

"That's not what I meant and you know it."

She'd been dreaming about sitting with Trisha Baxter after her husband had died, sitting in the warm May sunshine outside Trisha's house, drinking Coca-Cola and talking about nothing in particular, just feeling the bubbles on her tongue, the sun on her face, watching Lila playing in the dirt with a toy soldier army.

And when Trisha had gone in to check something on the stove, the old woman noticed the web sparkling in the sun, beads of dew like honeysuckle nectar on every strand, and the huge yellow and black garden spider hanging head down in the center. Wrapping something in silk, spinning the little insect body around and around, hiding it away and only bumps and ridges so she knew it was a grasshopper in there; when she'd turned around again, Lila was watching her, watching her watch the spider, and there'd been blood in the shape of a cross on her forehead.

And Lila had smiled and held one finger to her little girl lips.

The old woman licked her dry lips and thought about buzzing for the nurse to bring her a paper cup of ice water.

"I don't want you keeping that old shotgun in the house anymore," her niece had said and she hadn't argued, because she knew she wouldn't be going back to Cullom Street, because the eyes that had watched her from the kudzu had only laughed at the gun anyway, laughed at her, bony old woman. Laughed harder when she'd tried to aim at the winterbare tangle of vines, her shaking hands and their eyes she could only see because they were blacker than the dark, because they were places where there was nothing else.

The old woman closed her eyes, listened to her tired heart, and waited for the sun to rise.

5.

Niki and Spyder went home by themselves, Niki driving and Spyder talking for a while and then dozing off. Spyder had put on a Doors tape, had seemed in better spirits than on the trip up, as if the mess back at Dante's had cheered her up. It had left Niki confused, embarrassed and feeling useless again, eager to get out of the way before things got any worse. Claude had gone home with some friends he'd met at the club, said he'd get a ride back to Birmingham later, and Niki hadn't seen Daria again after they'd left the stage, had only talked to Theo. Theo like a human teakettle, so pissed she gritted her teeth and spoke through clenched jaws. Niki knew that Keith had taken off, and Theo said it was all his fault, because he was a junky, that Daria had finally kicked him out of the band and it was about goddamn time.

Niki blinked, nodded, too sleepy, reminding herself to get off at the next exit for coffee, sour convenience-store coffee, but maybe it would keep her awake until they got home. Jim Morrison singing "Riders on the Storm," and that song always gave her the creeps so she reached over and popped the tape out of the deck. Looked back at the road, broken yellow line tease and she rubbed her eyes. Spyder stirred in her sleep, dream mumbled, and Niki thought about waking her up, making her talk.

Let her sleep. God, she hardly ever just falls asleep without the pills, and Niki's eyelids fluttered, snapped open and fluttered halfmast again.

And something in the road, then, something big and dark that seemed to be moving slowly ahead of them, just inches ahead of the Celica's headlights; something too big to be real, but she snapped awake, full awake in a second and swearing, cut the steering wheel sharp to miss it and the tires crunched breakdown lane gravel as the car rushed past and over the spot where the thing would have been, if it had been anything but her exhausted eyes, weary, sleep-hungry mind.

Spyder opened her eyes and squinted at the road in front of them.

"What happened?" and Niki shook her head, "Nothing," she said, "I was half asleep and thought I saw an animal in the road . . ."

"What kind of animal?" Spyder asked and pushed The Doors tape back in.

"It was just my imagination," Niki said, but she was sweating and there were chillbumps under her clothes; suddenly even Jim Morrison's ghostly rumble seemed better than being awake alone with the cold Alabama night all around her.

"Stay awake for me," she said. "Talk to me, okay?" and Spyder nodded, sure, reached over and gently kneaded the knotted muscles at the base of Niki's neck with her strong fingers.

"It might have been a deer," she said, and Niki said, "Yeah, maybe so," and kept her eyes open for exit signs.

CHAPTER TWELVE

The Mules That Angels Ride

1.

Wham, wham, wham, and Niki woke up from a soft dream of the French Quarter and a girl telling her fortune with an oversized, dogeared pack of tarot cards, pretty girl in goth whiteface and eyeliner, *And this card,* she'd said, *this card, well, you* know *this card.* Woke up, groggy and she rubbed her eyes, realized she was cold and the bedspread was gone, and Spyder was gone, nothing left but the sheets.

Wham. Wham.

The rusty old alarm clock on the floor said a quarter past three and she closed her eyes again. Sunday afternoon; it had been sometime after dawn when she'd finally dozed off, after the long drive back from Atlanta and then sex, good sex even though she'd really been too sleepy.

Wham.

"Spyder?" she called, but no one answered her. "Is that you, Spyder? Christ, what the hell are you doing in there? Hanging pictures?"

She wanted to go back to sleep, wanted the girl in black lace and fishnets on her slender arms to finish the reading, turn over all her cards, wanted to feel the warm Gulf breeze instead of the clinging cold of the bedroom. Wanted the bedspread back and Spyder with it, Spyder warm around her, warm as any tropical evening.

"Spyder?"

Wham. Wham.

"Shit," and Niki ran her fingers through her hair,

shaggy mop she'd been thinking of cutting off short
again, kept meaning to ask Spyder if she cared or not.
She kicked the sheets away and slipped out of bed, bare
feet on the cold floorboards and she looked around for
her socks, none to be seen so she just tiptoed instead.
Out of the bedroom and it was even colder in the foyer,
tiptoed across to the living room but still no Spyder. The
television on and the sound turned down all the way,
silent MTV nonsense, gangsta rap pantomime; she had
to pee.

And there was the missing bedspread, huge white
crocheted thing stretched trampoline tight and hanging
in the air in the next room, the old dining room full of
Spyder's books; she stopped and rubbed her eyes. She
could see where two corners had been nailed directly to
the wall, big nails driven into the peeling wallpaper and
a third corner stretched over to a crooked shelf and held
in place with stacks of *World Book* encyclopedias. The
fourth was out of sight, around the corner, *wham,
wham,* and she knew if she stepped out into the middle
of the living room she'd see Spyder in there, hammer-
ing it to the other wall. But she didn't, too curious; Niki
knew that whatever Spyder was doing, she'd probably
stop the second she asked.

"Oh," Spyder would say, "nothing," so Niki kept her
mouth shut and watched.

An instant later and Spyder stepped into view, wearing nothing but the Alien Sex Fiend t-shirt she'd put on
after they'd made love, the shirt she slept in a lot but
never washed so it always smelled like sweat and
patchouli. Spyder was holding a bowling ball, a black
bowling ball with red swirls in it, so it sort of looked
like she was holding a strange little gas planet, ebony
and crimson Neptune; she held it out over the center of
the bedspread, set it carefully in the middle. The whole
thing sagged with the weight of the bowling ball,
sagged in the center until it was only about a foot off the
floor, but it didn't pull loose from the walls; Spyder
ducked underneath, came out the other side and she
stacked more encyclopedias to hold the corner that

wasn't nailed. She didn't notice Niki, standing alone in the TV glare.

Spyder disappeared, toolbox sounds, and when Niki could see her again, she had a fat black marker in her left hand, a yardstick in her right; she leaned over the bedspread, measured distance, colored careful dots, measured, black on the white cotton here and there, beginning near the edge and working her way in, toward the sucking weight of the bowling ball. Thirty, forty, forty-three dots and she set the yardstick and the marker on the floor, then, gone again and this time she came back with a blue plastic butter tub of ball bearings, different sizes, like steel marbles. She dug around, selected one, as if only that one would do, and placed it on the first black mark she'd drawn. The ball bearing made its own small depression in the bedspread before it started to roll downhill; Niki heard the distinct clack of steel against epoxy when it hit the bowling ball, loud sound in the still, quiet house.

Spyder selected another ball bearing and placed it on the next mark, clack, and she repeated the action over and over, clack, clack, clack, but never twice from the same mark, choosing each bearing and taking care to be sure it started its brief journey toward the center from the next mark in. Sometimes she paused between ball bearings, paused and stared at the bedspread, out the window and then back. Once or twice she stopped long enough to measure the shrinking space between the floor and the bowling ball with her yardstick. Spyder chewed at her bottom lip, something urgent in her blue eyes.

Niki's legs were getting tired and she wanted to sit down, too afraid of interrupting to even move. Her kneecaps were starting to ache. She wanted to say, "What the hell are you doing, Spyder?" What anyone else *would* have said right at the start, but then she'd never have seen even this much, and just because it didn't make any sense, that didn't mean it wasn't important. And if Spyder wouldn't tell her what was going on, all she could do was ignore her stiffening legs, be patient, watch, figure it all out for herself. Like a puzzle, like a child's dot-to-dot. Draw the lines and there's the picture, Mickey Mouse or a bouquet of flowers or whatever drove Spyder crazy.

There weren't many bearings left in the tub and Spyder had to lean way over to set them on the marks now, hardly any time after she let go before the clack of metal against hard plastic. The bedspread was almost touching the floor, and Niki could see where the weave was beginning to ravel from all that weight. Spyder worked like she was running out of time, just one or two bearings to go; Niki had to piss so bad she was afraid she was gonna have to show herself soon or wet the floor.

The last ball bearing glinted in Spyder's hand, dull reflection of the sun through the window, and there was a slow ripping sound. Spyder grabbed something off the floor, a moment before Niki saw it was a roll of duct tape, used her teeth to tear off a strip and she was reaching for the rift opening beneath the bowling ball when the bedspread tore all the way open, dropped everything out the bottomside. The bowling ball fell three or four inches, *thud* and barely missed crushing Spyder's fingers. Niki felt the vibration where she stood watching as the ball bearings spilled out and rolled away in every direction.

"Fuck," Spyder whispered and then she sat silently beneath the ruined bedspread and stared at the hole, the last ball bearing forgotten in her fingers.

One of the silver balls rolled into the living room, bumped to a stop against Niki's foot. She bent down and picked it up, not caring now if Spyder saw her or not, knowing whatever was happening had happened. One word, printed around the circumference of the bearing, one word that didn't mean anything to Niki, but she thought maybe she was starting to understand the whole thing, the dot-to-dot secret, the marks Spyder had drawn for her, and she wondered what was written on that last one, the one Spyder still held. And she realized Spyder was crying, softly, and went to her.

2.

Monday, another lazy short day that the winter-brilliant sun, warm and washed-out honey, made lazier, took its own sweet time getting up over the top of the mountain. Filtered down through the trees, all those TV towers, into the house, first the windows on the east side where Spyder and Niki were still sleeping sometime after noon. Spyder woke first, her arms around Niki, holding her close and the sun hung itself on the wall over them, big yellow-orange splotch like a saint's nimbus or halo and Spyder watched it closely, suspicious. Niki was snoring, not a loud ragged boy snore but the sort of sound a cat makes if its sleep is uneasy, and Spyder held her tighter.

She could feel the world still slipping away around her, not the jolts that had come at first; slow, steady creep now that didn't ever stop, or slow down, or get any faster, no matter how hard she held on. No matter that she sealed up the room. No matter that she watched the trapdoor to the basement to be sure it stayed closed. Spyder looked away from the sun spot on the wall, buried her face in the clean smell of Niki's hair. Robin's hair had always smelled of ammonia, hair dye, and Niki's hair just smelled clean, like hair and baby shampoo.

"Wake up," she whispered, too quiet to actually wake Niki, pressed her lips against an earlobe, gently tested the steel rings there with her teeth.

"Wake up, Niki," a little louder this time, just a little, and Niki mumbled something through her sleep and curled into a smaller fetus. Spyder kissed a spot on her cheek, next to her ear, felt the downy hairs there brush her own rough lips.

And that sensation again, less and less time between them every day, dizzy naked feeling, like she was falling and there was absolutely nothing anywhere beneath her, or above, like she'd fall forever. Spyder squeezed Niki, held on, waiting it out, the sensation, the sudden, hollow certainty, perception her doctors would have called delusion, or just panic attacks and tell her to take more pills to make it stop. And she wanted it to stop, but she wanted it to stop because it was over, because she'd found a way back, a way to put everything back right again, didn't just want to take pills that made it harder to feel, harder to trust what she felt and saw and heard, and knew.

And then it was gone again and there was only Niki in her arms and the sun on the wall, the itch beneath her skin that she couldn't ever reach.

"Niki," she said. "Wake up, please," and this time Niki rolled over and stared up at Spyder. Sleepy dumb grin and she rubbed at her eyes.

"Hi there," she said and nuzzled against Spyder's t-shirt, nuzzled in between Spyder's breasts. "What time is it?"

"I don't know," Spyder said. "Not too late, I don't think. Are you hungry?"

"Mhmmm," and Niki kissed her, slipped her tongue quick between Spyder's teeth and she was still surprised, even though Niki had kissed her so many times, and it still made her think about Robin and feel guilty.

"I meant for food," she said and Niki kissed her again, put her hands underneath Spyder's shirt, small cold hands against Spyder's chest, waking up her nipples, making them hard. "Coffee," Niki said and Spyder frowned.

"I don't drink coffee."

"Never mind then," and now her head was under the shirt, making Mr. Fiend's face bulge way out like he was pulling himself free of the cloth and silkscreen ink. Niki's mouth, warm and wet around her left nipple, teasing tongue, tooth play and Spyder kissed the top of her head through the shirt.

Niki sucked her nipple harder, wrapped both arms around firm muscle and the little bit of fat on Spyder's belly. Spyder let her own hands wander down Niki's back, no shirt in the way, just a bra strap before the small of her back, skin like satin, so much softer than Robin, no hard edges, no bones showing through.

And instead of the bottomless feeling, Spyder felt something else, something almost like the way she'd once felt with them all here around her, like things *might* be all right, if she could be sane a little while, careful, and then Niki's fingers were inside her boxers, tangling themselves in her thick pubic hair, her sex cupped in Niki's hand like fruit. Aching tingle when Niki's middle finger brushed her labia, velvet probe, and then slipped inside. Spyder shivered and there was simply no way to hold Niki close enough, to take her in and bind that sense of security, of oneness and belonging, so it wouldn't bleed away, wouldn't desert her, leave her dangling between the nowheres above and below and within when it was over, soon, when Niki pulled her hand away, pulled her head from under the shirt and went to make coffee. Everything was always already over before it began.

Niki laughed beneath the bulgy shirt and switched to Spyder's right nipple.

"Niki," Spyder said, "You're not gonna leave, when you get tired of the sex, or . . ." and then she didn't say anything more, wished she'd kept her mouth shut. Niki's tongue had stopped, and she pulled her head out, didn't take her hand away from Spyder's crotch, though. Her hair stuck out all over, static and bedhair, her dark, deep eyes, not hurt or pissed, wide and a little sleepy and no deceit in there that Spyder could see.

"I wasn't planning on it," she said, pretended to frown.

And Spyder looked back up at the sun on the wall, an inch or two lower, maybe, like the hand of a clock, sand in glass, nothing left behind as it passed. Except a cooling place if she put her fingers to the wall above it.

"I'm sorry," she said. "I know you're not *thinking* about going anywhere. Everyone always acts like it's gonna be forever, but nobody ever thinks about forever. We were gonna be together forever, Niki. I mean, me and Robin and Byron and Walter, like a family. Like a tribe . . ."

"I'm okay, Spyder," Niki said, and the way she said

it, Spyder could almost believe she knew what she was talking about. "*We're* gonna be okay, too."

"I want to tell you some things," and now Niki's hand did move away, left Spyder empty and damp between the legs, but she kept talking. "Not yet, but maybe tomorrow. Maybe soon. They're not good things, but maybe if we both know them . . ." and then she was too afraid to say any more and so she just stared at the sun on the wall, slipping down, like the world was slipping down. Falling, like the world was falling.

"Anytime," Niki said. "Anytime you're ready, I'll listen. And I'll still be here when you're done."

"We shouldn't make promises," Spyder said, "It's bad luck, I think."

*   *   *

The second time Spyder woke up, the sun was down, twilight tuned down almost to night and she could smell Red Diamond coffee and something cooking. She reached for Niki, but she was alone in the bed, and the spot on the sheets where Niki had curled next to her was cold. Like nothing could be left behind but body heat and the vaguest impression of arms and legs and heads in pillows. Spyder crawled out of bed and pulled on a pair of old Levi's, one of the buttonholes on the fly busted so her plaid boxers showed underneath.

She found Niki sitting cross-legged on the kitchen floor, some of Spyder's tools scattered around her. "Hey, sleeping beauty," Niki said and Spyder poked her in the ribs with a big toe. Niki slapped her foot and went back to what she was doing, stripping black rubber insulation from copper telephone wire with a pair of needle-nosed pliers, straightening the strands of wire again.

"I'm pretty sure I can fix this," she said.

Spyder didn't comment, went to the stove and lifted the lid on one of the pots.

"I found a bag of pinto beans in the cabinet, and a can of turnip greens," Niki said, began twisting the severed ends of the phone line back together. "Too bad we don't have stuff to make cornbread."

"Do you know what you're doing?" and Spyder tasted the pintos, added black pepper to the pot; Niki had already begun covering the spliced wire with electrical tape.

"I think so," she said. "I mean, it may not be the clearest connection in the world, but I think it'll at least work again."

"I wasn't talking about the phone," Spyder said. "You have to put salt in these, you know?"

Niki stopped and looked at her.

"And some onion wouldn't have hurt, neither. I thought people from New Orleans knew how to cook beans?"

"Yeah, Spyder. Whenever I wasn't too busy listening to the blues or chasing alligators down the street, I was cooking beans."

Spyder opened the refrigerator, began digging around behind six-packs of Buffalo Rock and Diet Coke cans, foil-covered leftovers, for the onion she remembered having seen a day or so before, found a little cardboard carton of mealie worms instead; she took it out and set it on the table. "I thought I threw these out," and she shook the carton, *shsssk-shsssk* rattle of sawdust and grubs. "I bet they're all dead by now, anyway," and she put them back in the fridge.

"Christ, Spyder. Please don't put dead worms in the refrigerator."

"I'll throw them away later," trying not to think about what the unused, uneaten mealies really meant, what they'd followed from and signified; she found the onion, white onion almost as big as her fist, hiding behind an old carton of buttermilk.

Niki stood up and dusted off her butt, lifted the receiver and held it against her ear. "Wow," she said, proud voice, "I did it. I fixed the phone." Spyder shut the fridge and clapped for her, smiled when Niki curtsied.

The receiver back in its cradle and immediately the black telephone rang. "Jesus," Niki said. "That's some good fucking timing, huh?" started to get it and "No," Spyder said. "No, Niki, don't answer it."

"Why? I just fixed it. That's probably someone that's been trying to call us for days."

"I don't care. Just let it ring."

Niki stared at the phone, strident box of noise on the wall; Spyder carried her onion over to the sink, ran cold water over the papery skin before she began to peel it. After the eleventh ring, the phone was silent.

"Are you gonna answer it next time?" Niki asked, sounding confused, disappointed, and Spyder shrugged, tossed the empty onion skin at the garbage. "Probably," she said, opened a drawer next to the sink and rummaged through the jumble of utensils and silverware inside until she found the knife she was looking for.

She sliced the onion on the counter, not bothering to get down the cutting board, not caring if she scratched the wood. So many scratches there already. Most of them there since she'd been a child and she'd never understood why her mother had always been so careful not to add any more.

"I was just trying to help," Niki said behind her. "You should've said something, if you didn't want me to fix the phone."

And then it rang again, third slice through the onion and Spyder almost cut her hand.

"Do you want me to answer it?" Niki asked.

Spyder finished slicing the onion, three more slices, three more rings, rinsed the knife under the tap. She carried a double-handful of onion to the stove and added it to the boiling pot of beans. And then she answered the phone, because she knew it was useless not to, just like she'd known precisely when the bedspread was going to tear, which ball bearing she'd be left holding, just like that.

"You don't have to," but she only stared at Niki, put the receiver to her own ear, spoke slowly into the mouthpiece. "Hello?" and nothing at first from the other end except traffic sounds, pay phone sounds that made her think of Byron and she almost hung up.

"Spyder?" Niki whispered and right after, in her ear, the familiar boy voice, "Spyder? Is that you?"

She pretended not to recognize him, watched the pots on the stovetop, the steam rising from the pintos. "Yeah, it's me."

"I know you probably don't want to hear from me," he said, Walter's nervous voice and he was at least half-wrong. Part of her wanted to hear him very bad, wanted to cry and smile and tell him how much she missed him, how she missed them all. Wanted to tell him none of it mattered anymore, not enough to justify the loneliness.

"So why are you calling me," she said and there was nothing through the line for a moment except the sound of him breathing, the backdrop of street noise.

"I left, Spyder. I got almost all the way to Chicago and came back," he said. "I've been riding goddamned buses for days and I have to know what's happening, Spyder. I think it's not gonna stop it from happening, or even stop me from going crazy, but I have to know, anyway. I have to know if all that shit Robin and Byron made up still means anything."

Niki took her other hand, held it tight, silently mouthed two words that might have been *I'm sorry*.

"Nothing's happening," Spyder said. "Nothing at all. Don't call me again, Walter."

"Please, Spyder. Please don't hang up on me. Christ, I'm fucking *seeing* things and I can't sleep anymore . . ."

"I've got to go. There's something on the stove."

"I'm scared shitless," he said.

"I'm sorry," and she hung up, shook her hand free of Niki's and went to the back door, out into the night, down the back steps and the screen banged shut behind her. Past the place where the kudzu came down from the mountain and swallowed the edge of the yard. No shoes and the leafsoft ground damp underfoot, rocks and sticks painful sharp, but she kept walking, climbing the hill, until the dark had wrapped itself all the way around her.

3.

The next morning, Tuesday, Niki sat alone on the back stoop of Spyder's house. No sleep all night, though she'd tried for a little while, had eaten supper by herself and then climbed into their thrift store bed, pulled the covers around her, left the light in the foyer burning and the bedroom door open so she wouldn't be in the dark room alone. But there'd been too much emptiness, inside and out, too much worry over Spyder and the memories waiting for her, and finally she'd started imagining that she was hearing noises under the floor, scritchy rat sounds and if she listened hard enough, the incessant mumble of voices, no single speaker but the softest curtain of indecipherable words and phrases, crowd mutter, and after a while she'd gotten up again, drunk coffee in the kitchen until dawn.

Now she stared at the gray tangle of the mountainside and cursed herself again, for not going after Spyder right away. For fixing the telephone in the first place. For not being perfect, not even close. She tried to concentrate, watching for any sign of movement, any evidence that Spyder was on her way back. She didn't like those trees, so close together and all those bare limbs that seemed to strain her way, crooked fingers restless in the cold wind, or the vines strung between them, drooping down to the ground, a sea of vines that she guessed was a smothering green sea of kudzu in the summer.

Spyder had told her it wasn't a good idea to go wandering around up there alone, especially at night or if you didn't know the woods already. Because there were a lot of old mine shafts and sinkholes that no one had marked or sealed up, deep pits left from the days when the mountain had been tunneled out for its iron ore bones.

"But they're really pretty neat, if you're careful," she'd said. "I'll show you one sometime. They're full of bats and I'll show you where to catch the biggest salamanders."

Niki wondered if Spyder was hiding in one of those old shafts now, or if maybe she'd stumbled into one of them in the night, if she'd been too upset to watch where she was walking and had fallen, had broken her leg or hit her head and couldn't get back.

"Christ, this is crazy," standing up, buttoning her army jacket, stomping her feet to warm up a little, get the blood flowing again. And then she walked to the edge of the yard, crunching over the frosted ground, stood ankle deep in kudzu vines and called into the trees, "Spyder? Spyder, can you hear me?" Somewhere down the hill a dog began to bark, and another one, farther away.

"Spyder!"

She looked back at the house, wanting to be inside, safe in its comfortable warmth and disorder, safe in bed with Spyder, turned back to the trees, the vines like a slumping wall before the copperhead mat of leaves began farther in. Took another step and this time her leg sunk in up to the knee and she almost lost her balance; off to her left, something rustled beneath the vines. "Jesus, Spyder, there's no telling what's living under all this shit."

Nothing to be afraid of, though. Rats maybe, possums or raccoons. Stray cats. Nothing that won't get out of your way if you just make a little racket.

"Spyder? I'm coming to look for you, okay?" and that sounded stupid, stupid as she felt wading around in dead kudzu at seven-thirty in the morning.

"It's okay," and Niki almost screamed, actually opened her mouth to scream before she saw Spyder huddled in the shelter of some fallen logs; narrow pocket in the vines like a child's teepee of quilts and blankets.

"I'm right here."

No coat, short sleeves and bare feet, and Niki thought she could see the white glitter of frost on Spyder's tattooed arms. "You've got to be freezing to death," she said, took another step and went in up to her waist this time.

"You can't get across that way. There's a ditch there."

"Great. Fucking wonderful," tried to plow her way through anyway, stopped when the vines were level with her chest and began to trace her way back out again, wishing she could quit thinking about everything that might be lurking in the kudzu, watching the half of her body she couldn't see, beady mean eyes that didn't mind the always-dark down there, red eyes, sharp white teeth.

"So where the hell *do* I get across?" and when Spyder didn't answer, Niki looked over her shoulder, caught Spyder staring up into the branches overhead, and she followed, like eyes could be a pointing finger, up, through the snarl and strangle, the draping leafless kudzu, up and there, maybe seven or eight feet off the ground, what Spyder was seeing. Niki rubbed at her eyes, rubbed them like a cartoon character to be sure it was real, those dangling arms and legs, limp and somehow stiff at the same time, sunken, black sockets where his eyes had been open wide and his mouth open even wider than that.

"Oh," and she felt like someone had punched her in the gut, had knocked the breath out of her, "Oh god, Spyder."

"How are we ever gonna get him down?" Spyder said, said the words so quietly that Niki almost didn't catch them. "I've been sitting here trying to figure that out, Niki, how to get him down."

Niki struggled, fought her way out of the kudzu and vomited in the frozen grass, puked coffee and mostly digested supper and the mess steamed in the morning shadows.

"Fuck," she said, over and over, and there was no way to stop seeing that face, the most frightened face she'd ever seen, no way to pretend it wasn't a dead face, no way not to see Danny Boudreaux up there. No way to get back to the moment before she'd turned around and looked.

No way except straight ahead.

"Spyder," and she had to stop, wait until the nausea

passed, and then, "I'm gonna go back to the house and call some help, okay?"

"No, Niki. You can't do that," a little louder now, a little urgent, "No one's ever gonna understand, not after Robin. I don't want to go to jail."

"Go to jail? Spyder, you didn't do that!"

Spyder didn't reply, gazed up at the dead boy in the tree like she was waiting for him to do something besides just hang there.

"I *have* to call the police, Spyder. He's *dead*."

"Then calling the cops won't make him any less dead, will it? You can come across down there," and she pointed to a spot a few yards away. It didn't look any different from the place Niki had tried to cross; she wiped her mouth, spit again.

"He's dead, Spyder. He's fucking dead."

"Yeah. I thought he'd just left town. I thought maybe he'd gone to Atlanta."

"Okay, well, then that's all you have to tell the police when they ask."

"We're not calling the cops, Niki," so final there was no way to argue, not now, anyway; nothing to do but go to the place she'd pointed, go to Spyder and get her inside before she froze to death or caught pneumonia. The wind rattled through the trees, dry, hungry rattle, and she realized the dogs were still barking.

Her feet only disappeared a little past the ankles this time, and the ground creaked beneath her shoes, tired wood creak, glimpses of weathered planks through the growth and Niki realized she was walking on some sort of bridge, probably rotten, and she tried not to think about that, either. Tried to think about nothing but getting Spyder out of the cold.

"Watch out," Spyder said. "There's a stump hole there," and then Niki was standing next to her, standing directly under the body in the tree.

"Maybe if we just pull on the vines . . ."

"I think we should go inside now, Spyder. At least warm you up a little bit. Get your boots and coat."

" . . . together. I tried it, but maybe if we were both pulling, the vines would come loose."

"We shouldn't do that," and she caught a hint of something bad on the air, ripe, meaty smell, and she told herself that it was too cold for the body to be rotting up there, knew that was total horseshit.

"You wouldn't say that, if he'd been your friend. I can't leave him there."

"If he was my friend, Spyder . . ." and whatever she was about to say, whatever was true and wanted to be said, no need for Spyder to hear it, and instead, "If he was my friend, I'd call the police."

Spyder stood, her feet raw, chapped pink, the palms of her hands the same color, the same painful shade across her forehead, under her eyes, around her mouth. But not a hint of frostbite gray, as far as Niki could tell; that was something, at least, something to hang onto. One way this could be worse.

Spyder grabbed onto one of the vines and pulled; Niki heard the limbs creak, the same grating sound the old boards over the ditch had made, same straining sound that might have been the last thing Danny heard after he stepped off the chair in his kitchen. "Help me, Niki," and "Spyder," she said, "Please," but Spyder only pulled that much harder, frowned and chewed her lower lip.

"If I could just reach his feet," she said.

The soles of the boy's shoes, swaying now because of all the yanking Spyder was doing on the vines, a bit of gravel wedged between the treads, a yellow-green wad of hardened gum. The vine felt utterly alien in Niki's hands, dried tendons from an alien corpse, something big as the mountain, old as the world. She pulled and way up high there were popping sounds, rippings, and Spyder jerked so hard Niki could see where the skin on her fingers was cracking open, beginning to bleed.

"And what are we supposed to do with him if we ever do get him down?"

Spyder put all her weight on the vine, lifted herself

off the ground a couple of inches. Loud crack and bits of oak bark fell from the sky, peppered their heads.

"We put him inside, where no one'll see."

Niki followed her example, cringed when the body sank a little closer to them.

"What then? I mean, you don't think you can keep him in there very long, do you? It's a corpse, Spyder. Sooner or later . . ."

"He'll have to be buried," Spyder said, and Niki didn't say anything else. Didn't want to hear any more of this. She tugged until her arms ached, white clouds of breath from the exertion, the cold making her sinuses hurt. And then the vines just let go, sudden slack in her hands and the body tumbled towards them, almost landed on top of her; he lay slumped against the trunk of the tree, head lolled forward now, one arm across his lap, legs splayed like the Scarecrow from *The Wizard of Oz* and she recognized him, the boy she'd watched across the smoky cave of Dr. Jekyll's. He'd been so wary that night, so pretty; the flesh around his eye sockets was tattered, torn and shredded by the careless beaks of hungry birds, but the face still looked wary. Scared and wary and sad.

"I can't do this," and Spyder shrugged. "Then go back to the house. I can carry him in alone."

She almost did, left Spyder to do this crazy, awful thing herself, left her to deal with that face, the hollows where his eyes had been. Spyder squatted beside him, brushed black hair from his face.

"No," Niki said. "I can't let you do this by yourself. Let's do it, now, before someone sees us up here."

"Oh, Byron," Spyder whispered, "I'm so sorry."

When she was ready, they carried the dead boy across the plank bridge and down to the house.

* * *

Spyder laid him on the kitchen table, asked Niki to get a washcloth from the bathroom, please, something to clean his hands and face with, to scrub away the dirt, the gore on his gray cheeks. His legs hung off the end, deadweight pendulums, but Spyder carefully arranged his arms at his sides so they wouldn't flop over the edge. Niki obediently brought her a washcloth, glad for something so simple to do, for those few moments filled with the imperfect illusion of sanity; Spyder soaked the cloth with warm water from the kitchen sink, wrung it out, and started to clean his face.

"We have to call the police now," and Niki was standing right by the phone, only had to lift the receiver and dial 911, but Spyder shook her head, wiped at a rust-colored stain on the side of his nose.

"No police, Niki. Didn't I already say no police?"

Niki looked at the phone, sick of the flat, helpless feeling, sick of walking on eggshells for Spyder, crazy Spyder, and this was going too far, humoring her this time, this was where she had to *do* something.

"I'm not asking your permission," as she reached for the telephone, "I'm just telling you what I have to do. You're not thinking straight right now."

And for an answer, Spyder set the washcloth down and picked up the big carving knife still lying on the counter where she'd sliced the onion the night before, stepped past Niki and made a loop of the bandaged phone cord, slipped the knife inside, electrical tape pulled tight around the blade.

"Put it down," she said, no malice in her, nothing but promise, and Niki understood the rest, put it down or there won't be a goddamned telephone to discuss, and the knife aimed straight at her heart.

"Spyder," and the cord pulled tighter, then, only a little more pressure and the blade would cut them off from the world again.

"When do I ever 'think straight,' huh? I'm taking my meds, and aren't they supposed to make me 'think straight'?"

"That's not what I meant and you know it," but she hung the phone up, stepped back, more distance between her and the knife, and Spyder glanced down at it. "Jesus, Niki, is that what you think? That I would ever hurt you?"

"Sometimes I don't know what to think anymore."

"If that's what you think of me, you don't understand any of this. If that's what you think, you should just get the hell out of here now," words pushed out hard and fast, indifferent cold melting away, and she dropped the cord, hurled the knife at the sink, and plates, dirty glasses and coffee cups shattered there.

"Everything got messed up, Niki. You weren't here so I don't expect you to know what I'm talking about. I tried to make it right again but I couldn't. This is all I can do for him. It's the last thing left and I have to do it."

"How am I supposed to understand when you won't tell me *anything,* Spyder? Am I just supposed to stand around and watch you mess your life up worse? Screw mine up with it? I do know that none of this is your fault."

"You don't know," Spyder said, like a sentence handed down, final judgment, *you don't know,* and she picked up the washcloth again, went to the sink, steaming water over glass and china shards, the window over the sink fogged opaque and she went back to Byron.

"I don't know how to help you," and Niki was crying now, hating herself for it, but she could not be this tired and scared, scared for her and Spyder, for them both separate and together, and not cry. Spyder began rubbing at the stubborn stain again, and already the kitchen was beginning to smell like death, sweet putrid death like bad meat and wilted flowers. Like breakdown, patient decay, disintegration.

"You can't help me. This isn't about you. Everything isn't about you, Niki," and Niki turned and ran, through the house and back to their bedroom, threw herself down on the bed and gave in to the tears, the exhaustion and rage. Her own madness inside and the certainty that Spyder was right; nothing she could do but intrude, act more like Spyder's nursemaid than her lover, or sit back and watch, wait for this shit to play itself out. She found Spyder's Klonopin on the floor by her side of the bed, pastel blue tablets inside amber plastic, had to wrestle a moment with the childproof cap: she swallowed one of the pills and put them back, wrapped her arms tight around Spyder's pillow, heavy feather pillow and its dingy, lemon-yellow pillowcase, as if cotton and the musky stink of old feathers could be Spyder. And she closed her eyes and cried herself to sleep.

4.

A long dream of candlelight on earthen walls and Jackson Square, the girl with her tarot deck again and still Niki didn't see the whole spread, *that card,* dream within a dream toward the end, that night on the beach in North Carolina, the strange girl named Jenny Dare, and Niki woke up slow, drifted up from the smell of salt spray and fish and the girl's wet clothes. Groggy and her mouth too dry, headache, and she remembered taking the Klonopin, that this must be what the doctor had called "rebound," like a hangover from the long benzodiazepine sleep. And then she remembered it all and wished she could close her eyes and forget again. Instead, she sat up, dizzy and so she leaned against the headboard and stared at the windows; not dark yet, but dusk, almost night.

Someone had undressed her—no, not someone, Spyder—had gotten her out of the bulky army coat and it hung on a bedpost now, and there was quiet music playing on the portable CD player, Dead Can Dance, cellos and violins, Lisa Gerrard's calming, ethereal vocals; the covers had been pulled up around her.

She could hear the television playing, too, a game show filtered through the walls. She stood up, cautious, distrusting her throbbing head, her rubbery arms and legs. No wonder Spyder hated taking this shit so much.

She turned off the music, set on repeat and no telling how many times the album had played through, getting into her sleep, coloring her dreams. The house was freezing and she guessed Spyder had turned off the heat. Niki slipped the coat on, zipped it closed, and went to find Spyder.

* * *

Spyder had not put on warmer clothes, too hot from the hours of work and finally she had stripped off the t-shirt and jeans, sat on the kitchen floor now wearing nothing but her boxers, sweat drying stickyfast on her pale skin. Watching Byron on the table, the package he had become, wrapped up tight. She'd started with plain white thread, four big spools she'd found in an old sewing box that had been her mother's, round and round his face after she'd stuffed the empty eye sockets with cotton wads from Tylenol bottles. And then she used the other colors, black and red and bright Kelly green, and she'd had to switch to yarn, orange and gold the color of grain around his narrow shoulders, and after that nylon fishing line and torn bed sheets and tape, whatever she could find, incorporated into the binding.

She'd been thorough, and no glimpse of skin showed through. His raggedy, filthy clothes were folded and placed together neatly by the body, ruined clothes and his shoes. She thought he might be safe this way, safe from her and the things the house remembered because of her. Safe from the sounds that had begun an hour ago, the things that made the sounds, bonemetal scrape and papery rustle from the basement below.

And she'd drawn a circle around the table, as perfect a circle as she could draw, crystal powder white of Morton's iodized table salt.

"Safe from me," she whispered, hugged the dream catcher close. Half an hour earlier, she'd pulled it off the boards nailed over her old bedroom door. Had carefully unwound each black strand of Byron's hair and laid them on his chest. Now the dream catcher was fraying, undone, lessened by subtraction and her busy fingers.

"Oh, Spyder. What have you done?" and she looked up: Niki standing in the doorway, beautiful confusion, rumpled clothes and hair, bags beneath her dark eyes, eyes puffy from sleep or crying or both.

"If I tell you," Spyder said, "you have to promise,

you have to fucking *swear* to me, that you're never gonna tell anyone else. No matter what happens, you'll never tell anyone else a single, solitary word of it." But Niki didn't promise, looked back and forth, from the pathetic cocooned shape on the kitchen table to Spyder sitting on the floor, like neither could be real, like there was a choice to make between them.

"I want you to go back to the hospital," finally, and Spyder said no, laughed and said no again.

"Please, Spyder. Jesus, you're frightening me." Niki took a step closer, moved so slow, one small step and another and she kneeled, close enough that Spyder could reach out and touch her now, would have if it could have done anything but make things worse; for a second, Spyder thought she smelled jasmine, maybe, but it was only the cleansers or bug spray under the sink.

"I'm not trying to scare you. I don't want to scare you."

"Well, you are. You've got me scared shitless."

"I'm sorry. I am sorry." She laid one hand palm up on the floor, empty, so Niki could take it if she chose.

"It's not too late to work this shit out, to get you out of here," and Niki did take her hand, squeezed it, twined their fingers together, weave of Spyder's pale, chilled flesh and Niki's duskywarm flesh. "I think maybe this house is making you sick, Spyder. Or keeping you from getting any better. Too much bad shit's happened to you here. It's no wonder you can't stop thinking about it."

It's not even half that simple, but all Spyder said was, "It's been too late for a long time," and Niki frowned, heat lightning flash of anger across her face and sudden anger behind her words, "Don't give me that crap, goddammit. I don't want to hear it. All you have to do is get up and let me take you to the hospital."

Spyder shook her head, let go of Niki's hand; the separation hurt, physical pain and pain inside that was worse, pulling away from the last bit of warmth in the world.

"Do you still want to hear what I was gonna say or not? I won't tell you if you don't."

"I want to *help* you, Spyder."

"Then listen, 'cause I don't think there's anything else you can do."

Spyder saw the moment clear in Niki's eyes, swollen moment of decision; saw it come like the shadows before a summer thundershower, lingering, sweet rain scent and ozone and the hair on your arms and the back of your neck prickling from the static charge, and then it was gone, and Niki sighed loudly, sat down next to Spyder and held her hand again. Decision made, and Spyder was glad for her touch, but couldn't look at her face, the fear and regret stamped there, stared over the edge of the sink and out the kitchen window instead, the cold night gathering around the house, taking its place, and when it had settled, when it was comfortable, she started to talk.

Not the night that he cut her face, a month later, maybe, and the cross scar between her eyes is bubblegum pink and fresh. And it made no difference at all, because the angels still haven't taken them all away, haven't taken him away and that's really all that matters anymore. But they sit in the basement, inside his charm, listen to two radios at once, one playing the preaching and the other playing hymns. The orange extension cords hang in loops from the ceiling so they won't break the circle; nothing must break the circle, ever.

The circle keeps out the monsters, the wicked things that are gonna crawl up from Hell at the end, will keep out the radiation when the bombs come down, when the sky burns and falls down to smash them and everyone in the world scorched flat. She isn't sure what radiation is, but he says it will kill her even though she'll never see it coming, and she doesn't want to know any more than that.

And this is the time that her mother didn't go down with them, the only time she said no and so he hit her. Her mother a ball on the floor, skinny arms folded like a shield over her head while he punched and kicked and Lila watched it all from the shadows in the hall. Obedient, good girl standing beside the trapdoor, waiting, praying that he'll stop, praying Jesus that he won't really let her mother stay up here alone to burn, to get eaten by the radiation monsters. That they'll make it down before the black sky outside begins to smudge and drip, squirming rain blood drops on the windowpanes; her mother begs *No, Carl, Please, she's watching. Please,* and he stops, steps back and looks lost, tired and lost and sad. Her mother holds her stomach where he kicked her, cries and says words Lila's not supposed to use.

"*Please,*" she says, "For God's sake, don't take her down there tonight!"

And he reaches down, helps her mother up off the floor, "I'm sorry, I'm sorry, my head hurts Trish or I would never hurt you, but my head hurts. It's too small to hold it all in, everything I've seen, everything I know."

"I just can't do it anymore, Carl. I just can't sit down there anymore. Please let me take her. Let us go."

"No," he says, turns around and looks at Lila, like she said something and he's trying to think of an answer, like he's forgotten who she is.

"We'll go to the church. I'll take her to the church, okay? We'll be safe there, Carl. You could even come with us. It'll be safe there."

"There's only one church," he says and her mother starts screaming, *fuck you fuck you fuck you you crazy drunk bastard shit she's my daughter* and there they sit, him in his chair, Lila in hers, her mother's chair empty and both radios turned up loud. He's been sitting for a long time with his head down in his hands, shaking hands, like his head's gonna fly apart if he doesn't hold it together and there's a muddy spot on the floor between his feet from the tears.

"They're tellin' me what I got to do," he says, and by now her mother's stopped banging on the basement door, she's stopped screaming at him to let her in. So the monsters must have taken her away, but Lila would rather believe she ran away to hide in the church, that Brother Taylor and the woman who plays the organ are watching over her.

"They're tellin' me, and I've been tryin' not to listen, Lila. 'Cause it don't seem right. It don't seem right at all." She can hardly understand him, he's crying so hard, wet face in the lamplight from crying and snot. "But it's the only way and this is the last night. They're runnin' out of patience with me. If I don't listen and the trumpets start, they won't take us with them . . ."

He stops, opens his red Bible and reads something from the back that she tries not to hear, locusts and seals, locusts and seals, and then she sees the jar beneath his chair for the first time when he reaches for it. Big Mason jar and something inside but she can't tell what, except it moves when he picks it up. Holds the Bible up in one hand and the jar in the other, holds them high up and he stands so that his long arms almost reach the ceiling. She watches his lips, moving and making words but no sound coming out until finally, *Please don't make me do this. Someone else, Lord. Not me.*

"Daddy?" and there's a sound above them like thunder and she's too scared to say anything else.

"You are not pure," he says to her, his eyes shut now, shut tight. "You have to be *made* pure so that the angels can carry us into Paradise before it's too late. It's not your fault, Lila," he says.

His arms come down slow, the Bible and the jar, and it's not one thing in the jar, a lot of small black living things, nervous things, and he sets the Bible in his chair. Tells her to go to her cot and then he counts backwards, big numbers she hasn't learned yet. And he unzips his pants.

"It's your mother. She's a sinner and now she's lost forever, 'cause she's too proud to listen, too proud to hear. She wants me to let her drag you down to Hell with her, but I won't, Lila. This is bad, but it's better than lettin' her have your immortal soul."

He bends over her and she can see inside the jar now,

can see the shiny black spiders and the red on their bellies. The bottom and sides of the jar covered with them,
clinging to glass and each other; he hands her the jar,
makes her take it in both hands and now she's too
scared to say no, too scared to scream for her mother
who wouldn't hear her anyway because she's dead
or run away. And her father puts his hands between
her legs.

"When I say, Lila, you open that jar."

All she can do is shake her head, *no, no,* she can't do
that, won't let them out; her grandfather taught her about
black widows when he taught her about rattlesnakes and
copperheads and poison ivy.

"Don't shake your head at me, little lady. You're
gonna do it when I say and then it'll be all right. Then
it'll all be over."

He touches her where she pees, slides two fingers inside her; it hurts and she can't help but cry.

"Open the jar, Lila.

"Open the jar."

And his fingers come out and something else goes in,
rips into her and she screams and he says it again, *Open
the jar. Now, Lila.*

The lid isn't screwed on tight, makes a gritty sound
when she turns it, and he drives the pain all the way in
before the lid hits the floor, rings like bells and the spiders flow out, tickling legs over her hands, down her
arms, onto her father.

"It's almost over, baby," her father says, and she
closes her eyes and waits for the end of the world.

Nothing Niki could say, nothing for her to do but sit
and wait for Spyder to finish. Or maybe the story was
finished and Spyder was waiting on her, for a sign, for
sympathy or a shred of consolation. Maybe Spyder only
thought she'd finished, and she sat for five more minutes, not speaking, face a white and empty canvas, until
Niki asked, "You've told your doctors all this?" and
Spyder's head snapped around, puppet-string whiplash,

and for a moment Niki was sure Spyder was going to hit her.

But, "Mostly," she said, instead of violence, the subtle, instant fury on her face, "But what the hell difference does that make? They can't undo it, they can't fix things so it never happened. They can't even make me forget about it, so what's the fucking point?"

And Niki didn't have an answer for that, either.

"My mother ran next door and called the cops and when they finally got here they had to use a crowbar to get into the basement, because he'd put so many fucking locks on the door."

Soft scrape against the floorboards under them, and Niki's racing heart, wanting out; a gentle thwump against the wall of the house and she opened her mouth to ask if Spyder had heard that, too, but Spyder was already talking again, and she made herself wait.

"I fainted or I was in shock or something. I don't remember that part. I don't remember anything else until I woke up in the hospital. They had my mother sedated somewhere and it was a week before I even knew he was dead, when my Aunt Maggie finally told me. It took him three days to die from all those bites."

That sound again, thwump, solid basketball thwump against the side of the house, the basement scrub brush sound right after it, and Niki pretended she hadn't heard, that there was nothing in the world now except Spyder.

"It's *hard* to get a black widow to bite you," she said. "You almost have to force them, Niki. And most people don't die, unless they're allergic or already sick from asthma or a heart condition or something like that. Something to weaken them enough the poison does more than make them wish they were dead. He must have spent days and days down there in the dark, catching all those spiders."

Thwump, and this time she looked at the wall, glanced back to Niki. "You're not hearing things," she said. "Unless we're both hearing things. I shouldn't be telling you this."

"It's probably just a dog," pretend certain, pretend composure, but Niki didn't look at the kitchen window, "or the wind."

"The wind," Spyder whispered, held out her arms, skin and ink, permanent, forever; turned them over to show her naked palms, unstained space but lines there, too, and she knotted her fingers together, lace of fingers, cup of flesh back behind her head, teeth gritting.

"They didn't bite *me,* Niki," almost a growl, throaty grinding up and out, leaking. "They've *never* bitten me."

"Maybe they protected you, then," and Niki as surprised as the look on Spyder's face, the look that said *How did you know, Niki? How did you know that?,* as surprised and she knew how important it was that she'd said that, even if she was just fumbling in the dark and confusion, needing to say something reassuring, anything right and comforting.

"Like a totem animal . . ."

The pain from Spyder's eyes, twisting under her skin so her forehead and eyebrows folded in like old, old mountains, so her lips trembled and she held them open a moment before she could speak.

"But they won't stop. They won't ever stop. They took Robin because they thought they were protecting me. They took Byron," and Niki didn't look toward the thing on the table.

"You need someone to help you make them stop, Spyder."

Thwump and the windows rattled; a coffee cup fell off the sink and shattered on the floor. Spyder covered her ears, hid her face between her knees, muffling what she said.

"Stop playing like you know what's happening, Niki. You don't know what's happening. If I let you stay they'll just take you, too."

"It's my decision," and she grabbed Spyder by the shoulders, pushed her back against the cabinet doors. "Look at me, Spyder. Look at me."

Spyder opened her eyes, stared out through her dreads, through tears and the roil behind the tears.

"It's *my* call. If I want to be here. If I want to help."

"It doesn't work that way," Spyder growled. "There's nothing in the whole fucking world you can do, even if I let you try." She closed her eyes again and began to pound her head against the cabinets, once, twice, the back of her skull against the wood, hitting hard enough that the cabinet door split the third time and Niki shook her.

"Stop it, Spyder! Stop it right *now*, goddamnit! You're gonna hurt yourself . . ."

Crack like lightning reaching for the ground and touching, splitting sound that wasn't the cabinet door or Spyder's skull; hungry light before Niki could shut her eyes, light that had mass and substance, cold as zero, broiling. And she couldn't let go, couldn't crawl away and hide in shadows that didn't exist in the blinding flash moment before it was over and the kitchen seemed so completely black there might never have been even the glow of a single candle in the world. Her hands came away from Spyder's shoulders with a sick and tearing noise and Niki crawled to the sink, felt for the cold water knob in the dark and held her scalded hands under the tap, tasting ozone and something like dust, tasting her own blood where she'd bitten her tongue.

And there was no sound but the soothing, icy splash of water from the faucet and Spyder sobbing behind her.

"It's still my call," she said, blinking, wondering if her eyes had burned away to steam, if there was nothing now but empty, red sockets in her face.

5.

Niki found Bactine in the medicine cabinet and sprayed some on her hands, the welt-red burns criss-crossing the backs of both, striping her wrists and forearms. Made bandages from an old bed sheet and then she sat alone in the living room, nothing for the pain but four extra-strength Tylenol, watched sitcoms with the sound turned too far down to hear. Her eyes itched and watered and there were still bright purplewhite splotches that danced about the room when she blinked. But the thwumping on the walls had stopped, the brushy rustling from the basement, and she could sit on the couch and watch mindless crap and almost not think about the familiar pattern the burns had etched into her skin or about what Spyder was doing in the kitchen or the racket when she wrestled the body off the kitchen table. The sounds the dead boy's swaddled heels made as she dragged him to the trapdoor and down. Not think about what had happened or what to do next, about the things that had happened in this house, had never stopped happening because Spyder had been scarred and so the house had scars, too. There would be time to think later, when her hands stopped hurting, when the splotches in front of her eyes faded.

The phone began to ring and Spyder let it, seventh ring before Niki got up and went to the kitchen (no boy mummy body on the table, no salt on the floor, no sign of Spyder, either) to answer it.

"Hello?" and there was sweet, faint music from the other end, The Smiths, maybe, and then Mort said, "Hey, Niki. You guys doin' okay?"

"Yeah," and inside, *No. No, we're not. Not even a little bit okay.* "We're fine."

"Well, look, I've got some bad news," and she thought she heard Theo in the background; Mort paused and the music went away.

"It's about Keith, you know, our guitar player," and "Yeah," she said, "Is he all right?" just as the basement door slammed closed. And then Spyder, standing between crooked paperback stacks in the next room, watching her: dirty hands, red dirt like rust or blood, dirty bare feet. A smear of dirt across her face.

"No," Mort said, "He's not," and Niki listened to the details, stared helpless into Spyder's expectant, nervous eyes and listened. When it was over, she hung up and sat at the table, just a plain table again, not a mortuary slab and all the salt and pepper shakers and bottles of hot sauce back in place. The plastic honey bear and the sugar bowl.

"What's wrong, Niki?" Spyder asked, cautious, sounding frightened again; Niki shook her head, no words left in her. She looked down at her ridiculous, bandaged hands, already beginning to ravel and when she began to cry, Spyder came and held her, wrapped her in consoling smells of mold and earth and sweat and stayed with her until she could talk again.

CHAPTER THIRTEEN

Sineaters

1.

The real funeral and the one in her head; Daria, sitting on her bed, sitting with her back to the wall and squeezed into the corner like a gunfighter so no more of this shit could come sneaking up on her, the real shit and the shit in her head; the shit since Saturday night and her laying down the law, the sentence, for the late and never to-be-great Mr. Keith Barry and the other shit like a 1950s Cold War big bug movie. That last kept for herself, her pearl, more secret than the guilt over Keith. Because she knew it was crazy, because she was too afraid to say it out loud, too scared to say words to set the nightmares loose.

Claude had gone out for more coffee thirty minutes before, only had to walk down to the Bean and back, *So where the hell is he?* and she watched the clock-radio and wished him home, wished herself back to Saturday night and Heaven and the time when there was still opportunity, a million other ways things might have gone down, if she'd let them, and none of the wishes came true.

Outside, the sun was going down, already, going down again, and that meant that she'd lived through one, two, three, four, and this had been the fifth day since Saturday night: Thursday, Thursday night creeping up on her like a fucking vampire that would take away nothing anyone could ever see, would leave her a little less alive, but still hurting. Hurting like she'd never imagined she could hurt, and empty, and sick and she thought she heard thunder.

She knew she looked like cold fucking shit, smelled just as bad or worse, maybe, same grody clothes, same underwear and no shower, so she smelled like sweat and puke and dried tears, old booze and stale smoke; mostly drunk since Tuesday afternoon, solid drunk since the funeral, drunk since the hours before his wake; hidden away in the apartment, sucking down the cheapest wine, the bottles of Wild Irish Rose and Boone's Farm and MD 20/20 that had been left behind after she'd chased everyone away from the wake, the precious numbing bottles she'd lugged back from Keith's old place in a huge, bulging paper bag.

Where are you, Claude? and she looked at the window, although she couldn't see anything for the bedsheet she'd made Claude thumb-tack over it, could only tell how soon it would be dark. *You fuckin' promised, man,* and Christ, she hadn't even wanted the fucking coffee.

"But you *are* going to drink it, and you *are* going to sober up," he'd said. "He's dead, not you. What happened to Keith, that wasn't about *you,* Dar. That was just about him, and nobody but him and all the shit he couldn't deal with anymore." And it hadn't mattered that she'd screamed at him for saying that, had hurled an ashtray across the room at him, dumping butts and ash and putting another dent in the walls.

He'd gone anyway, thirty-five minutes now.

She looked away from the window, tried not think about time or the setting sun, bad dreams or the distant storm sounds; *He'll be back soon,* and she looked into each of the room's three remaining corners, one after the other, corners Claude had cleaned so meticulously for her, swept away every trace of cobweb and sprayed them with Hot Shot; indulging her.

The thunder again, but no lightning, not yet, and the windowpane rattled a little. Daria lit another cigarette and waited for Claude, the can of bug spray gripped tight in one hand, and she watched the empty corners.

2.

She'd been at the Bean, one hour into her Monday night shift, when Mort had come in, stoop-shouldered Mort and Theo in his shadow, her eyes red, puffy, and that had been the first thing, the realization that Theo had been crying and Daria had just never thought about Theo Babyock crying. The coffeehouse was crowded, noisy, afterwork crowd, and she'd been too busy, still furious and pouring it all into the job, the endless procession of lattés and cappuccinos, double espressos and dirty glasses.

"We need to talk, Dar," he'd said, leaning over the bar so she could hear him over the Rev. Horton Heat and the beehive drone of customer voices.

"I'm busy right now, Mort. *Real* busy, so if it can wait . . ." but he'd shaken his head and reached across the bar, held her arm so she had to be still and listen, and Theo had turned away, wiped at her nose with a wilted Kleenex.

And she'd seen the red around his eyes, too, and felt sudden cold down in her stomach, belly cold, had set down a plastic jug of milk and, "Yeah," she'd said, "Okay. Just give me a minute." Had asked a new girl to cover for her and then she'd taken off her damp apron, followed Mort and Theo not to a booth or table (none were empty, anyway) but out the door to stand shivering on the sidewalk.

"What's going on?" and Mort had brushed his hair back, rubbed his hands together; Theo blew her nose loud, like a cartoon character.

"Keith," Mort said, "He's dead, Dar," just like that, no words minced; at least he hadn't fucked around the point, hadn't tried to break it to her gently. And then he'd said it again, "Keith's dead."

She'd opened her mouth, but nothing, no words, nothing but the ice from her stomach rising up to meet the cold air spilling over her tongue. And Theo made a strangled little sound, then, like someone had squeezed a puppy too hard and she walked away from them, fast,

chartreuse leather moccasins and the cuffs of her
chintzy aqaumarine bell-bottoms showing out from under her long coat.

Daria said something: "Oh," or "Oh god," "Oh fuck,"
something she couldn't exactly remember, only that
she'd made some sound, a word or two pushed out, and
Mort had looked down at his feet.

"We just found out about half an hour ago," he said,
"His aunt called me at the garage and we came straight
here."

She sat down on the concrete, weighted and sunk
down slow to cold that hadn't mattered anymore. No
colder than she felt inside, and she said, "How?" and he
coughed.

"The police found him in an alley, I don't know, somewhere in Atlanta," pause, and "He slashed his wrists with
his goddamned pocket knife," and then Mort sat down
next to her, put his hard drummer arms around her, em-
broidered cursive name tag on his gas station-blue shirt
and warmth and the safe smells of worksweat and motor
oil mixing with the coffeefunk that never washed out of
her clothes.

And she'd leaned against him, waiting for it to be real
enough that she could start to cry.

* * *

The next night, they'd gone together to the funeral
parlor: Daria, Mort and Theo, outsiders at the ritual, ex-
trinsic onlookers lingering among the chrysanthemums
and roses. Surrounded by relatives that Daria had never
known existed; she'd only ever formed the vaguest
sense that Keith even had a family, much less all those
tearful faces, and the feel and magnolia smell of Old
South money, fallen aristocracy and names that were
supposed to mean something. Eyes that looked back at
her through sorrow or obligatory sorrow or bored indifference, but all of those eyes saying the same thing in
slightly different voices: you don't belong here.

At least the casket had been closed, so she was spared

some mortician fuck's rouge and powder imitation of life. Only had to face the expensive-looking casket, almost buried beneath a mound of ferns and flowers and a Bible on top like a leather-bound cherry, the Bible and a pewter-framed photograph, cheesy yearbook pose at least ten years out of date. Keith before the dope, long, long time before her and anything that she knew about him.

His mother, old-young woman in heavy makeup, hugged her just a moment and left a mascara smear on her cheek, shook Mort's hand and said how good it was that he'd had friends that cared enough, enough to come. And the three ministers, Baptist fat and hovering like overfed crows, disapproving glances for Daria's crimson hair, Theo's clothes, Mort's simplicity. After that she almost hadn't gone to the funeral.

"They don't want us there," she'd said and Mort said, "But who gives a rat's ass *what* they want, Dar. What do you think he would have wanted?"

"He's dead, Mort. He doesn't want anything anymore."

But that was beside the point and she had gone. Borrowed black dress from Theo, something polyester and a patent black purse empty except for her cigarettes and Zippo, had refused to trade her boots or take off her watch. And Theo in a dress and black opera gloves, Mort in a gray suit with sleeves too short.

They'd come in to the memorial service late and taken seats in the back, Daria watching her hands until it was over, all that shit would have either made Keith laugh or pissed him off, the hymns and then back out into the parking lot and the procession to the cemetery, boneyard parade and the shitmobile stuck in the middle like an ulcer.

"You think he would have wanted any of this bull-shit?" she'd asked Mort, and no, he said, small, far away no, no he wouldn't have.

And there had been no rain, no clouds even, just that sucking vacant blue of a late Alabama autumn sky, and when it was over and they'd filed past the grave with the others, the hands dropping flowers, faces staring down that hole, Mort had taken something out of his coat pocket. Something rolled tight that caught and flashed back the weak afternoon sun and she'd realized it was just guitar strings, the strings off the busted-up Gibson. He dropped them in, funny metal noise before they slid off the lid into red dirt, and a man behind them frowned.

"That was one thing that was *wrong* with the boy," the man said and Daria stopped and glared up at him. Didn't tell him to fuck off or shove it up his tight white ass, just stared, and Mort's big hand on her shoulder, stared until the man blushed like a girl and looked away. And then she'd followed Mort and Theo back down the hill to the van.

* * *

Wednesday night, after the funeral, they'd finally gone back to her apartment, after driving around all afternoon, drinking beer and listening to bootlegged tapes Keith had made on Daria and Claude's stereo: bestiary of guitars through the shitmobile's tinny speakers: Hendrix and Page, Clapton and all those old blues guys she could never keep straight, Chuck Berry and the Eagles' "Hotel California."

"I tell you what he *would* have wanted," Mort had said, finishing another Bud and crumpling the can, tossing it in the direction of the kitchen sink. "What he said he wanted," and he told them about one night the summer before, July and him and Keith walking the rails alone, smoking pot and talking music shit. And they'd found a cat dead on the tracks, swollen and stinking on the oily ties and granite ballast, and for a while they'd just walked. And then Keith had said that when he kicked he wanted music around him, music and booze and people laughing, like they did down in New Orleans, you know. "Think of the most fucked up you've ever been, man, and get ten times that drunk and that's what I want."

"We're working on it," Theo had said and belched, still wearing her funeral clothes, the gloves bunched down around her wrists.

"No, we're not. We're just sitting around drinking. He meant he wanted a *party*."

And they'd both looked at her, like it was her decision, her call, whether or not Keith got his fête, his wake, and she was already at least twice as drunk as she'd ever been and her head still hurt from all the crying, just wanted to go to bed.

But "Sure," she'd said instead, "Whatever you think," and she'd opened another beer, had laid down on the floor and stared at a big water stain on the ceiling while Mort started making phone calls.

* * *

And an hour later, just before they'd left for Keith's apartment (she still had her key to the door downstairs), the phone had rung and Theo and Mort were already on their way out the door, Claude and his latest boyfriend, too, so she answered it, third ring and she'd held the receiver close to her face, so drunk she had to brace herself against a wall and said "Hello," had waited, listening to the nothing from the other end. Then, "Ah, yeah . . . I'm looking for Keith." A guy's voice and she'd almost laughed, had *wanted* to laugh but she wasn't quite that drunk yet.

"Keith Barry?" he'd said, nervous boy voice, and she rubbed her face. "You probably don't know me, but I'm a friend of Spyder Baxter's."

"Oh, yeah, uh, just a minute . . ." and Mort was watching her from the doorway, his tired face that said he was right there if she needed help, needed anything at all, and she tried to smile, easy nothing's-wrong smile for him, failed and said " . . . Keith doesn't live here," to the telephone; before the shaky voice inside could reply, she added, "Keith Barry never lived here," and hung up.

3.

Hours later and Keith's apartment was still empty, as empty as if all his stuff had already been carted away, as if most of the people Mort called hadn't shown: skatepunks and slackers, a few people from other bands and almost everyone with a bottle or two, a six-pack or a case of shitty beer. Daria sat on the old mattress, wedged into the corner and the sleeping bag across her lap, five times as drunk now as she'd ever been and she'd already puked once and started drinking again, looking for a place inside that was absolutely fucking numb.

The sleeping bag smelled like Keith, the whole apartment that same smell, that feel, and the pain faded and then welled back up, time after time, ocean tide, and she'd be crying again, and Mort or Theo or someone else sitting with her, comforting words and touches that could never really comfort, couldn't possibly touch the shattered place inside.

A friend of Mort's from work had brought a portable stereo and stacks of CDs, four speakers spaced around the room, and the music blaring so loud that the cops were bound to come sooner or later and run them all off, arrest them for the veil of pot smoke hanging in the cold air. Daria pulled the sleeping bag up to her shoulders and inhaled him, musky ghost, let him fill her up, try to take away some of the hollowness. And then she was over the crest of another wave, dropping into the next trough, tears hot and close, and she took another swallow from the bottle of Mad Dog, distant taste like grape Kool-Aid or cough syrup. A little dribbled down her chin and she wiped it away, as the forest of legs in front of her parted a moment and there was Niki Ky, coming through the door, someone handing her a beer immediately, and Spyder right behind her. The legs had closed again and they were gone.

Theo stooped down in front of her, Are you okay, Dar? Do you need anything? and she'd shaken her head

and smiled her goofy-drunk smile and fresh tears
streamed down her face.

"It's gonna be all right," Theo had said and hugged
her, sat down on the mattress; Theo without her opera
gloves now, a bottle of Sterling in one hand. Daria lay
her head on Theo's shoulder: that was what she wanted
to believe, that somehow it would *all* be right again,
that very soon she would pass out, slip away, barfing up
her guts in the toilet down the hall while Theo held her
head, whispered soothing words, and when she came to
she'd be in her own bed and all this just a vivid nightmare that would fade before she could even remember
the details.

"Niki and Spyder are here," Theo said, "You want to
talk to them?"

"Yeah," she'd said, wiping her snotty nose on her
shirtsleeve, "Sure," and Theo was gone, swallowed by
the press of bodies and back in a minute or two, towing
Niki through the crowd, Spyder still trailing behind.
Niki kneeled in front of Daria, weepy Buddha-Dar, and
said she was sorry, was there anything she could do?
Spyder looked at the floor or her feet.

"Not unless you can make me wake up, girl'o," Daria
said and Niki had said, "I would, Dar. I would if I
could."

"Hey there, Spyder," and Spyder had glanced down at
her, shrugged her shoulders and grunted something for
an answer.

"This is good," Niki said, "This party, I mean. Keep it
all out in the open, you know? Clean it all out."

Daria only nodded, stared up at Spyder.

"Guess we've both had a pretty shitty month, huh,
Spyder?" and Spyder's eyes narrowed, drifted around to
meet her own. And she'd seen the sharp glint there, sapphire flash of anger, had known she was too drunk to be
talking, that she'd done something wrong.

"I'm sorry," she'd said quickly. "I'm really goddamned shit-faced, Spyder, so just pretend I never said
that, okay? I'm sorry."

And Niki took her hands, and Daria flinched, hands

so cold, freezing; of course, it was only because they'd just come in, but she'd looked down and Niki's hands were too white, Spyder-pale and livid welts across their backs, crisscross of raised pink flesh, like fresh burns or keloid scars.

"Christ," she said, "what happened to your hands, Niki?" but Niki was already pulling them away, tucking them inside the pockets of her army jacket. "Oh, that's nothing. I had an accident in the kitchen . . ."

"*Jesus,*" Theo said, so Daria knew she'd seen the marks, too. "Have you been to a doctor?" and Niki had shaken her head, "No," she said, "It's really not that bad at all."

Someone changed CDs and there'd been a few seconds' worth of relative quiet, Daria looking at the bulges in Niki's pockets where her hands were hiding, aware that Spyder was still watching her, that her apology hadn't been accepted. And then the room filled with the sudden whine of bagpipes before thumping bass again, subwoofer throb, House of Pain, and the crowd began to jump up and down in unison, unreal trampoline dance, and she thought she'd felt the floor sway beneath them.

"I just miss him, you know? I just miss him," Daria said, bringing it back to herself, safer territory no matter how much it hurt. "It's such a fucking waste."

"Yeah," Niki said, and she put an arm around Spyder's legs, giving Daria another glimpse of her hand.

"I don't *want* to be angry at him," she said and took another drink from the wine bottle. "I don't want to be angry at him for being such a selfish fucking prick . . ."

"What do you mean?" Spyder asked, talking loud over the stereo and the pounding feet. "What do you mean, he was selfish?" and Daria looked back up at her, the anger still in her eyes, and "I *mean* it was a goddamn stupid thing, Spyder. That's what I *mean*. Never mind his friends, you know? Never mind me. He was a fucking genius, a goddamn fucking *genius,* and he pissed it away."

"It was his life," Spyder said. "He could do with it
whatever he wanted."

"Bullshit!" had slung the word at Spyder like a brick,
had known that Spyder was baiting her, no idea *why*,
but head clear enough to see she was. Just not clear
enough to keep her own mouth shut. "He had no fucking *right* to do that to himself, so don't give me that
shit, Spyder. No one has a right to destroy themselves
by shooting that crap into their body."

"You don't seem to mind pouring that shit into
yours . . ." and Spyder had pointed at the half-empty
wine bottle; Daria just stared at her, speechless, and
a new wave had risen up before her, towering black water rising, rising, and filthy foam whitecap up there
somewhere.

"Spyder . . ." Niki had said, sounding like maybe
she'd been afraid of this all along and trying to smile,
holding tighter to Spyder's legs.

"I'm sorry. It just sounds kind of hypocritical to me."

And Daria had tried to stand up then, the floor tilting
beneath her, the wall behind the only solid thing, and
"Goddamn you," she said, "God-fucking-damn you,
Spyder. You don't even know what the hell you're talking about," and Theo's hands trying to pull her back
down onto the mattress.

"Whatever you say, Daria." And Spyder half-turned
away from her, watched the dancing crowd of mourners.

"She really didn't mean it that way, Dar," Niki had
said, but Daria had braced herself against the wall,
enough support, and she swung a hard punch that
missed its mark and smacked Spyder in the throat.

Spyder made a startled choking, coughing sound and
stumbled backwards; bumped into the dancers and one
of them pushed her, mosh pit reciprocation, and so
she'd tumbled towards Daria, tripped by Niki's embrace
and the corner of the mattress. Sprawled into Daria's
arms and they'd both gone down, furious tangle of arms
and legs, kicking boots, Daria hitting Spyder in the face
over and over, Spyder's blood on pale knuckles and the
dirty wall. And Theo and Niki trying to pull them apart,

catching stray kicks and blows for their trouble. Some of the dancers had stopped to watch, had formed a tight arena of flesh around Keith's bed.

Daria's face, lip busted and sneering, teeth stained red with her blood and Spyder's, "Fuck you, *fuck you, fuck you,*" from her mouth and then Theo hauling Daria off and the toe of Spyder's right boot had slammed into her unprotected stomach. She gagged, wrestled free of Theo's grip and vomited on the floor, pure liquid gout of alcohol and bile that spattered them all.

"Christ," Theo said, and Niki, leaning over Spyder now, shielding Spyder, had said only "I'm sorry, I'm sorry," again and again.

"Just get her the hell out of here, Niki," Theo said, arms around Daria's shoulders as she'd heaved again. "Or I'm gonna finish what Daria started myself."

"She didn't mean it ..." Niki began, but Theo interrupted her: *"Now!"* she said, and Niki had helped Spyder up off the mattress, stepped in the way when Spyder tried to kick Daria again and caught the boot herself.

"Get her out of here, Niki!"

And Spyder growling, spitting bloodpink foam, and she'd said, "I'm not done with you, bitch," last word like tearing fabric and Daria could only cramp and listen and stare into the spreading pool of her puke.

"What the hell was *that*," Theo said and Daria shook her head, like she had no idea. The fury had already left her, left her scraped raw and a little stream of vomit from both her nostrils, her gut aching, throat and acid-burned sinuses on fire. When she could talk, "Make them all leave, Theo. Find Mort and make them *all* leave." And Theo had obeyed, reluctant, but doing it anyway; Daria sat back against the wall again, stared out at the confused crowd through watering eyes. They were trying not to stare at her, most of them, a few already being herded out the door by Mort and Theo. Someone had turned off the music. And then she'd closed her eyes and waited to be alone.

4.

Half an hour later, or an hour, outside Keith's building, locking the door and feeling like crap. Sick and drunk and bruised. Mort and Theo hadn't wanted to leave her, had offered to give her a lift back over to Morris, demanded finally, but she'd said the walk would do her good, that the air would help clear her head. And they'd gone reluctantly, leaving her to stuff the bottles of booze scattered around the apartment, the cans of beer, into a paper bag, leaving her to turn off the lights one last time and lock the door behind her. She'd stuck a couple of other things in the bag, too full, ready to tear and spill everything grocery brown paper, just some guitar picks from the floor, a t-shirt and a couple of his cassette tapes. Random souvenirs.

The key made a sound like ice or a camera click.

And when she'd turned around, he'd been standing across the alley watching her; she'd only thought it was Keith for an instant, impossible, dizzy instant, had almost dropped the clinking bag. But it wasn't him, wasn't anyone she'd recognized at first.

"What the hell do *you* want," she'd said, sounding as drunk as she was, sounding like a drunken old whore, and he'd looked both ways, nervous, up and down the alley, before crossing to stand closer to Daria. Tall, lanky boy with brown hair and a Bauhaus shirt showing under his leather jacket. Someone she'd seen with Spyder from time to time at Dr. Jekyll's, one of the shrikes.

"Before," he said. "When I called, I didn't know," and then she'd recognized the voice, too, shaky and scared, cartoon scaredy-cat voice from the phone. "I'm sorry."

"Whatever," she said.

"I needed to talk to him."

"Too late for that," and she'd handed him the bag. "Did Spyder send you around to kick my ass?"

He looked down at the bag, back at Daria, drawing a perfect blank with his eyes. "What?"

"Do you have a *name*?"

"Walter," he'd said, shifted the bag in his arms, "I used to be a friend of Spyder Baxter's . . ."

"'Used to be'?" and she'd started walking, him following a few steps behind, the bag noisier than their footfalls in the long, empty alleyway.

"I think that's what *she'd* say, if you asked her," he said, walking faster to catch up. "I'm pretty sure that's what she'd say."

"Spyder seems to have her little heart set on burning bridges these days," and she'd touched her swollen lip, but the pain couldn't quite reach through the boozy haze, far-off sensation, like the cold all around.

"She thinks I had something to do with what happened to Robin," he said.

"Robin? Spyder's girlfriend?" Daria stopped, and the shrike stopped, too.

"Yeah," and he'd looked back the way they'd come, anxious eyes, anxious tired face. "Did you?" but he hadn't answered, just stared back down the alley like he thought they were being followed.

"Why'd you want to talk to Keith?" and *that* hurt, his name out loud, from her lips, little cattle-prod jolt of pain right to the fruitbruise soft spot inside her, the place the wine and beer couldn't numb.

Walter shrugged, hadn't looked at her.

"I thought maybe he would help, because of that night in the parking lot, when he stuck up for Spyder and Robin. I thought he might know what to do."

"You're losin' me, Walter."

"Who was the girl that left with Spyder tonight?" he'd asked, changing the subject, starting to piss her off. "The Japanese girl?"

"Her name's Niki and she's not Japanese. She's Vietnamese and she's Spyder's new girl. She moved in with Spyder a couple of weeks ago."

"Is she a friend of yours?"

Daria had thought about that a second, thought about all the shit that had gone down in the weeks since Niki Ky walked into the Bean, almost a month now, and if she were superstitious . . .

"Yeah, she's a friend of mine," she answered.

"Then you ought to know that she's in danger."

And Daria remembered the welts on the back of Niki's hands, like someone had begun a game of tic-tac-toe on her skin with a branding iron, like the ink in Spyder's skin.

"Spyder's not right," he said.

"Spyder Baxter's a fucking froot-loop," Daria said and now she was staring back down the alley, trying to see what he saw, what he was afraid of.

"No. I don't mean about her being crazy. I mean, she's not *right*."

"Walter, will you please just tell me what the hell you're talking about and stop with the damn tap-dancing?"

And back in the shadows, then, a garbage can had fallen over, bang, and the sound of metal and rolling glass on asphalt, before something dark and fast had streaked across the alley. Walter almost dropped the bag, and she'd taken it from him.

"What the hell's wrong with you? It was just a cat, or a dog, for Christ's sake . . ."

"Spyder's not right," he said again, like maybe she'd understand if he repeated it enough times, "and if you care about your friend, you'll keep her away from that house. Robin knew and she tried to tell us, and now she's dead. And Byron believed her, and no one knows *where* the hell he is . . ."

"I think I'm way too drunk for this shit," she'd said, and started walking again. Walter hadn't moved.

"I'll wait a day or two," he'd said as she'd walked away. "Just a day or two, and then I've gotta leave. If you want to talk, I'll be around."

"Yeah, sure, whatever," she'd muttered, not caring if he heard, just wanting to be back in her apartment, just wanting another drink.

And the last thing, before she'd stepped out of the alley and into the cold comfort glare of streetlights: "I'm not crazy," he'd said. "I swear to God, Daria, I'm not crazy."

5.

She'd found Claude in her bed, making time with his boy and she'd made them move it to the sofa. Had found a cleanish glass in the kitchen and screwed the top off a big bottle of Jim Beam, filled the glass to the brim and set the bottle of bourbon next to the bed.

"Maybe you've had enough," Claude had said, careful, and a glare had been all it took to shut him up. He'd taken his boy and they'd left the apartment, left her alone. Her face, her hands felt fevery, wind-chapped, and her ribs hurt from Spyder's Doc. A miracle she didn't have broken ribs; wondered if maybe she was bleeding somewhere inside, and Daria took a long, burning drink of the Jim Beam and went to the bathroom to piss. Just beer piss, safe yellow. She'd finished the bourbon, filled the glass again, and laid down, head on her own pillow, soft and slightly funky, stared at Claude's big poster of Billie Holiday through the syrup-colored liquor. The sadness, the fight with Spyder, the weirdness in the alley with Walter, everything running together like candle wax, waxen weight pulling down, and in a few minutes she was asleep.

* * *

"I don't hate her," her father says, "I love your mother," and she looks up from her crayons, her color swirl under black wax and the lines she's begun to scratch into it with her nails. Outside the sky is low and she can smell ozone and the rain rushing across the Mississippi prairies toward them, can see the electric lizard tongue flicks of lightning on the horizon. The car bleeds red dust behind them, and she tells him that she knows that, that she never thought he hated them. Scratches at the rising welts on her arms and hands, and he puts his arm around her, pulls her close to him and the steering wheel: her crayons are in the backseat now, and she feels cold and sick at her stomach. The storm talks in thunder and the orange speedometer needle strains toward ninety.

"I'm gonna get you to a doctor, Daria, and you're gonna be fine. So don't be afraid, okay? You're gonna be okay. I swear I'd never let anything happen to you."

The world rumbles under the thunder and the car bumps and lurches along the dirt road.

"I should have listened to your Mammaw," he says, and she tries not to think about what happened back at the gas station, the old shed and the biting spiders all over her, in her clothes and hair and the look on her father's face as bad as all those legs on her skin.

"I was scared, Daria, I didn't know what to do."

Crack, sky cracking open like a rotten egg and blue yolk fire arcing over them. Blistered sky boiling and she closes her eyes; the blanket that the man at the gas station gave her father to wrap her in itches and she wants to kick it off but he's bundled her too tight.

"I just couldn't let her hurt you again."

She shivers, and listens to the thunder. And something else, wail like the storm has learned to howl, opens her eyes and looks over dashboard faded plastic and the stitches in the earth laid out before them, bisecting the dirt red road, iron spikes and steel rails and pinewood ties to close some monstrous wound up tight, and the train, crawling the tracks like a jointed metal copperhead, train so long, boxcar after boxcar, that she can't even see the end. Can see the candy-striped gate arm coming down in front of them ahead, red crossing light flashing useless warning.

Her father presses his foot down hard on the accelerator and now he's praying, praying loud, please god, please god, if we get stuck behind that thing she'll die. And the train bigger than God, the God that hides behind His storm up above and sticks at the land with hat pin fire.

"Daddy . . . ?" she says, but he's still praying, and the cyclops eye of the train through the gloom, engine jaws and spinning silver wheel teeth. And she thinks that it has started to rain, because *something's* hitting the windshield, ocher drops that the wind sweeps away.

Dry, yellow-brown drops before the shark snout of the Pontiac hits the gate arm and the wood snaps loud, flips up and smacks the windshield, spiderwebs safety glass as they fly over the railroad tracks, careening, jarring flight, and the train is everything on her right, her father everything on the left of her, the storm the world above, and they smash through the gate arm on the other side as the train roars past behind them.

The car fishtails, spins to a stop in the dust and her father crying, slumped over the wheel and crying the way her mother had cried when he'd taken her away. And the broken windshield beneath the rain, rain with tiny furred bodies and a billion busy legs.

* * *

And another night, Thursday night, Daria sat with her back against the wall, bug spray in one hand and a cigarette in the other, hours since she'd awakened in the early afternoon pale sun coming through her window, head throbbing from the bull-bitch of all hangovers and the nightmare memories that still hadn't faded; waiting alone for Claude to come back from the Bean, Claude who'd listened to everything she said, who'd fed her aspirin and coffee and cold glasses of tap water. Who'd helped her to the toilet when she had to puke again but hadn't thought she could walk that far, and who should have been back half an hour ago. Before it got dark.

She took a deep drag off the Marlboro, exhaled, and jumped when she thought she saw something move, half glimpse from the corner of her left eye. Something big leaning over the foot of the bed, but of course there was nothing there now, nothing but tangled sheets and her blanket, gray powder smears from where she'd hurled the ashtray at Claude.

"Fuck," she said, tried to laugh and take another drag, but the cigarette had burned down to the filter so she stubbed it out on the bottom of the Hot Shot can, flicked the butt away. "Fuck me."

Can't even tell the difference between a goddamn bad dream and what's real. Crazy as Spyder fuckin' Baxter, now.

She'd told Claude about her mother and father, talked for hours, through the pain and dread, about that day with the spiders and the train and everything that had led up to it. Her father's secrets, not other women but other men and her mother taking it out on her. So her dad had put her in his Pontiac and they'd driven, heading nowhere, just driving, and her not even eight years old. How she'd wound up in a Bolivar County, Mississippi hospital with twelve brown recluse bites and she'd shown him the ugly scars on her legs to prove it, the worst of the scars that she never showed anyone. Puckered-flesh proof that it had all happened, touch and go for a while, and afterwards, the divorce and the years before she ever saw her father again.

Claude had listened, kind and so good at listening but he can't walk a block down the street and back in forty-five goddamn minutes. And she hadn't told him about the other dreams, the dreams since that day on Cullom Street, not just the familiar race with the train, the threadbare echoes of her father and that one awful day, but the new dreams of fire and things from the sky, entrail rain and the silent, writhing angels, greased stakes up their asses while the streets filled with blood and the long-legged shadows that might be crabs or tarantulas big as fucking Volkswagens, under a sun the color of a nosebleed.

She reached for another cigarette but the pack was empty and she wasn't about to get up and look for more. Thunder, right overhead, and the windowpane shuddered.

And the lights flickered.

"*Christ,* Claude . . ."

Hadn't told him that she knew that Keith had been having the dreams too, or about her talk with dowdy, frightened Walter the goddamned shrike on her way home. Hadn't brought up the marks on Niki's hands or the weeping marks on Keith's face and ankles. Connect the dots, Dar, draw your fucking paranoid's connections.

A tickle on her cheek and Daria brushed at her face, brushed back hair and stared at the thing that had fallen into her lap, eight legs drawn up tight like a closed umbrella, spider fetal, and she almost screamed, thumped it away from her. Touched her face again, and there were others waiting there, running from her, and she *did* scream, then, screamed louder when she saw how the walls were moving, crappy old wallpaper seeping their thumbnail bodies, the floor alive and clumps swelling from the ceiling, hanging there until their own weight and gravity's pull had its way and they began to fall around her. The spider clumps made almost no sound when they hit the floor.

Daria beat at her face, her chest, the scream continuous now, waiting for their jaws, the hypo sting, waiting to drown beneath them. Remembered the can of Hot Shot and sprayed herself, the bed, stinking pesticide mist everywhere, wet mist falling with the recluse shower.

"I'm not done with you . . ." whispered next to her ear, "I'm not done with you, bitch," and she screamed for Claude, for Mort, screamed for Keith. They were inside her clothes, touching her everywhere, at every orifice and soon they would be inside *her*. So many legs moving together they made a sound like burning leaves. Daria bashed herself against the wall, spidervelvet-papered wall, head thump against the sheet rock and through the pain she saw her silver Zippo lying where she'd left it on the table by the bed.

Just like Pablo had taught her years ago, cans of hair spray or whatever and a lighter, just for fuckin' kicks, just to see the noisy rush of fire, Daria aimed the can of Hot Shot at the foot of the bed, thumb on the striker wheel and *fwoomp,* bright splash of flame, gout of flame and spiders crisping, curling to charred specks, charred lumps of specks. The blanket caught, the sheets, and she aimed the flame-thrower at the wall.

The can spit up a last dribble of fire and was empty,

but it didn't matter, because the flames were crawling away on their own, devouring a thousand fleeing bodies every second as they spread.

And then Mort, reaching through the smoke, strong boy arms, his hands, dragging her off the burning bed, bump, bump, bump across the floor like Pooh and she let him, let him drag her all the way across the apartment and out into the hall, too busy beating at the spiders still clinging to her to stop him, the spiders carpeting the floor. He left her lying on the landing, grabbed the cherry red fire extinguisher off the wall and rushed back inside. Muffled sound like a giant espresso machine steaming milk, steaming a whole goddamn cow, and he was right back, coughing, eyes watering, black smoke all around them.

"Get them off me," she said, begged, *"Please, Mort, get them off me,"* and he squatted down next to her, into the cleaner air beneath the smoke.

"Get *what* off of you, Daria? Tell me what the hell you're talking about," but she was raking at her face, now, raking at the spiders trying to burrow their way into her skin to escape the fire. And he slapped her, slapped her so hard her ears rang like Sunday morning bells and she fell over; Mort picked her up again, held her hands in his fists and talked slow.

"You got the fuckin' DTs or something, Dar. That's all. There's nothing here to hurt you. Whatever you think you're seeing, it ain't real, okay? I absolutely fuckin' swear it ain't real."

"No, let me go," fighting him, coughing and trying to pull her hands free before they were in too deep to pull out again, like they'd gotten inside Keith. *"Can't you see them?"*

"Don't make me hit you again, Dar. Please god don't make me have to hit you again." And he pushed her hands, her straining arms, down to her sides and held them there until she stopped struggling. Until she was only crying, sobbing, and she could hear thunder and the wail of sirens, end of the world wail.

"We gotta get outta here, Dar. You need a doctor and I couldn't get the fire out in there."

Mort picked her up, carried her down the stairs and out into the freezing clean night air, the water rain that peppered her skin like liquid ice, bringing her back. Back to herself and Morris Avenue, the buildings washed in scarlet waves of fire engine light, blue and white cop car light.

CHAPTER FOURTEEN

Orpheus

1.

Three hours sitting in the emergency room and if Daria had actually been hurt, she'd have died a long time before Mort finally lost his patience and demanded that a doctor look at her, yelled at a couple of nurses and stomped about. Nothing but scratches on her arms and face, though, welts irritated from the Hot Shot, eyes red from the smoke. A sleepy-looking intern had given her antibiotic salve for the scratches and a halfhearted speech about drinking so goddamn much, although he'd assured her that it was very unlikely that she'd actually had DTs; questions about acid and shit and she'd shaken her head, no and no, not lately or not ever, just booze, and he'd stuck a couple of Band-Aids on her face and hands and sent her on her way.

Out sliding glass doors into the cold again, past ambulances and other injuries to the van, waiting for them where Theo had parked it: vast and mostly empty parking deck, feeble yellow light and concrete, blocky red numbers almost black under the lights, to tell them the level and row, like they could miss the shitmobile. Mort helped Daria inside, into the passenger seat, and Theo climbed in the back.

"We'll go to my place, Dar," Theo said, "In the morning we can have a look at whatever's left of your apartment."

Daria shrugged, *yeah, whatever,* took a slightly bent cigarette from a pack on the dash and let it dangle unlit from the corner of her mouth. Mort opened the driver's side door and "You sure you're feelin' okay? What a useless bunch of sons-of-bitches in there . . ."

"I'm fine, Mort. Can I get a light?" she said and he reached in his shirt pocket, passed her his lighter; orange flicker of butane flame and then the reassuring smell of the Marlboro and she closed her eyes, slumped back in the seat.

"What time is it?" but she looked at her wristwatch before anyone could answer. Nine forty-five in oilgray and it felt so much later, forever since Mort had carried her down from the smoke and fire. The fire and the spiders going dreamy in her head, unreal and far away.

Mort tried to start the van and the engine hacked and sputtered like an old man with double pneumonia, was silent. "Fuck, fuck, and *fuck*," and he hit the steering wheel.

"That's gonna help a whole lot," Theo said. "It's just cold."

"It's just a worthless piece of crap," and he tried again, turned the key and the old man wheezed and coughed deep in his watery steel chest.

Daria squinted out at the parking deck through cigarette smoke and the van's dirty, bugsplotched windshield. Two or three other cars and the fluorescents left little space for shadows, for secrets or hiding places.

"Can we just sit here a minute?" and Mort sighed, big, exhausted puff of white breath, "We might not have a choice."

"I don't suppose you happened to grab my bass on your way out?"

"There wasn't time, Dar," he said. "I'm sorry. Maybe it'll be okay."

"Maybe," and she pulled another drag off the Marlboro.

"Are you sure you're feelin' all right?"

"Yeah," she said. "Sure. Just a little freaked out, that's all." And quick, before she could talk herself out of asking, "If you can get the van started, will you drive me to Spyder's house?"

An astonished, disgusted sound from Theo and "Christ, why in hell would you want to see Spyder Baxter?"

"I don't want to see Spyder. I need to know if Niki's okay."

Mort made a doubtful face, doubt and worry and he looked as bad as she felt, almost. "Wouldn't it be a better idea to call?"

"No, Mort. I need to *see* her. With my eyes. Just a simple yes or no, okay? I think maybe it's important."

"I think maybe Mort hit you a lot harder than he intended," Theo said and Mort glanced back at her, annoyed you're-not-making-this-any-easier frown.

"'Important' *how,* Dar?" he asked. "What are you talking about?"

"Look, it's probably nothing, okay," and she thought about Walter, again, had been thinking about him a lot the last couple of hours: rumpled and bleary-eyed, shivering in the alley behind Keith's, fear like fresh scars on his pale, thin face. The things he'd said, the things she hadn't let him say. "But I need to get some rest and I don't think I can sleep until I know Niki's all right."

"After that scene between you and Spyder last night, it just doesn't seem like such a bright . . ."

"Please, Mort. I swear I'm not gonna hit her."

Mort rubbed at his forehead above his eyebrows like he was getting a headache. "It's not you I'm worried about, Dar," and he gave the ignition another try. This time the shitmobile belched and grumbled, carburetor hack and piston hem, and the engine growled to life.

"Yeah, sure," he sighed. "Why the hell not," and Mort released the parking break, wrestled the stick into reverse.

"Thanks, Mortie." And she leaned over, hugged him, little kiss against his stubbly cheek.

"Yippee," Theo groaned behind them, "Yippee-fucking-ki-yay." The van lurched backwards, tried to stall and Mort pushed the clutch down to the floor. And Daria watched the beam of the headlights and the numbers painted on the wall, the banks of phony jaundiced daytime overhead, until they were out of the parking deck and under the city night again.

2.

Spyder sat on a wobbly stool by the bedroom window, no light but a candle on the floor, and she listened to the gentle, restless sounds of Niki sleeping, asleep for hours now and Spyder had noticed that she'd been taking pills from her Klonopin script for days. Traffic sounds from outside, another place too far off to be of consequence anymore, and the noises from the basement, and the noises from the yard. Her face hurt, swollen lips, black eye, and another pain, inside, pain that meant more than broken skin and bruises.

"I don't think I can stay much longer," Niki had said that afternoon, after they'd fucked. "I can't take much more of this."

"What do you want?" Spyder had said, knowing the answer, playing the game as if she didn't.

"I want you to get help. I want you to tell your doctor what you told me. I want you to tell her about the body you hid in the fucking basement."

"Or you'll leave."

"I love you, Spyder. It's not what I want."

And then she'd rolled over and Spyder had gone to piss. When she'd come back, Niki was already asleep and Spyder had sat down on the stool, thinking about the hospital and its sterile, numbing tortures, idiot questions from people who got paid to listen. And then she'd thought about being left alone in the house, alone *with* the house, and herself, everyone dead or gone away somewhere else. Nothing left but long days and nights and memories.

Bitch, I'm not done with you, bitch, her father said, mocking, laughing behind the closet door, *What you've told her, what she knows, and she's still going anyway.*

"I figured you out, too," she said and then didn't say anything else, nothing to be gained from talking with ghosts or voices that weren't there, remembrances like broken toys she couldn't put away, talking to herself and answering herself. Spyder dug down into her jeans

pocket for the last ball bearing, the one there hadn't
been time for before the bedspread ripped open and
spilled her life onto the floor. The one she'd written
Niki's name on, and she held it in her fist. Held it tight
and Niki stirred, eyelid flutter and she pushed back the
covers, rolled over so Spyder could see her breasts, perfect small, firm, the silver ring through one nipple and
the scar across the other.

If you died now, it wouldn't matter. And he was trying
hard to sound like he had before he'd started seeing angels. *If you'd died when you were supposed to we'd
have both gone up to Heaven a long time ago. But if you
die now, at least no one else will get hurt.*

She won't get hurt.

Spyder opened her hand and held the ball bearing up
so he could see it through the closet door. Faint steel
glimmer in the candlelight and a sound like autumn
crumbling or the smell of tears and he hissed, *They
won't let me come without you, Lila;* when she answered, Spyder spoke low, trying not to wake Niki, just
as careful to find the threat.

"Does it scare you, Daddy?" and she grinned at the
cringing shadows on the walls. "It should. It should
scare the fuck out of you."

And when she was sure he had gone, had slipped like
cold air back between the cracks, sifted down through
termite rot and dust and rusting nails, Spyder laid the
ball bearing on the windowsill, made sure it wouldn't
roll off.

Like a totem animal, Niki had said, like something
Robin would have said, something Robin had understood. And it didn't matter if it was factual, because it
was true, whether she'd chosen them or they'd chosen
her. Somewhere all those fine distinctions had been lost,
her and them, enemy and friend and lover, past and present, no difference anymore and no one holding onto
the leash.

I love you, Spyder, she'd said, and *It's not what I
want.* The last straw in that contradiction, the last silver
ball before the bedspread had torn, and the rage was

coming, rage that had imprisoned Robin and Byron and Walter in her hell under the floor, the rage that swirled around her, storm rage, virus rage, and she knew it had touched Keith Barry, too. And now there was no distinction, the rage and the world, and soon it would touch the girl sleeping on her bed, the girl who hadn't run *yet*, never mind what she might do someday. Her rage like the vengeance of her dead father's god, as bottomless, as all-consuming, as blind and it would take Niki apart, body and mind and soul.

Spyder got up from the stool, went to the bed and she kissed Niki lightly on one cheek, careful not to wake her. And then she began to unbutton her jeans.

3.

Mort drove slow to the dead end of Cullom Street, pulled the shitmobile into Spyder's dirtcrunchy driveway and they sat in the van, watching the dark house, motor still running, headlights shining off the rusty ass of the old Celica. Unsteady glow from a front window, and Daria couldn't help that it made her think of one dull eye open, sentinel eye of something with many eyes but no need to open more than one on their account.

"They're already in bed," Theo said, and Mort looked at Daria, tired what-next resignation on his face, too tired to argue. "I'll be right back," she said. "You guys wait here. There's no need for us all three to go tromping up there."

"Are you sure, Dar? You messed her up pretty good. I expect she's still pissed off."

"I'll be right back. I'm just gonna talk to Niki and apologize."

Mort switched off the headlights, left the engine idling in neutral, and Theo grunted, disbelief and indignation, "Daria, if you go apologizing to that bitch, I ought to kick your ass, on general fucking principle." But Daria's door was already open, the cold getting into the van and she said, "I'd like to see you try sometime, girl'o," and the door banged closed again.

So much different than the last time she'd stood in Spyder's yard, that day in the snow and everything so vanilla icing white, that day with Keith; a sprawling shadow garden now, bare tree shadows and unkempt shrub shadows, a million weedy shadows crowded around her feet. Standing at the edge of the porch and she looked back but couldn't see Mort, nothing but more dark behind the windshield. And at the farthest corner of her vision, sudden movement and she faced the porch again, stared into the junk shadows waiting for her and nothing else.

Christ, I'm still wasted, and that was almost reassuring, almost sufficient, and Daria took the steps one at a time.

Back in the parking deck, she'd thought about trying to find Walter, finding him and letting him talk out whatever he'd wanted to tell her. *I'll wait a day or two,* he'd said, *and then I've gotta leave. If you want to talk,* so maybe they could've found him, if they'd tried. And she'd decided it was a lot sillier than just having a look for herself. Seeing that Niki was all right and getting some sleep and later they could talk about Spyder and the marks on Niki's arms. The marks that had looked like someone had tried to copy Spyder's tattoos onto Niki's skin with a soldering iron.

Loud and woodsy porchboard complaints and Daria stepped over the spot where she'd sat with Keith, between the broken machinery and cardboard rags to the door. Raised her hand, cold knuckles, and then the movement again, subtle disruption somewhere past the corner of the porch, something big, there and gone again before she could turn to see. A rustle in the bushes and she knocked hard, so hard it hurt.

And no one answered. No sound of footsteps coming to open the door, nothing but the van grumbling unevenly in the driveway and so she knocked again, harder. "Come on, guys. I'm freezing my butt off out here," and that was true, the cold and her teeth beginning to chatter, but she knew it was also a surrogate, a shoddy excuse, not the real reason for the way her heart was beating or the dryness in her mouth, the dizzysick surge of adrenaline.

"Get a grip, chick," and she hammered at the door until her hand ached and little flakes of paint had peeled away and fallen at her feet. "Fuck this," reaching for the doorknob and the movement, again, closer this time, as she turned cold metal in her hand and the door opened.

The house was full of light, silverwhite light strung in shimmering garland strands or floating lazy on the air, lying in tangled drifts on the floor. And Daria opened her mouth, to call for Niki or just in amazement and heard the scrambling, the hurried noises at her back, coming up the steps, crash as something tumbled over and she didn't look this time, stepped across the threshold and slammed the door shut behind her.

Mort watched Daria cross the short space to Spyder's porch, waved when she paused once and looked back, but Daria made no sign that she'd seen him. And then she went up the steps and was lost in the deeper night shrouding the porch. Theo had climbed into the front, sat beside him now, holding his hand across the empty space between the bucket seats.

"This is *so* stupid," she said and he nodded. No doubt about that. He strained to catch a glimpse of Daria, a hint of her reflected in the faint, yellow-orange light from the window.

"I can't see her anymore," and Theo said, "It's too goddamn dark to see *anything* out there. You'd think they'd put a streetlight up here."

"Theo, I'm gonna go see if she . . ." and a flash of light from the porch, painful bright, Daria silhouetted there, paper doll cut-out in the brilliance. And then it was dark again, twice as dark as before. Theo whispered, "Jesus, Mort."

He shook his head, reached for his door handle and

she screamed, screamed and was thrown into his lap as
something slammed against the passenger side of the
van, hit them so hard the van rocked a few inches up
onto two wheels before it bounced down again and the
motor sputtered and died. A scraping, shearing sound,
metal raked over metal; Theo scrambled back into her
seat, reached behind Mort and pulled out the aluminum
baseball bat Keith had insisted they keep there.

"What the hell are you doing?"

"Mort, you didn't see it," and he'd never heard her
scared before, wasn't sure if he'd ever heard anyone
that scared. "You didn't see that fucking thing," and it
hit them again, Mort's side this time and he was thrown,
smacked his jaw on the nub end of the bat. Steel ping
and pop and the wall of the van bowed inward. Mort
tasted blood, bitten tongue or broken tooth, wrestled the
bat from Theo's hands.

"Lock the doors behind me and don't move," and of
course she said no, no and fuck you; Mort opened his
door, slid out and almost lost his balance on the loose
gravel under his boots, almost fell. He brought the bat
around, everything he had going into the swing, but
there was nothing there. Nothing at all, but the dark and
the scraggly bushes and the side of the van gouged in
like they'd been sideswiped by a bus.

"Come on," he said, spitting out blood and library
whispering like maybe he was afraid someone would
hear, unable to look away from the dent, paint and rust
scraped away to the raw metal underneath. "We're
gonna get Dar and then we're gonna get the hell out of
here."

"I'm right behind you," Theo replied, shaken, but almost sounding like herself again, and together they
crossed the yard to Spyder's house.

4.

Another bus station, *this* bus station again, and Walter sat by himself in the Burger King kiosk, sipping a
large Pepsi that had been watery and flat and warm for

thirty minutes but he couldn't afford another, watching the clock. Waiting for his boarding call and the bus that would carry him north, nowhere in particular, but as far away from Birmingham and Spyder as the hundred and fifty bills in his wallet, everything he had left, would carry him. *Crazy, coming back here to begin with,* he thought again, *like anyone was gonna listen, like Spyder was gonna talk,* but at least it was something. All he could do and he'd done it and whatever else, he wouldn't have to feel like a goddamn coward.

He fumbled with the safety cap on the bottle of pink hearts, half-empty already, spilled four of the pills out into his palm. He swallowed two, washed them down with another sip of the Pepsi, and put the other two back for later. All that later left ahead of him, all that sleep left to stave off as long as possible. Slipped the bottle back into his jacket pocket, and he saw the spider, hairy brown spider big as a silver dollar, crawling towards him across the garish wallpaper. Just a fucking house spider but he felt his stomach roll, grabbed his backpack and slid out of the booth, trying not to draw attention on his way as he walked quickly past all those faces to the rest room, to cold porcelain, cold water. Privacy if he was lucky, and he was, no one else at the row of sinks, at the urinal, no shoes or pushed-down, rumpled pants legs showing from under the stalls. Walter splashed his face and the nausea began to recede, turning him loose, so he wouldn't have to dry-heave again, nothing in him to puke up but the pills and Pepsi. He pulled a paper towel from the dispenser and rubbed it across his face, rough brown and the animal smell of his dirty wet hair, wet paper smell. Looked up at the face in the mirror, hardly a face he even recognized anymore. He was starting to look sick, like he had cancer, or AIDS, maybe, like he'd been sick for a long, long time.

Walter turned off the tap and behind him, the wiry, coarse rasp of hairs like porcupine quills drawn slow across clean, white tile, labored breath, and it was there in the mirror, squatted between him and the door. Between him and escape and he made himself look, made himself fucking stare and one of its fang-lipped mouths moved, said his name, "Walter," like something treasured and forgotten and just remembered.

"Walter, Walter," and there was still enough of them to know, what might have *been* them once, before this wrong and hurting thing, features blurred like melted wax, a green iris set along the rows of glinting black and pupilless eyes, cupid's bow and prettysharp nose mashed between nervous, restless chelicerae and meathook fangs. Three delicate and blacknailed fingers at the end of one jointed leg, and the voice, neither Robin nor Byron but both of them.

And, "What do you want?" he asked, voice so calm like he didn't feel the warm piss running down the inside of his leg, like he thought he was gonna walk away from the thing in the mirror sane.

So much pain in that one human eye and the lips moved, working silent a moment and he didn't turn around but didn't look away from the mirror, watched its reflection.

"*What?* What the fuck do you want from me?"

"Help," and it coughed something up and he had to look away, down at the sink, the spotless, safe sink, or he would have puked. "Help," it said again.

"I can't," he said. "I've done everything I could do."

"Please, kill her," it said, phlegmy voice that suddenly didn't sound like anyone he'd ever known and that made it easier. "Please help . . ."

"You're not listening. I didn't say I won't; I said I fucking *can't*. I can't kill anyone. There's nothing else I can do. And I'm sorry. I'm really fucking sorry."

And he turned the water back on, twisted both knobs all the way so the gush and splash covered up the sounds it had begun to make.

"Now leave me the fuck alone," and he looked at it one last time, backed into its corner, quivering bristles and thick tears from that one green eye, before he put his fist through the mirror. The glass shattered, big razor shards that rained down off the wall, broke into smaller pieces all around his feet, sliced at his knuckles and fingers.

He waited almost five minutes, and when nothing happened and no one came in to see what the noise had been, Walter turned around, and saw he was alone again.

5.

Niki's sitting with her back to the wrought-iron fence that surrounds Jackson Square like a spiked bracelet, silent, watching as the girl turns her cards over one by one. Wind in the palms, the sewermud smell of the river and the girl turns up The Hanged Man and there's only one card left. She points at the pretty boy dangling by one leg from the t-shaped tree, triangle of his legs pointing toward the earth, cross of his arms and the glow around his head, saint's nimbus, "Ah," she says, "That one," and "That one can be trouble." And nothing else, no insight or prophecy before she reaches for the final card, reaches for the outcome, before the wind gusts and scatters the spread along the paving stones. The girl runs after her cards, barefoot with silver rings on her toes and the wind making bat wings of her black shawl. Niki looks at the sky, clouds so low and black, yellow-green lightning lying up in there like electric serpents and she thinks she should get inside, leaves money in the girl's cigar box and when she stands, tries to stand, she feels the pain in her ankles, the bottoms of her feet, coursing angry hot up her calves.

She looks down and the stones are breaking up around her, busted apart by the writhing snarl of roots, roots as smooth as the slick bellies of worms, the red of naked muscle, the blue of naked veins: the roots that grow time-lapse fast from her legs and feet, holding her to the spot, that bury themselves, herself, deeper and deeper into the soggy ground beneath the Square, rich black soil and fat white grubs. The murmuring tourists who point and stumble past with their souvenir New Orleans Jazz t-shirts and plastic, colored beads, to-go cups

of beer, daiquiris and hurricanes, and she can see the
fear and the awe on their drunken, puffy faces.

And the sky begins to tear.

And fall.

She woke up and the room was still and quiet. A little
candle flicker from the floor that made it seem darker
outside and her head was full of the dream and the confusion the Klonopin left behind. A stickywet spot on her
pillow from sleeping with her mouth open. And then
she remembered the dead boy in the basement and the
mess at Keith Barry's wake, the things she'd said to
Spyder afterwards, the burns on her hands, all the things
that she'd gone to sleep to escape. Things that made the
nightmare silly, any lingering dread dissolved by simple
recollection, replaced, and she called for Spyder.

No answer and she sat up in the bed, headboard at
her back, and blinked at the dim light and shadows.
"Spyder?" and she saw it, then, a few feet past the foot
of the bed, mottled shades of sage and indigo, hanging
down from the ceiling from taut cords or ligaments the
same gray colors; beautiful and hideous and utterly unreal and maybe the dream wasn't over after all, just a
jump-cut to the next scene, new set and she only had to
wait for her cues.

"Spyder," louder now and still no reply from the
death-still house. And she couldn't take her eyes off the
thing, misshapen butterfly's chrysalis and she'd been
shrunk down to nothing. Except that she was beginning
to see the form beneath the glossy skin, familiar lines,
curves and hollows, wax-doll attempt at sculpture and
she heard the sound starting in her throat, small sound.
Faint shape of arms folded across its chest, legs up to
the straining umbilicus, the ceiling warped with its
weight, head a foot above the floor and thrown so far
back there's not much visible but neck and chin. And
whether it was a dream or real, the same thing now, and
Niki opened her mouth and let the small sound out.

6.

Daria stood in the acid light, sizzling cold fairy light from the strands filling up Spyder's living room, and she only had to let one of them settle on the bare back of her right hand to know that they cut. Another gash on her scalp before she finally stopped gaping at her wounded, bleeding hand held up and the light streaming through insubstantial flesh, x-ray revelation of bones and veins and capillaries hidden inside. She pulled her jacket up over her head, ducked and dodged as best she could through the living room, calling for Niki, cursing whenever the strands touched her. Less of the stuff in the next room, but it was still thick enough that she had to be careful, and she stopped, hands cupped around her mouth, "Niki! Niki, *shit . . .*" and she shook one of the strands off her arm, ugly S-shaped incision left behind in the leather.

"Niki!"

There were windows just a few feet away, past a low and uneven wall of paperback books, only patches of glassy night visible through clots of the stuff but still another way out, maybe, and better than trying to go back the way she'd come.

She heard the front door creak open, turned around and there was Mort, arm up to shield his eyes from the glare and she shouted, *"No!* Go back! Don't try to get through this shit," and he squinted in her direction, as if he could hear but couldn't see. "Mort, just get the hell out of here!" And he did close the door, then, backed out and closed it and she was alone again, alone and the sound of the strands falling around her was like the night it snowed, heavylight whisper of so many flakes hitting the window of Keith's apartment at once.

Don't think about it, chick. Think about it and you're fucked. Keep moving.

Taut and nearly solid web across the doorway to the kitchen and all that left was the hall, a darker place in the blaze, leading back to Spyder's room and other, unfamiliar, doors.

"Hell, I'm probably fucked anyway,"

She stepped into the hallway, narrow wallpaper gullet, wood and plaster, stepped careful over razor drifts and her hands pulled up inside the sleeves of her jacket so she could bat away the strands hanging from the ceiling. Daria saw the plywood covering Spyder's door, no time to understand or even wonder before she almost walked into the open cellar, its door laid back and nail studded, nails bent and twisted at vicious, crazy angles, stairs that led almost straight down and she would have broken her neck for sure.

"Niki!" Still no answer, just the snow sound and she peered down into the rectangular hole in the floor, warmer air rising up from the cellar and incongruous scents: mold and earth, jasmine and the sweeter smell of rotting meat. And the blackness down there toward the foot of the stairs imperfect, dim red-orange glow and *What if they're down there? Still feeling like a hero, Dar?*

Daria leaned over the hole, the smells so much thicker close to the floor and she almost gagged, swallowed and shouted, "Niki? Are you down there?" No reply, a crinkly faint sound that might have been people talking or radio static, and she knew if she let herself look back, she'd never do it, would choose any other way out of this and so she put one foot down into the dark, tested her weight on wood that looked termite-chewed, punky and ready to break.

And someone screamed, close and sexless painscream and she almost toppled headfirst down the hole, in the quiet space after the scream clearly heard the top stair crack, split loud under her foot and Daria stumbled backwards, away from the cellar. There was no mistaking the laughter filling up the emptiness beneath her feet, leaking from the open trapdoor, for anything else, no mistaking whether or not she was hearing it: many-throated patchwork of laughter that was lost and sad and utterly, hatefully insane. The way you'd laugh if there was nothing else left, if you heard the emergency broadcast system attention signal on television and there'd been no reassuring voice first to tell you it was just a test. The way you'd laugh at the very end.

"For fuck's sake, Niki, where are you?" hardly more than a hesitant whisper, and she realized she was afraid maybe something besides Niki, besides Spyder, was listening. Cold sweat under her clothes, chilling sweat and adrenaline enough to tear her apart, and the scream again, but this time she knew it was Niki. This time could tell that it was coming from a closed door directly across from Spyder's bedroom, the plywood where the door to Spyder's bedroom should have been. She used the cuff of her jacket to wipe away a knot of the strands and it still stung her hand when she tried to turn the doorknob, no good anyway because it was locked.

She pounded the door and shouted, hoarse from shouting, "Niki! Let me in! Spyder?" and Niki, then, echo-game mocking her, "Spyder," and that was worse even than the laughter from the cellar, no spook house creepiness to distract her, nothing but the rawest loss; scream like a missing finger, and Daria hit the door with her shoulder, hit hard and it shivered in its frame but the lock held. She stepped back, all the way back to the other side of the hall, winced when one of the strands sliced into her forehead and she let that sharp and sudden pain carry her forward, a wish that she was as big as Keith or Mort, as strong, and she threw herself at the door. The wood splintered, split layers, decades of paint strata and the door slammed open.

Spyder, what had been Spyder, dangling from the bedroom ceiling, Niki naked and kneeling below her, and Daria almost turned and ran. Never mind the butchering gossamer or the laughing hole in the floor, Sunday school demons next to this. A sudden loud rapping at the window across the room, *bam, bam, bam,* and whatever new horror she might have expected, might have imagined, it was only Mort and Theo; urgent motions for her to open the window and he looked over his shoulder at the night waiting past the porch.

The plaster had started to sag from her weight, cracks

and flakes in the old paint where the thing was attached to the ceiling.

Think about it later. Get her out of here now, her whole life left to think about it, and she knew that she would, would see Spyder Baxter every time she closed her eyes for the rest of her life, that it would always be there in the darkness, in her dreams, behind every un-opened door. But that couldn't be helped now; maybe Niki could. She ignored Mort, went to Niki, Niki with eyes shut tight, lips moving like silent prayer and Daria shook her hard.

"Niki. *Niki.* Look at me," and she did, opened her brown eyes, irises ringed red from crying and for a moment there was no recognition, blank unknowing and Daria thought maybe she would scream. And then, "Daria?" one hand reaching cautiously up to brush Daria's cheek, fevery touch, as if maybe she thought this part wasn't real, all the rest, but not this.

"Yeah," Daria said, "It's me."

"You see it, too," and yes, she said, yes, I do, "Let's get out of here, Niki."

"I can't just leave her. That's what she thought, that I was gonna run away again. That I was too frightned to stay with her anymore."

"I don't think you can help her now," Daria said, not knowing if it was true, hardly caring. She looked franti-cally around the cluttered room, saw Mort again, Mort and Theo both staring in at her: pissed, very scared. Five steps to the window and she tugged at the handles, fresh agony from her hand and it wouldn't open any-way, unlocked but it wouldn't even budge. One of the handles came off in her hand and she saw the nails, the sash nailed down all the way around the edges, proba-bly painted shut besides.

"Get away from the window!" she yelled, loud enough that they would hear and when Mort and Theo were clear, she picked up a stool by the window, swung it hard and the glass shattered on the first try, crash and tinkle as the shards rained out across the junk on the porch. The night rushed in, sobering cold and the flame on the candle danced and guttered in the breeze, set an example for the roomful of shadows. Daria dropped the stool and Mort was back at the window, "Will you please tell me what the holy motherfuck is happening . . ." and she cut him off with one finger held to her lips.

"Give me your coat, Theo. She'll freeze out there."

"There's something *out here,* Daria," Theo hissed.

"Just give me the goddamn coat."

"Daria, something tried to wreck the fucking van," but she was already taking off her coat, black vinyl handed past Mort, through the broken window. Daria took it and no answer for Theo. No time now for thoughts of what might or might not come later.

"Do you need help?" Mort asked, and, "Yeah," she said, "Wait there, and Theo, you go get the van started. And be careful."

"Yeah, fuck you, too," and Theo was gone. "Hurry, Dar," Mort said, "She wasn't shitting you. There's something out here . . ." Daria turned around and Niki was watching them, wiped her nose with the back of one hand, action so simple it was absurd and she said, "I need a knife, Daria."

"Put this on, Niki," holding out Theo's coat, "Put this on and let's get out of here."

"I *need* a fucking *knife.* Mort, do you have a knife?"

"Uh, yeah," but still looking at Daria, helpless and he reached into the back pocket of his jeans, pulled out the big lockblade, opened it for her.

"We can send someone back to help," Daria said, trying not to show how scared she was, how angry she was becoming; Niki was already getting to her feet, stepped around her and she took the knife from Mort. "Jesus Christ, Niki," and Daria followed her back across the room.

"She thought I was leaving," Niki said, on her knees again, "Just like he did. And that's what she was most afraid of, being left alone. Just like Danny."

"I don't know what you're talking about," and a gassy sigh and spit, then, stink like rotting peaches when Niki sliced into it, slit open a drooping thick spot where one shoulder should have been. Darker membrane underneath and Niki cut that, too; a couple of milky pale drops leaking out, falling to the floor and skittering swiftly away.

"Niki, *wait* . . ." but the blade sank in hilt deep and it split wide, melon tearing rip down the middle and the violent gush of a hundred thousand white bodies pouring out. A hundred thousand tiny specks white as new snow, covering Niki's arms and chest, burying her lap and Daria's feet up past her ankles.

"Fuck this," disgust and reflex, and Daria had already brought her boot down, crushed a few hundred of the spiders before Niki screamed, screamed for her to stop, please stop, and the alabaster tide broke and flowed away from them, mercury smooth movement toward the walls and open door back to the hall, beneath the bed and everything else. Niki folded open the husk, released the last wriggling clot, and Daria saw or thought she saw the impression of a hand inside, negative of Spyder's face, mold reflection, and she looked away.

"I wouldn't have left you," Niki said. "I wouldn't really have left you." And the last of the spiders squeezed themselves into the cracks between the floorboards and were gone.

"Come on," Daria said, "There's nothing you can do."

"There never was, was there?" and Daria didn't have an answer, helped Niki up and to the window. Mort waiting there, and Daria buttoned Niki snug inside Theo's coat while he cleaned the last of the glass away.

"Give me your hands," Mort said, reaching for her, and "Wait," Niki said, bent down, shaky, and picked something that Daria couldn't see up off the floor, blew out the candle and the darkness smelled like hot wax.

"Now," she said, taking Mort's hands, "Now, I'm ready."

EPILOGUE

Exuvium

"This breath is mine
Say goodbye
Fuck off and die
Say goodbye
Say goodbye"

"Iron Lung"
Yer Funeral

The week before Christmas, and they sit together in another diner, another truck stop breakfast. Fifty miles east of Denver and they'll see the mountains by noon, Mort says. Niki picks at her waffles and hash browns, brown foods, getting maple syrup on the shredded potatoes and grease on the waffles. Not as hungry as when she ordered it, not really hungry at all anymore.

"Anyone want this?" and Mort says sure, so she hands her plate across the table to him. Theo forks away the top waffle and he scrapes the rest on top of his own breakfast. Daria stops chewing her last mouthful of sausage and looks at Niki.

"You feelin' okay?" and Niki nods her head, "Yeah. I'm fine. Just not hungry. I'm going to the rest room," and she slips out of the booth, leaves them sitting there under the steer horns mounted on the wall and the moth-eaten jackelope with plastic holly and mistletoe tied in its antlers. Walks past the men sitting at the bar, truckers and locals and they watch her, uneasy mix of disdain and lust on their sleepy, sunworn faces. Past the cash register and gumball machines, the hall that leads back to the rest rooms. Out the door into the Colorado morning as clear and cold and dry as wine. Niki puts her hand into the pocket of the coat that Theo let her keep, shiny black vinyl lined inside with fake fur the color of blue Play-Doh. Checking to see that it's still there, her solid bit of certainty, like she's checked times past counting in the weeks since they left Birmingham. Her new secondhand boots, a gift from Daria, scrunch in the parking lot gravel, scrunch past pickups and the van and soon she's walking on chalky dirt and scrubby patches of grass and cactus. Thirty or forty yards and when she looks back, Daria is following her across the roadside prairie; she stops and waits for her to catch up.

"Where you goin'?" and Niki shrugs, looks west and the sky and the brown earth seem to go on that way forever, azure Heaven and the World below and her trapped somewhere between.

"I just needed to walk."

"Sure," Daria says, and "Would you mind some company?"

"I'm okay," and Daria apologizes, turns back toward the truck stop. "No," Niki says. "It's all right. You can stay."

"Thanks."

"You know we're almost out of cash again," Niki says.

"We'll all get jobs in Boulder. It's a college town; I'm sure there are plenty of shit jobs. Don't worry about the money, Niki."

"Daria, are you still scared?" and Daria looks east over her shoulder, the wind through her hair that's faded cinnamon and grown out blonde at the roots, and "Yeah," she says. "I don't think it just stops. You wanna walk some more?"

"No," Niki says and takes the ball bearing out of her pocket. "This is far enough, I guess." The constant caress of her fingers has almost worn away the ink, but she can still read her name in Spyder's handwriting.

"What is it?" Daria asks and Niki doesn't answer, holds the steel ball in her palm. It glints in the bright sun like old chrome and for a moment she just lets it catch the light, silver and the bright scars lacing her arm. And then she squats down and digs a shallow hole in the ground with the fingers of her other hand, places the ball bearing inside and pushes the dirt back into place over it. Stands up and taps the spot with the toe of her boot until it's smooth again.

"Nothing, anymore," she says, and Daria puts her arm around Niki and together they walk back to the truck stop.

"Heaven's net is wide;
Coarse are the meshes, yet nothing slips through."

Lao-tzu, *Tao Teh Ching*

Author's Biography:

Caitlín R. Kiernan's gothic and gothnoir short fiction has appeared in numerous anthologies, including *The Sandman: Book of Dreams*, *Love in Vein 2*, *Lethal Kisses*, *Noirotica 2*, *Brothers of the Night*, *Dark Terrors 2* and *3*, and *Darkside: Horror for the Next Millenium*. She also scripts *The Dreaming* and other projects for D.C. Comics. Caitlín currently lives in Athens, Georgia. *Silk* is her first novel.